FAR HORIZONS

The Stellar Heritage Series

by Bob Mauldin

Legacy

Spheres of Influence

Far Horizons

When One Door Closes

FAR HORIZONS

Stellar Heritage

Book Three

BOB MAULDIN

Publishing Company

Published in the United States by
Blade of Truth Publishing Company, Forsyth, Montana

Cover art: Covers by Christian

This is a work of fiction. All characters, places, and events
portrayed in these stories are either products of the author's
imagination or are used fictitiously. Any resemblance to actual
persons, living or dead, events, or locales is coincidental.

Contact the publisher via email at:
chadd@bladeoftruthpublishing.com

ISBN-13: 978-1-64248-014-6

PROLOGUE

Rentec do' Verlas stood on the bridge of the battlecruiser *Esmit do Caryl*, flagship of the First Shiravan Contact Fleet, and stared into the slowly rotating holographic display. There were times when his head still reeled from his appointment as Shiravan Ambassador to the human race, and this was one of them. Things tended to happen fast when humans were involved.

The system they had just entered was the seventh one in more than a turning since the contact fleet had begun searching for the homeworld of the recently discovered race of humans.

Derek Carter and Maggie Spencer, pod jockeys during the attack on Orion Base, had been rescued from their Korvil captors by a Shiravan Reprisal Fleet. They had recuperated on the Shiravan homeworld, teaching Rentec English in return for a trip home. Linnas des Harras, Matriarch of the Shiravan Polity, hoped that returning Derek and Maggie would create enough of a favorable impression that her ambassador would get a chance to investigate the possibility of an alliance to combat the Korvils.

At the same time, she and her advisers discussed possible responses to a number of scenarios that might accompany first contact with a race as young and volatile as this one seemed to be. Rentec assured Linnas that from what he'd learned during his language lessons, humanity as a whole *was* prone to violence amongst themselves, but they'd never met an alien race before. He explained that they tended to hide their violent behavior behind a facade of letting the other guy throw the first punch or claiming the higher moral ground, so some communication should be possible between the two races.

When the long-range scans had first imaged the yellow star and its family of satellites from the vicinity of the star known to humans as Alpha Centauri, Derek had known instinctively that this was the sun that had spawned his race. His certainty was so intense that Rentec ordered the corvettes to carry the location to both the homeworld and the Second Fleet. Only after the corvettes were confirmed clear had Rentec ordered the fleet to jump to the new destination.

Almost thirty days had passed while the Shiravan fleet ghosted through contra-space, that region of mathematical space humans called hyperspace. It had become ten self-contained worldlettes during this time, the inhabitants performing battle drills, eating, sleeping, and handling the minutia of nearly six thousand highly motivated lives.

Several things couldn't be done while one was in contra-space—checking what was happening in normal space being one, and communicating with another ship in contra-space being another. That was why the routine for return to normal space was to drop out well outside the target system, allowing the fleet to regroup and assess the local situation. As a rule, the computations for such maneuvers were a matter of precision, but the vagaries of solar wind, galactic drift, passing large bodies in normal space while in contra-space, and a host of other things could affect reemergence. Then, there could be trouble.

Their jump to the new star was as uneventful as such things usually were. The realm of contra-space seldom caused problems unless one spent too much time gazing out through one of the normally shuttered portholes. Then, one's spirit was all too likely to be sucked into the swirling grey nothingness and join with the Spirits of Space, the spirits of all ancestors who had gone before. That realm was left to the Spirit Witches, who kept a clear domed room on most ships of any size so they could meditate close to their gods.

The return to normal space was preceded by a call to stations for all hands. This was the system, after all, of a spacefaring race. Humans were new to space, certainly, but they'd started with a complete colonization ship. If humans were all as intelligent and determined as the two he'd already met and come to know, what was possible for an entire race to do with the information they'd received lately? Unfortunately, they'd only had access to the lost ship for a mere handful of turnings. Not much was expected, but with a little help, who knew?

Derek Carter stood beside Rentec and felt a glow of triumph suffuse his entire being as he recognized Jupiter's unique Red Spot and Saturn's distinctive rings. More than four years had passed since he'd last seen Earth, and there had been times when he hadn't expected to see it ever again. He searched for and found the small blue planet basking in the temperate zone of the bright yellow sun. It was only another dot on the velvet cloth of outer space, but it was home. His grin of victory changed to one that hinted at past pain, as well as the promise of revenge.

Rentec saw the expressions crossing the face of his human friend and thought, *It is well that we bring them home. I only wish I knew whether to hope that the stories they've told of the ferocity of their race weren't an exaggeration or that they were.*

Rentec returned his attention to the holodisplay and the problem glaring back at them. The fact that they were in the wrong place in relation to the system's primary happened often enough to be taken as the whims of the Spirits of Space. The real problem was that there was a full-scale battle going on, and they had just dropped into normal space directly in the path of the oncoming combatants. It was obvious that one side or the other would detect their presence within a matter of hours, if not sooner.

"We need to determine which group is the human one," Rentec said to the captain as he assimilated the data appearing on the holodisplay. "Assisting them is one way to show that we mean no harm."

"Unless," the captain responded dourly, "they have had enough of alien races altogether."

Rentec looked sharply at the captain. "And why would you come to that conclusion, Captain do' Sirkis?"

"Put yourself in their place, Ambassador," the captain said. Related to each other by a kinship string long enough to be purely coincidental, they had discovered mutual interests over the course of the voyage and become fast friends, allowing for a more informal, straightforward conversation than would otherwise have been possible. Still, in the public forum of the bridge, the captain maintained proper adherence to protocols and kept kinship out of the conversation. "If you'd found a construction vessel and had the chance to give your race a technology boost that was magnitudes beyond what you presently had, wouldn't you fight to keep it? Besides, the Korvils don't announce their actions. These humans have no way of knowing whether the ones they fight are the owners of the ship or not. For all they know, we could be reinforcements. In their place, I would assume anything *except* the possibility of friendly intentions. I advise proceeding with caution, Dom do' Verlas."

Rentec stared at the holodisplay without really seeing it. "Derek, how would you analyze this situation?" He switched to the human's language with almost no hesitation now.

"There's no way I can answer that with any certainty, Rentec. I know they're my people and all, but can you say how any specific group of your own people would react under specific conditions? I can guess as to what's going on here, but I can't be sure."

"I see your point, my friend," Rentec conceded. "But, as the closest thing we have to an expert on humans, what would you guess is going on?"

Before Derek Carter had time to answer, the navigation officer spoke up. "Captain! I have two drives powering up less than one million staka's sunward and heading at right angles to our course."

"Quickly, Derek. What would your people do?"

The dark-skinned human tried one final time to hedge his bets. "I'm not in charge, but if I was, I would have my forces retreating to one of our strongholds or back to Earth if they were getting whipped—a fighting withdrawal. So, my guess is that since everybody is outward bound, the four bigger ships are ours and the other two they're chasing are the enemy. I think maybe the two bigger ones you just found were out here to

5

support the little ones or pick them up."

Derek shook his head. "When Maggie and I got captured, we were just pod operators, remember. We weren't in on what the higher-ups were planning, aside from building several stations and then a bunch of ships. Where the stations are and what type of ships—not a clue. We were only there for the construction of the first base. The only thing I can say is that someone will be thinking that we *could* be friendly, but the final result is going to be to err on the side of caution. That tends to be a human trait."

The Nav officer spoke again. "I've identified four distinct and stationary power sources located roughly equidistant around the asteroid belt and seventeen drives that equate to battlecruiser size, as well as one larger drive and several dozen smaller drives of corvette strength, Captain." Almost as an afterthought she added, "That doesn't include the dozen ships the four battlecruisers are chasing or the two new drives now headed our way, all of which are distinctly Korvil, now that I have a better resolution on my scans."

"Seventeen battlecruiser drives?" asked the astonished captain. "That's almost a third of our battlecruiser strength, overall. Are you certain?"

"Yes, Captain, I am," the Nav officer replied without looking up from her screens. "And there appears to be some action taking place near the third planet as well. Also, we've just been scanned. Our presence is no longer a secret. You should also know that the four possible Terran ships engaging the twelve smaller ships have drive signatures that... fluctuate."

"Explain what you mean by fluctuate, Navigator," the captain ordered.

"I can't explain it, sir. In my experience, there's no

way for a ship to have the power signature of a full battleship at one time and a battlecruiser at another."

"A battleship running at lower power to mask its true strength?" the captain mused, more to himself than to anyone present.

"My sensors say that is not the case, sir," the navigator responded.

"These humans are full of surprises. Regardless, they are too far away for us to worry about now, but we should have expected the scans. They have the same type of sensors we do," the captain said. "It's the nearer two ships we should be concerned with right now. What are your orders, Ambassador?"

"Obviously, we need to do something," Rentec said quietly, "but having no previous contact with this race other than Derek and Maggie, I'm going to go with Derek's intuition. After all, he *did* pick this system from four lightyears out with certainty." He held his hand up to forestall objections. "I realize it could have been coincidence since this is the seventh system we've found that matched the parameters our scientists laid out, but it could just as easily have been Second Fleet that found it. The Spirits of Space have smiled on us through Derek, and I say it's time to take a risk. Besides, we now have our navigator's assessment that those are truly Korvil ships. Captain, bring the fleet to battle stations and prepare to attack the two larger ships approaching us. Hail them first, then attack when you get no response."

The one concession Rentec was making to analytical thought rather than superstition and two hundred and fifty years of ingrained hatred was that the Korvils had never bothered to respond to a hail. They merely attacked anything that moved through whatever space they happened to inhabit at the time. Hopefully, if the two ships were human, they would respond to a hail. "Considering the progress these humans have made in such a short time, they must have discovered the translation program in the ship's data banks and copied it to their other vessels. It's what I would do, knowing that another race exists out there somewhere."

CHAPTER ONE

Captain Robert Greene, commanding a four-ship battle group from the bridge of his own ship, the *Niven*, shook his head. "This just isn't getting any easier, is it?" he asked nobody in particular. "*Niven* to all ships: incoming hostiles. Launch all Mambas and assist your fighters. Do not, repeat, do not attempt to follow the larger ships at this time. *Niven* out." He sat back in his chair, studying the information that had been downloaded to his display. The distances were so close, it might as well have been in real-time. "Tactical, screens to maximum. Weapons, make them hot and prepare your gun crews. Comm, set up for a tight-beam message to the *Norton*. She is to be ready to jump for Earth at a moment's notice. Nav, what are the new ships doing?"

"Sir, the big ones we spotted are building up speed away from us. I have their course and drive characteristics locked into the computer. The new group is definitely ten ships. But they're just sitting there. No!" the Nav officer said, correcting herself. "They're powering up!"

"Okay, Nav. Copy all your data to Comm. Comm, encrypt and prepare to send to the *Norton* on my command." Intently watching the holographic display floating in front of him, he split his attention three ways. Facing the more immediate threat of the twelve surviving raiders that had turned to attack, he kept the other two groups under close scrutiny. Delegation of authority was all that let him spread his attention that far. Tactical was coordinating the ten Mambas from the *Niven* with the thirty others from the *Spica*, the *Capella*, and the *Norton* by way of her opposite numbers on the other three capital ships. Weapons was doing the same with the massed laser fire and torpedo assaults on the enemy ships. Fortunately, the new double-warhead missiles worked almost without a hitch, and bogeys began disappearing from the display, along with an alarming number of Mambas unable to get past the raiders for the easier stern shots.

Tactical, Navigation and Helm were all first or second-wave veterans well acquainted with their ship and its systems, allowing Robert to concentrate on the more immediate threat. Weapons, a high-scoring third waver, reported, "Sir, shields are heating up."

As Helm kept the larger ship at approximately the same distance from the attackers, maximizing the *Niven*'s fire. This move allowed the raiders to pinpoint Alliance ships as well, so there was a downside to the tactic. Shunting power from environmental systems and the ship's services to shields and weapons was their only alternative.

Robert Greene's ears caught the rising hum of the shield generators at the same time the report came to him. He winced as he saw icons representing one Mamba after another disappear from the display as well.

"Sir, report on the new group," Nav said. "Their course is toward the two escaping ships. Emission signatures look like they are powering up weapons." Voices fell silent for several seconds as everyone on the bridge absorbed the implications of this new information. The sounds of the ship reigned supreme momentarily— shield generators humming louder by the second; a high-pitched, intermittent whine, going beyond human hearing as the lasers fired and fired again; the dull thud of missiles leaving the ship at fractions of the speed of light; the bell tones, felt in the bones, of enemy hits on the screens.

The comm officer turned in her chair, saying "Sir, I'm picking up a transmission. It appears to be aimed at the two fleeing ships and coming from the larger group. Transfer to your station or play it aloud?"

"By all means, play it out loud, Comm, and record it for later analysis," Robert said, listening along with the rest of the bridge crew.

"Chap ara, Korvil! Mokara da est simu. Chap ara, Korvil! Shiravi korpa yefite!" A short interval passed before the message was repeated, another pause and another repetition, then silence.

"Sir, unknowns are launching Mambas," Nav reported. "Uh, not Mambas, but something similar with lower power outputs. I make it about twenty vessels. They're attacking the two ships as a group. I'm getting more on the ships themselves now. One has engine outputs that are almost identical to ours, four have larger outputs than any I've seen except aboard the *Galileo*, and the rest are slightly less powerful. The two ships running away are almost up to our outputs, but their signatures are… dirtier. Same as the ones we're fighting right now. I can't say it any better, sir. It's like their engines aren't tuned as well as ours or the new guys." A heartbeat passed, and she added, "Sir, the new guys… they're losing fighters and their small ship has been destroyed. No, make that two. Looks like they've lost their drive. They're sitting ducks."

Eleven Mambas had been completely destroyed by the time the last raider dissolved in a slowly expanding

11

cloud of plasma, while six others were damaged badly enough to require pick-up. And that didn't include the losses inflicted on the mysterious fleet that had appeared from nowhere. Scan showed that two of the six damaged Mambas were on a trajectory that carried them past the now-stationary group of unknowns.

Navigation, responsible for knowing where things were in the vicinity of the ship, reported, "Sir, I've got a beacon on my screens. It's like nothing I've seen before but on the same wavelengths we use. I think it's one of the small fighters launched from the unknowns. And six Maydays are coming in from our guys. Two of them are drifting into range of the unknowns."

Captain Greene, acting on a hunch, ordered, "Launch ten Mambas, two each for the four Mambas we can get to easily, and have the other two do a flyby on the bogey. Bring our guys in on capture fields. Have the pilots of the flyby report before committing."

"Sir, what about our other two guys?" Helm asked. "I can get us in close enough to handle a pick-up."

"Not without bringing us under the massed fire of eight ships," Robert said as he looked into the display. "I'm not writing them off, Helm; I'm playing a hunch. We're picking up one of theirs, and I'm betting that they pick our guys up."

Icons began moving around the display—green for friendlies and red for unknowns. Two green dots were surrounded by red and finally disappeared from the display. Another two green dots passed the lone red one drifting toward the Terrans and almost immediately the radio came alive. "Flyby reporting. This is Hothead. Looks like a weird Mamba, Control. One side is burnt off. No stabilizers on the port side and half of one engine is gone. I'm surprised it's in as good a shape as it is. Waiting for orders." The female voice could have been reporting on the condition of air filters on the engineering deck for all the emotion that came through.

"Hothead, this is the *Niven*. You are authorized to make another pass. Get closer, and get a look at the pilot, if possible." Robert released his mike button and waited.

"Roger that, *Niven*. Reporting in two." The static hissed as the pilot left her mike open while she turned her ship for another pass. "Dagger, this is Hothead. I'll make the pass. Hold off and cover me," came through in the same aloof voice.

An eternity passed aboard the four ships in the space of several heartbeats. Finally, the static ended as the pilot reported again. "*Niven*, this is Hothead. I am dead relative to the bogey. It's a Mamba, sort of, but definitely not one of ours. It's tumbling, so I can't get a good look at the pilot, but I can see a humanoid form. There's some type of helmet covering the head, like ours in a way. Can't make a positive ID. Sorry, *Niven*."

"Hothead, we understand. You and Dagger lock on with your capture fields and stop the tumble. Slowly! Bring it alongside for inspection by pod."

One of the four repair pods carried by all capital ships was waiting outside when the two Mambas brought the stranger alongside. "Bridge, this is Chief Wilson." The senior engineering officer prepared to do the inspection of the strange vessel himself. "Pilot appears humanoid, but I can't tell any more than that without opening the cockpit. Engines are definitely shot. This bird will never fly again without a trip through the nearest base. Power core appears stable. All voluntary control circuits are out. I think life support is intact. This thing is so much like a Mamba it's spooky."

"Very well, Chief. I have some ideas on that

particular subject. We can discuss them later. Have it brought aboard and crack that cockpit. Make sure that all personnel are either out of the bay or in pods."

"Aye, sir. But, if I may, I have a way to test for poisonous atmosphere before opening her up."

"Do it, Chief," Robert said. "Let me know as soon as you have something. Bridge out." He turned back to the holodisplay. "Nav, what are the unknowns doing?"

"Sir, they've picked up their fighters and our guys, too." The Nav officer tweaked her instruments. "Weapons are still hot, but there's been no attempt to lock on. Engine power fluctuations are consistent with station-keeping. We are being subjected to the same type of scans." She shook her head. "I can't tell you any more than that."

Commander Marian Farley and Lt. Commander John Evans found themselves drawn aboard one of the ships of the unknowns. Life support was the only system still functioning on Farley's ship, while Evans had gone to reserve air, and the temperature was steadily dropping in his cockpit. The two Mambas were placed side by side in a bay or hangar by the four little fighters that were so reminiscent of the ships they flew—or had flown until then. The two pilots watched as the bay doors rolled shut. Momentarily, sounds began to reach their ears, confirming that air was being pumped into the bay.

Able to see into each other's cockpits, Lt. Cmdr. Evans signaled his dilemma to his fellow captive. Unable to use her radio, Commander Farley shrugged her shoulders, unsure what to do. The bay their ships had been deposited in was barren of any living thing, but machinery along the walls was familiar in ways she couldn't explain. The dim red light that seemed to serve for illumination only added to her inability to determine anything concrete about their surroundings. As a pilot, she hadn't been required to service her ship, but it was customary for a pilot to know her ship's systems and know how to work on them if called upon to do so. Therefore, she had a passing acquaintance with the equipment in the *Capella's* bays. It was like looking into a slightly warped mirror, and it left her feeling queasy in a way she had never felt before.

Without any warning, her fellow pilot shrugged back at her and popped his cockpit. She watched in consternation as he removed his facemask and took a deep breath, then another, and a third. Finally, he grinned at her and gave her a thumbs up. Relief flooded her system, followed immediately by anger. Releasing her own seals and shock harness, she pushed straight up, standing as the canopy swung up and back.

The two Mambas had been set directly on the deck since their landing gear was unable to be deployed, so Commander Farley vaulted out of her cockpit and let her knees flex as she hit the deck, cushioning her dismount in the slightly lower gravity. One wall, she noticed as she looked around, had no fixtures or equipment against it. *That would be the hatch we came in through*, she thought. The other three walls were covered or lined with various pieces of equipment, some of which were familiar and some not. A slightly taller-than-normal door, reminiscent of the doors on the *Galileo*, was centered in the wall opposite the hangar bay door.

Farley turned her attention to her companion. Glancing at the name stenciled on the fuselage, she addressed him, unable to keep her temper in check. "Lt. Commander Evans, do you have any idea how stupid that was? Suppose the air wasn't breathable? I don't know how things are done on the *Spica*," she said, looking at his shoulder patch, "but on the *Capella,* we're taught to be a little less irresponsible."

"Do you have any idea how much air I had left, Commander?" the junior officer asked in return. "Look for yourself." He tossed the portable air bottle to the deck at her feet. "That's the only one in the rack. If I ever get back to the *Spica*, you can bet that somebody's ass is gonna be grass."

She picked the bottle up and glanced at the meter on the side. "Ten minutes. Okay, so you had cause. But this is part of your checklist," she said, tossing it back with force. "The only person you've got to blame is yourself. And I'll make sure to note that in my report." Evans caught the bottle and dropped it into the cockpit with a guilty look on his face. "Now, get down here. I think we should meet our... hosts... together."

Evans dismounted less acrobatically, swinging both legs over the edge of his cockpit and sliding down the side to the deck. "Looks like we finally get to see what the BEMs look like. I coulda done without the honor, for sure," he said caustically.

"BEMs?" Farley asked. "You're going to have to explain that one to me." She walked away from the ships and began examining the equipment along the wall near the door.

"It's an old science-fiction term," he replied, walking along beside her. "It meant 'Bug-eyed Monster.' I don't think you should touch that," he protested as she picked an object up off of a high bench.

She turned to face him, brandishing the thing in front of his face. "Don't tell me you don't recognize this. It's a *flux tuner*!" She laid it down and lifted a bulky item off of two hooks on the wall. "And this," she hissed, pushing it into his hands. "Tell me what *this* is."

"Uh, a flow compensator? It realigns the couplings between the core and engines, I think."

"So, they did teach you how to do more than fly that rattletrap on the *Spica*. I'm surprised," she said, acid in her voice.

"Hey! It's not my job to repair the damned things! Why should I know what this thing is? I just happen to remember it from training. What's it doing here?"

"But it *is* your job to understand as much as you can about the ship you fly, so getting your lily-white hands dirty…" She broke off her tirade and the two humans turned around as the door latches began to spin open.

Their surprise couldn't have been greater when the door swung open a few inches and a slight southern drawl spoke through the gap. "I'd take it as a great personal favor if you two would keep your pistols holstered. Mind if I come in?"

Captain Greene strode down the corridor known informally as Damnation Alley, an allusion that still eluded him. The previous four years had seen a revival of science fiction among Alliance personnel, and the name came from a novel he hadn't yet had time to read. The five armored and sealed doors on each side of the corridor led to launch bays housing individual Mambas, but due to the fighting, many were empty. That thought brought a constriction to his chest that he had a hard time setting aside.

He stopped before a door with a blinking red light above it. Fighting to get his emotions and voice under control, he pressed the intercom button connecting him to the repair pod. "What's the verdict, Chief?"

"My sensors say that his atmosphere is a little higher than ours in oxygen, a little less in nitrogen, and a few trace elements that would give the air a different smell. Nothing fatal, though. I've added oxygen and reduced the nitrogen a bit but otherwise left things alone. You're going to get an oxygen rush after a few breaths, sir."

"I'll keep that in mind, Chief. Thanks." Robert cracked the vacuum door and slipped in, shutting himself inside with the mangled fighter and the Operations Chief, who was busy climbing out of his now-deactivated repair pod. He pressed a button on the intercom and said, "Bridge, this is the Captain. I'm leaving this circuit open. Comm, wait for my signal to transmit unless something drastic happens, either in here or outside the ship. Then transmit and we'll worry about the consequences later."

"This is Comm. Understood, sir. And… good luck."

Robert turned to the ship sitting in the middle of the launch bay and nodded at the man climbing out of the deactivated pod. "I figured you'd need an extra hand, sir," the chief explained as he left the pod leaning against the wall. "The pilot of that thing hasn't moved since we shut the doors."

Robert stood there, hands on his hips, eyeing the sight before him, not missing the slumped form of the pilot through the darkened canopy. "How would you pop the canopy if that was a Mamba, Chief?" he asked.

The chief looked at Robert as if he'd sprouted a second head. "If that was a Mamba, there'd be an access hatch on the port side just behind and below the rear hinge," he said, pointing. He walked up to the side of the ruined fighter and stepped up on a jagged edge to reach the area he had just indicated. "Son of a bitch," the man muttered. He turned to the captain who was watching from below. "How'd you know, sir?"

"When did you join up, Chief?" Robert asked in lieu of a direct answer.

"I was on the crew that built Gemini Base. Why?"

"Well, Chief, I've been involved from the beginning, and the fighters we had at first looked exactly like this one. It was after Orion got shot up that we redesigned them and called them Mambas." The heaviness in his chest came back. "I think we've got one of the Builders in our launch bay, and I think we need to get him out of there. Pop it, Chief."

The Operations chief turned back to the access hatch and fumbled with it. "There's a handle in here just like on the Mambas. You sure, sir?"

"Not entirely, Chief," Robert admitted, "but what real choice do we have? Besides, he's just one individual and possibly hurt. And I'm hoping that the folks who picked up our guys are treating them as well as I intend to see this guy treated."

Farley and Evans looked at each other and both shrugged. "Doesn't seem like we have a lot of choice, now does it?" Marian answered for the two stranded pilots. "It appears that we're at your mercy."

The surprises continued when an obviously human black man stepped slowly through the door. Dressed in a grey one-piece coverall, he didn't resemble an Alliance member, and he was moving freely about an alien ship. Too confused to do more than stare, the two pilots waited for the stranger to speak.

The man seemed disinclined to speak for a moment as he stared at the faces of the two pilots. "God, it's good to see humans again. My name is Derek Carter, and I'll explain as much as I can in the short time before you meet the leader of this fleet. I'll be able to answer a few questions on the way up, but I'm really just an interpreter, if needed. Would you come with me? After you meet the Ambassador, you'll be allowed to call your ships and tell them you're alive." The man turned around and stepped back through the door, waiting for the pilots to follow. As soon as they did, he headed off down the corridor.

John, first to get his voice back, said, "I'm John Evans and this is Marian Farley. This looks a lot like the *Spica's* flight deck."

"I wouldn't be surprised," the man who called himself Derek Carter said as he walked along the deck. "It was probably built from the same set of plans that produced this ship. Elevator is right here." Pressing a control identical to the ones on all Alliance ships caused a door to slide into the wall.

"This is just spooky," Marian said, a slight quiver in her voice. "Where are we going? And why have you let us keep our weapons?"

Derek turned and looked at them. "Before we go up, I need to tell you a few things and answer a couple of questions. First, you're being allowed to keep your weapons because trust has to start somewhere. Second, we're going to the command deck. Third, you probably want to know why I'm here." At their nods, he just smiled. "That one will have to wait until there's more time. But most importantly, you're on an alien ship. I'm the only human aboard, except for you."

"So, where are all the aliens?" John asked. "We couldn't get a good look at the pilots of the ships that towed us in."

"You're going to start meeting them in just a few seconds," Derek answered as the elevator door opened. "They were asked to stay away so they didn't shock you before I had time to fill you in a bit." He stepped inside and turned to face the two pilots. "Come on. First you meet Rentec, and then you get to call your ships and let them know you're okay."

Marian watched closely as Derek placed his finger on a strip alongside the open door and ran it toward the top. "What did you mean by the 'same set of plans,' Mr. Carter?" she asked.

"Haven't you guessed yet?" Derek answered her question with one of his own, then gave her the answer she had shied away from. "These are the people who built the *Dalgor Kreth*, the ship you so aptly renamed the *Galileo*. All that you folks have built was designed by these people." The door slid closed and the floor pressed against their feet. "They're humanoid, with two arms, two legs, and a head. Eyes, ears and nose in all the right places and numbers. They just look different. The other race out there, the Korvils, have all the same physical characteristics—arms, legs, head, eyes and ears and such, but they're the bad guys. Ambassador do' Verlas and his people, the Shiravans, have been fighting them for over two hundred years. Now, you two aren't going to go berserk or anything, are you?" Derek asked, real concern in his voice.

"Is anybody going to… Hell! I don't know," John said in frustration. "This is a lot to take in, ya know?"

"Believe me, I know," Derek said with enough venom in his voice to draw stares from his companions. "I was captured by the Korvils right after Orion Base was completed. But you guys have an advantage—me. I'm telling you these people are *friends*. You're just going to have to trust me. They saved my life, and yours, too, and went to a lot of trouble to bring me home. Of course, they want something in return. But they need to talk to the boss."

The elevator slowed to a halt and the door retracted into the wall, giving the two pilots a view of another corridor. Not far off, two tall, thin beings were just disappearing around a corner. "They're red!" Marian exclaimed. "I mean, like, really red!"

"Tall, skinny, no hair," John remarked, a tremble noticeable in his voice. "Less exotic than what I've seen on television, and not as bad as I imagined. At least they're not slimy blobs or something."

The two pilots were led down a corridor that was strangely familiar yet eerily alien. The non-human origin of the vessel was becoming more apparent with each step the pair took, and the feeling of dissociation was compounded by the fact that they were following a fellow human who appeared to have the run of the ship. They walked past several open doors, commented on the higher ceilings, and got glimpses into open rooms. And, once, two beings walked past, glancing curiously down at them. This afforded them their first close-up look at their rescuers.

The aliens were somewhat taller than humans in general, which accounted for the higher doorways and ceilings throughout the ship and taller benches noted in the landing bay, and somewhat thinner of build. While they were indeed humanoid, with the proper number of arms and legs, eyes and ears—two each—as well as a head, nose and mouth—one each—the whole, when viewed from the perspective of the two pilots, was disconcerting. The skin was a bright red, even in the muted lighting common throughout the ship, leaving no doubt as to their alien origin. The ears were slightly pointed, apparently independently mobile, and located higher on the head than on humans. The nose was bereft of cartilage, leaving a mobile flap of skin below and between the eyes, while the mouth was probably the most normal part of the face. The eyes were what drew the pilots' attention, though. Pink eyes shading into rose glanced their way from one lofty face while the eyes of the other registered in Marian's mind as more salmon-colored than anything else.

Derek stopped in front of a door like all the others, knocked twice and opened it without waiting for a response. He stepped to one side and motioned for the pilots to enter. Hesitating for only a second, Marian looked at her companion, shrugged, and stepped through. John followed warily, taking in the room as a whole.

Two beings sat facing the doorway, one behind a desk and the other off to one side. As John stepped into the room, the one behind the desk stood up and stepped around it, approaching the humans slowly. From the doorway they had just entered, Derek said, "I'd like to present Rentec do' Verlas, Shiravan Ambassador to the human race. Mr. Ambassador, Doma Marian Farley and Dom' John Evans of the Terran Alliance."

The tall red man stuck his hand out, and with yet another surprise, said, "Dom Carter has informed me that it is the custom of your people to shake hands to show that one holds no weapons."

The captain and Operations chief stood on opposite sides of the stricken craft, and when the canopy jumped up the fraction of an inch that it always did on Terran Mambas, they pushed up and back, revealing the still

23

form of the pilot.

A helmet and grey one-piece suit covered most of the figure, but the hands were plainly visible. Immediately noticeable was the color of the skin—red, very red. It took a few seconds more for the other big difference to sink in. There was an extra joint on each finger. Robert's eyes riveted on the sight, and he felt a shiver run up his spine.

He looked over at the chief and said, "We lift to your side. When you have him stable, I'll come around and help get him to the deck."

The chief tore his gaze away from the hands and nodded. He reached in and hit the quick-release button on the restraint harness. "Just like on our ships," he muttered. The two men lifted and moments later had the alien flat on his back on the deck.

Robert raised his voice. "Comm, do you copy?"

"I do, sir."

"Very well. I want you to call the doctor down here and then transmit all data to Admiral Hawke on the *Rigel* via the *Norton*. Add this note: 'Mission accomplished. All enemy vessels destroyed. Cost: eleven Mambas, nine pilots.' *I hope*, he thought, "Add: major damage to two ships. P.S. I have an unconscious Builder on my flight deck. Would appreciate your arrival soonest.' That is all."

Five seconds passed, and the speaker broke the silence. "This is Comm. *Norton* away. Time to reception by the *Rigel* in Earth orbit is just over four hours."

"Damn," Robert said. Turning his attention back to the alien pilot, he laid a hand gently on its chest. "At least he's still breathing, I think. His chest is rising and falling. How can we tell how bad he's hurt or even what hurt is?" Robert shook his head in total bewilderment.

Before Chief Wilson could reply, the intercom squawked again. "Sir, this is Comm. We have an incoming transmission from the unknowns. It's in English, it's not our pilots, and they're asking for Captain Hawke. What are your instructions?"

"In English? How the hell is that possible?" he muttered. Aloud he said, "No response until I get back to the bridge. I'm on my way. Get a copy of the message downloaded to my comm link. I'll play it back on my way up." He turned to his companion. "Chief, can you...?"

"No problem, sir. The doc will be here in a minute. This guy isn't going anywhere."

Robert nodded his thanks and headed for the bridge as fast as he could. When his comm link beeped, he replayed the message that had been recorded by Comm. "This is Derek Carter calling Captain Hawke," a hesitant voice said in a definite southern drawl. "I am aboard the Shiravan flagship *Esmit do' Caryl,* accompanying Ambassador Rentec do' Verlas, who wishes to speak with Captain Hawke. As a sign of good faith, the ambassador has authorized the two Terran Alliance pilots rescued by his pilots to report their situation. As another show of faith, the ambassador has authorized the return of your pilots and myself. I was captured shortly after the *Galileo* left Orion Base for Earth. Unfortunately, their ships are too damaged to make it worthwhile to return. An unarmed shuttle will leave this ship momentarily. Carter, out."

The voice ended as Robert strode onto the bridge. "Comm, get me the signal and send this: 'This is Captain Robert Greene of the *TAS Larry Niven.* We've picked up one of your pilots as well. Unfortunately, your pilot appears to need medical attention. At least, we think so. If you have medical personnel aboard, they are welcome to accompany our pilots back to this vessel to administer aid and return your pilot as soon as they consider it feasible."

A red dot had separated from the swarm that was designated "unknown" while Robert was speaking. It reversed course, merging with the larger group, and minutes later it again headed slowly in the direction of the *Niven*. Robert returned to the flight deck and waited for the other ship to dock.

Marian stepped forward, trying to show more confidence than she felt. Warily eyeing the hand of the taller being, she tentatively reached out and grasped it. A thoroughly normal handshake ensued, followed by a repetition with John. The second being had risen at their entrance but made no move to come forward. "You speak English?" she asked, looking at Derek.

"I have a small understanding of your language, Doma. Dom' Carter and Doma Spencer have been excellent teachers. I'm afraid that I will be at a loss if the discussion gets technical, though. Your translation programs should be of enormous benefit in that area."

Marian shook her head. "So many questions. But Mr. Carter said that we would be able to call our ships and report in. I think that should be our first priority."

"And so you shall, Doma. I apologize for the delay in allowing you to do so. It was merely that my curiosity got the better of me. I've met only two humans before this moment. Now, Dom' Carter will take you to our communications station where you can speak to your commanders, and then we will return you to your people."

The two human pilots self-consciously exchanged pleasantries with the alien being and followed Derek out of the room. "Are we really going to be returned to our ships?" Marian asked the strange man leading them down an all-too-familiar corridor.

In response, Derek stopped and waved them into a room filled with communications equipment and several aliens. "Of course," he replied. "Ambassador do' Verlas wants the best relations he can get with the Alliance." To the aliens in the room he said, "Errocerra, ara eset Terrani simu yat mihara pukara, Dom do' Verlas."

An alien sitting at one of the stations held out a microphone and Marian hesitantly took it. She glanced at the black man and took his nod as an indication that it was all right to speak. "Uh, this is Commander Marian Farley, leader of Tiger Flight, call sign Tinkerbelle. I'm standing in the comm center of an alien battlecruiser of about the same configuration as the *Capella*. I have Lt. Commander John Evans of the *Spica* standing with me. We are alive and well. Evans would probably be dead now if not for the assistance we received. We have been informed that we are to be returned to our ships as soon as possible. Uh, that's all for the moment. Over."

"Commander Farley, *Niven* Control. We have received your message and will be trading the two of you for one of theirs. Congratulations. We lost a few good people, but with the assistance of your new friends, and at great loss to them, not one ship escaped. Control, out."

CHAPTER TWO

Robert hurried back to the hangar deck, listening to Flight Operations on his comm link as they talked the alien shuttle in. The thoroughly human voice with the southern drawl continued to speak for the shuttle all the way through its final approach and into shutdown. As soon as the status light over the door turned green, Robert spun the hatch locks loose, took a deep breath, and stepped inside.

The sight that met his eyes couldn't have been more normal. So much so, in fact, that for a second, he almost believed he had hallucinated the entire past few hours. A normal-enough looking shuttle ramp sat open in the bay, and the two pilots walked to the lower end, stopping just short of stepping onto the *Niven*'s deck. Commander Farley, saluted and asked, "Permission to come aboard, Sir?"

"Permission granted, Commander," Robert replied, returning the salute. "Report to the command deck and wait for me in my ready-room. Stop off in the mess hall first, if you need to. I'll be a while, I think."

The two pilots moved toward the hatch, the junior stopping beside Robert. He glanced back at the shuttle and said hesitantly, "Captain, you're about to have some pretty weird visitors."

"So I've been led to believe, Commander. But I already have a pretty weird one in another bay. Thanks for the heads up, though." Robert turned back to the shuttle sitting in his bay. *I'm not sure I'm ready for this*, he thought. *Any of it. It's just now sinking in that some people aren't coming back, and now I'm having to deal with aliens, for crying out loud. I think I can understand how Kitty felt after...* Cutting the thought off savagely, he turned back to more pressing matters.

Expecting to see someone like the unconscious alien pilot step out next, the appearance of an Afro-American man caused almost as much befuddlement as if an alien truly had walked down the ramp. The first words from the stranger confirmed his identity, as much by the accent as the words themselves.

"Sir, I am Derek Carter. I apologize for my haste, but Ambassador do' Verlas would like to see to his pilot as quickly as possible."

"Of course," Robert said quietly. His voice gaining strength, he added, "In his place, I would want to do the same. What's the procedure?"

"I assume you've seen the pilot?" Derek asked.

"Yes."

"Then you won't be too shocked to see three walking, talking members of his species come out now?"

"I guess not," Robert replied hesitantly.

"There will be two medics bringing out a stretcher, followed by the Ambassador. His presence is required, as he speaks both English and Shiravan." Derek turned and called out, "Chap ara. Terrani est sa aleren." He faced Robert again. "I picked up a little Shiravan as I was teaching the Ambassador English. Couldn't help it; it kinda stuck. Now, if you'll lead the medics to the pilot, sir?"

Robert hesitated when he saw the figures start down the ramp. The first two were dressed in greyish, one-piece coveralls and carried what looked like a standard stretcher except for the muted green color, while the third was dressed in a blinding outfit that appeared to be a turquoise shirt trying to hide under a yellow vest and a pair of trousers that matched the screaming yellow vest.

When he realized his mouth was hanging open, he closed it with a slight gulp and said, "Follow me, please." He walked to the door and turned to look at the odd procession. The two medics were directly behind him, being trailed by the garishly dressed alien and, finally, Derek Carter. He shrugged, more to himself than anyone else, stepped over the threshold and turned toward the open hatch of the adjoining bay.

Robert stepped through the bay door and motioned the two medics forward, a feeling of disassociation washing over him. He stood to one side and watched as the two beings set their load down beside the stricken pilot, and one opened a pouch at his waist. He removed a device and laid it on the pilot's chest, watching it for a few seconds. Obviously waiting for some reaction from the device, the Shiravan glanced up at the damaged fighter and then around the room. Returning his attention to the device on the pilot's chest, the medic pressed a control, and when it emitted a short, shrill beep moments later, the wounded pilot twitched, shivered, and raised his head.

"Su lapka? Domar foroset paka reth?"

"Par a Terrani dara foroset. Ep torbinasa pakara din *Esmit*. Terrani dara foroset."

"Now he's being told that your people saved him and that he is being returned to his ship."

Robert turned to look at the speaker and found himself looking up into a pair of unnervingly red eyes. "I am Rentec do' Verlas," the being said, holding his hand out. "I have been appointed ambassador to the humans by Linnas des Harras, Matriarch of the Shiravan Polity."

Robert apprehensively took the hand and felt the slightly higher temperature of the skin against his. Shaking it gingerly, he answered, "I am Robert Greene, Captain of this ship and a member of the Terran Alliance. Welcome aboard the *Niven*, Mr. Ambassador." A retreat into formality was all he could think of.

The alien gestured with his head and said, "My people are ready now to return." Robert looked and saw that the two medics had lifted the injured pilot and were waiting impatiently.

"Of course," he said. Leading the group back to the shuttle's bay, he stepped aside to let the medics carry the pilot aboard. "Will he be all right?"

"It is too soon to know, Captain," Rentec said. "As soon as I become aware of his condition, I will inform you. Your concern and aid are appreciated."

"Uh, sure. Thanks, Mr. Ambassador," Robert said, faltering and feeling more foolish by the second.

"Please understand, Captain, this is no more comfortable for me," Rentec said slowly. "Yours is the second race we have come into contact with and the first we have been able to converse with. The Korvils are not a social people. We can only assume that they hate all who are not Korvil as they attack you with the same…" He turned to Derek. "Kome esan dara eset jimana polika mehara?"

Derek answered with a single word. "Ferocity."

"Ferocity." The red man looked as if he were trying the word out in his mind. "A strange flavor to that word. And so compact for such a complex idea. They attack you with the same ferocity as they do us, it seems."

The two medics disappeared into the dim red interior

of the shuttle, and a moment later, one returned to stand beside the ambassador but behind by one step.

Before the ramp raised, another alien stepped into view. "This is my assistant, Doma Maratai kep Parrasine. Would it be proper for us to remain aboard your vessel and await the arrival of your Captain Hawke, whom Derek has told us of? We would speak with him on matters of great urgency."

When did I lose control of the situation, Robert thought? *Oh, yeah... just about the time I got out of bed this morning*. Aloud, he said, "Certainly, Mr. Ambassador. I think we could wait in my ready room, if that is agreeable with you. That's on the command deck. I've already sent a message to Captain Hawke—who's now an admiral, by the way—and expect his arrival within the next five or six hours."

By the time Navigation detected approach, Robert had been brought up to speed for the most part on the adventures of Derek Carter and Maggie Spencer.

"Once we were sure of the location of your homeworld, I dispatched a ship to report to my ruler and another to inform Second Fleet. Doma Spencer is aboard the *Chi Mara Vesh* to perform much the same function that Dom Carter has, which was to keep you from shooting at us before we could show our intentions," Rentec said.

"Apparently, Mr. Carter hasn't told you the story of the Trojan Horse, Ambassador," Robert said, a small grimace crossing his face. "Humans can be a very suspicious people, especially right now. Considerable damage has been done to our world, and people are going to be looking for someone to blame. At the same time, they… we… most of us, are going to have very short fuses."

"I beg your pardon?" Rentec knew he was using this phrase a lot of late. As soon as he thought he had a handle on these humans, something would get said that threw all of his assumptions into contra-space. "Trojan Horse? Short fuses?"

"It will take a history lesson to explain the Trojan Horse. Suffice it to say that it is a reference to an ancient war and subterfuge. As for the short fuses, it means that our anger is easily aroused, and sometimes we aren't too careful about how we retaliate."

Robert's comm link chimed. "Sir, this is Navigation. We've picked up the *Rigel* on long-range scans. Your orders?"

"Sit tight. I'll be right there. Call security and have two men posted at my ready room door. I don't want our visitors to be bothered by a lot of gawkers. And we're going to have to arrange for something for them to eat. We may have to have something brought over from the Shiravan ships."

Maratai turned to Rentec as soon as Robert's door closed. "It would appear that we aren't trusted, even after we aided them at considerable cost to ourselves. I think we may have been deluding ourselves that these humans would be willing to support us in our fight against the Korvils."

"Do not assume in haste, Doma kep Parrasine," he answered. "We have spoken only to this one officer. We will await the arrival of their Admiral Hawke."

"We should be wary of what we say, Dom do' Verlas," Maratai responded. "They could be recording us. It is what I would do if the positions were reversed."

Rentec nodded. "I agree, but remember that Captain Greene has said they don't possess any translation protocols. Somehow all of that was erased from the memory banks of the *Dalgor Kreth* when they took her over."

"So they say," she argued. "We have only their word on that. And Dom Carter has told us often of the human penchant for duplicity, which has been confirmed by this Captain Greene."

"Nevertheless, we will wait," Rentec decided.

The *Rigel's* speedy arrival meant that it had outpaced the laggard light-speed communications the Alliance was restricted to. The only information Simon had been privy to was what had been carried by the *Norton*— mostly a pure data-dump attached to Robert's announcement and a few cryptic remarks made since the *Rigel* had arrived. One in particular had caused Simon to smile: "Visitors in the parlor. Bring your wallet and leave your guns at home."

Sensors on full and weapons hot, the *Rigel* sat slightly apart from both groups of ships while Simon's shuttle docked with the *Niven*. Simon strode down the boarding ramp accompanied by Joanna Barnes, now the Alliance's science officer since Stephen's death. "Permission to come aboard, Captain?" Simon asked as he saluted Robert from the boarding ramp of his shuttle.

"Granted, and gladly, Admiral. I'm happy to have someone to turn this hot potato over to," Robert said, relief evident in his voice. "If you will follow me, sir."

"Captain Greene, Commander Barnes, our new Chief Science Officer," Simon said by way of introduction as the group headed for the midship elevator. "So, what can you tell me, Bob?"

"I can tell you that two of our people didn't die during the attack on Orion," Robert said. "They were captured and then eventually rescued by these guys—Shiravans, they call themselves, from the planet Shiravi. The two rescuees taught them English, and one of them is here as an ambassador to the human race, asking for help in their fight against the other ones, the Korvils. Sounds like science fiction to me." Robert laughed lightly at the old joke.

"We've all been living a science-fiction story for years, now," Simon answered, finishing the now-tired joke. "They can understand us, but we will have no idea what their transmissions say."

"Not entirely, sir. We do have Derek Carter. He's learned some of their language in the process of teaching them ours, and he should be able to identify intent if not content."

"I can work with this," Simon declared, "as long as there aren't any more surprises."

"Well, there is one more," Robert ventured as they left the elevator and started down the corridor.

"And that is?" Simon asked when Robert added nothing further.

"There are ten more ships headed this way with Maggie Spencer aboard the flagship. Once this bunch located Earth, they sent ships back to inform their homeworld and the *other* fleet that was looking for us."

"This just gets better and better, doesn't it?" Simon asked rhetorically. He stared into the bulkhead and beyond for the better part of a minute as his mind toyed with the various scenarios. "So, they know where our homeworld is. I'll bet that information hasn't been mentioned concerning their planet, has it?"

"Not yet, sir," Robert admitted as he stopped in front of his ready room door. "There's one other thing you should know, sir."

"Yes, Captain?" Simon prompted when Robert said nothing for a few seconds.

"You saw the data-dump?" When Simon nodded, Robert said, "Then you saw that they lost two ships taking out the two ambushers. Their arrival apparently flushed them out. They were closer, so they took them out. Been like this ever since."

Simon nodded slowly. "Common enemies make strange allies. Okay, let's do it." Simon waved Robert toward the door. "You get to handle the introductions, Captain, so lead the way."

I always thought this was supposed to be fun, riding around in spaceships, like Buck Rogers or something, Robert thought as he reached for the door. *I keep forgetting that even movie characters have problems*. He opened the door and stepped in and to one side, allowing room for Simon and Joanna Barnes to enter. The tall, red beings stood at his entrance and waited quietly.

Robert waited until the two parties stood a few feet apart and announced in a slightly strained voice, "Ambassador do' Verlas of Shiravi and associate." He'd only heard Maratai's name once and wasn't willing to mispronounce it and possibly anger his guests. "May I present Admiral Simon Hawke of the Terran Alliance and his science officer, Doctor Joanna Barnes."

Simon's sense of déjà vu was strained for a moment as his mind went back to a Montana mountain retreat over four years ago. The mood broke when the taller of the two beings, dressed in the most eye-blinding colors he had ever seen on a living being, stepped forward, hand out, and said, "I am pleased to finally meet you, Admiral. Dom Carter and Doma Spencer have told me as much about you as they knew and guessed. I have waited for over two turnings… years, for this meeting."

"I've thought about it, too," Simon confessed, shaking the proffered hand. "But I wasn't expecting this." He looked next at the Ambassador's companion and then at the table they'd been seated at. "It seems that Captain Greene has neglected to offer you refreshments," he said. "Can we get you anything to drink or eat?"

"Sir, we discussed that," Robert interjected, "and the Ambassador thought it best to wait for your arrival before sending to his ship for appropriate foods since it's most probable that what we have to offer will be unacceptable to the Shiravan metabolism."

"Okay, so you *have* been thinking about this. My apologies, Captain," Simon said. Turning to the alien, he said, "This takes some getting used to. Please, go ahead, Mr. Ambassador." Another shift of attention. "Robert, make sure Traffic Control knows to expect further arrivals from the Shiravan fleet. Oh, and order our ships to power down weapons," he said, almost as an afterthought.

Simon noticed the other occupant of the room. "Mr. Carter, is it?" he asked, reaching out to shake hands.

"Yes, sir. And glad to be home," Derek answered.

"We'll see about getting you back to Earth as soon as possible, Mr. Carter," Simon promised, "and if you still want to be a part of the Alliance, I'd be pleased to have you. You've certainly earned the right. For all that we've accomplished up until now, you've traveled farther than any other human in history. And you are due for a *lot* of backpay."

"I think that by the time Maggie arrives, she will have taken that title away from me, sir," Derek said self-deprecatingly. "But I'll take you up on your offer after I've had time to get reacquainted with home."

Turning back to the two aliens, Simon asked, "How can we make your stay easier, Mr. Ambassador?"

"I have already taken the liberty, as Derek would say, of calling my ship and ordering some food and drink to be loaded onto a shuttle," Rentec stated. "Do I understand you to mean that it is all right to have it sent?" Rentec held up a comm link similar to the ones carried by Alliance personnel. He looked at Robert. "Also, Captain Greene, while we were waiting for Admiral Hawke, I was informed by our medical staff that our pilot will be well after some time to rest. He suffered from lack of air. If your people had not taken him in, he surely would have died."

"You did the same for us already, Mr. Ambassador," Robert said with a dismissive wave of his hand.

"By all means, Mr. Ambassador, go ahead and send for your foodstuffs. How long do you plan to stay aboard, if I may ask? If you're going to be here for any length of time, you will certainly need it." He listened attentively as the alien spoke into his link. When Rentec finished, Simon said, "I think you are the real deal, Mr. Ambassador. Of course, I can't understand the words, but the flavor of your language fits in with the single recording we have of one of your people."

For the first time, Rentec's companion spoke up. "One of Shiravi, Admiral? How did you get… recording of one of Shiravi?"

Simon looked directly at the other being. "I don't think I got your name."

Rentec spoke before Maratai could answer. "This is my aide, Doma Maratai kep Parrasine. She is also special assistant to our ruler."

"*Doma*?" Simon asked, noting the stress placed on the word.

"Doma is a word used to denote respect to a high-ranking Shiravan female, sir," Derek said by way of explanation. "Just as Dom is used for males, as in the case of Dom do' Verlas.

"Ah, I see," Simon said, turning his full attention back onto the smaller being. "Well, Doma Maratai kep Parrasine," he said, stumbling slightly at this first pronunciation, "it seems that one of your people—most likely a crew person—aboard the ship we found left a message in the ship's computer. We didn't discover it until about a year ago. I would be greatly pleased if you could shed some light on what it says."

"That brings up a point we need to discuss, Admiral," Rentec said. "Captain Greene tells us that you do not have a translation program in your computers. All Shiravan deep spaceships have such a program imbedded in the basic matrix of the computer. Surely you must have found it by now."

Simon looked at Joanna, who tentatively leaned forward. All this time she had been carefully watching the interaction between the two leaders and wished more than anything that she could just stay quiet. "Well, uh, Mr. Ambassador, I guess you could say that I'm responsible for that. My field is… was… advanced cybernetics. That's the study of advanced computer intelligences. I was recruited early on to study the computer aboard the *Galileo,* and in my eagerness to discover all that I could, I'm most likely the one who opened the sealed case surrounding the computer core and exposed it to some form of viral infection."

Rentec shook his head, an almost human gesture. "Dom Carter has been very thorough in his teachings, but some of these words I do not know. Viral infections?"

"Very tiny lifeforms that can inhabit the blood of living beings like you or me, sir. In some cases, they have the ability to change the genetic structure of a person's DNA—the smallest bits of information in your body that tells it how to grow." Realizing that she was again going deeper than the two beings could understand, she tried again. "These tiny lifeforms have the ability to make you sick and die. It takes a doctor... one who understands the body... to know how to combat these tiny things. Among humans they—viruses—are the smallest living things we know of. In some cases, they've been responsible for killing off whole cities, even destroying countries, because not enough people were left alive to keep things going."

Rentec and Maratai spoke animatedly in their own language for several moments. "Excuse us, but we don't have the words to discuss in your language what we needed to say. What form does this... virus take? What did it do to the computer?"

"What form? I cannot say as it has survived to be studied in only two places, and I don't have clearance to anything but pictures. What it did was begin to wipe all information out of the computer, like taking all of your memories away. I managed to stop it by reprogramming blanked portions of the computer as the virus moved to other sections and got the computer to use its information-writing lasers to attack and destroy each viral piece as it tried to assault another portion of the computer." Joanna sat silently for a few seconds. "One of the things we lost was the translation program. We had it at first. We used it to put English names on all the controls so we could use them. But before we could find a user's manual for the ship…" She shrugged in defeat and sat back in her chair.

The faces of the two aliens couldn't be read by the humans in the room, with the possible exception of Derek, but their manner was positively agitated. "There is a…" Rentec paused, looking for words to express himself. "People lose their memories first," he said, trying again, "then their body stops doing the things it is supposed to do. Finally, they die, most horribly. This is not just one person, but many—first those closest to the first one affected, spreading outward in larger and larger circles. Strong things must be done to stop the spread of this… frenda vesh." He looked to Derek for help.

"The only thing I can come up with is the obvious," Derek said. "I'd have to say that he's describing a plague."

"Yes," Joanna said eagerly. "First it attacks the memory centers of the brain, then moves to motor functions—I'd guess at voluntary levels first and then involuntary, like breathing."

"Yes," Rentec said. "Breathing is one of the things affected by this… plague? In our earliest recorded times, it killed entire cities and was called frenda vesh, the death wind. Now, we also understand that it is caused by very small things that get into the blood. They can only be seen with the aid of devices designed to look at small things."

"Microscopes," Joanna said. "We tried that. But by the time we felt it was safe to take samples of the gel the computer is made of, we weren't able to find anything out of the ordinary—ordinary for the gel, that is."

"This is cause for great concern, Admiral," Rentec

said. "We take great precautions to make sure that nothing like this is allowed to get off of our planet. There is too much that can go wrong on a colony world without having to deal with a plague as well."

Simon shook his head. "I don't know what to say, Mr. Ambassador. We haven't seen any ill effects, but maybe your virus can't affect a metabolism as different as ours. I grant you that we breathe the same air, more or less, but we are just too different, I think."

"We have duplicated the original computer into all of our ships," Joanna said. "Smaller versions for our fighters, as well. That's almost two hundred different computers out there, and not one of them has given us any reason to suspect that the virus hasn't been completely eradicated."

Rentec tipped his head to one side, then the other, and said, "What cannot be changed, cannot be changed. I will call my ship and inform them that they are not to associate with any other ship, either by person or by exchanging supplies, until they are sure that the plague has not come to their ship from yours."

"Quarantine," Simon confirmed. "We have the same concept on Earth."

Rentec straightened up at the mention of Earth. "As troubling as this matter of plague is to us, we have another matter we wish to discuss with you, Admiral. That is the joining of our two races into a force that can defeat the Korvils. It is fortunate, in a way that they are between our two peoples. That way, they have to divide their forces to fend off possible assaults from both sides."

Simon raised his hand to stop the alien ambassador. "That's not a subject that we can discuss by ourselves, sir," he said. "It would be best if we include our Herald in any negotiations, Mr. Ambassador."

"Herald?" Rentec asked. "I do not know this word."

"The Herald is our ruler, sir," Simon told Rentec. "She should be present for any negotiations since she will have to make the final decision."

Simon thought he was beginning to get a handle on the facial expressions of these beings. The ambassador definitely looked confused. "We were told by Dom Carter that you were the ruler of your Alliance."

Admiral Hawke nodded, a strange expression on his face. "At one time, that was true, but things have changed in Mr. Carter's absence. Actually, the person we call Herald is the second to hold that title since it came into being." Simon went on to explain how the Alliance had copied their governmental style from the United States Constitution and Bill of Rights and gave a more complete picture of the Alliance's short history that brought Derek's information up to the present.

"We are amazed at the amount of progress you have made in the short time you have had possession of the *Dalgor Kreth*, Admiral," Maratai commented. "How is it possible? We have much trouble getting recruits for our ships."

Simon pondered the question for a time. "You have to understand that we are an inquisitive race, Doma. There's not much we won't stick our noses into. It's only been in the last sixty years or so that we discovered atomic power, how to release energy from the smallest pieces of matter. It's been less time than that since we first set foot on our planet's satellite. We are very new to space and really haven't taken our ships out of our own solar system yet. We probably would have, had it not been for these Korvils." Simon looked around himself at the ship's walls and the human and alien gathering, and said, "We have a form of recreation—fun," he said when he saw the confused look cross the ambassador's face, "called science fiction. It is an art form that consists of storytelling. Sometimes we read it and sometimes we watch it, but it's storytelling about how science will affect humans in the future. A joke we of the Alliance make among ourselves is that we are living in a science-fiction story come true." He paused for a moment, a little smile passing over his face. "And, of course, it doesn't hurt to have access to who knows how many young, adventurous, idealistic, science fiction nutcases who are willing to work in outer space for nothing."

The Shiravan edibles arrived, two small crates on an antigrav pallet. A crewman pushed it in, followed by a Shiravan. The Shiravan pulled out a tray, bottle, and glasses. "Ah, refreshments," Simon said. "That was quick. I'll get glasses for us, Mr. Ambassador, and then I'd like to introduce you to the human custom of the toast."

"I'm afraid, Admiral, that Dom Carter has already done so." Rentec smiled at the nearly identical flinch the Admiral shared with Derek when surprised.

CHAPTER THREE

'People' is the right word, Simon thought, studying the two aliens. *Just different-looking*. After some thought to keep the words simple for his visitors, he said, "It is my hope that this meeting will be a first step into a bright future for both our races."

Simon looked at the raised glass he held, duplicated five times by the people around him. "So, let's just get to it, shall we? Ambassador, what do you think the next step should be? I have my own ideas, of course, but it would be easier if we can start out knowing what each other wants, and as the guest, you should go first. Human custom," he quickly added to forestall any objections.

Everyone took a sip of the liquid they held, the aliens copying the gestures exactly. Simon set his glass on the table. "I never have figured out how to get from a toast to the more serious business that needs to be discussed."

Rentec looked around. "We would speak with your Herald to discuss the possibility of a partnership in our mutual fight against the Korvils." The statement, simple and straightforward, hung in the air for a few seconds.

"That's all?" Simon asked. "I'm going to make an on-the-spot decision here and say that the Herald will be rather upset if I say no to that. Granted, Ambassador. You and one ship can accompany us to Earth to advise the Herald. I imagine having a planet under your feet after all this time will be a nice change."

"That will be nice, Admiral," Maratai answered. "But why only one ship? We have seven other ships in need of the same chance to walk under an open sky."

"Because, Doma," Simon said, looking into the disconcertingly red eyes of the female alien, "after what my planet has just suffered, a large group of alien vessels suddenly appearing in orbit will cause much worry among our people. The damage has been too severe. They don't know that you aren't the enemy, but they will react as if you are because they have been hurt too badly, too recently. Another trait of my people is to look for someone to blame and exact revenge—make them pay a price for attacking us and killing our people," he amended at the blank stare that came his way.

Rentec glanced at his companion, then back at Simon. "It is easy to forget that such things exist when a person spends so much time away from a planet." He placed his hands together in front of him. "If I may ask, how severe was the damage to your world?"

"Only two ships made their way through the blockade to Earth," Simon said slowly. "But that was more than enough. One exploded its cargo above one of our continents, destroying an area of several hundred thousand square miles." He drew a circle on a piece of paper. "Our world. Earth," he said. Then, he drew South America inside that circle and a smaller circle inside the continental outline to show the devastated area. Drawing another circle, he said, "The other strike was here." Drawing more continents, he showed an area off the coast of Alaska. "One raider was shot out of the sky, and it fell into the ocean about here, five hundred miles from one of the regions that supply a large amount of the sea creatures—fish, we call them—used for human consumption. Tidal waves swept down the North

American coastline and inland as far as any river or tributary would allow up to about three thousand feet inland and sometimes miles. That affected millions of people in the United States alone. The tidal waves that resulted from the explosion at the depth of almost a mile killed people and destroyed property and manufacturing and agricultural resources all around the ocean's rim. The western rim took it the best because the energy from the explosion used itself up trying to move that much water that far. In all, it is estimated that over twenty million lives were lost, and our ability to recover from such a hit is… it will be years before the full effects are known. Nothing like this has happened within the recorded history of our race."

Robert pulled the paper to him, horrified both by the pictures and the words. "Sir, any chance that the reports could be wrong? We did lose most of our satellite network. Couldn't the reports be somehow exaggerated?"

"No, Robert, I'm afraid not." Simon's face mirrored the feelings roiling through Robert's mind. "The U.S. took the hardest hit. Almost every coastal town, including San Francisco and Los Angeles, is like a ghost town. The water just swept in and right back out, taking anything not nailed down and an unknown number of people with it," he said. "And we came close to losing our Japanese embassy. Some smart thinker turned on the force field in the nick of time, but the island itself will take considerable rebuilding. Then there was South Korea, parts of Russia, China, the Philippines, Hawaii, and Indonesia. Australia got off lightest of all because of Indonesia, but the west coast of the United States got hammered. Twenty million seems like a pretty small number when you consider the area affected. Doesn't make it any easier, though."

Robert's face paled at the recitation. "So, what will we do?"

"We'll rebuild, of course. The Alliance will contribute all it can to the effort, but we can't stop production on the fleet, either. We'll start sending entire asteroids to Earth for the *Galileo* to process in orbit, rebuilding what we can. The people and economy will recover eventually, but nothing is ever going to be the same. First off, we'll be handing out food processors wholesale. We'll split our people and start with Japan and the west coast of America."

Rentec didn't understand every word, but he caught enough to know that the humans had suffered greatly. "We are saddened at your losses, Admiral. It seems to me that the losses will continue unless we can come to an agreement. In the spirit of that thought, perhaps we can begin our journey to see your Herald?"

"Of course, Ambassador. I have been told of the losses to your ships. This saddens us, as well. Your sacrifice on our behalf is a debt that cannot be repaid. Would you accept the offer of repair and resupply for your ships? And I would be honored to have you ride with us back to Earth."

Rentec smiled. "I would be happy to ride with you, Admiral. It would give me time to learn more about your people. But I think it would require too much foodstuffs for us for the voyage."

Surprise crossed Simon's face. "Too long a voyage? How much do you folks eat? I can have you on Earth in three hours, tops." He turned to Robert. "Am I missing something, Captain?"

"I'm not sure, sir," Robert replied. He turned to the

ambassador. "I hope this isn't a stupid question, but how long would it take for one of your ships to reach Earth from here?

The puzzled look on Rentec's face was becoming a frequent occurrence. "At top in-system speeds, I would say about four of your days. That is just a guess since I am not trained to know these things. Why?"

"Because, sir, like I said, I can have you on Earth in about three hours. I'm at a loss here. We have the same technology. Surely your ships can do the same." Now it was Simon's turn to be confused. "Or is it a translation problem?"

"I will confer with the fleet commander about the repairs. I'm uncertain if he will be willing to split the fleet," Rentec said. "As for the question of how fast our ships can travel, I will speak to someone about it, but I am sure I am right."

After a short session making sure everyone understood each other's time systems, Captain do' Sirkis stood beside Rentec on the bridge of the *Rigel* and watched as the crew prepared to jump for Libra Base. Simon stood with his guests, letting the ship's captain do his job. The *Esmit do Caryl* would follow at its best pace. Simon was still perplexed as to the reason for the slowness of the Shiravan vessels.

The *Rigel* ran up to jump speed, followed closely by the Shiravan ship. As the otherspace barrier got closer, eyes started following the scans more closely to see where the difference lay. "Two minutes to barrier, sir," Navigation reported. She glanced at Helm's data stream. "Course laid in and locked."

"Very well, Nav," the captain acknowledged. "Take us to Libra."

The silence stretched out until Nav began the final

countdown. "Ten, nine, eight..." On the mark, the screens traded their view of the universe for the swirling, grey emptiness of otherspace for a few seconds before helm shut them down. "Translation complete," Nav reported. "Two hours, fifty-three minutes to breakout."

Simon turned to his guests. "Well, gentlemen, the hard part's over." He stopped speaking at the look on the Shiravan captain's face. *The guy is scared to death!* he thought. "What is troubling your captain, Ambassador?"

The aliens spoke together quietly for a moment, and the fear drained out of the Shiravan's face to be replaced with... resignation. "It has been so long that the rule of not using this level of space travel inside a solar system has been in place that no captain would think of ordering it. Neither of us considered the possibility that you would do so."

The alien captain spoke again, Rentec handling the translation. "Do you travel like this often?"

Simon's mouth quirked up at the ends. "As a matter of fact, it has become standard practice. Doctor Barnes said it herself: we didn't get the operator's manual. We had nobody to tell us it couldn't be done, so we went and did it. And it's so much quicker than the other method. Besides, we couldn't have done as much as we have in defense of our world without this trick. Don't the Korvils know about this either?"

"I would say they know about it now, if any ship has escaped with the information," Rentec answered.

"You have made changes to the engines, haven't you?" the Shiravan captain asked through Rentec. "I would like to see how you have changed the design. And I am interested in seeing what you have done with the parda kellin, the small fighters."

"We've changed far more than just the engines,

Captain," Simon said proudly after the translation. "I think we've found some applications for your technology that will surprise you. Sometimes it just takes a different perspective. I'd be happy to give you the grand tour. But first, we should consider getting the repairs to your ships underway. And you've got two of our fighters to tear apart and examine. But we can discuss those things another time."

While the Terrans were aware of the problems with positional accuracy inherent in the drives of their ships, the distance was relatively short—just over three billion miles—so the margin of error was considerably less. The *Rigel's* navigator dropped the ship back into normal space above Libra Base, well outside the plane the asteroids traveled.

In the twenty-four hours it took for the damaged ships to arrive, the *Galileo* docked with the Alliance base, and Simon was able to get the base commander up to speed on the next order of business—preparing for the arrival of the two alien destroyers. Pulling the specs out of the computer, Viktor McCord, Captain of Libra Base, set up the parameters necessary for the repairs to begin.

"You have done much with the technology, Captain McCord," Rentec said as he watched the process. "I am not very well acquainted with how these bases are operated, but I think that if the circumstances were reversed, we would be unlikely to have made as much progress as you have."

"Well, I guess you could say that we had a greater incentive than you folks did," Simon responded. "You developed the technology over who knows how many years and without much in the way of... innovation, if you will forgive me. We've been pressured from the very start, first by our own people and then by these Korvil folks. We *had* to produce quickly."

The Shiravans continued to get additional surprises as they awaited the arrival of their ships. A trip to the lower levels gave them some insight into one form of human recreation that amazed them. "We would not think of turning off the gravity matrix," Rentec translated for the *Esmit's* captain. "And you use the system to play games." He flipped his head from one side to the other. "And you use weapons in your play. This I find very... disturbing."

"Disturbing in what way, Captain?" Simon asked intently. "Disturbing that we turn off the gravity for fun or that we play with guns for fun? We consider both to be as much relaxation as training. And the guns are toned down. Even a direct hit on the eyes won't do more than cause a person to be blinded for a moment or two—about the same as walking from a dark room into bright light."

"I find the practice disquieting as well," Rentec said, his English improving at a phenomenal rate. "I recognize the necessity, but it is not something Shiravans would ever consider."

"Well, Ambassador, we humans have found out that if you disguise training as play, you tend to get a lot more accomplished," he said, defending the practice. "As a matter of fact, I think that throughout history—our history, that is—humans have gone to great lengths to make work of all kinds more interesting by adding an element of fun to things. Here, we are doing no more than letting our people relax from their daily chores. The fact is that it bears directly on space combat and hand-to-hand fighting. Do we point this out and take all of the fun out of it? I think not, knowing how our minds work.

Suppose a ship loses its gravity? Would you have your crew unable to perform their duties because of the disorientation from suddenly having to cope with zero-G? How about their ability to fight effectively when they can't even navigate their own familiar corridors without the benefit of gravity?"

Simon and Robert let Rentec and the alien captain finish their conversation as they guided the aliens, leaving Carter to translate as best he could. They led their guests through the forward partition and into the huge middle room. "This area we call the Projects Deck," Robert said. "It is where all of our R&D boys and girls put their little inventions together. Then, we can slide them out of the ship and tow them safely away for field testing."

Simon left the group and spoke to the flight operations officer quietly for a minute before making his way back. "I have another surprise for you, Mr. Ambassador," he announced. "I think we've made better use of some of your technology than you might expect. We found your... we call them capture fields... to be most effective for picking up asteroidal material and bringing it to the converter. We think that some industrious soul was told to figure out how to do that, and he or she did just that and no more. We experimented with it and found that these capture fields serve as a very effective shield against meteors and most projectile-type weapons, as well as reinforcing the walls of the bases and ships whenever necessary. In some cases, it is even possible to do without the metal walls altogether. It was all a matter of figuring out how to get enough power to the shields and learning how to manipulate them."

At a signal from Simon, the operations officer

activated the field and opened the outer walls as if they were going to move a piece of equipment out of the deck and into space. The expressions on the two alien's faces were becoming more readable by the moment. Total shock was evident on both as they gazed into the infinite depths of space, separated from it by the merest electronically generated field. "We've also adapted the same field to another use," Simon said offhandedly. With another wave, a Mamba that had been left sitting on the hangar deck for this particular demonstration was lifted by one of the internal fields and moved across the expanse of the hangar, setting down beside the group.

Simon walked over to the grounded fighter and climbed up to the open cockpit. "Those fields were not in evidence aboard the *Galileo* when we found her," he said, looking back down at his guests. "Some of our technicians figured out how to adapt them to interior use. Makes it a lot easier to move things around inside, don't you think?" He motioned for a waiting crewman to bring a rolling ladder for the others to use. "Captain do' Sirkis, you said that you wanted to get a closer look at one of our fighters. We call this a Mamba. It's named after a very poisonous reptile on our world, one for which most people have a very healthy respect. It's modeled after the fighters we found on the ship. Most of the modifications are to make it more comfortable for the human pilot, but we did make the engines more powerful and enhance the gravity-sump. We also added forward shields to protect the vessel from front impacts. Sorry, we have to make up our own words for all the new toys we've acquired. Anyway, our pilots are able to accelerate harder, faster, and longer than yours, I'll bet. Makes for a more agile ship, too."

The Shiravan captain looked into the cockpit of the

fighter, taking in the differences and making allowances for the smaller frames of the human pilots. "Different controls. What for?" he asked through Rentec.

Simon looked at Robert before answering. "Stronger engines and shields, and bigger grav-sump all require a different level of monitoring for humans. I must say that the neural connections in the helmets and bodysuits gave us some trouble at first. We're not as apt to trust a computer for things that we can monitor for ourselves."

Captain do' Sirkis walked around the lethal-looking ship. "Bigger, certainly," he said to Rentec in Shiravan. "One wonders what they've done to the weaponry since they've modified so many other things." He stopped at an access panel to the engine housing. Tapping on the panel, he got Simon's attention and cocked his head to one side.

"Apparently, the captain would like to get a closer look at the engines, Admiral," Rentec noted. "I believe that, as a youth, he would have been among the ones who were fascinated with over-powered hover cars. Now, he has a chance to see how someone else does it."

Simon waved an okay to the curious captain and continued talking with Rentec. "My people tell me they have already begun repairs on the most critical of your ships, Mr. Ambassador. Two weeks—three at the outside—will see both of them back in shape. In the meantime, we should probably head for Earth and meet the Herald. It *is* what you came to do, after all."

"Right now isn't the best time to be an Alliance member on Earth," Kitty said when Simon called her Zurich office from orbit. "World opinion, led by the United States, isn't giving us much of a break. I've recalled most of our people to active duty. The few who didn't want to crowd into the two embassies are aboard the *Galileo,* and I'll bet almost anything you want to name that they'll be *eager* to move upstairs very soon."

"I'm more concerned with your safety, hon," Simon replied. "Shouldn't you be aboard as well?"

The image of Kitty shook her head in Simon's viewscreen. "It wouldn't serve any good purpose, Simon, and it would just lower confidence in our people at this time. So far, I'm fine. Don't forget, I'm in Switzerland. They're famous for their neutrality. And I have the added bonus of being Freddie's guest. He, by the way, along with a whole battery of lawyers, is moving heaven and Earth to get things settled down. Most of the rhetoric is just smoke anyway. Things are being said like, 'You should never have taken possession of the ship in the first place.' Another one is, 'The United States takes the position that you aren't qualified to handle either the equipment or the situation.' And my personal favorite, 'We are aware of the imminent arrival of a representative of an alien race in Earth orbit. Negotiating with a possible enemy of the human race unilaterally is not an acceptable course of action. We insist on the right to have a representative on hand to greet the alien and assess the situation first-hand.'"

Simon looked at Kitty closely. "Why is that your favorite?"

"Well, it's the most pompous. And they're the ones who supported us the most," Kitty answered. "We gave them almost everything they asked for, and they go and lead the world in crying for our blood."

Simon shook his head. "We *sold* them almost everything they wanted. What they couldn't buy, they couldn't get, and that pisses them off to no end." He hesitated for a moment and added, "But that's not what I get out of that last one. What I want to know is: when and how did they find out about our visitors?"

Kitty had started to speak over Simon but stopped as the implication struck home. "We've got a leak?"

"Not just a leak," Simon noted. "This was deliberate. We have a snitch. And if it's someone who took a loyalty oath, I consider it treason."

Kitty had glanced away from the screen but jerked her attention back. "Treason! Simon, we can't do that! I mean the penalty is... I don't know what the penalty is, but we can't!"

"Relax, hon," Simon raised his hands at the screen in a protective gesture. "The penalty for treason doesn't have to be death. We haven't had to deal with the situation before, but I should have figured it would happen. We did figure it, in fact." He thought for a minute and then said, "No lives have been lost due to the leak, so simple expulsion would suit me... if we can figure out who our problem child is."

Simon, Robert, and the two aliens stood on the *Galileo's* bridge, awaiting the arrival of the Shiravan ship *Esmit do Caryl*. The captain of the *Esmit* had attempted the same jump maneuver the *Rigel* used to get to Earth orbit but caution had apparently played too large a role in his calculations. The *Esmit* glowed in the holodisplay just outside the moon's orbit, while most ships had a standard jump program that put them at fifty thousand miles above the surface. Then, the relatively short jump dropped down to assigned parking in geo-synchronous orbit at twenty-two thousand miles and a fraction.

"Maintain station beside the *Dalgor Kreth*," Rentec

told the *Esmit's* captain. "Doma kep Parrasine and I will go to the surface and speak with the leader of their Alliance. Our trip may be for an extended time, so one of us will keep in touch with you on a regular schedule."

The four beings walked into the *Galileo's* transporter room. Maratai looked around slowly. "It doesn't appear that you have made many changes on this vessel, Admiral Hawke. Why is that?"

"Well, Doma kep Parrasine," Simon responded, "this is the fount of all knowledge, so to speak." He waved his hand in an expansive gesture. "We didn't want to mess with it too much and maybe lose more of it, like we did the memory in the computer. Essentially, all we did was to change things to make them more comfortable for humans—lower the tables and chairs, add short platforms in front of consoles, that sort of thing. The major changes were incorporated into the new vessels we built."

"I would still like to see the engine room aboard your *Rigel*," Rentec said. "And I am sure that Captain do' Sirkis would like to accompany us on that tour as well." He glanced at the controls for the transporter and said, "I am full of surprise at how you were able to reprogram the computer to accept your language. It is my understanding that it is not a small accomplishment."

Simon smiled knowingly. "I've been given that same impression myself. I think that since Doctor Barnes felt responsible for the problem in the first place, she worked harder at getting things squared away than she might have otherwise. Sometimes, embarrassment is as much of an enticement to greater achievements as anything else. But in actual fact, when we got the ship, it already had every Earth language in its database. I believe it was the last survivor who managed to get your computer to do the translations."

"You may be right, Admiral," Rentec said, nodding his head in an entirely human gesture.

Simon entered the transporter, followed by the two aliens and Robert, and turned to the nervous technician manning the controls. "We'll be beaming down to the Zurich embassy, Ensign. Set us up for the Herald's outer office, please." He turned back to Robert and the two visitors. "I had thought to take a shuttle down so you could get a better look at our world, but this isn't the best time. Too many people are too upset at us for what they think is our fault." He motioned the rest of the group to the hexagonal spaces on the floor.

Maratai walked over unhesitatingly, as if she had done this countless times before. "We are concerned, Admiral, with the fact that your Herald does not speak for all humans," she said, taking her place on the appropriate spot. "On our world, we have had a single ruler for dozens of generations, and have a hard time thinking of any other system as... effective? Is that right?"

Robert spoke up. "That would be the right word to use, Doma. And we are surprised from time to time to find out that things work as well as they do with so many different groups advocating so many different goals. We are slowly heading toward a universal planetary government, but a lot of folks resist it, thinking they'll lose their national identity. They don't realize that real expansion into space will eventually require the concerted effort of the entire planet."

Simon took his place on the last hex. "We can continue this conversation downside, I think. We're expected soon," he said. To the young ensign, he just nodded. Seconds later, when the columns of blue sparks had faded away, they were thousands of miles away.

Rentec's awareness of his surroundings underwent the normal dislocation he always associated with beam travel. Seconds passed while he took in the new locale. Gravity was a bit higher than he was used to aboard the *Esmit do' Caryl*, but nothing that he couldn't handle with rest periods at opportune moments until he could get acclimated. The air was a trifle denser than he found comfortable and full of strange but not overly unpleasant odors. The room he materialized in was furnished with low-slung furniture indicative of the shorter stature of these humans and was occupied by one of the five humans present.

The seated human looked up from papers on her desk, and said, "Welcome to Alliance Headquarters, Zurich, Admiral. The Herald is expecting you. Go right in." She didn't seem to bat an eye at her first view of the two aliens.

Rentec thought, *I would imagine a different reception had we arrived without an escort.* Aloud he asked, "No more formality than this to get into the presence of your Herald? I imagined something more."

Simon started across the room, gesturing to the others to follow. "We don't stand on ceremony as much as some people might think, Mr. Ambassador. Our rank mostly serves to let each of us know who's in charge in a particular situation. To those outside our organization… well, they're used to pomp and ceremony, so we give it to them. Most people see what they want to, so we tend to reinforce some misconceptions for our own benefit. Besides, the Herald is my mate."

Rentec only understood about two thirds of the words

Simon spoke, but the inference was clear. "We, too, have certain things we do to make the actions between peoples go easier. Some make sense, and some are things we do because we have always done them so."

"Like not changing your technology for hundreds of years just because it works as it is?" Robert asked as Simon reached the door to Kitty's office. Rentec's answer was cut short as Simon opened the door, stepped through, and ushered the group inside.

"Madam Herald," Simon said formally, "I have the honor to present to you Ambassador Rentec do' Verlas of the Shiravan people and his aide, Doma Maratai kep Parrasine."

Kitty Hawke stepped around her desk and walked up to the two aliens as if she did this kind of thing every day. "Welcome to Earth, Mr. Ambassador," she said looking up enough to hurt her neck. "I have imagined this day for many years now and am very happy to make your acquaintance."

Rentec put his hand out in the human gesture and took her cooler one in his, shaking it carefully. "I, too, have thought about this moment for some time, Madam Herald, and am happy to meet you, as well."

Kitty waved at a cozy setting of chairs and tables, two of which were noticeably higher than the others. "Would you care to sit down? I would offer you something to drink, but I'm afraid we don't have anything you'd consider safe without a lab to test it first. Even our water could have harmful effects."

The taller alien moved to the grouping of seats, saying, "I took the liberty of having my aide bring beverages with us in the event that we were to be here for a time, Madam Herald. It is my hope that you are not offended?"

Before Kitty could answer, Maratai noted, "You have chairs of Shiravan design. How is that?" She sat on one of the cushioned seats as if it was going to bite her.

"When I knew for sure that you were going to arrive," Kitty said to Maratai, "I called the *Galileo* and had them make some chairs and a few other things from designs in the computer and send them down. My only worry was that you would bring more people along and I'd not have enough for everyone." To the ambassador she said, "No, I am not offended at you bringing refreshments. Under the circumstances, I would have done the same in your place."

The five beings settled themselves into the chairs, situated so that the aliens had a view out the picture window at the massive mountain range looming over the embassy. Kitty noticed Maratai's attention riveted on the scene. "One of our more impressive mountain ranges, I believe. I consider myself lucky to have that to look at. The place I grew up is more flat than anything else."

"I think your mountains are bigger than any we have on Shiravi. I think our world is an older one than yours, but I am not sure," Maratai said. "I have seen bigger on several worlds, but these have a..." she hesitated, looking for words in the strange language. "These have a bigness to them that I have not seen before."

Kitty let the small talk go on for a few more minutes before she got the group focused on the reason for this first official meeting between the two races. "I've been told that you're here as a representative of your ruler, Mr. Ambassador. I do not wish to appear too uninformed, but would you tell me in your own words just what your mission is?"

"Doma kep Parrasine and I were sent," Rentec started, "to find out if humans could become partners in our fight against the Korvils. That is the main thing we have been asked to do, after returning Dom Carter and Doma Spencer to you, of course. Our other goals are to assess your ability to assist us and help where we can."

Kitty leaned back in her chair and looked up at the tall, red alien. "I see," she said. "I know you've seen our ships in action against some of these Korvils and have been allowed to tour one of our bases. You also got to see how we've adapted some things, sometimes drastically. Are you willing to share with us some of your feelings now that you have had time to think about what you've seen?"

"We feel, Madam Herald," Rentec said, having trouble taking his eyes from the diminutive human with the amazingly white hair and disconcerting blue eyes, "that humans have the capacity to help us greatly in our fight to rid ourselves of this problem. Even though we have faced the Korvils for some two hundred and fifty of your years, we have not been able to do much to stop their raids on our space and peoples. Not until recently have we even done so much as find one of their bases. We have only been able to destroy a handful of their ships, and that only if they happen to attack while a sufficiently large force of ours is in the vicinity. And our win/loss ratio is becoming unacceptable."

Kitty nodded. "I see your point, Mr. Ambassador. We'd be grateful for any assistance you could give us as we prepare a larger effort to defend ourselves, but just how can we help *you*? You've been dealing with this problem for far longer than we have. How can we help as advanced a race as yours?"

Rentec looked to Maratai, who leaned forward, placed her hands together in her lap and, with an expression that Kitty read as uncomfortable, began to speak. "One of the things we were to do was find out what we can about your culture. We had only Dom Carter and Doma Spencer to go by, and they said that they were only—I use Dom Carter's words—just plain folks and not informed as to what you or other leaders might do or say when we arrived. We are happy to see that your Alliance is headed by a female, as that is how our culture is run, but we are troubled by the fact that you are a small part of your race and that the rest is so splintered. I wish Dom Carter could be here to help with this talk, but I am happy that he was able to go and reassure his family that he is still alive. We will have to make do with the words we have."

Rentec took the reins back. "Another thing we are to do is find out how much you have done with what you call the *Galileo*. We know that you have only had the ship for a handful of your years, and we thought that you would have done very little with it, even knowing what Dom Carter has told us of your plans. He and Doma Spencer were not high in your Alliance, so they weren't aware of your future plans."

"Which changed drastically," Simon interjected, "right after the attack that they got captured in. We began a massive recruitment and building campaign immediately afterward."

"As we would have in your place, I believe," Rentec said. "We are amazed at the amount of progress you have made in so short a time. To speak the truth here, we are also somewhat worried about the same thing. We believe that the Korvils—they called themselves something else long ago—stole a ship from us. It happens that a ship will not come back, from time to time. This is the nature of life in space, unfortunately, but in this case, some four hundred years ago by our reckoning, the Korvils must have come into possession of a ship, either the same way you did or by finding and killing the crew of a ship. We feel this to be the case because the ships they used when we first met them were almost identical to ours. Unfortunately, they do not have the same values we do. From that point, they used the ship they copied to expand their empire. We became aware of their existence when they started raiding our planets. At first, we tried to talk to them. They never spoke but merely began systematic attacks against us wherever our spatial borders met."

"So, you feel threatened by us for what we've done with your ship?" Simon asked.

"Not threatened," Rentec corrected. "At this time, we are happy to find another race we can speak to and possibly work with on friendly terms. We do worry about the future since the Korvils are the only other race we have met."

"It would be nice," Maratai added, "if humanity were to become our partners in wiping out this menace to our way of life."

"But you still feel threatened by us," Simon prodded.

Kitty raised her hand, stopping Simon from continuing. "Let me try, dear." She turned to the two aliens sitting stiffly in the over-sized chairs. "I think you see the similarities between us and the Korvils, don't you? The ability to take your technology and duplicate it for our own use, our lack of a unified government, our racial immaturity. These are the things you find that do not make you happy. I think it's time for you to know the whole story about us—as a race, how we came by your ship, and how we've arrived at this point. First, though, we should have those refreshments."

After glasses had been brought in by an aide and

everyone was again comfortable, Kitty started. "I'm not an expert by a long shot, but most people know enough about the beginnings of the human race that they can speak reasonably knowledgeably about it. There are actually two differing stories—one scientific and one religious. I'll leave the religious for another time. Our planet is about four billion years old, our scientists think…"

An hour later, with the help of Simon and Robert, Kitty summed up the situation. "Yes, we quarrel among ourselves. We fight each other and kill each other for a variety of reasons, some of which can be defended but not very well. We were in the process of growing into space—or we were until your ship came along and let us make a leap that would have taken hundreds of years. I'm afraid of what would have happened if we hadn't found that ship. The Korvils came anyway. They would probably have turned us into a hunting preserve or something, and that would have been the end of humanity, in the end. But they found us with the ability to defend ourselves instead. What would we have done against them if we hadn't possessed the technology we do—a question I'm glad we don't have to answer. Are we ready for this great step? I have no real answer except to say that some of us are but not all. Can we help you? Certainly, we can. It's how much help we can give and what kind of help that are the main questions. And one of your bigger worries—a female in charge. We have one now, but at one time it was a male," she said, nodding at Simon, "and under our system, it will be again at some time. We don't have anything preventing it. We believe too strongly in what we call equality of the sexes."

"We believe as well that it takes both male and

female in balance to make a unified, productive, rational race," Maratai said, her feelings eased somewhat by the history the humans had just revealed. They were as war-like as the Korvils, to be sure, but moderated by a sense of right and wrong that she felt in her soul. And they even spoke of a higher power! "We have come to believe in the moderating influence of the female spirit in our race. It lends itself, we believe, to a greater balance and greater sense of right and wrong as you say."

Earth's first official meeting with the Shiravan lasted well into the evening, exploring ideas and possibilities until all the participants were too tired to think straight. Kitty finally called a halt to the session, saying, "I think we have enough information to keep our minds busy for days to come, Mr. Ambassador. And while I agree that we need to do something together to end this menace to both our races, I think it would be wise to include some of the other leaders of our world in the discussions. Perhaps we could get together again in a few days?"

Rentec nodded his head, disconcerting his hosts with the humanness of the gesture. "I agree as well, Madam Herald. But if I may, Doma kep Parrasine has a question she has wanted an answer to since she first heard about the situation." The ambassador continued to refine his use of the English language, and the improvement was apparent even near the end of this first meeting.

Kitty nodded to the ambassador and turned her attention to the other alien. "If there is anything I can do, I will certainly do so, Doma kep Parrasine."

Maratai was beginning to feel the effects of the slightly higher gravity. Even so, she wasn't going to pass up this opportunity. "Ever since we heard that you have a recording of one of our people in the computer of the *Dalgor Kreth*, I have been eager to hear it. Is it possible to hear that at this time?"

Kitty nodded her head slightly, lips pursed. "I think that can be arranged. We've been anxious to find out what it says, too." She walked to the desk and pressed a button. "Diana, can you find the file from the *Galileo* marked unknown alien speech, please, and transfer it to my office?" Moments later a light blinked on her terminal, indicating the arrival of the requested information.

This was a file she had accessed so many times that she knew the alien sounds almost by heart. She didn't understand any of it, of course, but she knew the sounds. "I'm convinced," she said, spinning the monitor around so the others could see, "that this is the person my husband and I saw the day this all started. Please, move your chairs closer if you'd like."

"Most definitely a Shiravan," Rentec said as he examined the image frozen on the screen.

"And recorded on board the *Dalgor Kreth*," Maratai noted. "It appears to be one of the personal rooms, but I can't tell which. It appears that all of the furniture and decorations have been removed from the walls."

"That's how we found her, Doma," Simon interjected quickly, "with not one personal item to be found." He deliberately omitted finding the pendant. Just why, he couldn't say. A quick glance in Kitty's direction let him see her hand twitch slightly toward her neck, then drop back to her lap. "It wasn't until about a year ago that we discovered this recording after a computer problem. We believed it was a member of the race that built the ship, and it's nice to have our guesses proven true. Our hope is that we'll find out something useful about how our world was chosen by whoever that is," he said, nodding at the screen.

Rentec settled back and folded his arms across his chest. "We will do our best to translate for you, Madam Herald. I can think of no reason that you cannot hear what is said. Besides, you have Dom Carter to verify our words if you think we lie."

"Mr. Ambassador!" Kitty said, looking at Simon and Robert. "What have we done to make you think we wouldn't believe you?"

Maratai looked at the two human men. "When we awaited the arrival of Admiral Hawke, we were left alone for a time, but were kept under guard so that we might not explore the ship or speak to any of your crew. We find this to be a sign that you do not trust us."

Robert flushed to his collar. "Wait a minute! I didn't put you under guard. I was only trying to allow you some time to yourselves without being interrupted. You could certainly have gone anywhere you wished. But I was going to be right back with the admiral."

"And haven't you been shown everything you've asked to see since then, Doma?" Simon asked. "And been allowed to speak to anyone you wanted?" He turned to Kitty. "Not once have we done anything that wasn't for the good of our visitors, much less insult them."

"Let's not let things get out of hand here, people," Kitty said placatingly. "It could be something as simple as a culture clash. Mr. Ambassador, Admiral Hawke is under my orders when he's acting in his capacity as an admiral, but at all times, he is my husband. He's aware of what I will do to him if he makes a mistake on this matter. And Captain Greene is one of our most trusted officers. I'm equally sure that nothing he did was meant to cause insult. I would hate to have a possible alliance between our two races fall apart before it even got a chance to start."

Maratai looked at Rentec before speaking. "I would not like that either, nor would the Matriarch. I think we treated Dom Carter in much the same way at first to protect him from those who needed to see to believe. I should have not been so quick to speak."

Relief flooded through Kitty's body. "Thank you, Doma kep Parrasine. Now, if you'd like to see the recording?" When the two aliens nodded, Kitty hit a key on her console and the image came to life. Even though the humans had seen this same video many times, it was the first for the alien members of the conference, and they sat transfixed.

"Se el Trajo Kuria. Pela ben kala es Derol Kuria dep Gerra Kindara. Dumal subara set es kimro sparadimo ni apara torbinasa."

Rentec waved his hand and Kitty hit the pause button. "This says he is Trajo Kuria, son of Kala and Derol. He is from the Kindara region of our world, which is not far from the Stala Mountains where our Matriarch has her private residence. He also says that he is—was—a junior computer technician and the captain's shuttle pilot. Please go on."

This time, when Kitty resumed the replay, Rentec spoke over the sound, providing a running translation. "And this is my confession. I freely give up my honor, for I am guilty of the deaths of all aboard—not by my hand alone, but under the guidance of Isolationists, the same Isolationists who wanted to see this mission fail and told me that the explosives built into the ship when it was constructed were meant to cripple it and make it return to Shiravi. I was told that the Expansionists would see how deeply we had penetrated their regime and stop their expansion into Korvil space. I was lied to. The explosives were there, but just enough to rupture several containers of a deadly sickness."

Rentec raised his hand. "Please. Stop the recording." He took a drink from the tall, thin, wine glass, and stared at it for a moment. After a few seconds he looked first at Maratai and then the humans, and said, "I am at odds to explain why I can appreciate the gracefulness of this," he said, indicating the glass, "when I have just heard of the deliberate destruction of an entire crew. I knew some of those people. I was personal friends with the captain. He was the first male to command such a large vessel in our program to return our males to the workforce. Now I must tell his lifemate."

Kitty felt as if she were intruding on a private moment. She glanced at Simon and inclined her head at the door slightly, eyebrows raised. When he just shrugged, she said, "Mr. Ambassador, if you wish, we can leave you to listen to the rest of this in private."

Rentec sat up straighter in his chair. "No, Madam Herald. I'm sure the worst is past. The rest will be just details. Please, continue."

The recording continued, and so did the strained voice of Rentec. "I have had many nights and days to consider my situation and how I came to be here. I believe that I was used. This does not lessen my guilt, but perhaps it may explain it. I always believed in the Isolationist ideal, but when I was chosen from university to work on the new computers, I jumped at the chance to learn more about my profession. It would be a great thing to say to potential future employers.

"I was approached several times by a dockworker named Kinna Feras, but not until I met Rami did I begin to go to the meetings he had invited me to. It was at her urging, I now see, that I finally agreed to go. As our feelings for each other grew, so, it seemed, did her hatred for the Expansionist ways. When I was chosen for the next crew, I would have refused to go out of love for her. It was she who said that I could help the cause by damaging the ship from within, for explosives had been planted while the ship was being built, supplied, and inspected.

"It was she who convinced me, but it was still I who input the codes that started the Isolationist plan into action. Half a turning, they said. Half a turning into the flight, I was to send the codes to the explosives, and then the ship would have to return home. Only one turning would I be away from my beautiful wife. Yes, wife. We were married in a small place of worship in the Dukara Mountains overlooking the spaceport at Quillas." This was the point in the recording where Kitty had always felt that the being speaking was distraught. It would seem that she'd been right. She heard Rentec's voice falter and Maratai's sharp intake of breath.

"She gave me her family crest," the narration continued. "I could add kep to our family name. I was so proud that such a one as she would bestow such an honor on one of my birth." Resignation crept into Rentec's voice, matching the tremors in the recorded speech. "We, the captain and I, were outside the ship and managed to survive the infection. When the last crew were dead, we evacuated the air from the ship using pod suits and removed all the bodies and personal possessions, committing them to the Spirits of Space. Their names are twice recorded in the ship's journal. Then... then," the voice faltered and stopped for a few seconds. "The captain fell victim to the death, and I was alone. I searched for home after the captain died, but it was no use. While we were outside, someone removed all navigational data from the computer so we couldn't take a death ship back to Shiravi. But they needed to know, so I tried.

"Instead, I found this new world, inhabited by an intelligent race. Satellites in orbit say they are almost ready to step beyond their world. I give this ship to them in hopes that they can help topple the Isolationists that killed me, for I find that I now have the plague as well. I will take a shuttle to the surface and try to find someone to give our knowledge to. If not, the ship will stay in orbit until they can find it and enter it on their own. I will evacuate all the air to sterilize the ship one more time. A recall signal will restore the air, or a ship approaching will do the same.

"To all who hear this, know that no one was meant to die—not by my hand. Know also that the people of Shiravi are a good and kind race. Know as well that there are those amongst us who, while they are good and kind also, will do whatever they think necessary to forward their particular cause. Be it Isolationist or Expansionist, there are extremists on both sides." The figure on the screen broke out in a fit of coughing that left him visibly weakened. "All that I have said here, I have written down and placed, with additional proofs, with the ship's log. I go now to my fate. May the Spirits of Space forgive me, for I know no one else will."

CHAPTER FOUR

Tears rolled down Kitty's face while both Simon and Robert looked uncomfortable. Rentec took several breaths before he spoke. "I would find this journal as soon as possible. Whatever information it contains that you can use is yours, but the journal itself must be turned over to the Matriarch as soon as possible."

Simon looked at the humans present. "One of our standing orders is to bring anything like a journal or personal possessions to the attention of any officer so it can get to us for analysis. No record has been turned in. Where would something like that be kept?" This last was directed at the two aliens.

Rentec shook his head, adopting the human gesture for the time being. "I would not know, as I was never involved in the day-to-day functioning of any of the ships. The one to ask would be Captain do' Sirkis. But I can tell you why no personal things have been found. It is one of the customs of our people to take all of the things a person has gathered in their life and bury it with the remains. It was thought long ago that it would ease the journey to the next level of existence. Now, although we no longer believe that, it is a custom that continues. Also, anything that might hold the frenda vesh must be destroyed."

When contacted, do' Sirkis said, "There is a secure document safe in the captain's cabin, but the most likely place to find it would be in the side panels of the command chair. Most captains keep their logbooks there for easier access."

Simon shrugged at Robert. "As many times as I've sat in that chair, I had no idea there were hiding places in it." To the image coming from the Shiravan flagship he asked, "How do we open these panels, Captain?"

"Beneath the chair arms are two depressions easily reached by the fingers of either hand. The usual method is to press the rear one once, the forward one twice, and the rear one once again. This should open the compartment."

An hour later, the five beings were sitting around a small pile of material found just where the *Esmit's* captain said it would be. Rentec and Maratai pored over the heavy journal, commenting in Shiravan at times. The two aliens read the final pages in the journal and came to a separate packet. Opening it, they began to peruse the sheaf of documents inside until Rentec sat back in his chair, one hand loosely holding one of the papers. Every bone had been removed from his body, it seemed, and every emotion drained from him, he sat so still. It took a moment for his despondence to register with the rest of the people in the room.

Kitty touched Maratai on the arm as she read more of the hand-written notes inside the packet. When she looked in the indicated direction, Maratai put down the paper she had been reading. "Dom do' Verlas, Mr. Ambassador, what troubles you?"

Saying nothing, he handed the paper to Maratai. Her eyes flew across the document line by line, and she said, "It appears to be a marriage document between one Trajo Kuria and... and... Mr. Ambassador! Se el kuvai. I'm so sorry," she added in English.

Kitty asked, "What is so bad, Doma?"

"What?" Simon asked at the same time.

"This document," Maratai said, "says that our young man who was led astray by his feelings for a female was indeed married in a small chapel in the Dukara Mountains. It names both parties and their affiliations back three generations. It appears that the names here are legitimate, but one of them is of great concern to us. Trajo, we can discount as perhaps one who was used as he said. But the other—that is a problem." She turned to the gloomy-visaged representative. "Should I tell them, Dom?"

"I will tell them, Doma," Rentec said heavily. He sat up straighter in his chair and took the paper back from Maratai. "The second name on the document is the same as that of my lifemate, Ramannie kep Gillas. But it must be a mistake. How could this be? Proof must be gathered before I will believe this!"

"What would it take to make you believe this Trajo, Ambassador?" Simon asked.

"Every female, when she comes of age," Maratai said, halting over having to turn Shiravan into English, "is given a…" she hesitated for a few seconds, her eyes roving across Kitty's desk until she saw a pen. "May I use your writing instrument and something to draw on?" Kitty nodded and slid the pen across the desk with one hand, reaching into her desk for a legal pad.

Maratai fumbled with the unfamiliar pen until she made it fit her longer fingers. Simon, sitting beside her, watched as she drew a circle on the paper and began to fill it in with strange symbols and designs. "If Trajo truly mated with Ramannie," she said, her voice choking on the name, "then he should have had a symbol like this with him. It would be too important to allow it to be lost. There are also bad spirits," the red woman's voice cracked again, "associated with the loss or destruction of a bond symbol."

Simon watched with interest as the woman drew, feeling a strange tightening in his chest as she continued her drawing. When she finished, Maratai sat back in her chair, as drained as Rentec.

Simon picked up the drawing and stared at it for a moment. "Kitty, I think you should show your necklace to the Ambassador." He handed over the pad without another word and sat back in his chair.

Kitty took a long look at the drawing and pulled the necklace Simon had found in the little fighter craft during his early examination of the ship out from under her blouse, sliding the chain over her head, and hesitantly handed it to the Ambassador.

"It would seem that our Trajo has provided even that, Dom," Maratai said quietly, instantly recognizing the medallion for what it was.

Rentec's hand trembled as he took the solid disk and looked at it. "The kep Gillas crest, for sure," he said. Turning it over, he peered closely at the back. "To our daughter Ramannie on her twenty-fifth turning," he read. "This," he said to the humans present, "is given to a female on her ascension to full adulthood. Giving it to a male seals her decision to mate with that male. I had assumed it was because my family status was already higher than hers that she had never offered it to me, although she said it was because it had gotten left behind in one of her moves."

Kitty looked at the ambassador, sorrow for his plight coloring her emotions, but when she looked at the female, conflicting thoughts ran through her mind. Recognizing that the ambassador needed time to sort out this strange turn of events, she said, "Perhaps we should end this meeting for now. I'm sure that you both are as tired as we are after all this."

"That would be best, I think," Maratai said, looking at the slumped figure of the Shiravan ambassador. "Nothing more will be gained this day. How will we get back?"

"I see that you're both wearing wristbands like the ones we wear," Kitty said. "And you have already been through the beam process once, so you're registered with the computer. I'll personally escort you to the *Galileo*, and you can transfer to your own ship. I'm sure you'll be more comfortable there."

"I'm glad you're still here," Kitty said when she returned to her office. Simon and Robert seemed not to have moved from their chairs except for the refilled glasses sitting in front of them.

Simon snagged a beer from the mini-fridge and set it down on the table in front of her. "Your day is over. Now it's time to digest what we have here. There's more going on there than we can see, for sure. The ambassador took a hell of a hit just now, I know. It's a long way to travel to find out that his woman isn't the person he thought she was."

"But the woman—Maratai is her name?" Kitty asked. Simon and Robert nodded. "If she were human, I'd say she has feelings for the ambassador. It looks to me like we have a lot of similarities between our two races."

She took a long pull on the beer, made a face, and set the bottle down. "I still don't know all that happened to me in that chamber, but I do know that I seem to have lost my taste for this stuff. Maybe I'll just switch to tea." She leaned back in her chair, crossed her arms and legs, and asked, "Okay, guys, what do you think we should do?"

"Why are you asking us? You're running the show now," Simon pointed out.

"I am, indeed, and what I say will go," Kitty retorted, "until people stop doing what I tell them; then I'll quit. But I have a cabinet now, with people to advise me, and I'm going to take full advantage of that. You're my Secretary of War, Simon, and you Robert, represent your ship's crew. I want to know what you think we should do. Trust me, yours aren't the only opinions I'll be asking for."

"Well, I can only speak for myself right now," Robert said. "Until my people are in the loop on this, I won't have any idea what they think. My feeling is that we should keep on the way we have so far—looking into the possibility of an alliance with the Shiravans. And if things go as they have, in about a year and a half or two, maybe, we're going to have to face another attack by these Korvil guys. Each time the numbers and stakes have gone up, so what can we expect next time? Both of these races have been in space a lot longer than we have, and they have a numerical advantage, but I think we have a technical advantage. Look what we've done with the Shiravan stuff we've had—upgraded it so much that we amazed the original owners. All we have of theirs right now is mechanical, to one degree or another. What about values, ideas, other branches of science? I say we need the Shiravans."

Simon stood up and paced the floor for a moment. "I don't know much about the ambassador and Doma kep Parrasine yet, but I already think of them as people." Robert nodded vigorously in agreement. "There's so much that they can teach us. Let's start with simple things. What area do these Korvils claim? Just exactly where do these Shiravans call home, and what areas do they claim? We may already know more about them than they realize. For example, they have way more ships than we do. After all, they're sending out two fleets of ten major ships each to find us, which takes them away from system defense for their homeworld and colony planets. And they must still feel relatively safe or they wouldn't have released that many on speculation. On the other hand, even though they sent out that many ships, they still feel they need our help to defeat these Korvils.

"We know they have feelings and emotions just like we do, that they care about each other and put the safety of their race on a higher plane than personal survival. These are all evident from their actions and what we got from the ambassador's translation. We know that they're a stagnant and stratified society—"

"Hold it, Simon," Kitty interjected. "How have you arrived at 'stagnant and stratified'? And how will knowing this help us?"

"I don't know that it *will* help to know this," Simon said, walking over to the window and staring out at the slowly darkening sky, "but the old adage of 'knowledge is power' was never more important than right now. We are at the single most crucial event in human history." He turned back to his wife and friend. Leaning back against the windowsill he continued, "I said stagnant because they've been in space for over four hundred years, and the ambassador said they've been doing things the same way for a long time. No change. Things that work don't get upgraded to make them better—the old 'if it works, don't fix it' syndrome. The ambassador and captain were amazed at what we'd done to their equipment. Never even thought of it. So, stagnant."

Kitty nodded. "I'll buy that line of reasoning. But what about stratified?"

"Now, that one is more of a guess than anything else." He thought for a minute. "They refer to each other as Dom and Doma. Carter told us that's a sign of deep respect. Did you notice that they never once referred to the guy in the video that way? Maybe it's because they don't respect a mass murderer, but I get the feeling it goes deeper than that. Also, they're a matriarchy, which is probably why there was less tension in our meeting with them than there had been in some of our other interactions before now. It hadn't been enough to comment on, and I really didn't notice until we sat down with you. They've had a one-world government for so long now that I'd guess just thinking about how splintered our system is gives them the willies."

"I think there's more to the kep Parrasine woman than meets the eye," Robert said when it became apparent that Simon had finished.

Kitty looked at Robert sharply. "I had the same feeling, Bob. What did you get out of the conversation?"

Robert shrugged one shoulder. "It's not much. It's just that she was introduced as the ambassador's assistant. Plus, they've admitted to being a matriarchal society. It seems to me that she takes entirely too much initiative for an assistant. It could just be a quirk in their culture, but what else do we have to go on at the moment? If their society is stratified as Simon believes, then they're from different yet equal levels. What did you see?"

"Well, I see things from a woman's viewpoint," Kitty said. "I think she has feelings for him—ones she can't express because he's committed to someone else. But that may have just changed. Her personal world is in just as much disarray as his. And these are personal matters they're going to have to work out on their own. I just hope none of that will get in the way of why they came here in the first place."

"So, how are we going to use all of this to our advantage?" Robert asked.

"Simple," Kitty answered, taking a long pull on the beer and making a face. "I was right. This stuff tastes terrible now." She set the bottle down and continued. "We're going to throw a party. But that's a matter for tomorrow. Right now, it's getting late and I haven't eaten yet. And since we're both on Earth at the same time, husband..." The grin on Simon's face assured his wife that his thoughts had paralleled hers in the matter.

"Well, Doma kep Parrasine," Rentec said after they materialized in the comfortably ruddy light of the *Esmit do Caryl's* shuttle bay, "it appears that we have walked through the thitura's nest and emerged unharmed."

Maratai matched him pace for pace as they made their way to the captain's conference room. "Harm can come to a person in many ways, Dom do' Verlas. It would seem that I fared somewhat better than you." Her eyes flicked to the medallion he still carried in his hand.

Rentec looked down at the necklace, turning it over in his hand. "The finer details of the tragedy aboard the *Dalgor Kreth* will remain secret until I am ready to pass the story on to the Matriarch. I will accept responsibility for my involvement with Ramannie, either upon our return to Shiravi or when Policy Minister sel Garian arrives here with Second Fleet. I expect she'll take over negotiations with the humans anyway."

The pair arrived at the door to Captain do' Sirkis' conference room and entered to find the captain already there. "Well, Ambassador, it seems that you return intact. Did you find the *Dalgor's* log?"

"We did, Captain," Rentec confirmed, "and it appears that we have a greater Isolationist problem than anyone imagined. The crew was killed by the frenda vesh. During the construction of the *Dalgor Kreth*, Isolationist partisans managed to infiltrate the work details and plant vials of the plague to be released by an unwitting accomplice."

"But the accomplice would die as well!" the captain interrupted. "Not even Isolationists would throw their lives away in that manner."

"We have a video confession, Captain. In it, the traitor, one Trajo Kuria, claims to have been misguided about the level of threat. According to him, the ship was only supposed to be damaged enough to ensure its return to Shiravi before completing its mission. He was a pawn—a well-meaning one but a pawn just the same. He did manage to flush the ship of the virus, so there should be no chance of anyone aboard this ship becoming infected; however, we'll follow quarantine protocols for the next ten work shifts. No one from this vessel will come into contact with anyone from any other ship in our fleet. The medical staff will begin testing immediately to determine if any spores have been brought aboard. Doma kep Parrasine and I will be the first to be tested, and you will be next. In the meantime, we should discuss our observations of the humans before things begin to blur in our minds."

"I find them to be open and forthright," Maratai said immediately. "My greatest concern is that the Alliance itself is such a small group. Will they be able to provide enough ships and personnel to assist us when needed? And how will the fact that the vast majority of the planet is not aligned with the Alliance affect their decisions?"

"Unfortunately, those questions will not have answers in the near future," Rentec said. "I agree that they are a forthright people. It is also gratifying to know that their leader is female. It bodes well for negotiations with the Matriarch. I also note that the admiral is lifemated to the Herald. Such a close relationship between the topmost officials of the Alliance should provide for faster responses to most situations."

The Captain of the *Esmit* had listened carefully to the opinions of Rentec and Maratai, waiting for them to finish before offering his own viewpoint. "I do not agree that they are as forthright as you both believe. And I worry greatly about their ability to manipulate the technology aboard the *Dalgor Kreth*." When neither Rentec nor Maratai responded, he continued. "Forthright, in my opinion, means open. And I feel that the humans have not been totally open about their advances with our technology. By their own admission, they have only been in possession of the ship for a handful of turns, yet they have managed to build four bases and seventeen ships! Fourteen of those ships are Karda-class battlecruisers like this one, one is a transport, and two are a totally new configuration designed to carry fifty of their parda kellen each. They have strengthened our weapons and invented new uses for them like their shields. It is obvious that no single Shiravan ship could stand up to one of theirs unassisted. Worse still, their natural inclination to dominate could make them more of a problem than the Korvils. These things they have told us, even bragged about." do' Sirkis idly picked up a small statue that sat on his desk and rolled it around in his hands. "One thing they haven't even mentioned once, however, is their advances in weapons technology. Their ships do not sustain as much damage as ours. That is related to these new shields, and those are only a reconfiguration of capture fields. They project what is in reality a repulsor field around the entire vessel, except the stern, for maneuverability. And they inflict considerably more damage to an opponent's ships. Our analysis of the fight when we entered this system shows that they had lost fourteen of their Mambas but not one of their capital ships while destroying all of their enemy's ships—enemies that concentrated their fire on those same ships. Those ships were destroyed in a third of the time we could have done the same job, and they lost only the fourteen parda kellen."

"This can be explained by the strengthened shields alone, can it not?" Rentec asked.

"It is possible," the captain answered, "but not likely. It was commented on by Admiral Hawke that we had the remains of two of their Mambas. He neglected to ask for their return. I have had my engineers going over them in detail. Heavier engines, on a class with long-range scout vessels, let them accelerate almost to jump speed. Stronger gravity-sumps allow them to withstand the higher accelerations and, consequently, perform abrupt maneuvers more easily. What worries me the most is the weapons we found in one of the Mambas. And that is my reason for saying they are not forthright. The torpedoes those ships carry are equipped with anti-matter warheads! A most ingenious device it is, too," he added.

At Rentec's blank look, the captain explained, "The fuel for a standard torpedo is a small anti-matter power cell, and the main body of the weapon is equipment designed to detect and lock onto enemy engine signatures plus explosives to destroy the enemy vessel. These people have added a second power cell on the front of the missile as well to replace the explosives. My engineers say that since the field generator for the power cell is at the front of the missile, it will destroy itself on impact, the field will vanish, and the anti-matter will blow a hole in the hull. But remember the power cell on the other end. It passes through the first hole, and when its generator is destroyed on an inner wall, it blows a hole deeper into the ship. So obvious now, but no one ever thought of it before."

"It would appear that for all of our similarities," Rentec noted, "the minds of these humans work in ways that we must strive to understand. This we already knew from our exposure to Doma Spencer and Dom Carter, but now we have an entire race that thinks the same way. How we deal with this problem could determine the fate of our entire race."

CHAPTER FIVE

Simple wasn't a word that even came close to describing the process of getting a party set up the way Kitty envisioned it. So, she called in the experts—Baron Freddie and Margit. It would take time for the various dignitaries she wanted to invite to arrange their schedules, even for such a momentous occasion. *Especially* for such an occasion. Smoothing the ruffled feathers of those same worthies took most of her time, along with the help of Baron and Baroness von Schlenker.

The guest list included representatives of every government on Earth. Even the United States would be represented but by one person only—Brandon Galway. Kitty knew it was petty, but she couldn't help but thumb her nose at America at the moment. And considering the press this was going to draw, the slight wouldn't go unremarked.

Freddie's ballroom underwent a drastic make-over, debuting the new Alliance flag, thirty feet long by twenty high, hanging on the wall opposite the grand staircase. A midnight blue was background to a representation of Earth in blue and green centered with a small, stylized spaceship spiraled away from the planet, leaving a red trail behind it from its point of origin. Arched over Earth were the words 'Terran Alliance' in blocky silvery script and 'Ad Astra,' cradled the planet below. Kitty stood at the top of the grand staircase and gazed across the hall at the huge banner. Struck by the dichotomy of the ancient stone walls holding up the emblem of the future, she shivered. The hair rose at the nape of her neck as the weight of centuries yet to come settled more solidly onto her shoulders.

A week passed while various officials met quietly, if not exactly secretly, with Kitty and the two aliens. The purpose was to not overwhelm the aliens and to let them get used to interacting with a race that wasn't out for their scalps. Stress was put on the idea that these representatives were here to help humanity in their fight against the enemy that now had a name: Korvil.

Kitty passed the information to Sarah Parker, the Alliance's go-to journalist, that there were aliens on Earth, and they even allowed her to meet and speak with them for a few minutes. "There will be time for more later. I want you to have first shot at this, but I also want as much coverage of the party as we can get. That means that every reporter on the planet who can wrangle it will be here. Not to mention security. It's going to be tighter than…" Kitty was at a loss for an allusion. "You get forty-eight hours lead time, kiddo. Make the most of it."

Very little mention was made of the terrible losses Earth had suffered. Enough key officials in the major governments around the world had grown up with stars in their eyes, as well, and ungracefully accepted the keeping of the *Galileo* and her offspring in independent hands for the near future at the very least. Quiet talk was of another great step toward the realization of a one-world government. With the formation of the European Union, the world was quickly heading toward becoming a three-entity planet. The other two were the Pan-Asian group and the Pan-American Union. The smaller nations had to fall into one or another of the three or be left behind. There was even talk of the Alliance as an off-world branch that would be equal to, separate from, but ever connected to the Earth.

Kitty tried during the week between the first press release of the Shiravan's arrival and the gala that would actually introduce them to humanity to prepare Rentec and Maratai for the reality of human reporters and paparazzi. She looked for and found movies showing celebrities being mobbed by reporters and said, "There will be security present to protect you, but this is what you will have to look forward to until we can get inside the hall to meet the invited guests."

"Shiravans would never act in such a manner," Maratai asserted with a shake of her head, staring at the television screen Kitty had moved into her office.

"Actually," Rentec said, "I seem to remember a story about one of your own ancestors, Doma. Mondas kep Parrasine, I believe. He risked his life to prove the validity of his hypothesis that anti-matter was a viable power source. His return to Shiravi was met by thousands of demonstrators, both for and against the new technology. The Matriarch of the time named him a cultural treasure."

"And he never recovered from the fame thrust upon him," Maratai retorted, heatedly. "He died some turns later under circumstances that were never clearly explained to the kep Parrasine clan."

Rentec tossed his head from side to side, a Shiravan shrug. "Even so, there are things in our own past that parallel this kind of display." He looked closely at the television itself. "A most remarkable device, this television. We have something similar, but it is used only for direct conversations when the persons involved cannot be in the same room."

"We can do the same and use it for information dispersal, as well," Kitty said. "And entertainment as well as education, with special emphasis on entertainment. The scenes you have just witnessed are from a form of visual entertainment called movies— stories to amuse, accompanied by visual images. Definitely not scenes from real life, but close enough to give you a good picture of what you can expect from our people."

"As entertainment, this perversion robs individuals of the need to exercise their imaginations," Maratai said disparagingly.

Kitty gave the alien woman a calculating look and smiled approvingly. "Your English is improving, Doma. I congratulate you."

Maratai lifted and dropped her shoulders in a human shrug. "I only follow Dom Carter's advice to use a technique he called total immersion. I do not allow myself to hear the Shiravan language unless it is absolutely necessary. And I listen and try to relate a word to a meaning."

"It appears to be working well for both of you," Kitty said. "You speak much better than you did just a week ago."

The night Kitty referred to as the 'big event' arrived all too swiftly for her taste. She felt as if things were totally out of her control, a train racing downhill with no brakes. She began to second-guess herself. The decision to arrive with her alien guests in front of all the cameras began to look like a bad idea. "We could just go in the back way and let the invited guests meet with them," Kitty said to Simon as they dressed for the affair.

"It's your decision, of course," Simon said nonchalantly. He looked himself over in the full-length mirror attached to the inside of the closet door, brushing lint from his space-black uniform. "But you've already made the plans and informed the press. How will it look if you change things at the last minute?"

"It's not for me," Kitty said, pushing him aside to inspect herself. Her white dress was reminiscent of the uniform Lucy had worn to her first formal affair at Baron von Schlenker's castle. "I just don't want Rentec and Maratai to be any more distressed than they already are." She turned one way and another, looking in the mirror. "I think I should have more than just one dress for occasions like this, don't you?"

"Of course," Simon said in agreement, allowing Kitty her little white lie. "But they seem to be ready for the ordeal. I did get him to wear something a little less... outstanding. Turquoise shading into pure purple, I'd say. He called it night wear. I think he meant evening wear. It's kind of like a tux. Maratai seemed scandalized that he would appear at such a high-level function in what amounts to Shiravan casual wear."

Two light beeps sounded from the armband on Simon's wrist, and he glanced at the time. "Well, Madam Herald," he said, bowing formally, "it seems that time for primping and preening is over. Shall we go start the dog-and-pony show?"

Kitty punched Simon on the arm. "Primping! Preening! Who was the last one dressed?"

"Who hogged the bathroom for almost an hour before

I could get in there?" Simon said, retaliating. He stood beside her and looked into the mirror. "Hell of a contrast we make, I'd say." He laughed quietly.

"What?"

A smile ghosted across his face. "Any other time, we'd stand out like sore thumbs, dressed like this. But tonight, we're not going to get a second look after Rentec and Maratai make their appearance."

The last week had brought the two Alliance leaders into such close continual contact with the two aliens that a first name basis developed almost in self-preservation. The constant "Ambassadors," "Madam Heralds," and "Admirals" had gotten on everybody's nerves until Maratai quietly suggested the solution. "Please, Madam Herald," she had said deferentially, "call me Maratai," hoping that Kitty would reciprocate.

"I would like that, Maratai," Kitty answered. "And you can call me Kitty in private, of course. In public, we must remain Doma and Madam Herald."

"Of course, Kitty. I agree. But if I may ask, what does Kitty mean? You do not look like a small household pet."

Kitty burst out into the first real laughter she'd enjoyed in months. "No. It's the short form of the name I was given at birth—Katherine."

Maratai opened her mouth to answer, but no sound came out for several seconds. "If you will not feel offended," Maratai said demurely, eyes cast to the ground, "I will call you Katherine. It has a very Shiravan feel to it." Kitty noticed the hesitation but decided not to pursue the matter at that particular moment.

Simon's comm-link buzzed, and he answered it. "Ten minutes, Admiral. Your guests are already waiting at the south entrance."

Kitty picked up a small white handbag and headed for the door. "I just can't get the concept of fashionable lateness across to these people. They are much more literal than we are. And they don't have much sense of drama either. Looks like we've got a lot more to teach them than anyone realized."

Herald and Admiral made their way down the corridor and elevator holding hands all the way. The elevator settled into position, and Simon reached out and pressed the hold button. "You realize that this is going to be about the last personal time we'll have for a while?" At her nod, Simon bent down and kissed her gently, left hand at her neck. With his right hand still on the door button, he slid his left down Kitty's back until he cupped one taut cheek, feeling her heart race as his picked up speed to match.

"Mmph! My makeup!" she said, suddenly breaking free. "My dress! Be careful!"

"Lighten up, Kittyn. You look perfect. Any more perfect and I'd have to stuff and mount you."

"Simon!" Kitty slapped his arm playfully.

"Hey! What? I didn't mean... oh, hell, yes I did." He smiled boyishly at her, and as she raised her arm to hit him again, he took his finger off the button and the doors slid aside, revealing eight black-clad security personnel.

Four men and four women composed the detail that took great pains to make itself obvious to anyone who was watching. There were also several less obvious security personnel stationed along the short route the limo would take to the front of the castle, and still more were among the crowd already gathered there to film or just get a glimpse of the two beings for whom the party was being thrown.

Security surrounded Kitty and Simon and added the two aliens to their group as they met at the embassy doors. The crowd separated themselves out into the two vehicles at the curb—four guards in the lead car, and the rest packed themselves into the limo. Two practice drills earlier in the day made the process much easier for Rentec and Maratai, who were getting their first ride in an ordinary ground-effect, fossil-fuel-powered vehicle.

Rentec, taller than the rest, slumped slightly in his seat, his nearly neon suit riding up his legs, revealing shiny black footwear. Maratai, dressed in a suit of a pale shimmering material that changed color as she moved or the lighting changed, sat motionless beside him. The light green color that predominated when she sat still flattered the red of her face and hands, and, somehow, complemented the near purple of her companion. The combination added an extra dimension to the alien-ness they presented to the humans.

"Relax, now, you two. You look great," Kitty said as the limo rolled around a corner and the lights of the castle courtyard appeared. "Just the right mix of exotic and commonplace to keep people off-guard. Okay, boys and girls," she said into her comm-link, "it's showtime!"

The limo rolled to a stop between two groups of people and cameras being held back by red ropes hung from waist-high brass poles and several dozen very dedicated security personnel. First, the four guards from the lead car stepped out, and the driver pulled the car away. The limo driver moved up to center the vehicle's doors on the open space, and the four guards moved to preassigned positions, providing an extra level of insulation between the occupants and the curious crowd.

Captain Robert Greene, outfitted in his dress blacks,

stepped forward from among the dignitaries at the base of the outer staircase and opened the rear limo door. The roar of the crowd hit the occupants with almost physical force, and stepping out onto the red-carpeted walk was like moving through chest-high waters flowing the other way. Simon, first out after two of the guards, surveyed the crowd. Face impassive, he leaned into the limo and said quietly, "Okay, boys and girls, let's make history."

Simon stepped back and straightened up, urging Maratai out of the vehicle. Humanity-at-large would remember their first impression of two hands—one pink and one adding a new dimension to the word red—clasped together. Cameras flashed and video lights cast a cold bright light on the scene.

The sound swelled noticeably as people got their first look at a real, live alien on Earth's soil. Later, pundits would remark on the strangeness of her features and the serenity she exuded as she scanned her first crowd of humanity.

Voices yelled questions and hands pushed microphones forward while other hands continued to film the occasion. Simon nodded to Robert to step forward and take the arm of Maratai. The two paraded up the staircase, both led and trailed by two stern-faced guards, threading the gauntlet of humanity clamoring for a word from, or a look at, the real aliens from beyond the stars.

The Shiravan ambassador caused even more of a stir when he unfolded to his full height. The tallest human in sight barely reached his chin, and the bright purple suit brought voices to a halt in a spreading circle as he got *his* first look at humanity amassed. The voices started up again almost instantly, louder than before. Captain Gayle Miller, resplendent in her uniform, stepped forward to act as escort to the ambassador, and the second group followed Robert and Maratai, with two more guards immediately behind.

Simon stood to one side as Kitty emerged. He held his hand out and she took it until she got her balance, and then she turned to survey the crowd as well.

Admiral and Herald, husband and wife, walked hand in hand up several steps to a waiting microphone-topped podium and turned to face the buzzing crowd. He held up his hand for quiet as Kitty stepped up to the podium. A minute passed while she stood unmoving, refusing to answer any question or respond to any comment. Finally, the babble of voices stilled enough for her to speak and be heard. "I am Katherine Hawke, Herald of The Terran Alliance, and you have just witnessed the first public meeting of humans and aliens. The two beings you have just seen are called Shiravans after their planet, Shiravi. They are here tonight to meet with world leaders to discuss combating another alien race. The same race that has caused so much death, destruction, pain, and suffering to our own world has been attacking them for hundreds of years."

No sooner had that statement been made than the reporters went wild. Only parts of questions reached her ears.

"… they from?"

"How many…"

"… of weapons?"

"How long…"

Simon held both hands up and yelled, "Hold it!" several times, to no effect. Finally, he surreptitiously turned the volume control up, and in his best parade-ground voice, yelled, "Silence!" Getting the crowd's attention at last, he turned the volume back down to something approaching normal. "Later, there will be a press conference. The Shiravan Ambassador will make a statement, and then a very few questions will be answered. In your press kits, you'll find a card labeled 'question.' I suggest that you put your heads together and come up with four or five questions to ask. Otherwise, not much will be learned by anyone. We'll try to give you fifteen- or twenty-minutes' notice before they come back out. Until then, you are all invited to wait in the lower hall where you'll find refreshments and heat. Now, I have to go. No," he said, raising his hand again as the sound level rose. "I will not answer questions at this time."

Simon and Kitty met the others in the foyer as they rearranged themselves to enter the main hall. As visiting emissaries, Rentec and Maratai would lead, followed by Simon and Kitty. Normally the centers of attention at public events, the human couple were happy enough to let the aliens take some of the heat. They heard the baritone voice of Freddie's majordomo perfectly announce, "Dom Rentec do' Verlas, Ambassador of the Shiravan Polity, and his aide, Doma Maratai kep Parrasine."

Instantly, the background sounds of nearly three hundred people died to nothing as the alien couple made their way down the grand staircase and began the process of moving through the receiving line at the bottom. Seeing the pair acknowledging the customs of their planet, the noise began to rise again, stabilizing at a low murmur.

As Simon and Kitty appeared at the head of the stairs, a few heads turned to watch them move slowly down the steps. Shortly, they were moving among the crowd with glasses in hand, never far from the two aliens, occasionally entering one group or another to assess the reaction.

The Shiravan delegation to Earth, while officially consisting only of Rentec and Maratai, also sported three Alliance security officers on loan, as well as one or another of the various ships' captains who happened to be in orbit for the occasion. Over a two-hour period, most of the hundred or so invited guests found occasion to drift into the circle surrounding the two red beings, most merely confirming the facts with their own eyes and moving on.

During the evening, Rentec noticed the slow motion of groups around the room and around each other. *Almost like solar bodies*, he thought with some amusement. The laws of physics that governed that movement finally brought the group surrounding Rentec and Maratai into a corner of the room while stripping most of the idle onlookers away at the same time.

Maratai ran her hand over the wood and iron surfaces making up the centuries-old door that was half-hidden by two tall plants. "Did you know," she said in quiet Shiravan, "that the Herald's name is not truly 'Kitty,' which is a diminutive for a longer, more formal name."

Rentec fingered one of the leaves on the nearest plant. "Much like I would be called Rennie, or you might be called Mari?" he asked in return.

"Just so," Maratai responded simply without taking her eyes from the ambassador.

"I suppose I should ask what her proper name is," Rentec observed laconically. "Should I ask her, or do you happen to know what it is?"

Exasperation tingeing her voice, Maratai said, "Her

name is Katherine, Rentec."

Rentec was side-tracked by thoughts of his last visit to Quillas more than a turn ago at a gathering much like this one, with Ramannie glowing beside him. He suddenly froze and looked at his companion. "Kath-e-rin?" he asked incredulously.

"Yes, it sounds very much like Kath-e-Rin. A good omen, I would think."

"It does sound much like Spirit of Light," Rentec agreed.

Kitty appeared out of the crowd, ending their discussion. "'Ask and ye shall receive' is a phrase sometimes used when someone or something is being talked about and appears unexpectedly," she said cheerily, missing the exchange between the two aliens and only hearing what sounded like her name as she arrived. "Actually, I engineered this little breathing space."

Before she could continue, Simon arrived as well. "Looks like you two could use some rescuing," he noted. "How are you holding up?"

"All goes well, Admiral," Maratai answered in nearly perfect English. "We have functions similar to these on regular occasions. I believe that since we don't have your television, we participate in more social gatherings. The higher gravity is causing some discomfort though."

"I think our world would be a better place if we spent more time in the company of others rather than insulating ourselves from each other as so many do these days," Kitty commented.

"I think some people are better off left alone," Simon said.

"Those are probably the ones who'd benefit most by being brought into social events," Kitty shot back. "And if that doesn't happen, at least you can keep an eye on them." She turned to her guests and assumed a more formal posture and tone. "Please, let me apologize for tiring you out. I had thought that now would be a good time to escape from this crowd. Would you two like to sit down for a while and speak with some of the people you came here to meet?"

Kitty knocked discreetly on the door Maratai had just been examining, and after a few seconds' delay, it opened. "Mister Ambassador, Doma kep Parrasine, if you would follow me, please?" she asked formally, stepping across the threshold.

For the Shiravans, accustomed to a sun producing light in the cooler shades of red, the outer hall had been the optical equivalent of high noon in the Gobi Desert for humans. The darkened interior was an oasis for their eyes.

"Welcome, welcome!" The baron's hearty voice sounded from across the room where he stood pouring drinks into four glasses. Waving off-handedly in the direction of the lounging area, he said, "Sit, please. I have two special chairs for two special guests."

Four chairs sat side by side, the center two obviously having been built for someone with different bodily parameters, leaving the Alliance representatives sitting one to either side. The empty chairs faced an even dozen men from various extremely interested and influential nations and conglomerates around the world, although none were well known by many of their respective populations.

Simon ushered the Shiravans to the chairs so clearly meant for them and sat down on their right after making sure Kitty was settled. "Well, gentlemen, I think we've all met at one time or another in the last week. What say we get down to business?"

"Please, Admiral," the baron interrupted, "let's first toast the occasion." He turned from the side table carrying the four glasses on a silver tray. Stopping in front of Rentec and Maratai, he offered the two a glass from the front of the tray. They hesitantly took them, glancing at each other. "I assure you, honored guests, that this is something you will be able to drink." The old man offered glasses to Kitty, then Simon, and then moved to one side of the assembled group. Lifting his glass, he proclaimed, "To a bright future!"

All repeated the sentiment except one, who muttered, "Please, God, let there *be* a future."

Simon, stung by what he thought of as criticism, stood up and said, "To new friends, without whose help we may not have had any future at all," inclining his head and glass to Rentec and Maratai. The toast was repeated with a bit less enthusiasm.

Kitty, sensing the moment disappearing before it even arrived, stood up. She raised her glass and stared into each face before she made her pronouncement. "To hope, gentlemen! Raise your gasses to the hope that we survive this crisis as a race; to the hope that we make new friends across the depths of interstellar space; to the hope that our new friends survive as well; and to the hope, gentlemen, that the ability to cooperate is still within both our races, for we surely are going to need to do just that if anything is to survive much longer."

She drained her glass and stayed on her feet, glaring at the assemblage until first one and then the rest drank to her toast.

The following hours seemed at moments like a police

interrogation as first one alien or Alliance representative was quizzed and then another. At other times, it felt like a summit meeting of the world's greatest powers. The Shiravans answered questions about how they had first met the Korvils, found the two humans and, through them, Earth, and what they hoped to accomplish with this contact mission. Kitty fielded most of the questions directed toward the Alliance, with Simon, for once, staying uncharacteristically quiet.

In answer to one pointed question, Rentec made mention of the fact that Shiravi was a one-government planet. "Quite unlike Earth, as we understand it," he added. "Also, our colony worlds, while encouraged to handle their own affairs like internal disputes and trade, are tied to the homeworld in such a way that no one planet enjoys too great an edge over the others."

Members of the human contingent in the room looked at one another, the exchange not lost on the Shiravans. Finally, one who had remained conspicuous by his silence chose to join the conversation. "Your pardon, gentle beings," he said. "I am Eric Bader, recently appointed as Vice Consul to the German Chancellor. One topic of conversation that comes up at meetings of this kind in the past has been the formation of a one-world government much like yours, I would think. Not long ago, several of our countries in Europe formed a type of loose coalition that allowed us to standardize our currencies and brought us one step closer to that goal. It now remains for the Asians to complete their unification and for the Americas to finish what was started with NAFTA. After that, the only real holdouts will be the Arab and African nations. Smaller nations will have to fall into one camp or another or be left behind when the realignment occurs."

The story got picked up by the British representative. "Gordon Smythe-Blakeley of the United Kingdom, Mister Ambassador. It is the opinion of all here that events are about to start moving at a pace far in excess of anything imagined as recently as even five years ago. This is due to two events: the acquisition of your technology by the group that calls itself the Terran Alliance, and your own arrival. We, here, believe that the threat represented by these aliens called Korvil could be enough to push our world into uniting in such a way that a one-world government will be the logical outcome. It is deplorable, of course, that so many lives and so much property were lost recently, but they can serve as vivid reminders of what can happen if we do not work together, thereby making their sacrifices worth something."

Kitty set her empty glass down and leaned forward slightly. "Our Shiravan friends think they'll learn much about us by watching how we handle our internal affairs. And by 'us,' I mean humanity in general," she said. "And we've already told them that most humans, Alliance personnel not excepted, like to mask ulterior motives under the guise of altruistic words and endeavors." She leaned back and settled deeper into the chair, her body language telling all that she was settling in for a long talk. "What I want to know, gentlemen, is how you think the Alliance is going to fit into this new image you're planning for our world.

"I'm not saying that I oppose a one-world government, but I want to know just where we'll fit into *your* picture. We're already willing, as soon as this crisis is over, to take over all space-related services, such as launching satellites, building space stations, and moving people from one point to another. We'll consider leasing vessels to certain organizations and training pilots, freeing up Alliance personnel for other projects. We will, of course, continue to release technology to Earth, allowing all nations to share the wealth."

"Continuing to keep for yourselves the weapons technology and the secret of your propulsion systems, of course," accused the Chinese representative.

"First, the propulsion system is no secret sir," Kitty countered. "As we've said before—and proven on more than one occasion—the energy we use to power the drives of our ships comes from a carefully controlled matter/anti-matter balance. The material comes from the surface of the sun, and only we have the ships that can mine this material safely. Also, the conversion process has been deemed unsafe for set-up on a planetary surface except under very controlled conditions. I can cite several examples that everyone here should be familiar with by now. You're all aware of the huge hole in the ground where Camp David stands—I hear that it's now being called Lake David, by the way—that resulted from the release of energy from two small torpedoes and the power core from a mere shuttle. A mere few dozen *grams* of material in all. The devastation in South America was caused by what we believe to be a power core from a Korvil assault ship. That power core was either never installed or was removed for this occasion and used as a bomb. The explosion that caused the tidal wave that took so many lives all along the Pacific Rim was caused by the failure of the containment field around the power core of a single ship barely twice the size of one of our cargo shuttles. We feel that both of these explosions were caused by amounts of matter considerably larger than were present at Camp David. The destruction caused by the second ship was so great because the explosion occurred at a great depth, multiplying the power of the resulting tidal waves."

This particular conversation had been anticipated by Kitty, and she had earlier instructed Simon to answer the rest of the question when it arose, dividing the attention of the group sitting opposite them. While these men were of different countries, religions, even philosophies, they were the more-or-less secret cabal that worked behind the scenes to advance the concept of "one world-ism." Their faces and names seldom ever made the news, but their power was legendary, and was the subject of a few movies and many books. Their combined power would give many a world leader reason to pause were the reality of the situation known, and in this instance, they were as united as it was possible for them to be.

"We still maintain," Simon said, "that the weapons technology is too intense to allow on the planet in the hands of groups with so much mutual antagonism. The balance of power would change too drastically if we gave it to just a few, and if we gave it to all, it would get used. This would do for the Korvils what they haven't been able to do for themselves. We don't believe there are enough people off the planet yet to allow the human race to survive such a misuse of technology. Besides, you already have enough standard weaponry to destroy this planet many times over. Why do you need more?"

A dark-complected man, dressed as if he had just stepped away from a desert-spanning caravan, was conversing quietly with a man whose suit and coloration fairly shouted Mediterranean. The olive-skinned man, younger than the Arab by a decade or more, straightened up and asked, "What assurances do we have that you won't take your ships and leave when the going gets rough?"

Simon laughed out loud, earning a glare from the man. "First, where would we go, sir? This is our planet as much as it is yours. Every Alliance member was born here and has a birth certificate to prove it. Second, where would we draw our recruits from? Where would our replacement supplies come from? Third, where would our people go to retire or just plain quit? There are no human colony worlds to turn to yet. Give us a couple hundred years, sir, when there will be places aplenty to go. But right now? Our destiny is tied too closely to Earth to think of leaving. Fourth, everyone who chooses to return to Earth brings back with him or her all the knowledge they've accumulated, which will, of course, be made available to all the peoples of Earth."

Brandon Galway finally decided to speak up. "Madam Herald, Admiral, you both know me. Trust me when I say that I personally agree with your goals and methods. Officially, though, I'm supposed to convey the message that the president is rather upset at the international snub you handed him. The United States still maintains that none of this would have happened if you hadn't been so irresponsible as to keep the discovery of the ship to yourselves," he said. "Look at what has resulted directly from your decision. The world will never know the full number of lives lost. And to set yourselves up as an independent government with only the technology of one ship to back you up is ludicrous."

"I believe that you'll be able to appreciate the gravity of the fact that we have considerably more than the one ship you allude to, Mister Galway," Kitty answered carefully. "And we maintain that the devastation would have been much worse than it was because you would have proceeded considerably more cautiously than we did. It's our contention that you would have done nothing more than study the ship with an eye to its military applications for the United States and not toward what it could do for humanity as a whole. We further contend that the Korvils would have arrived regardless of who was in charge of the *Galileo*, and since you wouldn't have been building ships, the very first attack would most likely have gutted the one hope our race had to stave off total annihilation by the Korvils. Or worse. Neither we nor the Shiravans have any idea what the Korvils do with prisoners. Hunt them? Eat them? They don't communicate with us, so we have no way of knowing. I will say from what we've seen so far, they have no compunction about ridding the universe of our presence. Are we a threat to their existence? To their expansion? Or are they just xenophobes? We'll probably never know for sure. But I will say that since no one had any experience with this type of technology, we did at least as well as you and yours would have, and probably better." Her last words were a total condemnation of all that the U.S. stood for, and Galway's eyes showed his understanding. Secretly, she felt sorry for him. If she had her way, diplomacy was going to become a whole lot less complicated in the future.

"I have a question for you, Mister Galway," Simon interjected, happy to get another word in edgewise. "We're curious as to how the United States knew of the existence of the Shiravan delegation to Earth before we made the information public to the world at large. We had every intention of doing so, of course, but even before they set foot on Earth, we received a communiqué mentioning their presence. Are you able to enlighten us as to how this could be?"

The pensive look on Galway's face blanked, but Kitty noticed the expressions flowing, hard as he tried to conceal them. Damn all stubborn men. They'd been on again/off again enemies and associates almost since the beginning. Frenemies, if you will. "I saw the message before transmission," he said, "but I have no idea where the information came from. It was a first for me."

Simon nodded, accepting Galway at his word. He had earned it, along with one other U.S. agent. "I don't pretend to know what drives you, Mister Galway, but I believe you should make it clear to your associates that you personally are aboard the one-world train. You're free to either tell all or sandbag your boss. It really doesn't matter anyway."

"You'll appreciate that we're most concerned about the devastation that has recently been done to our world," another man said. "Can you give us any assurances that this won't happen again?"

"No," Simon said curtly. "We don't know how many ships these Korvils have or what type. Are they all raider-type like we've seen so far? Do they have larger ships? What kind of tactics will they use next time? How far are they willing to go before they break off an engagement? Do they think they're earning rewards in their version of heaven? These questions and more we won't be able to answer until it happens."

"Is it possible that our new friends can answer some of these questions? They have been at odds with these other aliens and should have some answers."

Rentec shifted in his chair. "Yes, we've been fighting the Korvils for over two hundred and fifty of your years. And they do have larger ships than you've seen so far. As far as how they fight, most of what we've seen is hit-and-run tactics. It appears that they don't normally want to commit their larger ships to a conflict, as if they don't have very many or don't want to risk them. We've lost a considerable number of ships over the years, but we have no way of knowing how many fell to the Korvil or how many wound up like the *Dalgor Kreth*—the ship you call the *Galileo*—or were just lost to accidents. The data you've shared with us concerning your encounters with the Korvils up until this time show an increasing amount of force with each new encounter, so it's safe to say that the next attack will be on a larger scale yet. To that end, I have authorized the entire remaining fleet to assist humanity in defending this system. That means eight more ships, thanks to the space docks made available to us by the Alliance, and ten more when Second Fleet arrives, bringing Maggie Spencer home."

Kitty glanced at Rentec, and, feeling that he was uncomfortable with being the center of this kind of attention, she spoke, transferring the group's attention back to her. "At this time, we have fifteen battlecruisers and two fighter carriers in service, with another battlecruiser due for completion within the week. With the addition of the Shiravan fleet, that brings our strength to over thirty major ships, along with hundreds of Mambas that can be committed to any defense of our system. We aren't yet counting the ten ships of the Shiravan Second Fleet since we have no idea if or when they'll arrive."

Seeing Rentec stiffen, she added, "It *is* possible that they could run afoul of a Korvil fleet or have some other reason for not showing up. The old saying is 'don't count your chickens before they're hatched.' If those ships don't show up, we won't have made plans that fall apart because of their absence. I will say that we're turning out a total of eight ships per year at the moment, but I feel that isn't good enough. I plan to authorize the *Galileo* to begin ship production immediately upon leaving this meeting, along with helping to build housing and other facilities for the Pacific Northwest."

Seeing Simon's head turn in her direction, she forged on. "I believe the *Galileo* is a resource that's been overlooked. She's a factory ship, designed to build the infrastructure for a colony world, and is perfectly capable of building ships just like one of the bases she's already turned out. As a matter of fact, considering her size, she should be able to out-produce any one base by two to one, bringing our total production to twelve ships per year. And the *Galileo* can stay in Earth orbit, letting her shuttles catch asteroids sent our way by ships from the belt. If the Korvils hold off for two years, as seems likely considering the distances involved, we should have over fifty capital ships defending this system by the time they arrive." On the heels of this optimistic view came a sobering thought. She leaned back in her chair and let it out quietly. But all in the room heard it nonetheless. "Of course, if they show up much earlier, we could become a footnote in galactic history."

CHAPTER SIX

Second Fleet exited contra-space and found themselves in the Oort cloud of the newest system on their schedule. They scanned thoroughly per standing orders and found significant traces of Korvil presence. "The fourth planet, sir," the scan tech confirmed a full day after arrival. "A third again larger than Shiravi, three moons, and six drive traces. That does not count any vessels powered down."

The fleet commander concurred with the assessment, and ordered, "Send a scout home with the location, immediately. I will not have this information lost to the vagaries of battle." His observation left no doubt as to his intentions. "Place the rest of the fleet under full alert and cloak. We will take a lesson from our enemy and accelerate for two hours, then shut down all power except life support and passive scans until we close to within ten thousand stakas of the fourth planet's outer moon."

He paused for a time, considering the lives about to be lost to his next commands—his as well as most, if not all, of the fleet if things didn't go well. "The *Marasel Sepis* and the *Kepara Lourbin* will target the planet. The *Kath-e-vesh* and the *Besserai* will target the moons. All other ships will attack any vessel in range. Particular attention is to be paid to any vessel under power, but do not hesitate to fire on unpowered ships if the opportunity presents itself. Once the fleet goes silent, no one will break the tranquility of space until I give the order to attack."

Marcad Korvil stormed through his palace, venting his frustration on any unfortunates who crossed his path. Most of his anger spilled onto the being shadowing him. "Tell me, war-Minister Darmag," he roared, "how it is possible for not one of almost twelve hands of ships to return from a simple reconnaissance in force?"

Shrewdness prevented the war-Minister from pointing out that Marcad himself had ordered the fleet into human space. Instead, he placed the blame on the one he thought his master would most likely believe to be the culprit. "Lord, Sept-Leader Vorkan's battle plan was to assault in three waves. Surely some survived to bring back word of what happened. Perhaps they are only damaged and taking longer than anticipated to return, or perhaps some unforeseen calamity befell them."

The gigantic figure, a cross between an enraged teddy bear and a furious panther, spun around in the corridor and pinned the smaller entity against a wall. "Sept-Leader Vor'an formulated those plans and submitted them to *me* before he left. I personally authorized them. There should have been less than a twenty percent loss on all combined ships. And at no time should there have been a point at which every ship was either destroyed or damaged too badly to return. At the very least, a large fraction of the first wave should have survived to make rendezvous with the host ships for resupply and return. And not even those host ships have reported in. Are you saying that Sept-Leader Vorkan and I devised a flawed battle plan?"

The lowered voice and nearly immobile posture gave

away Marcad's transcendence to hunting mode, a condition not lost on the Korvilene deputy. "No, Lord. I only suggest that there may have been incomplete information to work from. Perhaps a covert mission to ascertain the facts is in order. A smaller one that will not risk so many ships."

The massive leader moved with deceptive speed. Four furrows graced the left side of the war- Minister's face, narrowly missing one eye. "Covert! Smaller! Risk! You accuse me of cowardice? I will have your head on a pole before the day is out! I will eat your sons and use your cows to breed loyal Korvils to serve me and my descendants!"

A gesture from the maniacal monarch brought guards to surround the war-Minister and escort him to Marcad's Pit of Justice where his death would be carried out with all due ceremony, displaying for all the strength and bravery of their Lord.

The Korvil, flushed with anger at the insult to his Honor, stood in his Pit of Justice studying the prone body of the one who had lately been his war-Minister. He glanced at the sword in his hand and threw it contemptuously to the ground, spattering Darmag with sand. "Rise up and arm yourself!" he roared.

Darmag slowly rose from the sand where he'd been thrown by his guards and picked up the blade. Recognizing the dishonor of trying to talk his way out of his imminent death, he planted his feet firmly and hefted the weapon, getting a feel for the weight. Designed for one a bit larger than himself, it was a clumsy tool, but he vowed to acquit himself with dignity. He shrugged out of his vest, the attached Honors tinkling incongruously as it fell to the ground, and saluted with the sword. "Lord, what weapon do you choose?" he asked, seeing Marcad unarmed.

"Weapon? What need have such as I for weapons when dealing with you?"

Darmag finally got a glimpse of the madness lurking beneath the surface of the overbearing ego driving his Lord—too late by far to do him any good. He lifted the sword and felt himself snap into hunting mode.

Protective membranes slid into place over Marcad's eyes at Darmag's first move, sharpening his eyesight and narrowing his field of vision. He dodged behind one of the carved pillars that surrounded the Pit and grabbed a projection as he passed, letting his momentum alter his direction. Feet lifting off the ground, he spun around the column and slammed into the smaller being, knocking the sword spinning into the darkness.

Ribs cracked by the impact, Darmag fought for breath as his metabolism fought to deny the pain. Claws extended, he rose from the sand for the second time. Lips peeled back from his teeth, he scanned the Pit as he sidled toward the fallen sword. Eyes questing from side to side for any sign of movement, nose searching the air currents for the musky scent of a hunting Korvil, he crouched down and let his hand brush across the sand, feeling for the sword.

The backs of his fingers connected with the smooth metal of the blade, and he slid his hand along it, feeling for the hilt, but found instead only the point. Darmag slid his hand the other way, still wondering at the disappearance of his opponent. His fingers curled around the hilt, pulling it from the sand, and one of the pillars moved.

Marcad stood immobile, arms above his head and

hands planted firmly on the ceiling of the low-roofed Pit, watching his prey. He saw the hesitation in the movement of his victim as the sword was raised back to a guard position, and he felt a distancing. Time slowed as his hands came away from the roof, and he flowed across the three paces separating him from his quarry.

Darmag started to spin as soon as his ears heard the swish of feet through sand, but the motion was never completed. A huge hand lifted him from the sand by the neck, shaking him violently. The sword flew yet again into the murk surrounding the combatants, and he heard not the expected scream of victory, but, surprisingly, the raucous sound of a battle alarm sounding in the distance as darkness closed in on him.

Marcad turned from the still-twitching body of his former war-Minister, the victory howl caught in his throat. He pounded from the arena, struggling to reacquire a sense of perspective. He raced up the three levels to comm central, finding several Korvils moving about the room in extreme agitation. "Who sounded the alarm? I'll have another head on a pole! What excuse can you offer to keep it attached to your body?"

One technician turned from his console and saluted his master. "Lord, we are under attack! The outer moon reports several attack runs. Reports are coming in from the far side of Korvil saying the same thing, and all five ships in orbit are reporting Shiravan attack craft targeting them. We have lost contact with one ship so far and have confirmed two enemy destroyed."

Marcad studied the real-time display as his ships moved out to interdict the attackers. One ship down left the odds at six attackers to four defenders. If things continued at that rate, the ships not firing on planetary targets would soon be destroyed, leaving only a few ships to rout the balance of these krath-Shiravi. Power and weapons systems operating at full capacity, the four surviving Korvil ships plowed into the formation of Shiravan battlecruisers, scattering them.

The battle moved away from the planet's surface as Marcad watched. His anger at the unexpected development turned to joy as he saw his ships start to perform a reversal that would bring them behind the attackers, giving them clear shots at the relatively unprotected engine pods.

Before one shot could be fired by the defenders, two more Shiravan ships joined the fray. Fresh from their attack on the undefended outer moon, the two new ships saw the position their fleet-mates were in, and both captains elected to assist their comrades.

In a matter of minutes, the tide turned. Four defenders became two, and the odds were now four to one, having lost two more Shiravan craft. Twisting and turning, using the planetary gravity field to change directions in ways that fooled the Shiravan gunners and accelerating to speeds even gravity sumps had a hard time dealing with, one more Shiravan ship died as the Korvils fought with their typical fierceness and tenacity.

The last Korvil ship vanished from the screens in a flare of light, and Marcad raced out the front entrance and down the Boulevard of Skulls toward his personal ship, which was under orders to be crewed and ready at all times. Before he could reach the vessel, he was thrown onto his face by an explosion behind him. Climbing to his feet, images of his latest foray into the Pit flashing through his mind, he turned to look for the source. A series of detonations threw him back as extensive portions of his palace disassociated themselves from other portions, and still others caved in on themselves.

He looked up to see two Shiravan single ships moving away at speed. Attracted by the massive radio and scan traffic and active sensor arrays, they had destroyed generations of Korvil heritage in a matter of seconds. Spitting curse after curse at the krath-Shiravi, Marcad turned back to the waiting cruiser only to see it dissolve into a huge fireball, taking a large section of the landing field with it.

Pain finally worked its way through to his perceptions, and he looked down at himself. Blood coursed freely down his body from the numerous cuts inflicted by bits of rock and metal thrown about by the explosions. Numerous Honors earned in a lifetime of service to Korvilene were either damaged or completely missing from his torn vest. He shook himself, raised his bloody head to the retreating fighters, and roared his defiance.

Kitty sat at her desk looking over the progress reports for the rebuilding of the areas that had been devastated by the Korvils. She shook her head slowly, amazed at the things she was reading. Just a few years ago, no one would have believed it possible for the world to react so unanimously.

The anniversary of the first Korvil attack had passed almost without ceremony two months earlier. According to the papers sent to her office by the agency overseeing the actual work, virtually every nation of the world had contributed in some way to the reconstruction of the American west coast and the rest of the Pacific Rim— the larger countries with technical expertise and equipment, and the smaller with brute manpower. Earth movers and other equipment that had been built to construct the Montana facility had been moved to Portland, Oregon, and a large amount of the equipment that had been built and was no longer needed for the construction of Vesta was spread across the planet. American civil and military engineers had arrived to supervise the restoration of several dozen individual economic entities, and the world watched the extraordinary collaboration not seen since the loss of the World Trade Center just a few years before.

First, roads had been built to facilitate access to areas needing the most assistance. Then, hundreds of buildings needed to be erected—from family-sized dwellings to multi-storied structures to house the various governments and agencies that would be needed to help with the resettlement of displaced persons and the administration of aid that was beginning to make its way to the dislocated survivors. In large part, the workforce for this mammoth project was found in the very people it was designed to serve. It provided work, sustenance, and stability in a time when those were in short supply

Focusing on another part of the report, Kitty noted that dredgers from the United States had made their way to the waters surrounding Japan early in the restoration effort. They were still busy moving mud and other material from the ocean bottom onto the rocky protuberances that had once provided food for so many millions. Earthmovers from terrestrial organizations, as well as from the Alliance, were busily moving the piles of dredged materials to all parts of the island in an attempt to provide a new layer of what would become topsoil for the devastated country. Soon, the millions of Japanese lucky enough (or unlucky enough, as some maintained) to be away at the time of the attack would be allowed to return to their portions of the islands, take possession of their homeland, and start to rebuild their coastal infrastructure nearly from scratch. Tears ran down Kitty's cheeks as she thought of the vanished millions she'd never known and the few hundred of those with whom she'd had at least a passing acquaintance.

She put down the monthly report the World Restoration Organization had sent to all heads of state and turned to Alliance matters. In crises, one helps as one can, and the Alliance was no exception. As the only group able to take on the task of guarding the planet from attacks from space, Kitty gladly threw Alliance resources into the pot. The fact that that had already been happening from before the attack was given little consideration. The peoples of the world had finally seen the Alliance siding with the rest of humanity to stand against the monsters from space, throwing their support behind the effort. As a result, each time a ship was ferried to Earth to be crewed, the Montana training facility was able to respond almost immediately.

Twenty-four new ships had been projected for service by the time two years had passed, but only twenty-two had been built. The difference was made up for by the fact that Taurus Base had pulled the plans for a full-sized battleship out of the files, amended them to fit human standards, and, in two years, had turned out two. Named the *Antares* and the *Polaris*, these two ships boasted crews of over nine hundred. Smaller in size than the *Galileo*, they had equivalent engines, and there was considerably less automation aboard with correspondingly more weaponry, including new experimental particle beams, which necessitated crews on a par with the huge factory ship.

Vesta had continued to grow as well, one of the pleasanter parts for Kitty to read—not as much for the continued expansion of the hollowed-out asteroid as for the news of her friend, Lucy Grimes. Apparently completely recovered from her nervous breakdown, Lucy now headed the construction efforts on the new Alliance facility as its project director. She had the full support of the doctor who'd returned to Earth to assist with Alliance personnel suffering everything from agoraphobia to xenophobia.

The asteroid had been hollowed out by machines built from plans in the *Galileo*'s computer. Set loose under computer control and operating on broadcast power, the bevy of machines were busy carving the interior of the asteroid into forty separate levels except at the end opposite the entrance. There, the level count was only twelve to allow for the open spaces humans needed to have around them from time to time to prevent claustrophobia. A Parthenon-style building and a Roman-style Forum for plays and readings had been included. Mega-tons of pulverized rock were spread on the floors of these levels and mixed with load after load of dirt and topsoil brought from Earth by each passing ship. Seeded with trees and shrubs, grasses and plants of various kinds, these levels would be a small slice of Earth intended to soothe the nerves of those so many millions of miles away from home. Now that air and water had been added from ice asteroids found throughout the belt, people were beginning construction of the living and working facilities for the projected forty-thousand-plus inhabitants with an industrious bent.

Lucy still had her brother and two friends with her, Kitty noted, all working at meaningful jobs while providing strong support for the former Herald. Her brother, Bruce, was working his way up through the ranks of the Alliance, his skill in a cockpit somewhat of a surprise to all. Her friends, Amy Sparks and Carmen LeBoy, worked as administrative assistants to the project director. *All in all*, Kitty thought, *not a bad outcome, considering the possible alternatives.*

The engineer originally chosen for the job hadn't been able to continue functioning as over-all director due to a severe case of tunnel vision. As each new engineering obstacle arose—and there were many—he would tend to focus on that one rather than the bigger picture, letting the more mundane tasks associated with an effort of that magnitude go untouched. Supplies hadn't been ordered, reports hadn't been sent, questions had gone unanswered, and a myriad other things needed to be attended to. Lucy had eventually gravitated to the position by default and finally accepted the position officially after Kitty personally visited the installation to lean on her friend.

"Delegate, Luce," Kitty had told her. "You did it once, and you can do it again, on a smaller scale this time. Work your way back up, so to speak."

"Back up to what, Kitty?" Lucy asked snappishly. "Herald? Don't even think it, or I'm packed and out of here on the next rust-bucket back to Earth. Then who do you get to pick up the pieces? Who's going to understand them?"

Kitty smile ruefully at her friend. "If it wasn't for Shiravan technology, there's no way we'd have done something like this in just two years." She let the smile fade as a memory surfaced. "Do you remember Simon so long ago saying something like, 'Experience doesn't matter when no one has done anything like this before?' I'm sure I've misquoted him, but the idea's the same."

She waved a hand dismissively. "Of course, we wouldn't have been off-planet at all, and how would we have dealt with a Korvil incursion then?"

Linnas des Harras perused the report she'd been holding, mimicking the moves of her unknown counterpart many light years distant. "Tell me, Sitha," she casually asked the woman seated across from her, "what do you make of this report?"

"M-me, your Grace?" the young woman stammered. "I certainly wouldn't go so far as to express an opinion on a subject I haven't been fully briefed on."

"Since when has lack of complete information stopped a kep Parrasine from speaking her mind?" the Matriarch asked archly. She watched the conflicting emotions flow across the face of her assistant with amusement. "I need to gauge the response of the common person in this matter, Sitha. And while I know that the kep Parrasines are far from common, you have a better idea of how they'll react than anyone else I have access to at the moment."

"Well, Your Grace, it seems to me that most people will welcome the news that the human homeworld has been found. True it is that we all have our doubts because of our long struggle with the Korvils, but if these beings will be able to help us, much can be withstood. The only thought contrary to that is what if we wind up trading a thitura for a biroc?" Sitha's remark made Linnas consider the agony of the bite of a thitura and extended recovery therefrom as opposed to the painfully certain death of the innocuous-looking biroc.

"Your point is well-made, Sitha," the Matriarch said, "but I think it's a gamble that must be made. We do have the example of our friends Doma Spencer and Dom Carter to go by, so the risk is really less than one might think at first glance."

"So, what response to the courier-Captain, your Grace?"

Linnas des Harras, Matriarch of the Shiravan Polity and supreme ruler of fourteen subject worlds, picked up a gaily wrapped package. "Tell courier-Captain des Marach to take three days leave for herself and her crew; then, she is to return to Ambassador do' Verlas at all speed with this gift for the Alliance leader." She slowly added a small package to the packet. "And these are my express wishes. This package is for the eyes of Ambassador do' Verlas only. Under no circumstances will the existence of this packet be made known to anyone until after it has been delivered to the ambassador. Then he can decide what to do with the information." She leaned back in her chair and gazed at the lights dancing on the peaks outside the des Harras estate and sighed. "Now, go. Let the crew have their time with their families. It will be long before they will see their loved ones again."

Policy Minister Manura sel Garian read the dispatch handed her by the courier-Captain, who had finally found the Shiravan Second Fleet. "These coordinates are correct, Captain?" she asked in her gravelly voice.

"Yes, Minister," she answered. "I personally entered the figures into the computer before coming to you. Ambassador do' Verlas requests that you arrive with all due haste. Those were his exact words."

"Very well, Captain, then that is what the fleet will do," the diminutive woman said. "You have acquitted yourself well. You will resupply from fleet storage and rest for two periods, then make your way back to Shiravi with the news that we have been directed to the human homeworld. The Matriarch should be kept apprised of our actions at all times. Have you any news of the war with the Korvils?"

"None, Minister. We came to you as directly as possible. Following the schedule laid out to us by Minister do' Verlas, we checked each system on your projected list until we arrived here. There has been no word of any attack by the Korvils."

The old woman shook her head. "It is unfortunate that I have no way of knowing what's happening with the Reprisal Fleets. There is much to be said for staying on-planet when war clouds loom on the horizon. At least there I would have access to the latest information." A thought flitted through her mind. "Or perhaps, *my* being on the scene would be the greater of two evils in this particular case."

sel Garian left the bridge and went to her quarters after seeing that the fleet was headed for human space almost half a turn from their present position. She wasn't going to handle military duties as well as her other self-appointed responsibilities. It was merely a check to see that no one individual held too much power at once. For a time, she busied herself with setting her quarters in order, then went to her desk, pressed a button on her comm link, and waited for a response. When it came, she said, "Ask Chief Tekavey to come to my quarters at her convenience." Then, she sat back and waited for the kath-mora to arrive.

CHAPTER SEVEN

Even after two years, the memory of the Korvil attack on Earth was still fresh in the minds of humans, and the lingering effects brought more reported changes almost daily. Temperatures had dropped an average of three degrees worldwide, and growing seasons had changed. Deserts bloomed with new growth, and drought now threatened areas once thought to be ever fertile. The gulf stream no longer flowed all the way up into the northern Atlantic, and the jet stream moved farther south. And these were just the more visible signs.

To the overwhelmingly vast percentage of humanity, the double strike on Earth had been the first attack. To the ever-increasing thousands that comprised the entity known as the Terran Alliance, it was just the latest in a series of attacks that had started almost the moment they'd ventured into their own asteroid belt. They had "bullies" to protect themselves from, and that was why a siege mentality had set in upon Alliance Command. The average citizen of Earth began to be subjected to increasing amounts of propaganda, touting the need for a "retreat" to their own private asteroid to battle the double menace of aliens from space and a new ice age. Accepting the premise and acting upon it was going to be an uphill fight the likes of which the political world had never seen.

Polls taken by news agencies showed an increasing trend toward consolidation of forces to combat the alien menace, and closer to home, secondary effects from the attack continued to fuel the move toward globalism.

Entire species disappeared from the natural environment. Spotted owls, pandas, and migratory fowl of several varieties were only to be found in zoos and other protective environments around the globe. Plant species that had been abundant only two years before were now found only in greenhouses and carefully controlled environments. The polar ice caps had begun to grow at a rate not recorded since measurements first began, fueling the fear that Canada and the upper portions of the United States might become uninhabitable within a single lifetime if the effects weren't somehow reversed. Not so coincidentally, plans were already being drawn up to move the Worldwide Seed Storage Facility, which had spent many years above the Arctic Circle. The time to move it south might just be upon them. Corresponding latitudes worldwide experienced the same concerns. Several reporting agencies noted that the decline in the size of most glaciers had ceased, and in fact, most, if not all, had begun to increase in size.

And recruits flocked to the Alliance. As expected, most were young and eager, with sci/fi on the brain and almost totally useless until trained, but a smattering was able to be put to work almost immediately. From the first days after the attack that had finally gotten humanity to truly see the bigger picture the whole world over, the number of applicants accepted, given a quick orientation, and shipped out had jumped drastically. The four Alliance bases kept producing ships, Mambas, and probes at a rate no one had expected prior to the attack. A friend of Lucy's father had shown up in Zurich and begun to streamline the mess that was Personnel and

Deployment. Vesta, while still austere, was home to over four thousand Alliance personnel and would eventually be able to house ten times that amount. Most were construction workers, true, but a few of the training staff had arrived and were getting used to the layout before the recruits they had to teach arrived. It was going to be a matter of staying one chapter ahead for quite a while.

Construction crews had finished most of the preliminary housing and were busily crafting the park areas, the place the pond would be, and a nine-hole golf course able to be played backwards to get the full eighteen. Alliance command personnel were beginning to make their presence known as space was constructed for them, and scientists from all over the world were working in the Research and Development areas, expedited for the necessity of finding new and more powerful weapons to deal with future attacks. Supplies arrived almost daily from ships moving back and forth across the system.

Now information would flow to and from Vesta as it assumed its duties as the new Alliance Headquarters. There was no point in being an off-planet nation and having your capitol located on Earth. Technological updates made their way from Vesta to the four asteroid bases and were then incorporated directly into the newest ships. Now, the *Galileo* was going to become a full factory ship with no room for esoteric studies, and the new headquarters for Research and Development moved to Vesta.

Older ships were being retrofitted as quickly as they could be accommodated. Of course, ideas emanated from the bases as well since they were where the modifications were actually being put into effect. Joanna Barnes wove the disparate entities into a smoothly functioning whole.

The first clue that the Korvils were on the move came when a probe was activated by an incoming drive trace. The past two years had seen a quantum leap in the production of these small devices, as well as their distribution around the periphery of the solar system as ship after ship flew out of the yards, making their way to Earth for crews and moving off into the outer reaches of the system on shakedown maneuvers and patrols.

The signal was picked up by the newly commissioned battlecruiser *Predator* on maneuvers in the Oort cloud surrounding the solar system. Lying passively among the debris from which comets were thought to be born, the probe woke up when it detected a drive trace and recognized it as one of Korvil manufacture.

"It's just plain luck that we were here to pick up the signal," Captain Sierra Hawkins said as she looked over the shoulder of her comm officer. Standing to her full six-foot height, the captain turned to her bridge crew. "Standing orders, people. We set course away from the invaders and away from Earth. Maybe we can make them believe we aren't on to them. Helm, use your best estimates as to where another picket ship is or will be. Get us into range so we can transfer the message. They'll carry the word to Earth, hopefully keeping the Korvils in the dark as to the fact that they've been spotted. We'll just continue on patrol, looking like we know nothing. Nav, prepare the best set of coordinates you can from the probe's signal and send it to Comm. Comm, prepare to transmit to any ship we pass as soon as it can be identified as friendly."

"Even Shiravan, ma'am?" the Comm officer asked.

"I said friendly, didn't I?" Hawkins retorted testily.

"Any ship in this system that isn't Korvil is friendly and will be treated as such. Set up a translation program to send to any Shiravan ship just in case." Hawkins privately wondered about the wisdom of having xenophobes aboard ship. It seemed too many people just couldn't get over the fact that the Shiravans were alien—really alien. Movies like E.T. notwithstanding, a lot of folks just couldn't make the leap that would allow them to accept people as different as the Shiravans were. Even though racism was nominally on its way out on Earth, due to her own black heritage, Captain Hawkins knew from personal experience that it still existed. Now, with the Shiravans present in the system, bigots of all types had another target for their poisonous natures to obsess about.

Breaking out of her reverie, Hawkins strode to the Nav station and inspected the course that had been laid in. She clapped her Nav officer on the shoulder and sat down in her command chair. "Nav, send the course to Helm. Helm, execute as soon as you get the data. With luck, we should be able to pass this off to either the *Vega* or the *Red Shift* and set ourselves up for a combat pass if necessary as they go out-of-system." She heard the generators start to rise in pitch as the ship built up to near-jump speed on an oblique course away from the source of the captured signal.

The *Red Shift* dropped into Earth orbit at fifty thousand miles, as had become the custom for ships needing to come to Earth. The Nav officer, at his captain's orders, had sent the message off even before sending out the standard IFF signal required of all inbound ships.

Kitty dragged herself out of the warm bed she'd been

sharing with Simon for the first time in more than two months.

"Ma'am, I'm sorry to disturb you," her aide said. "The *Red Shift* has just entered orbit and her captain sends the code word 'whiplash.'" Diana Ross knew the importance of her message but still felt protective enough of her boss that she regretted having to disturb her at this ungodly hour.

"You did right, of course, Diana. Now, let me get dressed and we'll get this show on the road." The commander closed the door behind her as Kitty yawned hard enough for her jaw to crack and yanked the covers off her mate. "Rise and shine, husband mine. We've got trouble, and my guess is that it's spelled with a capital K. Let's get the ball rolling."

She let her eyes roam over Simon's lean body, regretting the late night that had gotten her to bed too late to do more than cuddle a bit before falling asleep. Now, she was going to be up informing leaders of the world about her impending actions and, hopefully, heading off a case of mass hysteria.

Two years distance from the event had taken the edge off the sense of righteous indignation that had blossomed early on. Xenophobia, from mild to extreme, had replaced the first feelings of violation, and fear fueled the rage that eventually burned low in a large portion of humanity as no further attacks were made on Earth. Pundits tried to warn people that the distances involved in interstellar actions dictated long periods of time in which the combatants would evaluate their next moves in relation to their previous losses or gains. Eventually, the feeling of innate superiority that mankind perhaps unwisely aspired to, coupled with the lack of another assault, had led the majority of people to believe that the enemy had been vanquished.

Most Alliance citizens had managed to avoid that particular pitfall. Because of the indoctrination they received upon joining and the constant reminders during training and after, Alliance personnel knew that another conflict was inevitable. Most were eager to confront the enemy that had tried to destroy their homeworld, and all were more than aware that much time would pass between incidents. They also knew that they might never again see the blue skies of home.

Those who didn't share this fervor usually tended to last a short while and then return to Earth. While considering themselves to be citizens of something greater than just one world, Alliance citizens nonetheless saw the world of their birth as sacred, and, to a man, were ready to take the fight to the enemy, reinforced by the fact that the damage to Earth was so very evident from their vantage point of several thousand miles above the surface. While the islands of Japan, just now beginning to green up a bit on their westernmost shores, and the Pacific Rim countries didn't show much damage from space, the huge defoliated area in the middle of South America was a constant reminder of how vigilant they all had to be. That determination was about to be tested.

The Korvil fleet commander had left Korvilene with the information provided by his Lord—that this new race of beings was to be treated with extreme caution. They were to be exterminated, for sure, with the slow pleasure a hunter takes in the doing. The caution was because an entire fleet had not reported back from this system.

Sept-Leader Grimat studied the screens before him.

His claws dug into the specially padded armrests as he assimilated the information that was passing across the glowing plate. He'd been expecting to meet two hands of ships and a fraction, maybe a few more. He also expected to face Shiravan tactics. A veteran of many attacks on krath-Shiravi ships and worlds, he had arranged his attack fleet to meet what he could only think of as more of the same. The drive traces his analyst had read out were identical, so how could the tactics differ?

The problem lay not so much with the types of vessels in the new system but their sheer number. Where he'd expected what humans would call a dozen, he'd found more than ten hands of ships of varying sizes, and they crossed the system in regular patrols, extending into the cometary belt where he had grudgingly hidden as he studied the situation. While he felt some trepidation at the prospect, his orders were clear, and Honor dictated that he and his Sept make the attempt. And should the unimaginable happen and they fail, then at least the second fleet would have much less to deal with.

Sept-Leader Grimat gave the order, and ten highly modified battlecruisers headed in-system surrounding his flagship, one of Marcad Korvil's greatly prized battleships. Never had so much power been concentrated in one place. Grimat wondered at the reasoning behind the necessity for a brief moment, but then went about the business his Lord and his Honor demanded. One small cruiser stayed behind, and her officers and crew were unhappy at the prospect of not being able to fight. Instead, they were loaded primarily with sensor gear strong enough to detail the coming battle. Her mission was to record the conflict and return to Korvilene.

Simon strode through the corridors of TAS *Red Shift*, a sense of foreboding following his every step. He still felt uncomfortable with the deference accorded him and wondered again if the right thing had been done eight years ago when the *Galileo* had first fallen into his and Kitty's hands. At times like this, he'd run the entire scenario through his mind again and come to the same conclusion, which never seemed to make things any better.

He came at last to a door marked Astrogation, took a deep breath, and walked in. "As you were," he said as the three men in the room came to attention. "Let's see what we have here, gentlemen."

The Navigation officer, Parker, by his name tag, moved over to a console. "Sir, we've backtracked the data dump from the *Predator* and have a target system that it is possible they originated from, but there's no guarantee it's good data. We also have some stuff we stripped from Hubble, showing the in-bound formation."

Simon looked sharply at the Nav officer. "How did you get anything from Hubble, for crying out loud?"

"Well, sir, we sorta commandeered it, you might say," the officer said, squirming a bit. "McReady, here, hacked into its systems. We pointed it in the right direction and got some stills for our own use. As long as it's pointed away from the sun, there's no damage to the unit, and it's one of the few things that didn't get whacked when the Korvils came through before. Just seemed right to use it to help us out now."

Simon shook his head ruefully. "That's one I wouldn't have thought of." He chuckled slightly. "Why didn't you just use Astrogation's systems? I believe they're a couple of orders of magnitude better than Hubble."

The hacker's face fell. "Uh, I just never thought of it, sir," he confessed. "I am kinda new here and don't really know the systems all that well."

Simon tried unsuccessfully to keep a straight face. "Commander," he said to the Nav officer, "I expect you to see to it that all of your people are fully conversant with the systems they have access to. It's going to be a matter of life or death, and a whole lot sooner rather than later, I suspect. Am I understood?"

"Sir, yes, sir," the officer acknowledged sheepishly.

"Okay," Simon said, relenting, and hooked a loose chair over to sit in. "However you got the information, let's see it."

Twenty minutes later, Simon left the *Red Shift* considerably more worried than when he'd arrived. Looking at Kitty on the screen in his launch, he said, "We've got all the trouble you mentioned earlier, hon. A group of eleven ships as far as we can tell. Too far out and too close together to tell more at this time, but it looks like a lot of tonnage. And if these guys run true to form, there's at least one other around somewhere. I don't know whether to call it a taskforce or a battlegroup or what, but we've got to put something together quickly to meet it."

Kitty's visage gave away her concern. "You're in charge of system defense, Simon. Do you think we can do it? Will we need the Shiravans? I don't know what else to ask at this point. Just be careful, will you? I thought I lost you once."

"And you got even by taking a nap for almost a year," he retorted, a smile on his face. "I don't want to have to go through that again, either. I'm going to talk to Rentec and do' Sirkis. I still think they should just act as scouts. They don't have the shields our ships do, not to mention the armament. In the meantime, I'm going to institute one of our contingency plans. Since the Korvils don't seem to want to jump around in-system, it's going to take a while for them to get to our inner system. I'm sending a dozen ships into the belt to hide until they pass and jump them from behind. Two of those will be carriers—I think the two new ones, *Castor* and *Pollux*. My hope is that the Korvils won't even see them because they're too far apart, but there's no telling what their sensors are like. Besides, they should be too busy worrying about the dozen more that will be waiting in plain sight."

Kitty glanced off-screen and back again. "I think I wish I had your job. I just got word that the Security Council is almost ready. I've got to go. At least your opponents are faceless, and they don't ask questions, either."

"Remember, dear, fearfulness and helplessness tend to make people more unpredictable than usual. And considerably more dangerous," Simon warned. "Make sure you've got a full guard detachment with you. When are you going to create a position that will do these kinds of jobs for you?"

"Just as soon as I no longer need to have such a position, dear," she answered sweetly. "Do you really think I'd put this off on someone else?"

"If you had answered any other way, I'd have to wonder if you were really you. You just be careful, too. I'll be in touch as soon as I have something to report. I love you." Waiting just long enough to hear Kitty's response to his last words, Simon cut the screen and stared at it for a short time before beginning to issue orders.

Some of the twenty-four ships of the Alliance were alerted to the impending attack through the simple expedience of contact. For others, too far out for laggard light-speed communications to be of any use, warp-capable shuttles were dispatched with word to bring themselves to red alert and position themselves for the approaching encounter.

Rentec and his captain, do' Sirkis, watched Simon leave the *Esmit's* ready room.

"I'm not happy to be taking orders from the humans, Dom do' Verlas. I feel sure that the Matriarch would agree with me in this matter as well."

"Do you object more to taking orders from the human or to not being allowed to participate in the coming battle?" Rentec asked pointedly. "As Admiral Hawke said, we've lost ships and personnel in their defense already. It's time to let them stand for themselves, Captain. And is it not effective to act as scouts on the fringes since our vessels don't have the shields and weapons to match either the Korvils or the humans?"

"Of course, it makes sense to stand off while the two stronger groups decimate each other," the captain said testily. "It's just galling that we, who have been in space for so much longer, must take a subservient role in this." The Shiravan fleet commander paced the room, a habit picked up from humans. His expression was that of someone who has just eaten something not to his liking. "That brings to mind another thing, Dom do' Verlas. The humans say they will upgrade our ships, but I haven't seen one of our fleet get these upgrades, yet. In truth,

I'm not certain that I want humans wandering through our ships, but since they already have all the specifications, I can see no reason to stand against it if we benefit from the exchange."

Rentec sat slumped in his chair. Slowly swirling a milky liquid in a blue-tinged glass, he answered as if preoccupied. "I understand your reticence, Captain. But, remember, both I and Doma kep Parrasine have had far more exposure to humanity than you have, and we both agree that there is nothing here. The delay in upgrading our ships, I like that word—upgrade—has a peculiarly human flavor. The delay is due to the ongoing effort to make all of their ships combat-ready. And it appears that time has run out for both them and us.

"Eleven ships of the line, Captain. Eleven! When has a Shiravan fleet ever met a Korvil fleet that strong? And what have we accomplished against any fleet we've encountered of whatever size, with the notable exception of the raid that netted us Dom Carter and Doma Spencer in the first place? Our losses have always been in the three- or four-to-one range."

"But those were *our* fights, Dom. We fought those fights and learned from them. Now we are ready to carry the fight to the Korvils." The fleet commander stood his ground, facing his superior without apology. "We fought two ships and lost one for one in the last encounter. Our tactics continue to evolve, and we grow in experience with each encounter."

The ambassador set his drink down with a pensive look on his face. "By your own words, Captain, those ships were lightly armed due to the fact that they were designed as support vessels for the long-range assault ships the humans finished off as we entered the system. And," he added before the captain could continue, "those two ships were doing something no other Korvil ship has ever been seen to do, along with the ones being chased by the humans—they were running from a fight! Have we ever caused a Korvil to do anything but fight to the death, Captain? Could that be what has aroused you to such heights of passion against these humans? I believe you might be suffering from what humans call xenophobia—a fear of that which is strange, or in this case, alien.

"Admiral Hawke has told me of the phenomenon among humans. It is true that there are those among them who hate us just because we aren't human. It does not matter to these individuals that we are friendly. It doesn't matter that we have no intention of taking anything that belongs to humanity. It just matters that we are different. Tell me Captain, do you have that failing?"

The fleet commander started to speak, then sat back in his own chair. A look of embarrassment crossed his face.

"I must admit that the idea has not crossed my mind, Dom. Perhaps I should examine my motives before I continue this conversation." The embarrassment changed to a look of wry amusement. "I certainly would not want to be accused of having the same failings as humans."

"Just so, Captain," Rentec countered, some sarcasm tinting his light rebuke. "Think about what they can teach us, as well as what we can teach them. And think as well about the fact that it would be better to have these people as friends in our struggle rather than as a second enemy. One thing I have come to see is that they are a volatile people, Captain. They hold their loves and hates close to their hearts. You would do well to feel sorry for the Korvils rather than hate them."

This pronouncement uttered, Rentec got up and strode from the captain's ready room without a backward glance.

CHAPTER EIGHT

Simon Hawke was no strategist, but after eight years of dealing with sniper-type fighting, massed formation attacks (suicidal) or guerrilla, he knew where to find one when needed. As a matter of fact, strategists and tacticians were running out his ears. Games theorists, game players, and numerous people of all kinds had flocked to the Alliance banner, and not one was allowed to go to waste.

Over the last two years, scenario after scenario had been run on the massive organic computers of the Alliance, first aboard the *Galileo* and then everywhere one of the cloned copies managed to wind up. Of special note to Simon was the different pattern of attacks after the first hit-and-run attack. Rentec and company had arrived with footage of the attack that had rescued Derek Carter and Maggie Spencer, so people now knew what the enemy looked like. They also represented just about the only combat experience that the officers and crew of the First Shiravan Contact Fleet could "recall" from the files aboard the various ships in Earth's system.

Some scenarios were set up with the Shiravans as the enemy as well. After all, who knew for sure? Other scenarios depicted the Shiravans and Korvils as allies against humans, since the Alliance only had the Shiravans' word that the Korvils really *were* the enemies or even truly existed. All were assigned degrees of probability and filed away, never to be seen by their new allies.

Now, one of those scenarios was pulled out, dusted off, and put into play. Twelve Alliance ships short-jumped into the asteroid belt, hopefully ahead of the Korvils' ability to detect them, with all the other traffic about to clutter things up. Twelve more moved into position just on the Earth side of the asteroid belt, making a target of themselves that it was hoped couldn't be resisted. According to the Shiravans, the Korvils had either a high tolerance for battle damage or a lower opinion of life, depending on how one viewed it. In either case, the usual battle scenario ran to a three- or four-to-one loss ratio in favor of the Korvils. One possibility for this particular ratio was thought to be a higher tolerance for gravity than Shiravans. Another was that their grav-sumps somehow worked better than the Shiravan's.

The one time that had not held true was when a Reprisal Fleet had caught a Korvil clan unawares and sucker-punched them. And still the Shiravans had lost two capital ships to two Korvil light attack craft.

Best guess said that the reason humans had fared so much better was that they'd started out getting punched in the nose immediately and began to expand their weapons arsenal. Listening to the Shiravi tell it, both sides had reached a certain level and just kept on slugging it out. Too hide-bound on both sides, most analysts said, and both sides seemed unable to really get behind the fact that humans had been able to innovate as quickly as they had.

Of course, that was because ever since the very first man stepped out of the trees and onto terra firma, he had been looking for better ways to "protect" himself with a "bigger club." And that fetish followed him through millions of years of evolution. So, yes, humanity was ready to bust out of its little blue egg and let the universe know it was ready to meet the rest of its playmates.

Simon wasn't one to let any resource go unused if he could help it, and human ingenuity was one resource he relied heavily upon. The four bases were so inundated with older ships coming in for upgrades to weapons and shields that special shifts had been instituted to handle them while the main business of construction went on. Still, a significant number of Alliance ships weren't fully refitted to the newer weapons.

When the Korvil fleet crossed into the area of Mars' orbit, the obstacle they openly faced was comprised of the newer Terran ships equipped with the latest hardware—third gen torpedoes that carried both shield generators covering an anti-matter warhead, as well as anti-matter propulsion, plasma bombs, or just plain nuclear warheads. Tractor beams and pressor beams to use against smaller targets, and more sensitive targeting systems had all been incorporated into the newer hulls and not a few of the older ones. And not one of these weapons had been divulged to the Shiravans. Simon hoped to get a lot of information about the Shiravans from their reactions to the new weapons when they questioned things later.

As the Korvil fleet approached the human one, it began to spread out, most likely to allow for fields of fire that wouldn't intersect other Korvil ships. The Alliance fleet, long since assigned to particular drive traces, much like a basketball team goes one on one, spread out to meet them. Simon, aboard the *Rigel*, was kept to the rear of the formation, much to his chagrin. "I have my orders from the Herald and the Council of Captains," the *Rigel's* captain informed him. "The admiral is to be kept out of harm's way if at all possible. Personally, I'd rather be out there, too, sir. She gave me this to give you at this time."

Simon took the proffered envelope with ill grace and tore the end off. "Simon, if you are reading this," it began, "it's because you're too stubborn and dense to recognize your value to the Alliance that *you* started— not necessarily as a tactician or strategist, of which we have plenty, but as a driving force, a symbol of what we can be. If I said it wasn't also because I'm afraid of losing you, I would be lying, but that isn't the only reason. It's the main reason for Kitty, the wife, but not for Katharine the Herald, and while I am both, I must now think of the Alliance first and myself second. In either case, you're too valuable to be put into jeopardy unless it's absolutely necessary, so the *Rigel's* captain has orders to hold his ship back unless it is, in his estimation, necessary to step into the fray. I realize this hurts your pride, but I pray you'll see the logic and accept the decision that had to be made.

"As Herald, my prayers go with you. As your wife, more prayers and all my love go with you as I stay behind and worry myself to death, waiting for the outcome."

Simon crumbled the paper in his hand and slid it into a pocket, his expression unreadable. "Captain," he said, "you will hold the *Rigel* in reserve and order the *Venture* and the *Aldebaran* to move into position to take on the bigger ship. Relay to all ships: 'Launch all Mambas and attack. Carriers move back and prepare to pick up survivors.'"

Simon found a vacant seat in a far corner of the control room and tapped into the main battle computer to keep himself apprised of the developing situation and was as surprised as any when the eleven ships they faced suddenly sprouted multiple signatures. The modified battlecruisers had each piggybacked six light attack craft to the combat area, and when action seemed imminent, they separated and set off under their own power. Soon Alliance sensors registered over seventy different drive traces.

Countering the tactic, of course, was the launch of all the Mambas in the Alliance "forward" line, representing well over three hundred vessels in total. Simon ordered the Alliance fleet to engage the Korvil attack force and waited to see what transpired. According to the plan developed months before, the overt opposition launched two hundred Mambas from the two carriers and another hundred from their ten main battlecruisers. As soon as the hidden Alliance fleet saw the deployments, they would do the same and attack from the rear. Given the speed of light, the blocking fleet would deploy first, hopefully attracting the attention of the invaders, and the second fleet would be able to approach from the enemy's blind spot. Taking into consideration the enormous amount of energy pushing each ship forward, sensors had an unusually difficult time peering directly astern. He hoped that the superior numbers would overwhelm the Korvil sensors and combat computers if they actually had any, but the result was going to be in doubt all the way up until the last moment. Their sheer numerical superiority did nothing to allay the knot of fear that settled into the pit of Simon's stomach and refused to go away.

Simon's experience (actually the Alliance's experience, limited as it was) had been confirmed by do' Sirkis—these Korvils were hard to kill. Several other things had become apparent as well after Simon and several Alliance captains started attending briefings on the aliens almost two years ago—that the Korvils had no desire to talk, that Shiravan opinions about humans approximated those of humans for Shiravans, and that Shiravans in general feared the humans more than humans feared the Shiravans.

As a rule, Alliance pilots felt more comfortable around the red beings than most other humans, Simon noted. This probably stemmed from the close working relationship both groups had with space—the Shiravans from so many years associated with it and the humans from their constant exposure to it as they trained incessantly.

Simon, reduced to waiting and watching, turned his attention back to the screen. It was now in the hands of the individual captains and group commanders as the two fleets merged. Each red dot, representing the enemies, was surrounded by as many as five green ones within a matter of minutes, and Simon could only sit there and watch the train wreck happen.

The Shiravan captains had taken great pains to explain just how tenacious and resilient the Korvils could be. At meeting after meeting, Simon and his staff had been regaled with stories of how Korvil ships in ones and twos had driven larger Shiravan forces from an area. With pictures of a dead Korvil—the one Carter and Spencer had been rescued from—displayed on a back wall, Shiravan captains had extolled the fierceness of the enemy they faced.

Simon had studied the scene and come to another conclusion. Held up by three Shiravans, the dead Korvil was still virtually the same height as the Shiravans, who were so obviously discomfited by their role in the video. Alive, the creature would have stood eight feet tall and weighed at least five hundred pounds. Covered in a light coat of short, bristly hair, the body had the normal two legs and arms, one head, forward-peering eyes and a set of teeth a lion would have been proud of. No clothes covered the body, and this was apparently normal, according to the briefing, with the exception of a short-pocketed vest bearing badges or medals of some sort and a belt that held a laser pistol almost any human would have had to wield two-handed.

Even in death, the face bore a look of defiance—at his killers, Simon wondered, or at the universe in general? Vaguely bear-like in appearance, the opinion most thought of on first seeing the picture was that a wolverine or some related animal that had managed to rise to primacy as humans had on Earth and now sought to rise further still at the expense of humanity and Shiravans alike. *A young species*, Simon thought. *As much younger than us as we are than the Shiravans*. He shook his head slightly at the thought. *We* should *have more in common with these Korvils than with the Shiravans*.

Unable to do more than watch, Simon read the notes flashed onto his screen about the battle—numbers of enemy destroyed or wounded, numbers of friendlies killed or missing from the screen, names of ships that became either drifting hulks or rapidly expanding spheres of energy. Slowly, after what seemed hours, the tech advantage of the human fleet finally began to make itself felt.

Experience on the part of the Korvils allowed for a higher initial kill ratio, but the newer, more powerful weapons of the humans started to take their toll. Torpedoes carrying generators and bombs together made a greater impact on the overly-thick, double-hulled

Korvil ships than in previous encounters.

Simon watched as one Alliance captain used a newly installed pressor beam to start one derelict hull drifting out of the field of combat. He glanced at the display and stiffened as the name *McCaffrey* added itself to the list of dead or disabled. Fists clenched, he pounded on the arms of the chair until he felt eyes upon him and forced himself to relax. Only days before, he and Kitty had hosted Marsha Kane and the *McCaffrey's* officers at the Zurich facility, and he could only sit, his breath catching in his throat and his heart seeming to quit beating, as her lifeless ship tumbled out of the battle comp's range.

Sept-Leader Grimat stared in confusion at the battle screen before him. More heavily armed and armored, his ships should have been able to withstand all that these humanz could throw at him. After all, not only were they using technology not of their own devising, but they hadn't been in space long enough to learn how to use what they had. Or so he'd been told in the short briefing he'd gotten before leaving on this mission. Besides, right was always on the side of the strong, and having seen videos of the creatures captured by the leader of a now-defunct sept, how could these puny beings hope to best a Korvil warrior? He, himself, weighed at least three times more than the male creature he'd seen. And it looked so weak.

He'd entered this battle as a graltha would enter a pira den, knowing he'd get scratched and bloodied but would come away well fed. Now, all but a double handful of raider-craft were debris—no Honors for their battle vests, no glory for their names, no prestige for their sept. And only four capital ships were left of the more than two hands of ships Sept Grimat had been provided for the campaign.

His head deserved to be added to the Boulevard of Skulls for allowing himself to be tricked so handily. The small fleet of ships that had come out to meet his outnumbered him by one, but their size gave them no advantage. He'd ordered the deployment of the raider-ships to strike fear into his enemy and throw them into confusion with the larger number of targets he knew would appear on their screens. This same order sent every Korvil to his battle station in readiness for the chase ahead. But, from that point on, nothing had gone as it should.

The humanz launched raider-ships themselves. Smaller than his, certainly, and most likely crewed by single individuals, they very nearly overloaded his own battle computer with their sheer numbers. And where had they all come from? He could only hull-mount six raider-craft on each of the ten battlecruisers in his fleet, while the single main battleship, his flagship, carried none, its sole purpose being to provide backup power, should it become necessary.

Grimat looked around his bridge at the officers directing the battle. Quiet orders were issued while icons on screens moved into new positions, all the things he was familiar with. Everything running smoothly as it always did, he relaxed in his command chair, knowing from experience that the loss ratio would strongly favor his fleet.

As the two fleets met, Grimat felt the blood course through his veins, just as it did in the hunting parks back home, but he didn't let it cloud his judgment. The initial figures began to come in from the first pass and that was the first moment that an inkling of what was to come entered his mind. Too many of the enemy's shots were hitting home, and the missiles were of a kind he hadn't seen before, causing more damage with each strike than he'd had any reason to suspect. Also evident was the fact that his warriors, seasoned veterans all, didn't seem to be able to make as much of a dent in their opponents as usual. Rage at letting himself get caught between two opponents coursed through his brain for a single instant, and then relief at the fact that no other Korvil would know of his folly. His rage had made him forget the watcher left hidden in the outer system. Not only should his head grace a pole for failure, but it should do so because his overconfidence would be the instrument of his entire clan's destruction. Still, he thought fatalistically, to make the journey into the next world more palatable, one took as many enemy dead along as possible.

Simon walked up behind the fleet commander's Tac seat and looked into the more comprehensive display. "I just don't see why they don't retreat," he said, shaking his head slightly. "Rentec said they won't back off, but we had the last bunch of them running, which surprised him and his top officers. Now this. I wish we could get a handle on how they think. I want them dead, but this just feels wrong somehow."

He watched as hit after hit got through the screen of destroyers and cruisers surrounding the one massive vessel. He'd figured the sheer number of Mambas and opposing main battlecruiser of First Fleet would make his enemy think that was all it faced, making the appearance of Second Fleet a complete surprise—so complete, in fact, that pilots and gunners managed to knock out three of the five main engines on the monster ship, leaving her a barely navigable hunk of metal. She was still highly dangerous but pretty much target practice for the Mamba pilots who continued to fly sorties against her.

"Captain, order a flight of plasma bombs and see if they will do any good. It's one tactic we've not tried." A number of the newly developed missiles got through several rudimentary or totally nonexistent shields and effectively stalled almost half a dozen ships that began to tumble, proving to be more of a hazard to the enemy than to humans. Simon wanted this to end. The rage he'd felt in the beginning and re-experienced every time these guys showed up had turned to quiet determination, but even so, this was too much like beating up a cripple.

Almost four hundred Mambas had launched against the Korvil fleet, with a few left behind, redlined for maintenance. At this point, just over three hundred pilots continued to fly mission after mission against the huge ship. Simon watched a lucky shot took take out one ship as it tried to get close enough to lock on and deliver the newest weapon in the Alliance arsenal. The other four ships in the flight wove through the return fire and launched their torpedoes directly against the enemy's hull.

The effect was spectacular. The energy bombs spread out across the hull of the enemy ship, glowing in colors that had to be seen to be believed. Rippling in waves from the points of impact, multihued lights flared up wherever two separate ripples met. Two more flights passed the doomed ship, directing their fire at the suspected location of the enemy power core. Their efforts were finally rewarded when one missile drove deeper into the heart of the giant ship and disintegrated the generator that was powering the anti-matter containment field.

Simon sighed in relief at the sight of the last enemy ship disappearing from the screen. Now the cleanup and retrieval could begin. Of the almost one hundred Mambas taken out of action, only a dozen beacons flared red on the screens. Of the twenty-four Alliance ships to enter the battle, sixteen returned, and two of those were the carriers that hadn't gotten close enough to the fight to be damaged. In all, eight ships had been lost, but only three didn't need repairs. Of the eight destroyed ships, only the *McCaffrey* survived long enough for her remaining crew to be evacuated by courageous shuttle crews flying into and out of her empty launch bays before her containment fields went down.

The badly mauled Alliance fleet dispersed among various bases and Earth according to the severity of their wounds. Simon rode the last shuttle to leave the *McCaffrey* as it flew into the *Galileo's* bay, rushing the *McCaffrey's* captain to the most advanced medical facilities available. A lucky shot had taken out the *McCaffrey's* antigravs, and Marsha had suffered several broken bones since she hadn't strapped herself into her chair, but most disconcerting was the growing lump on the back of her head. He escorted the stretcher to the med lab and saw to it that Marsha was put onto one of the tables in much the same way Kitty had been. There, a surgical team—now a standard part of the ship's medical department—worked on her mangled body.

For almost three hours, the team worked to stop Marsha's seeping blood. They taped ribs to help prevent a ruptured lung, while repairing torn muscles and suturing wounds. The most imperative task, that of removing pressure from her brain, was temporarily accomplished by simply inserting a needle through the crack in her skull to drain a bit of the fluid collecting at the point where her head had contacted the ceiling. The other procedures could then be accomplished without the additional burden of a time limit staring them in the face. To Simon's way of thinking, the amputation of Marsha's right thumb and forefinger was worse than the opening of her skull to reposition the pieces.

The entire operation had been videotaped to see if and when the cylinder would appear. As in Kitty's case, the doctors and nurses finished their work and stepped away from the table. This time, cameras captured the process as the two transparent pieces closed over Marsha's body and the concealing mist/liquid slowly engulfed her form.

"You what?" Kitty exploded out of her chair when Simon told her of Marsha's situation. She moved around her desk, an elemental force not to be denied. "You had no right to put her through that! There was every reason to think she'd survive without the assistance of... of... the ship," she finished lamely but no less angrily. "You have no idea what you did."

Simon, no less elemental, stood his ground defiantly, forcing Kitty to stop just outside his personal space. "Yes, I do," he answered quietly. "How many conversations have we had about what happened to you? Besides, I had every right to make that decision. The doctors told me there was no real hope that she would ever regain consciousness, and even if she did, they didn't hold out much hope that she would be anything more than a drooling idiot. This was our only chance to improve that prognosis. The fact was that this time, we knew what to expect. We have it all recorded, and the particular section of the computer involved is being monitored several different ways. Besides, no kin could be contacted in time to make the decision for her."

Simon spread his hands helplessly, and Kitty moved in to put her arms around him, reaching deep for the feeling of rightness and safety she always found in his embrace. "I'm sorry. It's just that I can still recall almost all of what went on inside there," she said into his chest. "I know I turned out all right, but it's not a guarantee that she will, and I just can't…" She broke off and cried, shoulders heaving in misery. "I guess all we can do now is pray."

The two stood silently entwined for a few more minutes, and Kitty finally broke away, somehow refreshed from contact with her other half. "She had an uncle on board, you know," she choked out. "Was there any sign of him?"

Simon shook his head. "Yeah, I know, and I looked. His name didn't come up among the *McCaffrey's* survivors. We checked out the launch bays pretty thoroughly. The main deck took a pretty hard hit but maintained structural integrity. She'd lost about half of her grav fields, and it made for a hell of a time searching. We found a few bodies, but his and four others weren't accounted for. They were listed as missing in action."

"Oh, God," Kitty cried. "I almost hope she doesn't wake up to that news. They were close." She walked over to the window and gazed out into the night, her reflection staring back accusingly. Silence reigned as two minds worried at the problem. "Both shuttles were still aboard?" Kitty asked, turning back to her husband.

"Right," Simon confirmed. "And we checked both of

them. There was no one aboard either ship. What are you looking for?"

"I'm not sure. I just have a feeling. Why just five bodies missing? And why was one of them Marsha's uncle?" She sat down at her computer terminal and turned it on.

Simon just shook his head, at a loss for ideas. He walked around Kitty's desk and watched as she brought up the *McCaffrey's* crew list. Kitty looked up at Simon and arched an eyebrow. He pulled himself back from a distant place and read off five names from a piece of paper he'd fished out of his pocket.

Kitty typed them into the computer and followed them with the command: Associate. Immediately, the screen vanished to reappear bearing the same five names. Beside Marsha's uncle's name was the legend: Assigned *TAS McCaffrey*, Chief of Flight Operations. Beside each of the other four names was the phrase: Assigned *TAS McCaffrey*, Emergency Repair Services.

The cursor blinked steadily for a full twenty seconds before Simon said almost abstractedly, "Chief of Flight Operations is also head of Repair Services."

Kitty finished the thought, "They took the repair pods out to try to get their ship back under power."

"And the *Spica* used their pressor beams to push the *McCaffrey* out of the area of combat. That had to throw the pods loose," Simon said, surmising. He pulled out his comm link and connected with the *Rigel's* captain. "Return to the original combat coordinates and run the entire scenario again. This time pay special attention to all movements of the *McCaffrey*. Extrapolate what her position would be if the *Spica* hadn't pushed her out of the combat area. Follow that heading slowly, sensors on full."

"What am I looking for?" the captain asked.

"You'll know," Simon replied firmly. "I'm betting on five emergency signals."

Unnoticed, a single drive powered up well past Pluto and disappeared into the depths of space.

CHAPTER NINE

The fleet moved slowly through the Oort cloud of the new system, sensors extended as far as the powerful generators could send them, disregarding the effects they might have on other sensor systems. On the contrary, they actually hoped to make contact.

Policy Minister Manura sel Garian sat in the captain's seat of the fleet flagship *Kath-e-Shiravi*. Three months into the voyage to the human homeworld, the *Kath's* captain had mysteriously died of an as yet undetermined malady. The ship's surgeon could only assure the crew and officers that there was no trace of plague. sel Garian, stepping outside the accepted chain of command, had assumed full command of the fleet, as well as the mission, combining the command structures of both the military and the contact team. Such was her power that no one dreamed of pointing out that it was strictly prohibited for a civil leader to directly command military forces.

One ship on the outskirts of the formation had picked up a probe's transmission when it sent off its report. Transmitted to the flagship, the signal pulled the fleet toward the probe. Once aboard the service deck, it was dissected and the report sent to the bridge.

"It appears to be a common marker probe," the terrified technician reported. Rumors floated throughout the fleet about what happened to those who came too close to the person of the Policy Minister. "There are some unusual differences, though."

"And what might those be?" grated out of the device strapped to sel Garian's throat.

"Larger than normal power core, odd configuration of components, unintelligible source coding, and such," he managed to get out. "Mostly, there's just an alien feel to the device. We *have* noted that the device seems to work with a much higher degree of efficiency than an equivalent device of our own."

A distracted flick of sel Garian's wrist sent the terrified tech back belowdecks, grateful to escape with her life. Lost in thought, sel Garian left the bridge, not bothering to turn command over to the exec. That officer gingerly sat down in the command chair and nodded to the helm officer. "Continue your previous course," was all he said, though his eyes contradicted the confidence in his voice.

Manura sel Garian entered her quarters and knew immediately that she wasn't alone. It wasn't that anything had changed; it was simply a feeling developed over many years of cunning and deception on her own part that let the minuscule clues send the proper message to her brain.

The suite was austere for one so high in the des Harras government. In one room was a desk, overflowing with the one enemy even sel Garian could never defeat—paperwork. One room was her sleep chamber, a luxury afforded to one so high. Another room held a couch, a low table, and a few chairs. No pictures or other color graced any of the gray metal walls of the suite. She turned into the common room, where she faced a robed and hooded figure. The dark figure rose slowly once sel Garian entered the room.

"The Sisterhood would have a report, Policy Minister."

"When I send for someone, kath-mora," she hissed, angry that even a member of the Sisterhood would violate her inner sanctum, "I expect them to arrive promptly and wait outside my personal quarters." She was angered as well by the fact that her visitor's tone of voice had been more of a command than a request.

"We have arrived," she said after a slight delay. "A probe has been found that is neither Korvil nor Shiravan. It bears striking similarities to one of ours but with distinctive changes, some say improvements." She poured a blue liquid into a small glass, deliberately not including her visitor in the small end-of-day ritual that always set her mind at ease. She sat down facing her uninvited guest, her dispassionate stare hiding her emotions.

The robed figure, hood thrown back, leaned forward. Her collar opened to reveal the rank and insignia of a weapons tech. "The Sisterhood requires that contact with this race be cut off at the earliest moment," she said quietly. "Use whatever means you can find to extract the two fleets from human contact."

sel Garian sipped from the tiny glass. "You still haven't convinced me that it's in the best interests of the Shiravan people to do so." She looked down, apparently absorbed by the lightly glowing liquid. "I have given my oath and life to the service of the Matriarch. Her desire for the Shiravan people is to expand into the universe, spreading ourselves far enough that no group like the Korvils will ever extinguish the light of our race. I deem that to be a worthy goal. What arguments can you present to make me break an oath strong enough to estrange me from clan and family for over thirty turns?"

"I can offer you no arguments to break a solemn oath; I only present the truth. Choosing to realign yourself must come from your heart. And for that to happen, you must see the error of your ways." The robed woman began to pace the floor. "Look at what the Korvils have done with the technology they stole from us. They hurt us badly at every turn, and they barely maintain their equipment at the level we had it at almost four hundred turns ago." She turned and looked directly at sel Garian. "And now these humans have not only stolen the technology but have even improved on it. What does that portend for us?"

"We don't know that the humans will do the same things the Korvils do," sel Garian countered.

"We don't know that they won't either," the kathmora shot back. "Do you want to wait until it's too late to find out?"

"You're condemning an entire species because of the actions of another," sel Garian noted quietly. "Is that the reaction of rational beings?"

"Is it the act of a rational being to condemn a third of her clan to death for an idea, Butcher of Harusel?" the robed woman retorted venomously. "Who is to say what is rational and what is not? At some time and place, any action could be considered rational. And we do not condemn them entirely on the basis of what they might do. The presence of only two humans on our world had already begun to cause problems, even before our departure. Both males and females have begun speaking of equality of the sexes. Young females wish to walk the streets unescorted. Males are being allowed into the workforce even more than before. If we are to allow such perversions of our traditional ways, where will it stop?"

sel Garian snorted, a chore for someone equipped with an artificial voice box. "The idea of equality of the sexes has been around since before the arrival of the humans. The earliest beginnings of the war effort brought the phenomenon into the open when unattached males and females were thrown into contact on a regular basis. And what young woman wouldn't like the freedom to go where she wishes when she wishes, like her Chosen Sisters? This, too, has been an outcome of the war effort, not of the arrival of humans."

The kath-mora looked daggers at her adversary. "You would bring us into contact with a people where males govern. We have seen the follies of that particular philosophy in our society, and now we will expose some of our most impressionable people to more of that after we have finally stamped it out. Contact with these beings will destroy the very fiber of our society."

sel Garian sat silently for a moment, pondering the line of reasoning of the Chosen Sister. "I will grant that there is some merit to your case. A bare kernel of truth if the diatribe is pared down. Still, my oath binds me to the Matriarch's goals. And it is my view that it is better to *have* a society, however badly fractured, than to have no society at all, which is what the Korvils intend."

The sorceress turned to face sel Garian, a strange glint in her eye. "The Sisterhood does not believe that either the Korvils or these barbarian humans will be able to destroy our society. Shiravi will prevail."

sel Garian stared back at the kath-mora, recognizing the look in her eyes for the madness that it was, and said, "The only way Shiravan culture will survive is through force of arms, through military might. And since we've steadily been losing planets and ships to the Korvils, I seriously doubt we'll be able to survive without outside assistance."

The robed figure drew herself up to her full height, believing it to give her a greater air of authority. On some, it might have worked, but sel Garian had been playing the game since before this one had been born. "We of the Sisterhood have meditated long on this very subject," the kath-mora intoned. She faced sel Garian, arms at her side, palms out. "I myself have spent days on end in the sacred chamber, meditating and communing directly with the Spirits of Space." sel Garian's visitor flushed an even deeper shade of red than was her norm. Her eyes glowed as with a fever, and she raised her hands to waist level, making fists. "And the Spirits dictate that you join us in our effort!" Finally, she placed her closed fists on her chest, wrists crossed. sel Garian recognized the ancient gesture for what it was—an order to obey—and knew then just how well she had wrought.

"I've been in that room you call a sacred chamber," sel Garian said coolly. She looked the kath-mora priestess in the eyes. *Who else would know the old signs?* she asked herself. *Certainly not one of the lower orders. She must be a priestess at the very least. I accomplished more than I knew when I assigned this one to the fleet.* Aloud, she continued, "Some say it gives you access to the Spirits; others say it sucks the soul out of you." She inclined her head, first left, then right, a Shiravan shrug. "All I see is the swirling mist of otherspace. I don't see any Spirits, and I'm not even sure they exist. So, I'm surely not going to follow the dictates of beings who might not even exist."

"Blasphemy!" the weapons tech hissed, stepping closer to sel Garian. "Remember, Policy Minister, it is by the hands of the kath-moren that you sit in the fleet commander's seat, and the hands of the kath-moren can remove you from it. You know not our power or reach!"

"On the contrary," sel Garian fairly purred through her throat box. "Do you truly think that the Butcher of Harusel, as you named me, who led the resistance that killed almost a third of my clan to protect the Matriarch would come aboard this vessel, this fleet, without knowing exactly who each and every one of the personnel were? And what their affiliations were? Or without protection?" She stood and faced the larger woman. "It was my signature that brought each and every member of this fleet's crew together. Even yours, High Priestess Masendi.

"Yes, I know who you are," she said to the surprised expression on the weapon tech's face. "I now know every kath-mora in the fleet and their affiliations, and if I were you, I'd be very careful about the threats I made. Now, I make one."

She reached out and grasped the robe with the fingertips of her right hand, feeling, testing the quality of the material. She looked into the astonished face of her antagonist. "Knowledge is power, *Sister*," she said sarcastically. "Your rank and affiliation, I was only able to guess at first. How much more do I know, you wonder?" The old woman just smiled, the merest twitch of her lip.

The beginning of the end for these fanatics, she thought triumphantly.

"That you will only find out as time passes," sel Garian said. "Now, if I see one more robe walking the decks of my ship, or hear of one on any other vessel in this fleet, or hear personally, or have reported to me even one similar conversation, the death of the previous fleet commander will be as nothing to the purge I will initiate. Remember well, Spirit Witch and tell your Sisters. You know I speak the truth, for as many of Clan Masendi died at Harusel by my hand as did Clan sel Garian. Remove yourself from my presence, return to your duties, and don't bring yourself to my attention again."

"If they're Shiravan," Simon asked, "why are they just sitting there?"

"It's possible," Captain do' Sirkis answered, "that the commander of that fleet is wary of entering a system with so many active warships moving around." He thought for a minute and said, "Regular maintenance, weapons checks, battle drills. They'll probably have their weapons powered up, but this is supposed to be a friendly system, so they'll probably not be actively seeking targets."

"Possible and probable are not among my favorite words right now," Simon noted dryly. "We should send one ship out to meet them and escort them to Vesta." He turned to Rentec. "Maybe, Mr. Ambassador, you'd like to go along for the ride? Perhaps assure whoever is in charge that the natives are friendly?"

Rentec shook his head, adopting the human gesture. "No, Admiral," he said. "Doma kep Parrasine has requested that privilege. I believe she's had a travel pack ready for some time now. Will you be accompanying the contact ship?"

"I had planned to, yes," Simon confirmed. "I'd like to oversee their arrival at Vesta. Also, since we know they're coming, sending our top military person to meet them is proper Shiravan protocol, according to Doma kep Parrasine."

"You're what?" Kitty demanded. She took a moment to get her voice back under control. "Simon, you can't. I forbid it as Herald."

"And who else would you send? You know what we've learned about Shiravan protocol. It has to be our highest-ranking military person—me." Calm reigned on Simon's face while his thoughts roiled. The thought of going to confront ten armed alien ships with just one tended to make him nervous.

"And what if they're not Shiravan? You'll need backup or something, won't you?"

Simon smiled at his wife's image in the viewscreen. "Taking a few ships will do as much good as taking one, and taking enough for a real fight would be an insult to the Shiravans. We got away with it when Rentec and company arrived because we were in the middle of a fight when they showed up. Besides, this way we only lose one ship if something goes wrong. And any commander who won't lead from the front is not one to follow." He reached out and touched the screen, watching her do the same. "More to the point, they're here to bring one of our own home, remember? And according to Rentec, this sel Garian wants to discuss an alliance against these Korvils. That's what we've been waiting for—the most senior players. So, there's not much chance that I'll be in any real danger."

"Initial reports show that they're communicating with their own people and with some of our higher-ranking officers on the scene," Kitty told Simon. "As a matter of fact, it looks more like a staring contest is going on right now. These guys have to know that we sent a ship to Earth to report to, well, us, dammit. So, they must know that the fleet they face is waiting for orders."

While Manura sel Garian's Second Fleet sat waiting for a response to the dissected probe's inbound signal, all sensors at maximum, section leaders saw to the routine maintenance of the fleet. Though certain chores could not be performed while the fleet ghosted through the realm Shiravans called otherspace, generators were realigned, field coils were retuned, magnetic containment vessels were recalibrated, and during all this, battle drills were being run.

sel Garian called her top people together. "It was never my intention to keep control of this mission," she said when all the ships' captains were present. "I now have the information I needed to apprehend the killer of Fleet Commander Keffis and will now proceed to name a replacement." With no more preamble, she said, "Binmith kep Parrasine, you will turn command of your ship over to your second and move to this vessel and take command of the fleet."

Operating on the better-safe-than-sorry principle, Simon ordered the *Rigel* to drop out of hyperspace several light-seconds away from the assumed Shiravan fleet. At the Herald's insistence, he told the captain, "She would prefer that we not lose another ship, if at all possible."

"I'm all for that, sir," the young captain muttered, staring at the holodisplay. "Tactical, your assessment of the situation?"

"I have eight ships confirmed, sir—six ships of the *Heinlein* class, one our size, and one a bit smaller. One of the *Heinlein* class ships appears to be damaged.

They're beat up but not helpless," the Tac officer said offhandedly. "I'd say stay powered up, though. We've got the legs to outrun them if we have to."

"Okay," the captain said decisively. He hit the all-ships intercom. "All hands, this is the captain. The ship is at yellow alert. All personnel to assigned duty stations. Section Chiefs, power to all weapons systems, torpedo rooms to standby. No one is to actually target any ship out there without my direct order. Engine room, prepare to go to emergency power on my command, pulling as much power from life-support as you can without killing us." He cut the circuit and turned to the bridge crew. "Helm, lay in a course directly through the center of that formation and label it 'cut and run.' Tactical, you are assigned to cripple as many of the opposing force as possible during cut and run. On my command, execute without delay." He thought for a few seconds, and asked, "Admiral, what are your orders?"

Simon shrugged, a half-smile on his lips. "I'd say we should answer the door, Captain. We've kept our visitors waiting long enough." He held up his comm link. "I'm tied directly into Communications." Pressing a button on the link, he said, "I am Admiral Simon Hawke of the Terran Alliance. Please state your race and business." He shut off the link and waited.

More than the estimated six seconds for a reply went by before the com screen, centered on the part of space holding the alien fleet, changed to a view of another bridge. Eerily familiar and lit with a dim red glow few aboard the *Rigel* besides Simon had ever seen, the scene was just a backdrop for the small red woman staring back at him. "I am Manura sel Garian," the image said in strangely accented but understandable English. "I am Second Voice of the Shiravan Polity. I return one of your people, stolen from you by the Korvils, and bring greetings from Domagera Linnas des Harras."

"Welcome to human space, Doma sel Garian," Simon answered in Shiravan. He continued in English, "While some of our people have made an intensive study of your language during the time your First Fleet has been in-system, I haven't had that luxury. I would prefer to either speak English or speak through an interpreter, whom I just happen to have beside me. You are acquainted with Doma Maratai kep Parrasine, aide to Rentec do' Verlas, Shiravan Ambassador to Earth?"

"I am, Admiral," came back six seconds later, the sound grating on Simon's nerves. "Would you and your aide join me aboard my flagship, the *Shumara Vacht*, to discuss matters of mutual concern?"

"I would be most happy to, Doma," Simon replied. "How will my pilot know which ship is yours?"

The image stood motionless for the six-second time lag and then said to someone outside the viewscreen's range, "Chia a ret. Suba ven gerat." She looked back at Simon and said, "I have ordered my ship to move slightly ahead of the remainder of the fleet. By this you will know. I await your arrival."

"Sir," Tactical reported, "I have ship movement. One ship moving forward and stopping."

"Acknowledged, Tac," the captain replied. He turned to Simon, "That sounded like an order, sir. Are you going to let her get away with it?"

"I'm going to let her think so for a short while, Captain," Simon said, a small smile flickering across his face. "So, she wants to play power politics, does she? I guess it's up to us to teach her a new concept—home court advantage." He stood up, straightened his shirt, brushed an invisible speck from the sleeve, and announced, "She'll get her reply when our shuttle leaves the flight deck, which we should probably be doing." He turned to his aide. "Please inform Doma kep Parrasine that I'll meet her on the flight deck."

Simon watched until he moved out of sight and said to the captain, "You have no discretion with respect to this next order, Captain. If things should for any reason go south on us, you are to keep your ship and crew alive to report back if at all possible. Your cut-and-run routine is more last-ditch than anything else. Remember, it will leave you with any surviving enemy between you and home base. I don't think there'll be a problem, but you never know with our own people, so how can we be sure about aliens?"

Rentec turned slightly to view the cut of his brilliant saffron coat in the mirror. "One thing I will never understand about humans is their ability to put their personal tastes aside and wear all that dull black clothing."

"Think of it as insignia carried to extremes, Ambassador," Maratai said as she surveyed herself in the same mirror. Her aqua gown matched the piping on the Ambassador's coat and trousers. "The militaries of all the various Earth countries have their own distinctive regalia. Even civilian groups demonstrate their affiliations in the same manner. Police uniforms vary from place to place but are easily recognizable as police nevertheless," she noted. "Even their sports groups exhibit the same inclination." She nervously straightened the small ensign on her collar, denoting her status as a member of the Matriarch's personal retinue. "sel Garian truly commands Second Fleet?" A quiver raced through her voice.

"So it would appear," Rentec confirmed. "When Admiral Hawke announced our presence, it was she who answered." He shook his head in the human manner. "I confess that I can see no reason for her to have usurped the military's role in this matter. Court intrigue is her forte, not interplanetary warfare."

"We will know soon enough, except that the only difference between the two that I can see is scope," Maratai replied, temporizing. She looked up at her companion and placed her hand on his arm. "If what you say is true, let our friend Simon find out just how dangerous she can be, Rentec. Don't get caught between them."

Rentec covered her hand with his. "I haven't been away from court so long as to forget the basics, Doma," he said formally. "Your concern for my well-being is appreciated, but I intend to stand by and let these two particular brekkis butt heads until there is only one left standing."

He smiled at the memory of a trip with his father many years before. Kirel do' Verlas had taken the young son he was pleased to have sired on an outing into mountains so remote they were merely numbers on a map. During their two-week stay, Rentec had seen two male brekkis fighting over territory and reproductive rights—the winner being the one to withstand the repeated high-speed head impacts with another five-hundred-pound, heavily-horned brekki.

Focusing his attention back on the present, Rentec opened the door leading into the corridor, breaking the contact and putting an end to the moment. "But why you would feel so about a junior minister, appointed to a unique post for what is certain to be a limited time, is a mystery to me."

"Perhaps," Maratai answered, trying to put an air of the very mystery Rentec referred to into her voice, "it could be said that I find myself respecting the fortitude you have shown during this most uncomfortable situation. Integrity, honesty, and perseverance, notwithstanding, I find myself admiring your dedication to your Matriarch and convictions, and the ability to integrate them into a whole you can work with. Especially considering your extenuating circumstances."

Shiravan culture prevented women from making overt bids for male attention. That was normally handled clan-mother to clan-mother. With so few men in the populace, there were economic advantages to having a male in one's household, but so few were born. Only in the last fifty years or so had the figures for male births begun to climb again. But so many of the old traditions continued, even after males started to enter the workforce.

The actual verbal reference to Rentec's situation was unheard of in polite Shiravan society, female-dominated though it was. She moved out into the corridor, effectively ending the conversation and leaving Rentec confused at her deliberate snubbing of all Shiravan custom.

Simon elected to approach the Shiravan fleet in the captain's gig—a small shuttle capable of holding two pilots and a party of eight—and completely weaponless. Rentec and Maratai, last to arrive, seated themselves at the rear of the passenger compartment near the door, filling out the four chairs facing each other. "Glad you decided to come along, Ambassador. Our other two personnel are a surprise, if your Doma sel Garian doesn't object," Simon half-explained when he noticed the Shiravan's curious glances at the two extra personnel. "If she does object, they'll never leave the shuttle."

"What are their duties?" Maratai asked, making note of the fact that these two did not carry the usual sidearm affected by most Alliance personnel. As a matter of fact, neither did Simon nor his aide, Captain Goldman.

"Call them harbor pilots," was all Simon would say.

The *Rigel's* gig drifted out of its berth in the battlecruiser's docking bay and passed through its shields. The pilots brought the inertial compensators online while the ship's computer acquired targeting data. Chosen for their ability to speak Shiravan as much as for their flight expertise, the two pilots locked on to the flagship and hailed her. "*Shumara Vacht*, tiso heppis *Rigel*. Sura vir tenara Admiral Hawke, Captain Goldman, Chudara Rentec do' Verlas, es Doma Maratai kep Parrasine."

Simon understood enough Shiravan to know that the pilots had just identified themselves, the shuttle, and its occupants. Even knowing that the flight should take no more than ten or fifteen minutes, he kept one ear tuned to the cockpit traffic.

"Tep'a ah musaret hisaro." The copilot had requested docking instructions in accented but recognizable Shiravan, and Simon smiled as the delay in reply time lengthened past the time a ten-thousand-mile separation and light-speed communication would normally account for.

The pilots finally received clearance and manually moved the little ship into one of the bays of the Shiravan flagship. Unused to the process since Alliance ships had internal capture fields to handle the chore, more time was spent warping the shuttle into the bay than getting from the *Rigel* to the Shiravan ship.

The larger ship had none of the forcefields over the bay openings that were standard on Alliance ships, so the occupants waited while bay doors closed and the pressure equalized. It was obvious when that had occurred since a side door opened, allowing a small group of Shiravans to enter the bay. Per orders received earlier from Simon, the pilots opened the hatch and let the door become a short ramp.

Simon's rise to his feet was a signal for the rest of the party to do the same. Only Kitty could have recognized the nervousness in him as he readjusted his uniform and wiped at nonexistent bits of lint. "Well, people, it's showtime," he said and stepped to the hatch. Moving past the hatchway, he noticed the difference in gravity. At about the time Rentec and his fleet had shown up in Earth's system, engineers in the *Galileo's* Research and Development section had finally figured out how to adjust what they called the gravity field gradient. From that time on, all Alliance vessels carried an Earth-normal gravity.

As he moved the few paces to the bottom of the ramp made by the gig's open hatch, Simon became aware that not all members of the group awaiting him were Shiravan. The sixth member was human. Margaret Spencer, if he remembered her name correctly.

Followed by Rentec, then Captain Goldman and Maratai, Simon walked over to the waiting group. Taking advantage of a short course in Shiravan protocol hurriedly pressed on him by Rentec and Maratai, Simon stopped in front of the fleet commander and gave a measured head-nod, granting her the status of equals.

Familiar with the makeup of both fleets, Rentec had said, "This commander will outrank Captain do' Sirkis. Her appointment to fleet commander of a battle group escorting Policy Minister sel Garian guarantees it, both militarily and socially. She will be the supreme Shiravan military officer in the area, and, as such, should be accorded every courtesy given to any visiting general or admiral of one of your own military forces." His voice had taken on the detached quality it always did when he was thinking. "I am surprised, though, to find that a kep Parrasine is fleet commander. It was my understanding that a Commander Keffis was to be commander on this mission."

Simon looked up at the taller being and decided that a little more distance between human and Shiravans would do wonders to prevent neckaches. Through a translator, he said, "Welcome to Alliance space, Fleet Commander. I'd like to express the Alliance's thanks for the safe return of Lieutenant Commander Spencer. Our facilities are at your disposal for anything you need to refit and repair your ships after their long voyage. As for the rest, I'll let your own people fill you in on that."

CHAPTER TEN

"I want the *Galileo* and the *Mira* back here ASAP," Kitty said into a her comm link. "We need to get those NASA guys back to Earth, and I want to get the *Mira* crewed up." She listened as a tiny voice acknowledged her orders.

"And now that we know the identities of the newest batch of visitors to our system, we can stand down from general quarters. But I want an eye kept on them until we are more certain of their motives. I'm still a bit unhappy that we repaired two of their ships after that last attack, but to be fair, they earned it, sticking their necks out without knowing for sure which way we would jump," she said to Captain Thomas Breen of the *Deneb*.

Second-waver that he was, he had excelled in all respects and received his comets just before the first Korvil attack. Sitting in an office on Earth while all of his friends got to go kick some alien butt galled him, but the reports of what had happened to the *Clarke* still sent shivers down his spine. Knowing that he was more of a courier than anything else didn't sit well, but the speed of light almost dictated using warp-capable ships for message carrying, even at just planetary distances, so there were two ships usually in orbit at all times. The *Shasta* would remain in orbit until another ship took the *Deneb's* place and would take her turn ferrying information and orders from place to place.

He turned his full attention back to the Herald. "This sel Garian person is the one Rentec said would show up and take over negotiations with us," Kitty said quietly. "I'd prefer to meet her on neutral grounds, but there aren't any, so we'll use the *Galileo* instead. She should feel more comfortable there anyway."

"You're not concerned that they'll find a way to take control of the *Galileo* while on board?" Thomas asked

"I'm only concerned about the medical section of the computer, I think," Kitty said. "We've never really understood what goes on in there, and it *is* a section that's still encoded with the Shiravan codes since we couldn't erase them without losing all the medical data, too. Simple solution was to limit their access to that which we don't understand *until* we understand it. Besides, with Marsha still inside one of those..." she let her voice trail off.

Thomas thought her fears justified but forbore to tell her so. Instead he asked, "So, what message am I to deliver to Admiral Hawke?"

"Tell him to delay twenty-four hours and then escort Policy Minister sel Garian and her flagship directly to Earth where the *Galileo* will be waiting to accept her entourage."

Thomas stood up and said, "Yes, Ma'am. Anything else?"

Kitty reached into her desk, brought out an envelope, and slid it across the desk. "Deliver this to Simon personally before he talks to the new ambassador, and time your arrival for about twenty-four hours from now." Thomas took the envelope, nodded, and turned to leave. "Have to have the gravity lowered for her, I guess," he heard just before the door closed.

An officious-acting young second lieutenant bent over Simon's shoulder and whispered in his ear, "Admiral, you have an urgent communique from the Herald. Should I wait for a response?"

Simon tore the flap open in frustration, read the contents, and looked up at the messenger. "There will be no response at this time. You may go." The now-deflated young officer crossed the room as everyone sat in total silence, apparently waiting for him to leave. Once the door closed, Simon waved the paper in the air. "This has just arrived from the Herald. Her respects to you, Policy Minister, and her apologies for not being able to be here in person. She requests what I have already offered, but now it is official. You, Policy Minister, and your flagship will be escorted to Earth by the *Rigel* and the *Shasta*, assuming you agree, of course. She adds," he said, reading further, "that the *Galileo,* or *Dalgor Kreth* as you know her, will be in orbit and can serve as a sort of neutral ground for your first talks."

"And how long until this meeting can be held?" sel Garian asked through her translator.

Simon just smiled. "Rentec, explain that we aren't afraid to short-jump within our own system. If she will allow two of my crew access the *Shumara Vacht's* Helm and Nav stations, I believe we can be in Earth orbit within two hours."

sel Garian's response was voiced at the same time that Fleet Commander kep Parrasine spoke up. kep Parrasine was visibly shaken at the old woman's curt acceptance of the request. Simon merely whispered into his comm link and told Rentec to tell sel Garian that the two harbor pilots were on their way to the bridge.

"Tell me," sel Garian asked, "where will you be

while your crewmen are controlling my ship?"

"Why, right here beside you, Policy Minister," Simon said pleasantly. "I wouldn't want you to think we were going to pull a fast one on you."

"Pull a fast one?" Rentec asked blankly as he struggled with the idiom.

"Trick you or try something sneaky," Simon explained. Rentec whispered in sel Garian's ear, who thought for a moment and then just nodded.

Simon, through Rentec and Maratai, had explained the idea of harbor pilots by the time the two officers arrived. They scanned the room until they found Simon. Guessing correctly that the person next to him was the VIP they had to impress, the senior of the two saluted and asked in stilted yet perfect Shiravan, "Commanders Matthews and Ivanov reporting as ordered. Permission to enter the bridge?"

Impressed, but trying not to show it, she merely said, "Granted. You may take your positions and report when ready. My officers will stand ready to assist in any way they can." This last was offered as a not-so-veiled threat that nothing besides the approved maneuvers were to be attempted.

The two officers, both women, went to what was to them over-sized control panels. Helm almost effortlessly began to access the strange ship's engines, drawing a mutter of astonishment from the alien crew. "I have control, sir," she reported in English to Simon.

Nav made several attempts before saying, "I need an access code to do this any time soon." She looked at the alien whose place she had taken and asked, "Erocerra, Doma. Se el tugara fet yefite?"

Rentec hadn't wanted the word 'yefite' to be used at all. Its usual tone carried the weight of an order, but the woman used the class-conscious Shiravan's own society against them, deliberately speaking in everyday equal-to-equal mode. This took the sting out of the order and relegated it to a very urgent request.

The alien looked at the other human—who was already deep into the systems of the ship and showing every sign of knowing what she was doing—leaned over the human's shoulder, pressed a series of buttons, and then stepped aside.

A few seconds of work and the second pilot reported, "I'm in and accessing primary targeting systems." Several seconds went by. "I'll bring her in to one hundred thousand first before acquiring a fix on a spot big enough at the fifty thousand marker."

Helm said, "Receiving data dump from Nav and applying coordinates." Several seconds went by before Helm reported, "Course laid in and locked, Captain."

Simon looked at Rentec. "We're ready to go. I know you guys have a problem with this. There's still time for her to change her mind and go the slow way."

"Oh, no, Admiral. Policy Minister sel Garian and Captain kep Parrasine spent the better part of last evening looking forward to the experience, it would seem. Definite military applications. See? Already you affect our way of thinking."

Rentec didn't bother to tell Simon that he and Maratai had been integral parts of that discussion, the early part of which had felt more like an interrogation than anything else. Neither held back anything they'd learned about the humans during their time together. Indeed, they'd been spoken to strongly by Simon before retiring for the night. "Now comes the big interview, Mister Ambassador," Simon prophesied as he nodded at the retreating backs of sel Garian and kep Parrasine.

"You've probably figured out some things we'd rather you didn't know about us, just as you fear that we have done the same about you. Let me just say that while I really don't know your culture as well as I'd like, I believe we have more in common than we suspect. Tell your boss the truth as you see it."

"We've been shown every courtesy possible, with the exception of places called secure facilities, which we believe to be military bases for protection from each other as they are still a one-planet, power-driven, tribal culture. All other facilities of a civilian nature were shown to us—hospitals, prisons, transportation control centers for their ground-based and air-based traffic systems. All of their industry is based—was based—on the consumption of fossil fuels." Rentec reached for a small cup and took a sip for his dry throat.

Maratai took up the story before he could settle back into his chair. "All of the construction you see about you includes four functioning bases, dozens of ships, literally hundreds of advanced parda kellin, upgraded to almost warp-level capabilities and carrying strange, stronger weapons. Also, it seems that they take less damage when in a conflict. My suspicion is that they've taken another of our technologies and twisted it to a more unique, more advantageous use. Most of the changes they've made have been predictable in hindsight, like adding another power core to a ship's systems."

She stopped, obviously embarrassed that she had run on so long. Rentec said, "No, Doma kep Parrasine, please continue."

Reassured by the lack of rancor in his voice, she went

on. "They are a secretive people by nature. I have learned that one of their favorite sayings is, 'Knowledge is power.' They still are splintered into many different factions on the planet's surface, though those who have moved off-world seem to be united in their desire to pursue a space-borne lifestyle and may be able to help in our war against the Korvils in more ways than we can yet guess."

Simon was already familiar with the reaction Shiravans had to in-system hyper jumps, but he watched these two especially closely. As Helm ran the ship up to jump speed, Nav said, "Sir! I have just acquired a Mayday. Orders?"

Simon looked briefly at the actual captain, and said, "Identify Mayday and authenticate ASAP, Commander."

Manipulating the superior scanning system built into this larger vessel, Nav quickly said. "Authentication confirmed, sir. I have five construction pods interconnected and putting out a weak Mayday. Orders?"

Simon turned to Rentec. "Tell your Policy Minister that those are five of my people thought killed in the past action. Ask if she would mind if we divert and rescue them."

Rentec spoke quickly to the elder of the two women. After a short exchange, he turned to the distressed Simon and said, "It is always in a Shiravan's nature to deal solicitously with those in distress. Stop and rescue your people, of course," Rentec translated.

Simon nodded to his Nav officer, who started sending new coordinates to Helm. In a very few minutes, the huge ship was on a course only slightly askew from their original heading. Simon felt the vibrations cease through the soles of his boots and correctly deduced that they were at the scene of the Mayday.

He turned to the ship's captain, only to find her speaking into her wrist comm. He waited until she was finished and let her speak to Rentec. "Your people are even now being brought aboard. As soon as the air can be restored to the bay, you may see them," he translated.

"Okay, then," Simon said. "Helm, recompute course for Earth orbit and send to Nav. Helm, wait until I return to proceed. I'm going down to see who we just brought on board. Rentec, will you show me the way?"

Rentec escorted this alien who had become his friend during the past year, looking down at the erect frame and stoic bearing and fighting hard, even with his longer legs, to keep up. "Your determination is admirable, friend Simon, but your crew will either be alive or dead. No amount of hurrying will change the situation."

"I don't have a choice, Rentec. They're my responsibility, and I must reassure them that they're safe, if they're still alive. I don't guarantee their actions if I don't speak to them personally. Besides, I also wonder what happens when I leave two unknown aliens in control of your number two's flagship while I go gallivanting off to see who we just saved."

"I see," Rentec said slowly. "They may think they've been captured by the Korvil. Won't they remember the pictures of Korvils we gave you?"

Simon smiled crookedly. "You've only known us for about a year now, Rentec. We have a long history of distrusting new things. Believe me, this is the best way."

Simon stood outside the docking bay that held the five interconnected construction pods, waiting the seemingly interminable time it took for the air to be pumped into the room. As soon as the lights changed, he pressed the open button and waited restlessly as the round wheel in the center of the door spun of its own accord. The wheel stopped spinning, and when nothing further happened, Simon pulled on it hesitantly. The door swung open as soundlessly as any aboard the *Galileo*, he noticed almost absentmindedly as he walked over to the cluster of pods deposited in the middle of the bay.

Looking over the names stenciled on each suit, he knocked on a pod and wiped the frost off the outside of the forward viewport. Simon saw a human face looking back at him and tapped his own ear, hoping the man inside would turn on the suit's external speakers and microphones. "Chief, this is Admiral Hawke. I need you unsuited and out here as soon as possible. Understood?" Getting a nod back, Simon stepped back a few paces and waited for the center suit to open of its own accord.

Marsha's uncle looked first at Simon and then Rentec. Simon cut him off before he could ask any questions. "We are aboard the flagship of the second Shiravan contact fleet, Chief. Right now, I need you and your men to maintain discipline in here until we reach Earth, which should be in about two hours since we have to run back up to speed. You'll be transferred to the *Galileo* almost as soon as we arrive."

The chief just looked at Simon for a few seconds as if he were processing the information. Finally, he nodded. "As long as we've got air, we can handle a couple of hours cooped up in this one room. For sure, it's more than we've had for some time now."

CHAPTER ELEVEN

Simon followed Rentec back to the bridge, looking intently all about him. He wasn't looking at the crew as Rentec thought but at the ship itself—fittings, signs of aging, disrepair, neglect, anything that might give him some indication what kind of readiness level these overtly pacifistic people were at.

All signs led him to the conclusion that this particular bunch of Shiravans were at a high state of readiness in a fully functional and battleworthy vessel. "Unless you're not allowed to speak on the subject, I notice that these Shiravans seem to be at a higher state of readiness than you tell me most of your people tend to adhere to."

Rentec looked down at his human friend. "I'm sorry if I gave that impression, friend Simon, but the truth is that most Shiravans, those planet-bound or just being transported from one place to another, are of a different mindset than those you see around you. We who actually travel between the stars as a part of our service to the Matriarch are truly humbled by the size of the universe and tend to maintain our vessels quite well."

Simon stepped onto the bridge and said, "Nav, you may execute your orders." Nav ordered Helm to execute her assigned course. It was at this point that most of the bridge crew finally realized for sure what the humans were up to.

Quiet pandemonium broke out, and Nav bellowed in her best parade ground voice, "Stimara!" The use of senior-to-junior mode stunned most of the red aliens into silence, as was intended. "Tiso serama. Everything's normal. Earth tiso serama yat."

Rentec, long since accustomed to the human usage of the concept they called short-jumping, immediately recognized the reason for the bedlam. Convention among Shiravan ship handlers said that one just did not short-jump inside a planetary system. The particular convention in question was never questioned or analyzed. The fact of the matter was that the Shiravan system didn't have two massive bodies like Jupiter and Saturn sweeping the outer system clear of stray material, and the moon, much more massive than either of the two that circled Shiravi, served as another gravity well, attracting most of the rest of the larger incoming material.

Humans, noted for not respecting convention, had ignored this one without even knowing it. The peculiar conditions that let them operate so effectively in their own system would one day become recognized as unusual in the extreme, but in this one case, it proved to allow strategies neither of the other two species would ever have thought of.

It would have been nice to keep that particular piece of information quiet, Simon thought. *I'm glad we aren't overemphasizing the fact that aside from the obvious alterations to the capture fields, they haven't noticed that we have a full set of shields against anything in their present arsenal and a way to counter their shields when they figure them out and implement them.*

Rentec spoke sharply and quietly to the captain and her superior, sel Garian. A moment later the captain said, "Stimara! Par'a Terrani sec ferrada, korpa daesta."

Simon looked from the captain to sel Garian to

Rentec, unsure what to do. Rentec finally said, "The ship is under your command, Admiral. Please take us to Earth."

Simon shook his head slightly and turned to his Helm officer. "If your course is laid in, Commander, you may execute."

Merely nodding, the woman turned to the oversized console, moved two controls slightly, and said in accented Shiravan, "On my mark. Three, two, one, mark."

The twisting feeling Simon could never quite shake passed in a matter of seconds, and he looked up at the display. Even eight years later, he was still able to tell, with the altered Shiravan color scheme, when they had arrived. "Doma sel Garian, Captain kep Parrasine, I would like to be the first to personally welcome you to Earth," Simon said with a small smile on his face. "Nav, Helm, turn your stations back over to their proper operators please, and report back to the shuttle." He turned quickly to the two Shiravans. "If that is all right with you, Doma sel Garian?"

Nonplussed by an alien giving orders in her presence and then asking permission, she nodded and waved a hand in the vague direction of the doorway to the bridge. Her eyes were still glued to the screens before her. Normal bridge patter, albeit Shiravan, began to pass back and forth among the crew, breaking the spell for the Policy Minister. With great difficulty, it seemed, she asked, "How soon will I be allowed to meet with your Herald?" the artificial voice grating more than usual.

"The *Galileo* should be in orbit, Policy Minister," Simon said. "The ship you call the *Dalgor Kreth*. The Herald will beam aboard it, it will move into transporter distance of this vessel, and we can all go visiting."

Rentec and Maratai, as interpreters, would accompany the Policy Minister's staff. sel Garian played another card in her arsenal. "I have ordered my shuttle readied to carry us to this historic meeting, Admiral. I'm sure you won't mind," Maratai interpreted. "It would be so much better for all of your Herald's visitors to arrive at the same time, don't you think?"

"I have no problem with that at all, Policy Minister," Simon replied. "You might want to add a few people to go over the ship to see that we haven't damaged her to any degree. And I'm sure they'll be quite interested in some of the modifications we've made." Anyone who knew Simon would have heard, just barely, the smirk in his voice. None of that made it to his face, though, as he gave the old woman what she wanted even before she asked for it, or worse, before she tried to find out by sending people skulking around what he still considered to be his ship, never mind the fact that it would have to be returned in the now-foreseeable future. "Of course, my gig will carry the rest of my crew back to their ship."

The old woman looked as if she had just eaten whatever passed for lemons on Shiravi, and Simon hid the grin on his face by turning away slightly and speaking into his comm link. "*Galileo* Control, this is Admiral Hawke. What is your status?"

The response, calm and professional, monitored by the *Shumara Vacht's* comm station came across clearer than the signal across his link. "Admiral, this is *Galileo* Control. We have the Herald aboard, moving to the one-hundred-thousand-mile orbit and will take position one thousand miles ahead of you. We will await your signal for transport."

"*Galileo*, be advised that there has been a change of plans. Prepare the starboard Projects Deck to receive a shuttle from the *Shumara Vacht*."

A slight hesitation preceded the puzzled response. "Starboard Projects Deck available for docking, aye, sir."

The old woman—small, Rentec had described her—stood nearly eye-to-eye with Simon and tried another way to assert her dominance over this alien being who seemed to have no fear of her position. "You won't mind, I'm sure, Admiral, if my crew stays on alert, weapons ready, in case of further Korvil attacks? None of your ships will be targeted, of course."

"No more, Doma," Simon shot back, "than you will mind when my flagship enters Shiravan orbit someday with its weapons sealed, trusting in the hospitality and ability of Shiravi to protect it without question."

The two leaders spoke no more for a time as they led a fair-sized contingent of people down to the docking bays. "See what I mean about a pair of brekkis fighting over territory?" Rentec said quietly as they lagged behind the two a bit. "Very interesting to watch but only from a safe distance."

"The problem is," Maratai mused, "that we won't be that far away from either of them."

"Oh, I've been meaning to ask," Rentec said conspiratorially. "Have you told the Policy Minister the Herald's first name yet?"

Maratai chuckled lightly. "There hasn't been time, it seems, to inform the Policy Minister of that little detail. What with worrying about Korvil attacks and not yet having met these new aliens, as well as keeping track of some sort of situation almost minute to minute, she hasn't asked too many questions."

Rentec nodded at the door ahead of them. "You have

precious few minutes to inform her of this not-so-little detail, Doma kep Parrasine." A look of worry crossed his face. "One thing I know is that it is never a good idea to get on Manura sel Garian's bad side. This will definitely do the job, embarrassing her in front of everyone who has any idea what is happening, the humans notwithstanding. She will have someone's head for that."

Maratai only shrugged. "I'm not worried. Her wrath can't touch me. And it is fun to take the wind out of that one's sails occasionally."

"Well, her wrath can certainly reach me," Rentec groused. "I hope you know what you're doing."

The group arrived at the door, and Captain kep Parrasine opened the hatch leading to the shuttle bay, the act coinciding with the arrival of the small party escorting Maggie Spencer to the shuttle. She carried only a small handbag slung crosswise from her left shoulder to right hip.

There was no more time for talking as the two groups combined and a few moved off out of the bay while the rest moved aboard the shuttle that was taking up most of the bay. Simon contrived to sit next to the ostensible main reason for this voyage. "Maggie Spencer, right?" he asked.

"That's right," she answered cautiously. After a short time, she said, "Derek and I talked about this moment. Am I in trouble, or what?"

Simon could just stare at her for a few seconds, and then he broke out laughing. When he got his mirth under control, he said, "Trouble? Not at all. As a matter of fact, your name and Derek's are probably almost as well-known as mine. Derek has been back for quite some time now, and if his story halfway matches yours, I'll personally see to it that you both receive the Solar Cross and get posted to our Alliance-Shiravan protocol team, assuming you wish to stay with us," Simon added hastily. "If you do, you get unlimited leave to recuperate from your ordeal and reunite with your family. Just press the red button when you're ready," he finished with a grin. "One way or another, we'll pick you up."

The shuttle carrying the party transferring to the *Galileo* filled up quickly. As there were twenty seats, all tailored for a Shiravan frame of course, Simon was surprised to see the shuttle full. He counted his own group—himself, Rentec, Maratai, sel Garian, and the *Shumara Vacht's* captain. Along with Maggie Spencer, that made six. The rest, he was sure, would fan out through the ship, examining everything they could.

Simon waited until the shuttle docked inside the *Galileo* before springing his last card on sel Garian. "You will understand that I can't yet let your people into what we've come to think of as our computer. Personally, I hate the idea that anything but pure fear motivates that requirement, but so it must be for the time being."

"I fear the same," Maratai translated for sel Garian. "But what you've done with our technology far surpasses what the Korvils ever did. You have actually improved upon many of the designs in our basic systems. We had very little wreckage of the two parda kellin we picked up, but even that small amount showed us that you are far more inventive than the Korvils and, therefore, far more to be feared. They at least just copy old technology. You look at something and ask, 'How can we make this more useful?' Or perhaps, 'How can we make this more powerful?'"

The shuttle was pulled through the forcefield and deposited on the deck with one door facing a group of humans. The pilot, without waiting for orders, pressed a button on her panel and opened the hatch, letting it become the ramp that was standard among Shiravan shuttles.

Shiravan protocol demanded that the closest to equals should meet first, so Kitty, resplendent in her white formal dress and marked even more by her solid white hair, stood at the bottom of the ramp slightly ahead of her top officers. During several short comm calls between the two ships, Maratai had wound up as designated interpreter for Kitty, so she hurried off the vessel and stood beside Kitty while the rest of the passengers disembarked at a more sedate pace.

Rentec, performing the same duties for sel Garian, took a deep breath and announced, "Manura sel Garian, Policy Minister for the Shiravan Polity and Second Voice in Council, requests permission to board your vessel, Madam Herald."

Kitty smiled up at the old alien. "I guess, technically, you don't need permission to come aboard your own property, Doma sel Garian, but please, be welcome. I am Herald of the Terran Alliance, Katherine Hawke." She stopped and let Maratai translate her welcome, then went on. "Each of my officers is fairly fluent in Shiravan and are at your peoples' disposal for their inspection of the ship. Now, if you will come with me, I can provide better accommodations than a docking bay."

Protocol holding him back, Simon rode up to the command deck in the second elevator, acutely aware that his wife was alone with three aliens in their own ship, and he had no control over the situation. Relegated to the purely military, he rode up with the Shiravan fleet commander and one interpreter while the rest of the Shiravan delegation fanned out through the *Galileo* with their escorts.

Unbeknownst to Kitty, a storm was brewing amongst the three aliens in her lift as stares and glares passed literally over her head. She thought the overly pungent odor might be because there were three Shiravans together, but she remembered many times in the past two years that that had been the case, and not once that she could remember had she ever smelled anything quite like this. Even among larger groups than three, she had never noticed this particular odor—not particularly repellent but one she certainly wouldn't like to spend much time with in such a confined space.

The lift doors opened onto the command deck, and Kitty, as host, waved her charges out of the lift ahead of her. It was then that she noticed that the peculiar odor was emanating from the Policy Minister. She stepped out last, and the door on the second lift opened, disgorging several more people, including, she saw with relief, Simon.

An awkward silence followed until Kitty whispered in Simon's ear. Simon finally noticed the tensions between the newly arrived Policy Minister and Rentec and Maratai. *Change of orders*, Simon thought. *Maybe we should give them time to talk before we start anything serious*. Aloud, he commented lightly, "We could only guess what some of these rooms were originally designed for, but we have set up one of the suites as guest quarters. An escort will be posted outside your suite to bring you to the Captain's Lounge when you've had time to freshen up and catch up before going any further. We will wait there. Ensign," Simon said to a young man at the back of the group, "please wait outside this door and lead our guests to the lounge when they're ready." He turned away, then back to the ensign, "Or to any other part of the ship they wish to visit before joining us. There will most likely be several different Shiravans reporting here from time to time. Render them any assistance they ask for. Do you have any questions?"

"Sir, no, sir," the ensign shot back immediately. He moved to stand beside the door, hands behind his back, feet spread about shoulder-width, relaxed—at ease, the position was called in the U.S. military.

"You will have a small staff of six new recruits sent up immediately to use as gofers should you find it necessary," Simon added to the ensign, "and you will stand four hour shifts as long as our guests are aboard. Second and third shifts will be informed of their new responsibilities before you go off-duty. "You, Ensign Randall," Simon said, reading the nametag on his victim, "will be the officer in charge of guest security while they are aboard, so all of these new people will be looking to you for guidance. At no time is any guest to be considered restricted from any part of the ship except the computer. Access to that area will be on my personal authorization and physical presence only, understood?"

"Sir, yes, sir," the young man answered, saluting crisply.

Simon suppressed a silent sigh and returned the salute. "Everyone chosen for this distinguished duty," he said, acutely aware of the translation murmur going on even as he spoke, "will have at least one criterion in common—they will all be able to speak Shiravan to some extent. They will serve as guides for whichever Shiravan wants to visit whichever part of the *Galileo* they deem necessary, answering all questions fully and truthfully. Do you have any questions?" Simon's voice had changed from the authoritarian tone he was used to wielding to one of almost sympathy.

"Sir, no, sir," the young man answered.

Simon turned to sel Garian. "Will that be to your satisfaction, Policy Minister?" he asked formally, bowing slightly as he did so.

The old spymaster, perhaps caught off guard at the openness these Terrans showed to total strangers, answered, "For the time being, Admiral, until I think of something else." She led the way into the quarters set aside for her and her delegation. As soon as the last Terran left, she ordered, "Full scan of all rooms and surrounding rooms will commence immediately. Captain kep Parrasine will post a schedule that will repeat those scans at irregular times on an ongoing basis."

sel Garian ordered all nonessential personnel to take a rest, deciding that it would be she who dictated the timing and structure of the forthcoming meeting. Several hours passed while she, herself, laid down and let her mind wander before she ordered the first shift awakened and brought in for a war council.

"These are barbarians," she told the officers of the Second Fleet. "Clever barbarians, but barbarians nevertheless. This Terran Herald is but a child when it comes to the use of our technology, and her abilities in the political arena will doubtless be just as inadequate, despite the testimonies of Doma kep Parrasine and Dom do' Verlas."

The old woman paced before the gathering. "And this Kath-e-rin thing as the name of the Terran Herald, for

Spirit's sake. I know something of the older teachings, and while Kath-e-rin is described as small, fair-complexioned, and white-haired, nowhere does it say that she will look anything like a human, Shiravan, or anything else. And while I'm not especially sure that I even believe in the Spirits," she said quietly, "there's no real evidence that they don't exist, either."

She squared her shoulders and said, "Until I have evidence to the contrary, I'll treat this individual as I would any head of state. I'm extremely grateful that this is only the second sentient race we've discovered, and I'm grateful that they are so helpful. Since we have no real protocols to go by when dealing with interstellar sovereigns, we'll just have to improvise."

Rentec said, "It has long been the custom among our people to have the visiting ministers speak first and present gifts. Perhaps we can use that as a starting point and explain that we are a people steeped in tradition and out of our depth."

sel Garian grimaced. "I will never publicly admit that we are 'out of our depth,' but I *will* propose a mutual trade and defense pact. Though they seem civilized, I remain unsure. I have the reports from the technicians studying the two human crafts. Between the two, we can get one intact craft and begin to reproduce it, giving us equal status with the humans."

Maratai stood up, interrupting sel Garian, an almost unheard-of phenomenon. "We have had almost two Earth years to study them, and they us. These are a young and vibrant people, prone to rash decisions and hasty judgment. But they are not to be underestimated. Ever. Remember, these people have, with only a few years' possession of the *Dalgor Kreth*, managed to survive three Korvil attacks, actually beating back two of them." She looked around the room at all of the royalty and near-royalty present and said, "And they have done something in that short a time that we have never been able to do—make the Korvils retreat."

Maratai got an embarrassed look on her face and sat down self-consciously. sel Garian looked at her with something akin to respect and nodded. "You speak truly, young kep Parrasine, but you don't look to the future. How long will it be before we are the subservient race?"

"Subservient?" Rentec laughed aloud. "You will find this people already less than subservient. And that is an understatement. The very most you will get out of a bargaining table will be equality. And if you start off trying to sound superior, you will wind up with even less. These people are a truly multicolored race, totally able to interbreed but different colors due primarily to the climates they live in. They have a long history of fighting for equality, and I would steer clear of anything that even sounds like superiority. They may be new, but look at what they've accomplished," he reminded the old woman, astonished that he really was speaking to her so. And surviving. "Remember," he said, allowing a hint of warning to creep into his voice, "their entire history is one of violence and conquest. At this point in their development, they have finally come to see the wisdom of valuing words above war but are not afraid to be even more aggressive than we are when it comes to defending themselves."

CHAPTER TWELVE

"This sel Garian is going to be a tough nut to crack unless we come up with just the right hammer," Simon said to his assembled captains and Kitty as he paced back and forth in the Captain's Lounge on the *Galileo*.

Kitty looked around the room before speaking, "Since she is Shiravi's second in command, we can't just brush her off. Their Matriarch chose a male to head their delegation out of respect for our traditions, so why is she here? I'll tell you why," Kitty said, answering her own question. "She's here to see with her own eyes just how much progress we've made, and she'll report to their Matriarch, most likely by saying she's been away from her own post for too long."

Simon nodded. "Hopefully, she'll take just one ship back with her, if and when she goes. Eight Shiravan battlecruisers are a whole year's production for us." He added, "With the continuing buildup of Terran forces as ships come off the assembly line and get crewed, we'll have a major advantage in our own tiny little section of space no matter how many ships they really have. And most of them will be on picket duty defending colonies against attack since most of those same colonies haven't reached the point where they can build ships to defend themselves."

Robert Greene, recently arrived in Earth-space in response to a summons from Kitty, added, "And soon, we'll outnumber them so badly that they won't dare oppose us. At least here."

"We will *not* be making enemies of these people," Kitty said forcefully. "They know their own technology far too well for us to become adversaries. Remember, they've been in space for over four hundred years."

"But we've made so many advancements," Gayle, also newly arrived, exclaimed. "Surely they can't hope to oppose us if we should decide it's in our own best interest to make unilateral decisions."

"Suppose they decide that our advancements pose too much of a danger to them?" Simon asked quietly. "I think that if they choose to do so, they can field enough ships to take us out, regardless of the innovations we've made. *If* they're willing to pay the price in people and ships."

"Well, it looks like we're going to find out soon enough," Kitty said, closing the note that had just been delivered to her. "Policy Minister sel Garian requests our attendance in the briefing room immediately. Before we go in there, I just want to point out that the eighteen Shiravan ships you see in our system represent just a small part of their space fleet. And while there are surely many more tied up dealing with the Korvils, I'm certain the Shiravan leader has enough reserves to come stomp on us if she pleases. Remember, sometimes numbers do overcome technological superiority. You have only to look to our own planet to see dozens of examples of just that situation occurring."

"This is still our home territory," Simon declared. "And I, for one, will not heel to the beck and call of the second in command of another star-faring race. Besides, we still have some points to go over ourselves." He turned to the message runner. Writing quickly, he handed a piece of paper to the ensign. "Take this back to the Policy Minister immediately," he said.

"What did you just do?" Kitty asked, her voice approaching belligerence.

"I merely told the Policy Minister that we were still discussing policy from our own point of view," Simon said innocently. "What you don't seem to understand is that all of this is just jostling for superior advantage. I, for one, am not willing to concede that position in our own space as long as we have the firepower to enforce our decisions."

Kitty looked at her husband, thought for a moment, then said, "As long as I am head of this Alliance, those decisions are mine to make, not yours, Admiral." The stress on the last word was not lost on anyone in the room. "I admit that in this case, I agree with you, but do not presuppose that just because we're married you can make certain decisions without clearing them with me first." This was the closest thing to a reprimand she felt capable of giving her husband in front of witnesses, so she moved on from there.

"I need to impress on this sel Garian woman that we can be of assistance in their war against the Korvils. I don't want more of their people to die than have to, or ours either, naturally, but I agree with Simon that this is an issue of who's in control of what, and even though we're the new kids on the block, remember that it's the Shiravans who have come to us for assistance. We know from some of what Rentec and Maratai have let slip, and what we've learned from other Shiravans as our people learn their language, that Korvil space is between us and the Shiravans. Or more precisely, Korvil space touches Shiravan space, and we are *in* space the Korvils claim as their own. The fact that we don't choose to be a part of the Korvil Empire just means that we will have to fight for our right to be here and control our own destiny."

The actual meeting between the two leaders came about forty-five minutes after sel Garian's directive was delivered. Kitty knew from security reports that sel Garian's party consisted of four people, Rentec being one. That left the other two to be her chief, Kitty reasoned, so she decided to bring Simon as head of the Alliance military, Robert Greene, a captain of a Terran ship, and Joanna Barnes, science officer, to meet with Policy Minister sel Garian, along with Maratai as possible interpreter.

Taking time to fully discuss the possibilities inherent in any joint venture between two such different cultures over a not-too-leisurely lunch, Kitty finally wiped her mouth, stood up, and said, "I believe we've kept our visitors waiting long enough. Let's get this dog-and-pony show on the road," she said copying one of Simon's phrases. She pressed her comm link. "What is the status with the Shiravan delegation, Ensign?"

They all heard the tinny voice announce to the waiting room, "As far as I can understand Shiravan, Madam Herald, if somebody doesn't make an appearance soon, somebody else is going to blow a gasket."

Kitty stood up, smiled, flicked at a crumb or two. "Thank you, Ensign." She turned to those present. "Just about to reach a boiling point, I figure. Time to take some of the pressure off." She looked around the room. "Simon, of course you're with me, as is Robert and, I think, Dr. Barnes. We'll also have Maratai with our entourage, which makes one more than our visitors." She turned to leave, then turned back. Unstrapping a pair of miniature laser pistols from her forearms, which had been hidden by the voluminous sleeves of this particular dress, she tossed them on the table. "No weapons will be carried into the conference room."

Simon stood up and unhesitatingly removed the low-slung .45 that had become a permanent part of his uniform. "I'm not sure I agree with this move, but we *are* aboard the *Galileo*, and you're calling the shots here, so I won't argue the point."

Kitty smiled and said, "No such request was made of the Shiravan delegation, Simon. Good faith has to start somewhere." Two more pistols joined the others on the table as the room emptied and the lights, now unnecessary, turned themselves off.

Simon, a little put out at not having any weapon at hand, followed his wife down the *Galileo's* corridor until she reached a door simply marked 'Conference Room.' He watched as Maratai used her own link to announce their arrival to their opposites waiting at the other entrance. Shiravan protocol would prevail in this first official diplomatic meeting between the two races.

The two doors opened simultaneously, and Simon immediately stepped through, seeing the captain of sel Garian's flagship do so from the other door. As the hosting culture, Shiravan protocol specialists had to dig into the far past, before space travel, to find a relevant situation. So it was that Simon introduced the Terran Herald to the Shiravan military commander, Captain kep Parrasine, just before she introduced Parrasine's superior to Kitty, who had entered the room upon hearing her name.

Manura sel Garian, the Butcher of Harusel, entered fourth, feeling like she had lost a battle before she even knew it had occurred. Her opinion changed somewhat at the first sight of her counterpart. Small, even by human standards, this creature who called herself Kath-e-rin stood just inside the other door, as protocol dictated for a superior accepting the presence of an inferior.

Not wishing to initiate an interstellar incident if it could be avoided, sel Garian bowed to the level of equals. She was surprised, therefore, when the tiny human bowed even lower.

"Please, enter and make yourselves comfortable. I had some Shiravan furniture refashioned as soon as I was certain you would arrive." Kitty went about preparing drinks for all, having learned from Rentec and Maratai over a two-year period just what kind of foods Shiravans would be comfortable with and letting the food processors do all the work. Now, using Maratai as her interpreter, Kitty continued, "I have asked Dom do' Verlas and Doma kep Parrasine to program the computer with quite a variety of dishes acceptable to Shiravan tastes, so feel free to order whatever you wish."

sel Garian settled into a chair, motioning to one of her assistants. Whispering tiredly, she sent the assistant off to speak to Maratai. Soon, a quick call to Engineering caused a noticeable lowering of the gravity in the room. Where Rentec and Maratai, among others of the first fleet, had accustomed themselves to the slightly higher gravity humans were used to, this was a first encounter for the entire Second Fleet with extended periods of higher gravity than *they* were used to. Almost immediately, the new arrivals began to show some of the vitality they had originally exhibited upon their arrival.

"Doma sel Garian," Kitty said, letting Rentec speak the rest in Shiravan as she settled into a chair opposite the Policy Minister, "let me apologize for not having the gravity reduced before your arrival. With all that's been going on, it's sometimes hard to remember the details. Even my assistants missed that one."

"A reasonable lapse, Herald," sel Garian said. "Let it be as if it never were." Changing subjects quickly, the old Shiravan asked, "How is Doma Spencer settling in with her family after all this time away?"

"They had long since accepted the death of their daughter, so it was with a great sense of joy that they found out about her survival. You've been personally invited to several homes of relatives of Miss Spencer, and should you choose to accept, know that these are sincere requests. There are quite a few people who wish to express their thanks personally. It's a human characteristic."

"Not unlike our customs, in some respects," the gravelly voice grated out of sel Garian's artificial voice box. "As senior civilian authority here, I suppose it is my duty to speak with those who wish to speak with me. But you and I, Doma Herald, will then have to sit down and explore the unique qualities each of our races would bring to an alliance between us."

Bowing to the dictates of human protocol, Minister sel Garian shuttled down to the human homeworld using a ground-effect vehicle of Shiravan manufacture for the express purpose of keeping the gravity lower long enough for the old woman to hold up under full Earth gravity. Once there, she met with Maggie Spencer's family—almost all of them. Upon hearing that the alien who had saved their beloved Maggie was coming, Spencers and Spencer-kin began arriving in record numbers.

A local park had been taken over for the occasion, and while police kept most unwanted visitors out, their main function was to keep the press away once they got wind of the meeting. Rentec accompanied the Minister to interpret for her, but it was still with some apprehension that she got out of the vehicle at all.

Standing up to her full height of six-foot-two, sel Garian, considered small amongst her own people, clearly could see all the throng awaiting her arrival. The silence that greeted her appearance was momentary. First, those closest started clapping, and then expanding outward, all the rest joined in.

"A human sign of welcome and respect," Rentec said quietly.

sel Garian chuckled quietly. "I've spent my whole life living and working in the shadows, and look at me now. I suppose I'm expected to say something?"

"It would seem, Minister, that they wish to hear you tell how you saved their relative. I'm merely here to translate."

"How I saved…? Is that what they think? We'll see how much of a hero they think I am after they hear what I have to say."

Walking over to a small stage, Rentec took the microphone and stand and set it to the back of the space. A strange smile on her face, Manura began to speak quietly. Rentec, eyes almost closed, hurried to translate as she spoke.

"I did not personally save your daughter. She was saved from our common enemy, the Korvils, who had enslaved her and one other, by forces of ours who managed to catch a manned outpost unawares. My participation in the matter came in when it was pointed out that it might be advantageous to have allies in our fight. The fact that you, too, were already doing so, made it obvious that we should ally ourselves. I authorized the return of your kin for political motives as much as anything else. Their return was our show of goodwill toward the chance to negotiate an alliance between our two peoples."

The next twenty minutes were spent speaking with Maggie and her immediate family a bit aside from the rest. "Thank you, Doma sel Garian," Maggie said. "It meant a lot to my parents and family. You may think that your political motivations disqualify you from this kind of respect, but we feel any reason that brings about a good result is a good reason. Now, I know you shouldn't subject yourselves to our gravity any longer than absolutely necessary, so feel free to leave at any time."

"Trying, most trying," the Policy Minister said to Rentec after her visit. "There was a sense of family, of unity, that I haven't felt in a long time, and I find that I miss it." She climbed into the back of the specially adapted vehicle. "Please set up an appointment with The Herald for later this evening if she's free and return me to the shuttle," she told the human driver, hardly caring if she was understood or not. "For now, I wish to be alone with my thoughts."

The scene was anything but a pleasant one. Kitty and sel Garian were to meet to formalize relations and establish some sort of mutual defense pact. Rentec and Maratai were present as the two best English speakers among the Shiravans, and Simon escorted Kitty as moral support and as her expert on Fleet matters. Rounding out the group, Fleet Captain kep Parrasine was present as the expert on Shiravan military matters.

"Korvil space abuts Shiravan space, and your system is in the far reaches of their territory," sel Garian started out, knowing as she said it that the humans were quite familiar with the location of the various territories claimed by each group. One of Rentec's suggestions had been to be as open as possible about Shiravan matters, including the precise location of the Shiravan homeworld.

Red dots designated known interactions with Korvils. No home planets were noted, except the one Carter and Spencer had been rescued from, and that was only given a tentative confirmation. Blue dots represented Shiravan ships and planets, the Shiravan homeworld being identified at last. The pitifully few green dots representing human ships were added to the spatial terrain, and humanity got its first really good look at what they faced.

The red dots were hazy, for lack of a better term, while the green and blue were crisper. "All data that is not conjecture is distinct—known vessels and planets, both ours and yours. The Korvils," sel Garian said as her head made the side-to-side shrugging motion, "are more difficult to pin down.

"It has long been assumed," sel Garian explained, "that the Korvils got their spatial technology in much the same way humans did." The old woman held her hand up to forestall any interruption. "We know humans took possession peacefully, but we believe the Korvils took their ship by force. Perhaps an exploratory ship that landed on their world was overwhelmed, and the Korvils—at that time they called themselves something else—took possession and began duplicating the technology."

The old Shiravan woman went on, only stopping while Rentec translated for her, "For now, the Matriarch will not contest ownership of the *Dalgor Kreth*," the old woman said, her words surprising all present, "as long as her use is directly related to the destruction of our mutual enemy, the Korvils. These words I am required to speak from the Matriarch and then determine for myself if that is the case."

Almost absent-mindedly, the Policy Minister took a small, wrapped box from one of her aides and continued her pacing. "Your rapid and highly effective use of our technology, along with the obvious upgrades I've already seen, could induce me toward either of two choices—to isolate you and hope the Korvils finish you off before you can become a threat to us, or ask that you join us in defeating them as a mutual foe." She stopped in front of Kitty and Maratai, making a small motion for Kitty to rise.

Kitty rose at Maratai's gesture, wishing she weren't beating the path in interstellar relations. She gazed up into the old woman's eyes, somehow redder than she had ever noticed on another Shiravan, and wondered what was to come.

"I have arrived at my judgment." Rentec's translation made the statement sound as if it were part of a ceremony of some sort.

Kitty looked quickly at Simon, who, poker-faced, gave her no help at all, and then back at the second in command of an entire spacefaring race. Feeling that some response was required, Kitty asked, "What decision have you reached, Policy Minister?" She already knew, really, from some of the previous conversation what the outcome was going to be, but she assumed this was an occasion where some form of protocol must be observed.

The older woman stepped forward, holding out the wrapped box as if it were some sort of treasure. "It is the wish of the Matriarch, Linnas des Harras, leader of the Shiravan Polity and fourteen subordinate colonies, that you," Kitty clearly heard a catch in the voice, as well as an odd intonation, artificial though it was, "Katherine Hawke, leader of the Terran Alliance, would consider entering into an alliance that will forever defeat our common foe. As a token of her desire and respect, the Matriarch has gifted you with a double set of kemwood cups. You, of course, will not be familiar with the properties of kemwood, but suffice it to say that any liquid poured into a kemwood cup can be drunk without any harmful side effects." She handed the box to Kitty, who looked around, shrugged and opened the wrapper. Inside was an ornately carved box with no apparent lock and two hinges on the back side. Kitty opened the lid slowly, wondering what she might see. Inside were four small cups, each identical one to the other, that almost seemed to glow with an inner light.

One more surprise waited for Kitty. Taking another small box from the same aide, sel Garian handed it to Kitty. "The cups are a gift from the Shiravan people. This is a gift from the Matriarch herself. Her family privately owns the only land on the entire planet where this particular type of stone can be found. It is extremely responsive to body heat and will glow if held or placed on a pendant around your neck. As one leader to another, the Matriarch personally went into the mountains and selected the stone you hold in your hand. Normally, a stone like this would be circled by the house sigil belonging to the dominant house of the woman giving it as a betrothal gift. And while there will certainly be no marriages between our two races, the Matriarch had the crests of all the major families on Shiravi who agree to this alliance etched in miniature, hoping that you'd join in our mission to exterminate these Korvils. You will come to note," she said acidly, "that House sel Garian has declined to allow their crest to be added. Whether you know it or not, this is one of the gravest insults one clan can give to another. Wars have been fought over much less." She quickly added, "That has not happened for almost a thousand years, though, since females took control.

"These gifts in no way diminish the assistance you have rendered our First Contact Fleet—building two entirely new ships to replace the ones lost defending your homeworld, resupplying ships in need of organics or new power cores, and even providing space on your newest endeavor, your Vesta Project. You've let our people have some room to stretch, so to speak, even extending these gifts to the Second Fleet, though they have done nothing to earn such largess."

The old woman stopped her pacing and looked directly at Kitty. "It has been brought to my attention that your world has lost almost twenty million individuals due to attacks by the Korvils. Of course, our Matriarch does not yet know of those losses, but I'm sure that when she learns, she'll mourn as strongly as you." After a short pause in which the old woman seemed to get lost in her thoughts for a moment, she added, "I mourn, as well, the loss of so many innocents. It has happened often enough in our own territories."

Kitty sensed that it was time to refocus the attention of this woman onto the present. She looked down at the pendant, beginning to glow in her cupped hand. "How lovely!" Kitty exclaimed. "It looks like the same kind of stone on the pendant Simon found."

"Pendant?" sel Garian said, turning on Rentec and Maratai. "Is this the same pendant you showed me upon my arrival? Does she understand the significance of what it represents?" Her voice, harsh and grating, was almost unintelligible to the translator whispering into the earbud—the Alliance's most recent innovation—that was covered by Kitty's hair. This old woman wasn't the only one who could play at spying. Kitty had had the room wired and was, up until that point, getting simultaneous translations in each ear—one from Rentec and one from a quiet human voice in her other ear. So far, both had seemed to dovetail almost perfectly. Rentec nodded, shamefaced, to the older woman.

Now, a microphone handily near the alien trio let her eavesdrop on the altercation going on in fast-paced Shiravan. The gist of the conversation was all she wanted anyway. She interrupted in stilted, childlike Shiravan. "I will speak now," she announced, standing up at the head of the table. sel Garian had tried to turn the far end of the table into the focal point of the meeting, but Kitty kept drawing attention back to herself and the Alliance that backed her.

"For two of our years now, Rentec and Maratai, along with all the hundreds of members of what we call the First Shiravan Contact Fleet, have been busily trading knowledge with us while we quietly spied on each other. Maybe 'spying' is too strong a word. Coming to conclusions drawn from what was said or not said in any given situation might be a better way of putting it since we, the Alliance, are working mostly from conjecture. We've heard references over those two years that have led us to the conclusion that your planet is not quite as unified as you would have us believe." Now Kitty took her turn pacing near her end of the table. Energy fairly crackled in the room, all participants lending to the charging of the atmosphere. "You know that we represent a very infinitesimal number of individuals compared to the planet we come from. You also know that we are still restricted to that one planet, and you know that we have more different governments down below than you—coming as you do from a people with a single, unified governing body—can begin to contemplate."

She turned in her pacing, letting her gaze slide across the Shiravan end of the table. "We have deduced from dozens of comments, mostly from early on, that your unified government isn't as stable as you would have us believe. Why, I don't know, and I don't care. I only care about getting these Korvils off our backs so we can relax and explore the potentialities of our new technology. We've been led to believe that the Korvils' territory lies between your space and ours, and that our space is actually *inside* a loose area these Korvils have claimed as their own. Well, we won't just roll over and play dead for them." She practically leaned on the table, slamming her open hand on it with enough force to cause a loud cracking sound, making everyone present jump. "One thing Earthmen are good at is war, Policy Minister. I fear that our beginnings are closer to the Korvils' than they are to your race, and we've never managed to agree on anything long enough for us to become a one-world government. It always seemed that someone would come along with enough power to disrupt any peace talks, and fighting would break out somewhere on Earth. I'm not even sure when the last time was that there *wasn't* some kind of armed conflict going on."

She sat back down in her chair, far enough away from the Shiravans that she didn't have to look up much, and said, "Our experience tells us that it's about time for a response to our last clash with the Korvils. Since, as far as we know, no ships escaped to tell about the battle, the next attack will be a feint, possibly with more punch in it than last time, but enough to cause us some severe losses, since they don't seem to—at least until this last fight—back off as long as they have an operational ship. It's almost as if they have Spartan orders. Mothers of Spartans would tell their sons, 'Come back with your shield, or on it.' They meant don't retreat, don't give up, and don't give anything less than your best.

"If you want an alliance with us, I will gladly accept. We are familiar with the concept of a two-front war. The main problem is going to be getting any information on where their planets are. It almost seems, from what we've overheard, that they move around, much like the gypsies of our past, the difference being that they only leave ruin in their wake." Kitty hesitated for a moment. "As far as tactics and such are concerned, those things I leave in the hands of my husband, Admiral Hawke, and his competent staff. I do know that we have a technological edge on these Korvils." The implication that that same advantage was held over the Shiravans as well appeared to go unnoticed. "How long that will last is anybody's guess, but if we are going to start attacking on our own accord, we need to get more ships built and crewed as fast as possible, and we'll probably require the assistance of some of your fleet, as much as you can spare, to start to heat things up on this side of Korvil space. Of course, we need hard data to go on. We can't be sending ships out to just anywhere. With the innovations we've added to the newer ships, I think we have a chance to stand up one to one with anything of equal mass that we might come up against."

This drew a murmur from the assembled Shiravans as soon as they heard the translation. Kitty's earbud told her, "That last statement has some of them jazzed, and others worried that you will become the next Korvils."

sel Garian looked at Kitty after the translation and said, "There is an old saying among my people: 'The enemy of my enemy is surely my friend.' I only hope this will be so after the Korvils are defeated."

Kitty, astounded that these people would consider humanity a threat after so short a time, thought furiously for several seconds. Most of what came to mind were old history lessons she'd studied in school. Romans, Greeks, Egyptians, Turks, and Asians came to mind from her lessons, but she had lived to see her own United States embroil itself in some of the messiest—in all of that word's connotations—fighting in all of recorded history.

She shook her head, clearing it of all those images, and cleared her throat before answering. "I'm going to see to it that you get to see recordings of some of our wars. From one called the Viet Nam Conflict all the way up until today, we've had the ability to record visually and let the people see instantly what was happening. We have footage from our greatest war, one that happened over fifty years ago called World War II, and it eventually involved almost every nation on the planet. These will by no means be shown to you as a threat but only to show you what humanity is capable of in its youth, inexperience, and anger. But look at what we've accomplished as well. Not all of us are out to destroy. There are a large number of people down below just itching to get into space, no matter what the cost, so we have no lack of recruits when we need to put a crew into space."

She seemed to wilt inside her clothes as she continued. "See? We've even carried that natural inclination into space. When our first station was attacked, we used your plans to build bigger and better fighters and started upgrading the weapons and defensive systems we inherited from you. That's one place where humans excel—taking something and making it better, stronger, faster, more deadly. Both you and the Korvils seem to think that if something works, just use it as it is.

"Humans are always trying to improve on the abilities of things. It doesn't matter if it's a booklight or a space torpedo, somebody is going to say, 'I can make it do this. I can make it better.' This is where I see the difference between our two races coming into conflict. You seek to preserve the status quo far more than we do, thinking that if something works it's good enough. We, on the other hand, seek to improve almost everything we come in contact with. The status quo is never good enough for us. We humans always try to push the envelope, the idea being that maintaining the status quo is just stagnation."

Kitty looked at the Shiravan Second Voice bluntly. "We, as human beings, have never found a problem to which we couldn't find a solution; otherwise, we wouldn't be sitting here today. On our world, we've arrived at the top of the food chain. Some creatures we needed to kill to eat and some just to keep them from killing us. We didn't have the armor, claws, speed, size, or whatever to take these creatures on one on one. So, we learned early on to work as groups. But we do have an inventive, curious nature. And let's not forget a nasty streak a mile wide when we're crossed. And, personally, I have a score to settle with these Korvils. The Terran Alliance stands ready to manufacture as many ships as we can and then begin using them offensively as soon as we get some hard data on where to best aim our efforts. Just going from one world to another…" she faltered, looking for the right words, "would be like looking for a needle in a haystack." This last allusion had to be explained. Her wry smile was noted by both species present, and a small round of laughter ensued, the Shiravan version sounding like a high-speed hiccup fit.

She'd taken something Simon had taught her long ago and bluntly used it, hopefully to her advantage. Her opponent had been in the negotiating business far longer than Kitty had been alive, so it was possible that it would be seen for what it was, but one made the best of what one had at hand. He'd told her once that if you stared directly at the spot between your opponent's eyes, it would look like you were giving him your undivided attention, and in many instances would throw the other person off just enough to gain some small advantage.

"Of course, we haven't been in space for very many years yet, so that could change. Thanks to our fortuitous acquisition of the *Galileo*, we're now able to step outside our own solar system at will, although we haven't yet done so other than for training flights, and even then, we haven't gone more than one or two lightyears from our own planet.

"I still see a number of ways the universe could hand us our heads on a platter, but at no time while I control the Terran Alliance will it ever become something *you* have to fear. Of course, to be honest, we have no way of knowing how long we'll live or who our successors might be, so you shouldn't think that we'll be a static equation at any time."

CHAPTER THIRTEEN

Manura sel Garian sat quietly, absorbing what the human leader had just told her. True, most of it had already been said by both Ambassador do' Verlas and Doma kep Parrasine, yet still she was troubled by the volatility of a race such as this, and one who's female leader readily admitted their bloodthirst, if somewhat apologetically. They were less predictable than the Korvils, of that she was certain, but a true threat to the Shiravan race? That was the question she had to wrestle with, along with the fact that since this race was still divided, only the spacefaring portion would truly be able to assist Shiravi in its time of need.

The old woman looked into the white-haired human's eyes. They were a light blue, she noticed, adding to the alienness of this creature she was negotiating with. She came to a decision. "Before females took control on our world, males ruled, making war indiscriminately, and except for one opportune incident, our history could have been as volatile as yours. The last such war almost totally decimated our male population, allowing females to take control completely and without question. It has only been recently, in the last hundred turns or so, that males have been allowed back into the power structure of Shiravan society. Our natural inclination in recent history is one of distrust for anything male-dominated. Your culture, apparently heavily favoring females even though some males rule small portions of your population, leads me to the conclusion that yours is a culture to be trusted. For we, ourselves, have just recently reinstituted the presence of males in positions of authority."

sel Garian leaned back in the chair/couch that had been provided for the Shiravan guests. The humans sat more upright and on couches that were lower to the ground than Shiravans would find comfortable. She'd tried furiously to figure out what it was about these humans that caused her to accept their leader at her word. Was it because their small stature, particularly that of their Herald, made them seem childlike and therefore to be protected? And believed? She shook her head slightly. "The offer you have just made is one that I, as Second Voice, have been advised to accept. I can and do agree to the joint operations of Shiravan/human forces in this sector of space. And I further decree that those forces be commanded by a human. It is, after all, your system. We will provide any logistical and tactical support as we are able, considering the distances between us. I authorize the entire First and Second Contact Fleets to remain in human space under the command of the supreme human commander. This ship, the *Shumara Vacht*, will carry the Herald to Shiravi to meet in person with the Matriarch and formalize relations between our two cultures."

A portion of Kitty's brain shut down momentarily while the full implication of what she'd just heard finally became clear. Ever since she'd first sat in the shuttle's pilot chair, she'd dreamed of setting foot on an alien world. All humans did. But the time had just never seemed to present itself. "You want me to go to Shiravi to formalize relations with your people? Actually *go* to another world?" Without discussing it with her cabinet, she immediately agreed to the deal offered her.

Predictably, Simon immediately objected. "You can't just go off to who-knows-where without a full meeting of the cabinet, Ki... Madam Herald. This isn't a time when it would be advisable for the head of the Alliance to be out of public view for an undetermined amount of time. We need to show a united front during the repercussions that we're bound to experience because of what's already happened. There's no reason to believe that even this many more Shiravan ships will make a difference against an aggressor willing to spend the lives of his subjects just to get information."

"If what you say is true, Admiral," Kitty said, her heart ached at the formality she had to assume in this situation, "then my presence would neither make nor break us. Besides, I have a person in mind to replace me for the length of time I'll be gone." She turned to the Policy Minister. "And just how long are we talking, round trip? While I agree with my senior military commander in spirit, I do believe that I should accompany you to Shiravi. I'll detail a complement of two battlecruisers and one carrier to accompany us. It should give your peoples' spirits a lift if we show them just a small part of what we have already wrought."

Familiar with the standardized construction of most vessels, she pressed several oddly scripted panels and buttons, calling up a view of the near galactic neighborhood. "Here is your sun," she said, making one star shine more brightly. "Here is ours." Another light, more yellowish in color than the first, grew brighter. "Between the two homeworlds lies Korvil space."

"This is the area where we're sure the Korvils are," sel Garian said. An area around the space between the two, designated orange, began to glow with a more reddish cast. "This second color represents the areas where the Korvils and Shiravans are in active contention." The redder area seemed to be a bit smaller than the orange, but not by much, and the orange actually overlapped the star the old woman had said was humanity's star.

sel Garian seemed even older, if that was possible. Kitty felt, as she listened to her translator and the timbre of the Policy Minister's voice, that the woman felt as if she had no choice in her decision. "Let me make myself perfectly clear, Policy Minister sel Garian, that the defense and preservation of the human race is my first priority. Even so, we'll still assist you in whatever way we're able to finish this war with the Korvil. We can see that our race is on the cusp of needing new territory to inhabit. We'll expand into Korvil space, taking what we win and making it ours. There are enough factions on that mudball below us," her derision showed itself, finally, "that we can dole out habitable planets to just about anyone who feel that theirs is the only right path.

"Expansion is our only option, as I'm sure it was for your ancestors hundreds of years ago. That's why you have fourteen colonies now, correct?" Kitty continued before anyone else could get a word in. "We've been in space, or studying it, long enough to know where we are in relation to the rest of the galaxy. And we—the Terran Alliance—have figured out for ourselves that just about the only places to expand are inward, toward the galactic center, rather than outward. The inner stars are older, more settled, one might say, and hopefully more civilized. To me, that means probably more advanced, if life evolved on them at all. We still have people on our own world who believe that both you and the Korvils are works of fiction, mere flights of fancy. Twenty million or more dead and a hole in the South American ecosystem that will take centuries for nature to repair, and still they refuse to believe." She shook her head sadly. "And that doesn't even begin to cover the costs of repairing the infrastructure destroyed by that last attack."

Kitty turned to the Policy Minister. "If you're here to judge us, then do so on what we've done to repair the damage done to our own planet and peoples and the help we've unstintingly given to your people and ships. If you haven't noticed, the two ships we gifted to First Fleet were reconstructed on Shiravan body heights and also incorporated numerous changes that you'll find most effective—all things we wouldn't do for anyone but friends. If you're here to help us defend ourselves from the Korvils, then point us at a target and watch us work." Three million years of sapient aggressor looked out of her eyes as she stared at the old woman sitting at the far end of the table. "We have an old saying ourselves: You're either for us or against us.

"I'd like to believe from our short association with your First Contact Fleet that you'd welcome us with, if not open arms, then at least without your guns drawn." It took a few moments of whispered consultation to get the idea across from English to Shiravan.

Manura sel Garian sat, stunned. It was as if she'd been personally accused of not trusting these humans. Granted that the Korvils were the only other race Shiravans had to use for a reference, and the reception the two fleets had received in human space should have defused any possible worries on the matter of where human loyalties lay. But still, she had no answer to the accusation that she didn't trust humans. Even when she had the head of the Terran Alliance in her grasp, she didn't trust.

Of course, that might be because Kitty had outmaneuvered the old woman and announced the existence of a human fleet to accompany the Alliance leader before such measures could be brought up by the Shiravans and dismissed as unnecessary. Manura wasn't used to being outsmarted, outguessed.

Used to statecraft, and seeing herself sinking beneath its waves, she acquiesced in a manner that saved face if not status. "In the name of the Matriarch, I accept your offer of alliance and give you my personal oath that your life is to be held as more sacred than my own while we are responsible for your safety. Should anything happen to you while you are away, it is my life that will be forfeit. I so swear upon my oath of fealty to our Matriarch. I will also dispatch a courier ship that will announce your arrival about two weeks before we actually arrive in orbit."

Also notifying Shiravan military authorities that the alien ships that will be arriving with them are not to be fired upon, I hope, Kitty thought. *Maybe these guys aren't so advanced as we thought.*

"I'll need about a week to hand over command to my successor," she said aloud. "And she isn't going to like it." At the Policy Minister's strange look, she explained with a wave of her hand, "I have a certain group of people whose sole job is to protect me, no matter what. I find it unfortunate that the rules that allow me to occupy this position also require that I have this level of protection. I've learned to act like they aren't even there most of the time, and they have specific orders to never speak of or reveal in any other manner what they see or hear while in my presence.

"If I make a quick jaunt across town, six armed guards accompany me. I never step out first and must wait while someone else decides whether it's safe for me to leave the vehicle. A contingent of these will accompany me, I'm sure. Even though I'm the leader, we have a council, and a few of whose members will be accompanying us as well. They can veto my decisions if they feel I've overstepped my authority, which is clearly spelled out in our version of another document called the Constitution. So, you see, in the final analysis, I'm really *not* the head of our Alliance except in times of emergency when one voice is what is needed, and even then I have to defend my actions later on."

Kitty smiled broadly at sel Garian and her Fleet Captain, kep Parrasine, while wondering if she was closely related to Maratai. She hadn't said one way or another.

A voice in her earbud said, "Rentec correctly translated your words, Madam Herald, but he added that he felt there was a measure of sarcasm in your voice and that you somehow felt no threat going to Shiravi."

Kitty's fingers had been flying over a keyboard in front of her. After determining the distance and travel times, and allowing ten percent for unexpected occurrences, she arrived at a figure and whistled. "This is somewhere near eleven Earth months, one way."

"That's almost two years away from Earth, not counting negotiating time," Simon stated. "I'm not sure that your disappearance for that length of time will do much to bolster the courage of those on Earth who feel less threatened because the Herald is here to keep the peace."

"Admiral, you seem to forget that it's my decision to go or stay." Kitty's flat, cold voice cut through the beginning of Simon's tirade. "Your job is to protect this system from further depredations by the Korvils while continuing to build and train our fleets. I will speak for myself."

She turned back to the Policy Minister and said, "I agree. This is too important to leave to anyone less than the two leaders themselves. It's unfortunate with so much turmoil between those of us who are in space and those still living down below. They are my responsibility as well, even though they don't know it or acknowledge it."

She paced briefly and turned back to her guests. "I have in mind a person who should fill the position admirably. Doma sel Garian," she said, turning to the Policy Minister, "tonight I will spend with my husband as I so rarely get to do. Tomorrow, I'll take a ship out to Vesta to personally ask Lucy Grimes to fill in for me here now that she's back on active duty."

CHAPTER FOURTEEN

Kitty stepped out of her shuttle to the bombardment of some vaguely familiar martial music. She stared at the group of people before her, her mind's eye picturing the bunch behind her, and had trouble keeping a straight face. She decided to let the leader of this group have the honor of speaking first. For some reason, she felt she shouldn't have to ask permission to come aboard one of her own bases. And Vesta was just another base as far as she was concerned. She let her eyes roam over the half dozen people mustered for her unexpected arrival. Without saying a word, she out-waited the music.

After several awkward seconds of silence, the senior officer—a full commander—stepped forward. "Welcome to Vesta, Madam Herald. How can we help you today?" She noted the green strip around his collar and knew instantly that he wasn't a line officer, green having been designated for Supply. This was all they could scrape up on such short notice?

Well, to be honest, she hadn't let them know she was in the area until just before penetrating the defense perimeter, so she wasn't going to be picky about protocol. Besides, she hadn't moved her flag here yet, and there was no reason to have very many officers of line rank. "Thank you, Commander," she answered. "I'm here specifically to see the Project Director. Would you be so kind as to inform her? And I'd like to wait somewhere more comfortable than a landing bay." She realized as soon as the words left her mouth how she sounded, so she did her best to mend the fence before it could be completely knocked over. "I'm sorry, Commander. I've had a very rough day, and I shouldn't take it out on you. Please, forgive me." She placed her hand on his arm and looked up, farther even than with Simon—who topped out at six foot.

With her tiny frame, Kitty had often been called an elf, a situation that on more than one occasion had led to bloody noses when she was younger. Now, though, with her white hair, she knew she looked even more elvish (if that was a word) and more childlike, which encouraged cooperation. It was a situation she had learned to take advantage of shamelessly over the past two years or so, and it stood her in good stead now. The pained expression on the commander's face disappeared, replaced by one of relief. "Let me escort you to the director's personal quarters, Madam Herald. I've already notified her of your arrival, but she's off-base at the moment, racking up some flight time."

"Oh, is she now?" Kitty responded sweetly, following his lead toward the elevators. "Then she must be running ahead of schedule, or she wouldn't take time out to keep her license valid. How goes the installation of the park?" she asked, quickly changing the subject.

The commander, whose name was LeCroix, answered, "We still need several more water asteroids to fill out the lake, but the bushes and trees are doing quite well with the subsurface irrigation system and the artificial sunlight. It will take several asteroids to completely fill all the reservoirs aboard the base. Of course, we're getting regular shipments of soil, and the planting of air-ferns and hydroponics is ahead of schedule as well. We're still a little behind on the factory section, not being real certain how compact or how spread out we should make the factories."

"Keeping them close together will minimize movement of material from one place to another," she noted absently.

"True, in essence," the commander said as he led Kitty down a long hallway. Her entourage consisted of six guards and the current captain of the *Rigel*, Thomas Breen. "But the director has the idea that if we move them a bit apart and put park-like areas in between, it would lessen the overall view of the area as a factory complex. Even the buildings will have different shapes, blending into an aesthetic whole. All will be connected by underground corridors to bring in raw material and taking out finished product."

The commander stopped in front of a door. Palming it open and stepping to one side, he said, "The director's quarters won't hold all of you. Guest quarters are here. The main room is the common area, and six private bedrooms open onto it. Four of you can accompany me."

Kitty said, "I really don't need anyone, but Thomas can come along if he wishes. Of course, two of my shadows will accompany us to fill out the quota."

"Three," one of the guards said. "One of us will be stationed outside the director's quarters."

Kitty sighed. "One of these days, I'm going to be done with this job for good, and someone else can deal with the headaches." She followed the commander further down the hallway, where he palmed open another door. He ushered the group in and followed, closing the door behind him. "This is the director's outer office. Considering the small size of her personal office, I suggest you wait in the guest lounge." He motioned the startled secretary back down into her chair and opened a door at the side of the room. "My datalink says the director will be landing in about twenty minutes. She will surely want a quick shower before she meets with you, so make yourselves comfortable. Guest bar is behind this wall." He pressed a button and a section of wall slid aside, revealing a full bar and refrigerator. The refrigerator held several varieties of beer and nonalcoholic canned drinks. The commander edged toward the door. "If either I or Miss Bartholomew can be of any assistance, please let us know immediately."

Kitty stopped him with a lifted hand. "A datalink," she said, recognizing the term from one of the Research and Development reports she'd read late one night. The details of what it exactly was slipped her mind in the moment. "Refresh me."

The commander reached up to his left ear. "This is a datalink," he said, taking the device off. A simple hook held an earpiece that looked like some kind of molded gel-like substance and a small boom microphone. "All of the UMC, ultra-micro circuitry, is actually inside the frame that goes over the ear and into the stem of the boom mike." The whole thing, when fitted in place, looked almost inconspicuous. The mike molded to his jawline and was almost hidden in his sideburns.

"It's both a transmitter and receiver of information to the central computer, allowing me instant access to whatever I need using these." He reached into a pouch at his waist and pulled out a pair of glasses. "VR, virtual reality, glasses. In combination with the datalink, this gives me deeper access to more information than anyone who hasn't used one will believe. Besides simple computer access, with the right access codes all of Vesta is laid out like an onion, if you so choose. Deep access requires specific codes, but almost everyone has access to communication Earth-side, even when Earth is in opposition. All traffic is routinely recorded and run through a special filter, looking for coded messages, both inbound and outbound."

He put the glasses away, making sure the flap was sealed. "Latest thing out of R&D," he bragged. "Completely eliminates the need for a keyboard or any other kind of hardwired access. A captain could be anywhere on her ship and be in as much control as if she were on the bridge."

"Full core access?" Thomas Breen asked, incredulous at the thought of the sheer volume of sensitive data available to just anyone.

"Oh, no. Not necessarily," the commander answered. "The codes can be set at various levels just like the wristbands, allowing the user access to certain portions of the computer only. These will be available to everyone in the near future, letting them interface with their systems more intimately and therefore more quickly. They'll even replace the wristbands eventually, we believe. Some people envision implants just behind the ear within the next few years, if we get lucky."

The conversation petered out, and finally, the increasingly uncomfortable commander said, "Flight Control reports her Mamba on approach right now. If you will excuse me, I should be there to meet her." Not waiting for anyone to say otherwise, the man, who'd been conveniently standing near the door, was through it and gone.

"That's one man who has a problem with authority figures," Thomas said casually. "I wonder what his job performance ratings say about him."

"Probably that he's reasonably good at his job but has problems with authority figures," Kitty responded. "Let it go."

"You're probably right," Thomas agreed. "Here, being a commander is more like middle-management, and those types are always nervous around their bosses. Besides, Lucy will be here shortly."

Lucy headed her Mamba back toward Vesta, suspicion weighing heavily on her mind. She kept abreast of what was going on, and she knew the second Shiravan fleet had finally arrived, especially since tall red beings were beginning to make occasional appearances around the hollow asteroid. They'd brought Maggie Spencer home, sure, but according to Rentec, whom she'd met on several occasions, they also brought the Shiravan second-in-command to survey the situation and make an onsite assessment of humanity's ability to help in their war against the Korvils. That assessment would surely include eighteen new ships in two years, two of which were built especially for the Shiravans to compensate for their losses.

After a quick shower and change, Lucy hugged Kitty and shook Thomas's hand. "Glad to meet you, Captain. Now, if you will excuse me for being rude, Kitty wants something, or she wouldn't be here." She turned to her friend and boss and said, "Spill it." She listened impassively as Kitty outlined her plans to travel to Shiravi to meet with their Matriarch. After Kitty finally ran down, Lucy asked, "And how is this going to affect me?"

Kitty grimaced. "You always do go right to the heart of the matter. That's what makes you so good at everything you turn your hand to."

"Nowadays, I get awfully suspicious when I start

getting praise heaped on me out of the blue," Lucy retorted.

"Just can't take a compliment between friends?" Kitty asked playfully. Turning grim almost as quickly. "I know how hard it was for you in the early days, but now we have a Council of Captains to shoulder a large part of the burden, and a better chain of command, as well as more people. I need someone who can ride herd on this bunch while I'm gone."

"But two years, Kitty. I'm not sure I can expose myself to that much sheer humanity if I have to climb back into the spotlight."

"Don't worry about it," Kitty responded instantly. "Keep your offices here. Anyone needing to see you badly enough can book a spot on one of the weekly shuttles."

After listening for a few more minutes, Lucy stood up, opened the door she had entered by, and said, "Private conference." She looked at the guards. "I hope you'll excuse us for a few minutes." She turned to Kitty. "Madam Herald, if you please?" When one of the black-clad security detail tried to pass, Lucy put a hand on his chest and said, "Private conversation means private conversation. I don't care what your instructions are." Such was her manner that she was able to get the door shut and locked before the guard could react.

"Now, that's exactly why I need you for this job. *I* can't even get those guys to do that," Kitty quipped before Lucy could explode.

Lucy ignored the attempt at humor with a vague wave of her hand. "You expect me to just take the reins back while you go play interstellar negotiator? Just how much of me do you want, Kitty?" Anger, surrounding a bit of hysteria, could be heard in her voice.

"Lucy, please, settle down," Kitty said in a calm, quiet voice. She pulled her friend over to a couch and gently pushed her down onto it, taking a place not too far away but safely outside Lucy's immediate reprisal zone. "It just seemed like the right choice. You've had the job before, and now it really *is* easier. No more micromanagement like we had in the beginning. You'll have a full staff to handle all but the worst problems, of course. Only the biggest stink gets to the top of the heap. That's where you and your previous experience come in. Hand down a decision from on high and remain behind your cloud of anonymity from millions of miles away. I'm just not willing to leave Earth without a seasoned veteran to run the administrative side with everything in such flux and us not knowing if there'll be another attack."

Kitty spent several more hours with Lucy. Finally, she took a break and went to Vesta's comm center to send a message to Simon. "Mission accomplished. Spending the night. See you tomorrow. Love, Me." She spent the rest of the night watching Lucy getting pleasantly lit, talking about the old days as if they were fifty years gone.

The next day, after a long and tearful goodbye, Kitty hopped the *Rigel* back to Earth. Within hours, she was repeating her conversation with Lucy to Simon, who was still showing great opposition to Kitty's proposed trip.

The translation sel Garian got repeated Kitty's words almost exactly, but Rentec said hurriedly, "This is not about you, personally, Policy Minister. We've spent countless hours with these two humans, and we believe this tone of voice she's using is just a ploy to get a personal point across to her husband in a formal setting."

"Admiral," sel Garian said, quietly, "your Herald... your mate... will be accorded the same degree of protection and reverence we would afford our own Matriarch. All who accompany her will have that same guarantee. Once we leave here and translate into contra-space, nothing can touch us. If you've had time to experiment with the warp drives, you'll have determined that once a ship enters contra-space, no other vessel can contact or influence it in any way until it emerges. And I promise you we will not emerge until we are safely within Shiravan territory."

"Admiral... Simon," Kitty didn't know which way to speak to him, especially in front of crew and aliens alike. "You can't take all the chances. This is a matter of statecraft, and it's a job I have to do because you, among others, put me here. Now you reap the rewards of what you've sown." Sorrow tinged her words. "It doesn't make me all that happy either, but look at the adventure. I'll be only the third human to set foot on an alien world. If it'll make you any happier, I plan to invite Baron von Schlenker and Maggie. Their opinion and insight will be an invaluable aid to me if they'll agree to go."

"I see you've already thought this out," Simon said sourly. "I've learned not to go against you when you get like this, Herald or not, so you go ahead and go. I'll do all I can to maintain security and keep our ship production up."

"You're partly right," Kitty replied. "I have thought this out. At some time or other, the leaders have to meet personally. If you'd been sitting where I am, you'd have seen that, I'm sure. You let your priorities get out of order, and for that you'll have to pay a small price. You'll direct the standing fleet, both human and whatever

"Shiravan ships Policy Minister sel Garian decides to leave in place. Ship production will continue to be in the hands of the various base commanders, and you're directed to stay out of their way. Recruitment of crews is also being fielded by our new Personnel Department, so that's one more thing you won't have to worry about."

She realized that if she didn't put restraints on him herself, Simon would take on too much and alienate half the people he needed most. Delegation of authority—that's what he'd taught her almost from day one but kept overlooking himself. This wasn't a situation where micromanagement was going to be very effective. She felt bad about using it against him, but not so bad that she'd let him ruin all they'd worked for by trying to be in too many places at one time.

"You just make sure the fleet is supplied and ready to fight when the time comes. Work on possible strategies, stage war games, and begin sending out patrols just as soon as you're ready. Look for evidence of Korvil habitation or visitation until you can get a lock on one of their base worlds. Then, take them out by whatever means necessary. Work on fitting the newer ships into the standing units and see about setting up those wolfpacks you mentioned so long ago. You'll notice that's what I plan to take with me to Shiravi. You can also work on getting as many of the Shiravan ships upgraded to our level as possible, too." She chose not to notice the grimace that passed across the face of the Policy Minister. "Those are your sole responsibilities as Admiral while I'm gone, except to accede to the orders of Lucy Grimes, who has graciously agreed to take the reins one more time. She'll hold the title of Deputy Herald and hold all the powers I have right now. Do you have any questions about what I want?"

When Simon slowly shook his head, Kitty relented a bit. "As my husband, you're allowed to worry about me just as much as I'm going to worry about you, and if things get too out of hand, you can always declare martial law and take those powers onto yourself, but you'd better be able to defend your decisions to a jury of your peers, not just me."

The Policy Minister slapped her left shoulder with her right hand, the Shiravan method of clapping, and hiccuped in laughter. She said something the translator hesitated over but finally translated.

"She says that you have him... I think she means well-trained, but the translation comes out 'housebroken.'" Rentec did his best to hide a smile, and Maratai only let out two small hiccups in surprise.

Simon's cheeks burned a furious red, and for once, he grudgingly chose silence.

CHAPTER FIFTEEN

Simon sat at a table looking at a replay of the old Shiravan's holodisplay. Now they more or less knew where the attacks were coming from, and learning that they were inside the area claimed by these Korvils rankled him like nothing ever before in his life. Somebody was about to get their noses bloodied... badly.

In the past two years, eighteen ships had come out of the docks, even with the *Galileo* producing at almost twice the rate of the bases. Three of the new ships were carriers, one of which was going to make an extended trip to Shiravi with the Herald, bringing the total up to five. There were enough battlecruisers around to start exploring the neighborhood with an eye towards, first, where the Korvils might have bases, and second, places where humans might start colonies of their own, which was going to require an entirely different type of ship later.

As soon as information started flowing both ways in this new frontier, expansion was going to be impossible to stop, even if stopping them was someone's goal, especially the Korvils. That still left enough human and Shiravan ships to begin to explore farther systems in groups of five, always weighted three human ships to two Shiravan. And ghosting along with the squadron would be two ships under full cloak—a hidden asset, so to speak.

The higher firepower of the human ships, along with the secret of real screens, started proving their worth almost immediately. A wolf pack and two Shiravan heavy destroyers that had recently been upgraded with the new screens had met eleven heavily armed Korvil destroyer-class ships as the squadron entered their third system. The Korvils were headed in-system for reasons of their own. The *Shasta's* captain led the fleet as they slowly emerged from the Oort cloud surrounding this new system. No one had even bothered to name it, since its only reference was a number in a catalogue.

Normally, passive scans swept the system, sometimes taking days to get full returns on the entire solar area, but this time Korvil engine signatures popped up mere hours after they'd arrived. The *Shasta's* captain had taken the gift handed to him. He ordered all sensors online and a cloud of fighters to launch, but he also ordered them to maintain strict silence and remain close enough to the carrier to cover the fact that they were in fact not one target but seventy once the Mambas from the two battlecruisers emerged as well.

Whisker-laser transmissions let the five ships coordinate their actions as they moved along a course that forced the Korvils to have to slow down to intercept. The *Shasta* waited until it was too late for any of the eleven enemy ships to veer off before springing the hastily planned trap. The carrier *Antares* began to back away from the fleet, leaving a shell of fighters that would register as one ship on almost any screen.

As soon as the Korvil craft were within range, the Mamba Strike Commander sent a single laser transmission to the five flight leaders. They each tight-beamed the individual members of their flights, and the battle was officially underway, except that the Korvils wouldn't find that out until they started losing ships. Sensors were notoriously ineffective directly astern due to the strength of the drive emissions, making it a perfect place to ambush the enemy.

Each flight had been given a specific mission to target one ship together and take out the engines for sure, in addition to as many weapons pods as possible. The enemy had gone into immediate disarray. Five Korvil ships had died in the first pass, and the extra flight from the battlecruisers got their shots in. Six of the enemy ships had been drifting hulks before they even began to fight back. This was the signal for the battlecruisers to power up their forward shields and begin firing on remaining targets, pinning the survivors between two superior forces. The antimatter-tipped warheads had torn broad holes into the sides of the Korvil destroyers, some even breaching the power cores and blowing entire ships.

Within a matter of less than an hour, the five-ship fleet had taken on and destroyed more Korvil major vessels than the entire Shiravan military had in over one hundred years. Losses were one hundred percent for the Korvils, and five fighters for the Alliance fleet—three to either superb or lucky marksmanship and two that forgot where they were and flew into someone's backwash.

The *Shasta's* captain was sorry about the losses, of course, but he wasn't too distressed over two of them. *The only truly capital crime in the universe is stupidity. There is no recourse and no reprieve. The sentence is death, and God have mercy on their souls*, he thought.

He turned the small squadron towards Earth to pass on the news after giving his gunners some target practice blowing apart anything big enough to hold any data on how this massacre had come to be.

Shasta Group (each patrol was named for its command ship) returned to Earth space full of glad tidings. They stopped in the outer periphery of the system to gauge their location exactly before moving on to Earth and performing the usual scans. Much to the surprise of Shasta Group, they found ten drive traces. They were throttled back to low but still emitting that drive signal peculiar to Korvil ships. Scanning said that they were all destroyer-class or better. Shasta Command ordered one of the Shiravan vessels—the one commanded by the more adventurous of the two captains—to hyper jump directly to Earth with the warning that the next invasion wave was underway and to deliver the particulars. Shasta Group would stay behind and harass the incoming enemy for as long as they were able. Shasta Command next informed the other Shiravan vessel to hyper jump to Earth if it became clear that the battle was going against the human ships.

The close departure signature of a large vessel registered on the Korvil scans, even though it happened from behind them through the interference of their drives. The tight-knit Korvil formation started to disperse, the signal for the carrier to drop Mambas instantly, holding a ten-percent reserve for emergencies. The two battlecruisers dropped their Mambas, adding another twenty to the melee, and attacked the two closest Korvil ships.

The Korvils hadn't had time to completely rid themselves of their forward motion, so they flipped their ships end-for-end and began firing at the approaching human ships. Their drive trails spewed out behind them as they fought to bring their ships back onto an attack heading using forward momentum to increase their options.

The forward shields of the two human ships shrugged off the torpedoes thrown at them as if they had never been fired, while their own projectiles, antimatter-tipped and powered, met no resistance at all as they impacted with the forward sections of the two Korvil ships.

The standard torpedo carried by all ships and Mambas was already a bomb in its own right. Destroy the generator for the containment field powering the missile, and a blast was the result. Period. End of sentence. The humans that copied these straight out of data files just added another bit of antimatter onto the front of the missile, thinking of the first bit as just the power source needed to deliver the package they'd attached to the front end. The innovation let the first piece of antimatter penetrate the hull of a shieldless opponent, while the second piece, the power plant, exploded deeper within the ship, multiplying the damage.

Ten torpedoes flashed from each of the two human ships, self-guided spears that had no chance of missing at this distance. Both Korvil craft ceased to be as their magazines took three hits apiece. Other hits to other parts of the hulls were merely icing on the cake.

The other eight Korvil ships gave themselves over to combating the swarm of tiny ships literally overwhelming their scanners, stinging at will. Any time one of the speedy craft came within range of a Korvil laser emplacement, that pest was destroyed immediately. But they kept the Fleet from reaching the two fighting warships, now turning to choose new targets among the quickly disappearing Korvil fleet. Even the Shiravan captain took on an opponent, emboldened by the shield strength displayed by their new allies. The Korvil Fleet Commander was "lucky" enough to be in one of the last ships destroyed. He lived long enough to realize that the Korvil reign was at an end.

The carrier *Antares* stood off and let the battle work itself out, needing to stay and pick up survivors and casualties. She couldn't enter the fighting proper. What she brought to a battle—more small fighters than either other race had seemed to deem necessary—caused her to have to give up space for things like mounted weapons, although she did carry torpedoes for both the Mambas and a dozen missile tubes of her own.

The two human battlecruisers almost immediately took out their primary objectives and turned to their secondaries. This was the point where the Shiravan commander called on the Spirits of Space to protect these brave and daring people who were fighting such a one-sided battle. The Korvil ships, realizing the havoc these two ships could cause in their midst, concentrated their firepower toward the two major vessels. Those two ships diverted power from their life support and engine modules and passed it into the system that was powering the shields. Only a direct hit from the rear would be able to get past the shields and destroy one of the human ships.

Under normal conditions, which these weren't, the two human ships would have stood up for perhaps only a few minutes against the massed attack of eight Korvil destroyers, shields not excepted, but the distractions of the Mambas and the Shiravan battlecruiser began to make themselves felt almost at once. Firing into the stern of the enemy ships, the Mamba swarm was attempting to take the power core away from each vessel. Faced with the infernal torture of the tiny ships on one side and the apparent invulnerability of the three larger ships and heavier firepower, the eight remaining ships, breaking hundreds of years of Korvil conditioning, tried to run for open space.

Under normal conditions, it might have worked. Earth had found enemy ships lurking around just one time too many to let the matter go. Alerted by the first Shiravan vessel, eight battlecruisers and one more carrier flashed into existence surrounding the struggle. The Korvils, upon seeing so many more ships, essentially committed suicide. They attacked any ship near them and either destroyed it or was finally destroyed itself. The final count left all Korvil craft destroyed at the cost of one rammed and destroyed battlecruiser and three others seriously damaged, one of which required a tow back to base. The Mamba cost was severe as well, with over forty more destroyed in this single assault. In the two incidents, humanity and the Shiravans had accounted for twenty-one attack craft, and in the process had lost one battlecruiser and forty-five Mamba pilots. That translated into almost six hundred humans dead, but what was the real loss to the other side? Had those twenty-one ships represented a major portion of their fleet? Enough had been destroyed in the five years leading up to this moment that one might think so.

The humans began to see why the Shiravans feared these beings so much. The sheer ferocity of the attack when the Korvils learned that there was no way out stunned the humans, who had used those very tactics innumerable times in their own past. Even the wolverine, one of the fiercest animals on Earth, gave up ground, if only grudgingly. Here there was no attempt to retreat or minimize damage to oneself, only the desire to crush all that stood before them.

The meeting was a subdued one. It was also not open to the public, considering that it was held on Vesta. It had become common practice for the Alliance to hand out press releases on a regular basis from the very beginning of their open-embassy policy. Now, with so many affected, apparently because of a lack of vigilance by the Alliance, countries from all around the Pacific Rim, even those with only minor damage, wanted answers. And scapegoats. Preferably rich ones. Simon was determined that the Alliance not be the scapegoat.

He looked out at the faces before him, just like so many times before, only this time the faces were of ships' captains, base commanders, embassy heads, and several dozen other people closely tied to the Alliance who'd come to Vesta for this one reason. There was Baron von Schlenker, all the way from Earth, and with him were several people he'd come to know as representing their governments in semi-official capacities. To see them there now was a bit of a shock but nothing he couldn't handle. He let his eyes meet each one of this group, recognizing but not acknowledging Brandon Galway. Three ships had been in orbit, and the baron must have leaned on one of the captains pretty hard to get this group out there so quickly.

Also not normal for a meeting like this were several Shiravan faces in a small group off to one side.

One other abnormality was the camera, red light showing in record mode. "I want to thank each of you for being here at this most auspicious of times," he began. "The recorded version will be sent out immediately, but you who happen to be here at this time deserve to hear two bits of news. First comes the good news. Shasta Group, consisting of a wolf pack, two Shiravan escorts, and two cloaked battlecruisers, ambushed eleven Korvil destroyers in the third system they entered at a loss of only five Mambas. The surprise was that complete. But on their return to bring the news, Shasta Group happened upon a ten-ship destroyer convoy inbound for Earth. The bad news is that even though this enemy convoy was completely destroyed, it was at a cost of forty-five pilots, the entire crew of the *Vengeance,* and several dozen from two other damaged ships."

Simon let the muttering go on for a few minutes before continuing. "I know. We all have friends among those lost. That's just how it is with a group as small and tightly knit as ours." He stood silently for a few seconds and then said, "Grieve for your friends. Take what time you need to do so, but if possible, make it fast, I'm sorry to say. Then turn that grief outward toward the enemy that has caused so much loss here and on Earth. Our losses are in the hundreds, but our *world* has lost millions. There are so many volunteers clogging the system down below that we're actually turning people away after taking a number they can be reached at."

He took a deep breath and went on. "Shasta Group's success was, according to her own group commander, mostly pure luck. Their arrival in the third target's system dropped them just outside the local Oort cloud. Their slow progress inward let them detect the Korvil battle group before being spotted themselves. *Shasta's* tactics, while somewhat less than conventional—if I can use that word in a venue almost totally new to us—let us destroy all eleven ships with only a five-Mamba loss. This shows us that these big, bad boogey men aren't so invulnerable after all."

The translators finished Simon's words almost as fast as he said them these days as familiarity gave greater confidence and competence to the interpreter corps, both human and Shiravan. The Shiravan delegation began to slowly clap their left shoulders with their right hands, at one and the same time a show of respect for those fallen in battle and sorrow at the losses sustained.

The human delegation surrounding Brandon Galway looked perplexed—all except Galway. Wasn't it enough that they had handed the Korvils their heads on a platter? Again? And for what? The fourth time now? Anybody else would back off and lick their wounds. But that was human thinking. Most people kept attributing human motives to alien machinations; after all, that was all they had for reference.

But Simon and his leading military officers had spoken at length with the Shiravan captains, during which time a speedy little dispatch boat arrived, dropped off a sealed communiqué for sel Garian, and then, after only one rest period in which all of her systems were tested and tuned as necessary, returned to the Shiravan homeworld. Whether or not the message had been replied to wasn't discussed during the next highly anticipated meeting between the two leaders.

Now, he got to drop a small bomb among the humans that would be certain to stir the hornet's nest down below when they returned home. "Now that our homeworld is known to the Shiravans, they've started sending messages back and forth between the supreme commanders of both factions. Unfortunately, Earth has too many voices for them to hear what we have to say. Their system is a one-world government, or more correctly put, a one-race government, and they're spread out over fourteen colonial worlds."

He let that sink in, distracting them for a short time, until he decided it was time to hit them with another dose of reality. "In short, ladies and gentlemen," he said, raising his voice to be heard over the babble of two different languages, "the Shiravans refuse to have any dealings with Earth except through the Alliance, and then only as long as a woman holds the reins of power. They will not accept any less and we have agreed, in the name of humanity, to abide by that decision *for the time being*."

He raised his hand to stave off the babble of questions that were fired at him. "Gentlemen, ladies, we had two options—one, agree to their demand, at least for the time being, or two, have all contact between the two races cut off. It appears that, as a rule, we are too much like the Korvils for their liking. Apparently the Korvils are a male-dominated society as well, and the Shiravans, for reasons explained to us in the past, distrust that kind of system. After all, look at how the Korvils most likely got the technology in the first place—murdering the crew and then, after retooling their lower technological facilities, reproducing the destroyer. We believe that to be the case, because up until recently, we haven't seen any indication that they were working on innovations. Destroyers don't have the database to do more than repair and reproduce themselves, which is why all you've seen so far are vessels slightly smaller than ours—more heavily armed and armored than we ever saw them in the databases, but I think that's one indication the Korvils aren't just some jumped up predecessor to a thinking, reasoning being. They may be a little closer to their ancestral roots than we are, to be sure, but still capable of rational thought, by their own standards."

Simon paced, thinking of Kitty and how she chastised him for it. He had never paced before finding the *Galileo*. "We've given the Shiravans some indication of what we're capable of in the attack Shasta Group made on the Korvil convoy. Granted, they weren't expecting it, but still, eleven destroyers down. And more good news, this time from the Shiravan side of the equation. The Shiravans have located and attacked what appears to be a heavily settled planet deep within Korvil-held territory. They used two entire—as I understand the translation, Reprisal Fleets—catching many ships on the ground, several unpowered ships in orbit, and a huge construction facility on one of the two moons of the planet, along with a smaller facility on the other moon.

"Unfortunately, the fleet was only able to make one pass, but it's believed that a significant amount of damage was done. Using that planet as a central focus, we—Shiravans and humans alike—are going to start attacking any world in the vicinity of that particular planet after verifying that they're inhabited by Korvils. If it isn't their homeworld, it isn't far from it, at least in terms of where it is in the colonization chain. Their courier arrived earlier today, and the coordinates of the planet have already been downloaded into the *Galileo's* battle computer. Ship captains need only query the *Galileo's* computer and the information is yours as well."

He finally sat down, an audible sigh of relief going up as he did so because it usually signaled the end of a briefing. "Policy Minister sel Garian will be heading back to Shiravi to help begin the coordinated attacks against Korvil planets and interests." An unpleasant look crossed his face. "For the record, the Herald and a handpicked team of negotiators will accompany the Policy Minister back to Shiravi, setting the rules for further contacts between our two races. Mister Galway, I'd be honored if you'd accompany the group to oversee Earth's general interests in the discussion that will take place. Make sure you have your own interpreter on hand, or you'll have to make do with what we tell you was said and agreed to. I'd like to talk to you about that later, if you please."

Galway, singled out, looked at the members of the Earth delegation. Getting blank looks in return, he turned back to Simon and nodded his head once, slowly.

CHAPTER SIXTEEN

"You know what happened in the recent past concerning me and my wife," Simon said, looking Galway directly between the eyes. "First, I thought I lost her in that damned machine, and now she's going lightyears away from where I can do anything to protect her. I can't send any overt protection, since that would be a slap in the face of the Shiravans, but someone trained to look for the less than obvious might be able to steer her on a straighter path than she otherwise might follow, if you know what I mean. And I don't mean influencing her in her talks with the Matriarch. *I* can't even do that, and I sleep with her."

Galway looked at Simon across the expanse of the desk separating them and smiled at the joke. "Of all the people I've met in the past few years, you and your wife seem most capable of taking care of yourselves. I'm no diplomat, but I still have a job to do. It will be an honor to watch out for her, Simon, but I'll try to talk the Matriarch into dealing with Earth directly, if I can. All in the spirit of friendly competition. That I can promise you."

"I guess I can't ask for more than that," Simon admitted ruefully.

"I hope not," Galway said with a small laugh in his voice. "We're going to be totally surrounded by aliens over forty lightyears from any help and no sidearms as a show of good faith. Watching her back is about all I'll be able to do for her." He sat silently for several seconds. "You know we're going to see to it that this Matriarch understands that your Alliance doesn't speak for the balance of humanity, don't you?"

"I wouldn't expect any less from someone who considers himself a principled man, Agent Galway. Besides, they already know that, almost from the first moment of contact," Simon answered.

"Brandon, please," Galway said. "If we're going to be working as closely as I expect over the next few years, not counting our time away, of course, then we should be on a first-name basis, don't you think?"

Simon stood up and held out his hand. "I agree completely, Brandon. Until I get bitten, of course. Then, the rules will change automatically. Every relationship has to depend on trust. I'm going to do my best to keep my word. Should be easy, since I do have the technological edge. But I don't want you to forget, ever since we've taken possession of this ship, I've done a lot of reading. And I do mean a lot. Lord knows there have been enough times when I've had nothing else to do. One thing that keeps jumping out at me is how the technologically backwards people have wound up absorbing their conquerors throughout history. There's no way you could have missed that one, Brandon. Just sit back long enough, and all things will come to you. You have to have cultural anthropologists working on any number of scenarios, and that one would probably be near the top of the list."

Galway had the decency to look embarrassed, but he neither confirmed nor denied the charge.

"I know you, Simon Hawke," Kitty accused, shaking her

finger in the face of the admiral of the most potent fleet in human history. "If I don't find some way to keep you under control while I'm gone, there's no telling what might happen. So…" An almost satisfied sound coming into her voice. "I've talked Lucy into taking the position of *deputy Herald* in my absence. Forget administrator. We need the office of the Herald to be active while I'm gone. She has also been given very explicit instructions on how to deal with you. We women have to stick together, you know. The only difference between us during my absence is that you won't be getting any from her. She'll handle the overall situation from Vesta, and you'll be in charge of handling fleet matters. And it will let you focus."

She watched the expressions pass over his face. "Look at it this way, hon. It leaves her free to deal with the intricacies of global politics, which she's good at, and you can concentrate on military matters, which you're good at. Delegation of authority—something you taught me almost from the beginning of this whole thing."

She moved into his arms, letting them automatically close around her. "You know, this is the almost the last time I'll feel this for nearly two years. Let's make it count, Lover." Kitty shamelessly used her ability to distract her husband, ending the discussion for all practical purposes.

Simon stood in the *Galileo's* viewing dome as the convoy carrying his wife, friends, and opposition forces got under way. He watched them move off into the blackness of space, standing alone and looking at the exact spot in space for several minutes before he let the malaise he felt wash out of him. Duty called. His job was to mold the new ships into the existing fleet, along with the Shiravan forces left behind as a gesture of good faith.

He got distracted by the images he began to see on the inner surface of the dome. He'd come to recognize that this was something other people couldn't do—see the future's infinite possibilities. In some sets of images, he never saw his wife again, and in some others, at a great distance, the human race no longer existed.

In other images, he could see the two of them walking arm in arm along an alien shore, watching a nearly blue sun set into an azure sea. His dilemma was to decide which set of images were the ones he needed to follow for the best interests of the human race. He shook his head wistfully. Working for that idyllic sunset tempted him desperately, but the corresponding image for humanity was of a universe devoid of human life.

Deep in thought, he let his feet carry him to the *Galileo's* transporter room and absently told the duty tech to beam him to the *Rigel*, which was presently acting as his flagship. He called the *Galileo's* med lab to inquire about Marsha Kane's status. He'd made it his job to check on her progress in the *Galileo's* healing chamber—as the strange device had come to be called—at least once a week.

It was with a great deal of relief that he learned Marsha had been decanted only hours before and had been moved to intensive care, not that she needed it after a sojourn in the healing chamber. She would be allowed to have visitors sometime the next day.

His next act after Kitty and her escort was gone was to put in a social call to the new deputy Herald. He walked into her anteroom, and her secretary almost couldn't get her words out. "Ad… Admiral. We had no idea you were coming."

"That's all right, Darlene," he said after a quick glance at the nameplate on her desk. "Please inform the deputy Herald that this is a 'Simon' visit not an 'Admiral Hawke' visit."

She looked first at her desk datalink and then at the door she knew her boss sat behind. "Go on in after a quick knock, Darlene," he said. "I know her. Just tell her Simon is here, and let's see what she does."

Less than a minute later he sat in her office with his feet propped up on a table covered with some of the latest magazines from Earth's newsstands. "So, what got you to come back into the fold, Luce?" he asked bluntly.

"I have your wife's assurance, and therefore yours by default, that this is the last time I'm going to have to fill this post. I was quite happy hiding out on Vesta, and I think I'll keep Alliance headquarters here." She looked at Simon for a minute, evidently gauging what she was going to say next. "My doctor said I was almost ready to reintegrate into society. Not at this high a level, but in some visible capacity. We intended that I work my way back into full-time service. Sick, crazy, whatever, I still have the same dream all the rest of us do—to take our place among the star-faring races of the galaxy. One step at a time, of course. One mustn't act too uppity, you know."

"Races?" Simon questioned. "I thought there were only three races in this part of the galaxy. We're pretty far out in one of the arms, after all."

Lucy shook her head. "I've spent several years out here now, treating a lot of our visiting alien friends to dinner and, in effect, interrogating them. One of their concepts I've tried to follow has been their references to the Spirits of Space. It seems to be a universal, almost religious thing for most of them."

Simon interrupted. "What does that have to do with anything?"

Lucy saw unease appear in his eyes. "It has everything to do with Kitty's mission to Shiravi," Lucy said, looking uncomfortable.

"Well, don't keep me in the dark, Luce," Simon demanded.

"It's not that simple, Simon," Lucy said, regret tingeing her voice. "I know that you know they speak of something they call the Spirits of Space. We just got through talking about it."

"Yeah? So? They talk about them like they really exist. Some of them claim to commune with these spirits in the observation domes during hyper-drive."

"Simon," Lucy said, intent on getting and keeping his attention.

It seemed that her ploy would work enough to let her get the last of her information out without interruption, because he stopped dead and waited for her to speak. "The Shiravans have two major Spirits of Space. One of them is Kath-e-vel, the Spirit of Darkness and Deceit. The other is the Spirit of Rebirth and Victory. That spirit is called Kath-e-rin. Katherine, Simon. Most of these Shiravans think Kitty is the personification of the good Spirit of Space come to help them overcome the dark forces afflicting their world."

Simon sat stunned into silence, a sight Lucy had seldom seen. Finally, after a time, he was able to get enough air to ask, "Are you telling me that my wife has gone off with a bunch of people who think she's some kind of goddess?"

Lucy looked uncomfortably around the room, which

was currently serving as her office until she could get moved into another part of Vesta. "Well, that's not exactly true, Simon."

"Don't you keep me in the dark on this, Lucy Grimes. Deputy Herald or not, I'll go after her with everything I can put into space if you don't fill me in, and fast."

"You've got to give me your word that you won't go off half-cocked," Lucy insisted. "That you'll listen to what I have to say and then sit on it for twenty-four hours before we talk again. Right here in this office."

Simon shook his head. "I'm not going to promise any such thing without knowing at least some of what's going on," he said stubbornly.

Lucy sat up straighter in her chair. "You *will* give me your word, Admiral, or I won't tell you anything. And those are the Herald's orders, not mine." She looked him straight in the eye, not flinching from the stony gaze he laid on her.

Simon stared at a spot one inch above and directly between Lucy's eyes. The effect was that of giving her his complete and undivided attention. Most people couldn't take that kind of attention for long. Lucy, though, had been warned by Kitty about Simon's tricks—not that she didn't know some of them herself. After all, she'd been serving with him in some capacity for almost eight years now.

"Policy Minister sel Garian personally oversaw the reprogramming of some of the *Shumara Vacht's* food processors so our delegation wouldn't have to carry too much in the way of rations," Lucy said, trying to change the subject.

Simon saw what she was doing but let it slide. After all, Lucy had been prompted by his wife, and he never could stand up to her logic in the long run, even secondhand from Lucy. "Okay, I promise," Simon grated out. "No matter what you tell me, I won't go off to save Kitty, at least for twenty-four hours. Now, what's the deal?"

Lucy hesitated for a minute, sizing Simon up. "I've never known you to go back on your word. I'm going to assume that when you say you won't go after Kitty, you won't stay here and send other ships after her. We may well need the resources in the not-too-distant future. The Korvils could strike again at any time."

"Okay," Simon reiterated grudgingly. "I stay here, and all ships stay here. Now what's the deal?"

"Some of the Shiravans think Kitty is a goddess, yes. The problem is that some of them think she could be this Kath-e-vel in disguise." Lucy was quiet for a second, gathering her words. "In the last meeting I had with Kitty before she left, we speculated on this, but this new information has just come to my attention. sel Garian doesn't seem to believe either way, I suspect, but she has leanings that her culture bred into her. She'll protect Kitty with her own life, if need be, if for no other reason than her own personal honor. There *is* some danger for Kitty on this trip, but somehow, I feel safer knowing that she's traveling with sel Garian."

Lucy picked up her datalink when it buzzed on her desk. After listening for several seconds, she said, "Thank you. Tracking can go back to normal scan." She turned to Simon. "Tracking says that the *Shumara Vacht* and her escort have just entered hyperspace on a course that would take them directly to the star sel Garian designated as their homeworld. Of course, they could change direction after a while, but that's all we can go on at this time."

Simon, discomfited by his wife' traveling so far without him, made perfunctory goodbye noises at Lucy and walked out of her office deep in thought. He didn't like the turn of events but had to defer to Lucy, who said she was only following Kitty's orders in the matter. That left him with nothing to do but work on the thousand and one things he had on his list.

Recruiting wasn't going to be a problem after the dual disasters that had recently affected Earth, but keeping the ships coming out of the yards was a challenge. Theoretically, if he increased the number of shuttles flying collection missions, ships could be built faster. But he had to figure in the people factor as well. Everybody needed a rest now and then.

Production and crewing were supposed to be under the control of another department, leaving Simon free to integrate the new ships and crews into the existing fleet. This worked well in theory, but Kitty seemed to have forgotten that base captains and commanders fell under the purview of the admiralty, for lack of a better word, because they were in the military chain of command.

Simon used this lapse shamelessly over the next two years, building the fleet into something that could be used to protect or attack, or both. The Shiravan ships were what made the difference. Patrolling the various sectors of the Alliance, namely those areas Simon and his command staff had delineated around the spatial vicinity of Earth and her sun, became routine during Kitty's two-year hiatus. In effect, he was carving out a small empire for humanity, saying, "Cross this line and you'll get your nose bloodied, bad."

CHAPTER SEVENTEEN

During Kitty's hiatus, all the Shiravan vessels were equipped with the new shields and some of the upgraded weaponry. Certain types of firepower, such as the plasma cannon, were still top secret. "'Politics makes strange bedfellows,'" Simon told Lucy one day in her new office on Vesta. "That' saying's been going around for almost as long as politics has existed. It just means that today's friend might be tomorrow's enemy and vice versa. Let's not give away all we know, shall we?"

Simon had sat in on various meetings and expressed his opinion openly on the need for a buffer zone around Earth. "The Shiravans have one, and it would behoove us to emulate our benefactors," he said at one meeting Maratai attended.

During one of those meetings, the question of whether or not the Shiravans were prosecuting their portion of the war came up. "We've not received one single report since the *Shumara Vacht* left for Shiravi," Simon declared, his concern for his wife just as strong as his need for intelligence. "I personally think we should have some kind of continuing chain of incoming reports about how the talks are going and what steps the Shiravans are taking to relieve some of the pressure on us while we start raiding into Korvil space. I particularly want to hear from my wife or any of her escorts that she's okay and that talks are proceeding smoothly."

Maratai leaned forward and said, "I'll send a dispatch

ship with your request immediately. I'm sure your concern for Katherine and the progress of the talks will make an impression on the Matriarch. But you must understand that the travel time will be the same, and Katherine is not due to stay an overly long time."

"What the hell does that mean?" Simon asked himself as Maratai sat back, apparently thinking she had rescued the situation. Simon looked Maratai in the eyes, the red still discomfiting him somehow. "If we don't start getting reports back soon, I'm going to begin sending out my own dispatch ships," he said quietly.

Joanna Barnes noted, "If a courier leaves Shiravi as soon as your wife arrives, it will still take almost a year for it to arrive and another to return. The courier could pass Kitty on her way back."

Simon just grunted unhappily.

Kitty received sel Garian's summons to her stateroom just before the convoy was due to move into hyperspace, the same area known to the Shiravans as contra-space. Surprised at the timing, she slipped her shoes on and followed the Shiravan aide to sel Garian's quarters.

Not entirely surprised to find Rentec there, she looked questioningly at sel Garian. In highly stilted Shiravan, she asked, "You wished to see me?"

"Yes," sel Garian said simply. "Please sit and drink with me for a while. There are some personnel adjustments being made before we jump for Shiravi. You and your people have been kind enough to tell us stories about your race. Some were designed to impress us and some to scare us, I think. Propaganda, it is called." Rentec worked furiously to interpret sel Garian's words.

"Let me tell you a story." The old woman got up and

poured an Earth wine into two wooden cups, polished to a high gloss by the thousands of hands that had held them over the years, and handed one to Kitty. "This is one of the best things about your culture," she said, slowly swirling the cup and smelling the wine within. "Long ago," the old woman began without preamble, "our world was dominated by males. Bigger, stronger, and faster than females, they dominated our culture for most of our recorded history and apparently all of our unrecorded history until about a thousand years ago when the males started a war that lasted almost two hundred years. Because women were so precious—after all, we were the ones to give birth to the next generation of warriors—we were kept out of the fighting."

sel Garian took a sip from her cup. "The females of the warring factions realized that if something wasn't done, all the males would wipe themselves out and the Shiravan culture would have committed suicide. They set up a situation where the males almost completely wiped themselves out in one cataclysmic fight, at which time the females stepped in and took the reins of power. That's a really simplistic view of what took over fifty years to accomplish, but we'll have many opportunities to talk later in the voyage, I'm certain."

The old woman took another swallow and continued. "The males tried to stop us, of course, but by the time they realized what was happening, there were too few of them, and more died in the fight to regain male dominance. The females had done their homework well. During the war, many females became legislators, and others secretly trained to fight like the males. We managed to rewrite the inheritance laws while the men fought, allowing property rights to reside in the female line so possessions were handed down from a mother to her firstborn daughter.

"And we saw to it that more females were born than males. Shiravans had become supreme geneticists, and we females were able to make sure that male births were kept low enough that they could never affect politics again. The problem was that some of us—the females—were psychic. Able to see into the future, albeit cloudily, we foresaw this war, although a thousand turns ago we had no idea what we were seeing. Now we know, and the belated realization could be our undoing.

"As with any group of people, there were numerous ideas of how to take advantage of our new-found power. We believe it was somewhere during this time that the Korvils got hold of one of our ships and began to duplicate it. It was almost two hundred years before we were directly affected, once they'd taught themselves how to operate the technology they'd stolen. By this time, the Korvil shipyards were fully functional, and we were left to deal with the situation." No hint of comparing humans to Korvils had entered sel Garian's voice.

"It was at this time that the anomaly of the kath-mora showed up. We have long had females who could read the future and make predications for matrimonials, births, deaths, and other such events, but it wasn't until this time that their success rate blossomed. On one of our early vessels, we placed a dome, like the ones on the *Kreth* and the *Shumara Vacht*, to study the realm through which we traveled. On one such excursion, a kath-mora, a Spirit Witch who'd been trained as a physicist, rode in the dome, making observations and transcribing them into permanent records. After a particular flight, the Witch claimed she was able to commune with the Spirits of Space, and they told her that it was time for the

Shiravan people to begin to retreat from their expansionist tactics. This was shortly after the first contact with the Korvils, who called themselves the Borgan at that time. It didn't help the Expansionist movement that the experience somehow heightened this kath-mora's power, and this Spirit Witch began the Isolationist movement that still thrives today. It is with great shame that I tell you that particular witch was a sel Garian."

Kitty must have looked confused because sel Garian said, "I was the one to make crew selections for this particular mission, and I saw to it that all the top-ranking witches were aboard the two Contact Fleets. While in your system, I reassigned all the witches from Contact Fleet One to my own fleet. Now, the witches from both fleets will be given the extra ship we brought along."

Kitty had wondered about that extra ship, as well as the overcrowded conditions aboard the *Shumara Vacht* since sel Garian had adamantly assured the humans that all Shiravan ships would stay in-system until the human shipyards could turn out enough ships to protect themselves. "The last ship, the *Cara Set*, will be used to house all of the Spirit Witches we brought with us, and they can find their own way home. When they get there, which will take some time as there are certain repairs that need to be made before she is otherspace-worthy, I think they'll find that the political climate has altered, and not in their favor.

"In the meantime, the Matriarch's forces will only have to deal with a disorganized smattering of witches totally bereft of their leadership. When I bring this last bit of evidence," sel Garian said, dangling the pendant Kitty had worn since Simon had discovered it aboard the *Galileo* all those years ago, "to the Matriarch's attention,

261

she will surely outlaw the kath-mora forever. The back of the resistance against our expansion into space will be forever broken, and we will soon remove the blight of the Korvils from the universe, along with the help of our new human allies, of course."

Kitty, not really knowing how to respond, merely grunted slightly as she took a sip of the wine in her cup. *Perhaps the old woman's getting a little dotty in her old age. After all, she's closing in on the three-hundred-year mark.* A few more minutes of banal comments and Kitty stood up, made her excuses, and left to think about the things she'd heard.

Brandon Galway felt distinctly uncomfortable seated across from the old Shiravan woman. Could he be, after all this time, a xenophobe? He had met and talked with dozens of Shiravans before Second Fleet had shown up, but it had usually been in a setting where there were more humans than aliens. So, he'd had "home court" advantage, so to speak, by being on Earth. Now he was in a room alone with two aliens aboard a spaceship that was taking him farther from Earth than all but two humans had ever been before. Granted, he knew Rentec, who, as interpreter, otherwise distanced himself from the conversation, but sel Garian was still a mystery to him.

"Would you like something to drink?" she asked. The mechanical voice grated on his nerves, but he refused to let it show.

Instead, he merely shook his head and answered, "No, thank you." Then, silence descended on the room as red eyes stared into brown ones. Galway was troubled by the invitation since he was only along in a mediocre position with the Earth delegation. One thing he was sure of was that he wasn't going to be first to speak.

After a decade or two passed, sel Garian broke the silence. "I've been told by the Herald that you are the true head of the human delegation to the Matriarch. I am told as well that you don't agree with what the Alliance is doing with the technology they've inherited. Are both of these statements true?"

Shock ran through Galway's system. His had almost always been a covert life, and to have information disclosed in such a fashion was unsettling. His mind raced, looking for an answer to the woman's question. He finally decided on a unique tack—the truth. "Let me address the second statement first, if you will," Galway said. When all he got was a slight left/right shake of her head, he looked to Rentec.

Rentec had begun to explain the difference between a Shiravan nod and a human one when sel Garian made a cutting motion with her hand. The old woman picked up a cup that sat before her, twin to the one in front of Galway, sat back in her chair, and motioned for him to continue. Galway tried to choose his words carefully, recognizing the minefield he was walking through. "First, let me say that we know yours is a one-government world, something some of us are striving for on Earth, while others seek to stop it in an effort to retain their own power. At present, there are over two hundred different nations on Earth, each ruled by an individual or coalition."

He looked at the woman on the other side of the desk and made up his mind. "Most people these days think of the Alliance as the saviors of humanity. They will take us to the stars, give us planets, make us rich. But most of those people aren't in government or military service. None of them understand the implications of dealing with an alien race, much less two at the same time. It's a basic tenet on our world that the majority rules, and these people who call themselves the Terran Alliance have taken it upon themselves to appropriate the ship they found and use it for their own purposes."

The red eyes bored into his. "Are you saying the Alliance doesn't represent the majority of humanity or the majority of humanity's governing bodies?"

Galway thought furiously. He'd decided on the truth and couldn't turn back now. "They do represent the majority of humanity, if their motives are pure. Otherwise, they don't. And they certainly don't reflect the opinions of the leaders of the various nations."

"When," the old woman asked, "did you get to be the majority's arbiter on this matter?"

"When I was assigned the job by my boss," he answered immediately.

"Who is, by your own admission, only one of over two hundred differing factions," sel Garian noted. "Your delegation consists of only six individuals. Are they representative of the rest of your world?"

"As humans, yes," Galway admitted. "Humanity is always looking for a way to better itself, and the technology aboard the *Galileo* would go a long way toward doing that. Again, when you put these few people up against the rest of the planet, the data becomes skewed, since each one of us is trying to come to some kind of unique understanding with you Shiravans. It might be of note to know that my boss is the leader of the most powerful nation on our world."

"A world that, by your own admission, he's unable to unite under one banner, and a world that will bicker and fight over each coveted point of order to get concessions they don't deserve. The Herald tells me," sel Garian stated, blatantly changing the subject, "that the knowledge aboard the *Dalgor Kreth* would be sequestered for decades before any of it got to the planet at large if taken by Earthbound humans. Is this true?"

"Well," Galway temporized, "we'd need to study it intensely before just starting to push buttons, which is exactly what the Alliance did. That's irresponsibility of the first order. Of course, military applications would be considered first. Protecting the source would be of paramount importance, and no knowledge of the find would be allowed outside of a small circle of scientists and military heads."

Galway was sure the old woman was scowling, although after all this time, he still wasn't quite sure which facial expressions meant what. "So, the find would be sequestered, wringing all possible military advantage from it before turning it over to civilian scientists?"

"Well, of course," Galway said vehemently. "First, we protect our country, then we advance our knowledge of the universe. Human history abounds with ideas and products that were first military applications that finally filtered down to the general populace."

"And history abounds with civilian applications that were used by various military organizations on our own world as well as yours. Just take the invention of dynamite, for example," the old woman retorted. "I sometimes think, from what Doma kep Parrasine and Dom do' Verlas have told me, that our races parallel each other in many ways. We started out first, but you are fast catching up." She sat silently for a moment, eyeing the human. "And that scares me. Besides, had the Alliance not gotten there first, there would probably *be* no human race."

Galway had no response to sel Garian's statement, so he only nodded his head once in recognition of the comment and waited for her to continue. "Tell me, Mister Galway, what do you think the Alliance will do with all its ships after this war is over? Do you fear they'll come back to Earth and take over? They certainly could." She smiled at the look of astonishment on his face. "As a matter of fact, if Shiravi should decide to back out of the fight now, you and the Korvils would bleed each other dry and we could take all the worlds of both races. Now, that seems the more opportunistic way to go."

Galway's mouth moved, but no words came out. It was virtually the same thing his bosses had come up with and the main reason they'd sent him on this mission at all—to gain at least a portion of the Shiravan's sympathy to Earth's side of the ledger. Finally, he was able to speak. "We would hope that that wouldn't be the end result," he said. "But in light of the fact that we really don't know the power, capabilities, or the intentions of Shiravans, we have no choice but to work under a worst-case scenario."

"Which is self-defeating," the old woman said. "That kind of thinking is what led to the War of Ascension, when women took the reins of power. Only recently have we begun to lift the restrictions placed upon our males. And if it weren't for the Korvils, we might not be lifting them even now. If you walk into a room expecting a fight, it's more likely that you'll find one than if you enter the room looking for ways *not* to fight."

Galway resisted the ideas the Shiravan was putting forth. "You should still be prepared for as many eventualities as you can. Letting your guard down can get you killed."

"I said nothing about letting your guard down," she replied. "Only that you not go looking for a fight." She let that sink in for a moment and added, "Fortunately, intelligent individuals know when enough is enough. We've tolerated Korvil depredations for so long that a movement to suppress expansion into space was growing almost daily. I'm taking care of that little problem with the *Cara Set* as we speak."

"And we have suffered at the hands of the Korvils as well, from the first attack on an Alliance space station to two surface impacts that killed over twenty million people and will continue to cause environmental problems for years to come," Galway asserted.

"So now you put yourself on the side of the Alliance," sel Garian said tartly. "You really must get yourselves under control. Look at our history if you wish to see one of the possible paths open to your present methods of governance." Her stress on the plural did not go unnoticed. "With a little less luck, there might be no Shiravan race to sit here now. It would seem, Mister Galway, that you really have no idea which side you're on."

As a chime sounded softly in the room, sel Garian started and said, "We'll have more time to talk on the way to Shiravi, Mister Galway. Right now, I have an appointment, and you must have much to discuss with your delegation."

Brandon walked back to his cabin bleakly, thinking, *Well, at least we get a vacation from the rat race. I'll just spin our losses as a woman-to-woman thing. We never stood a chance.*

Manura sel Garian sat and thought as she sipped a tangy

liquid from her wooden cup and wondered how much to reveal to these humans. Granted, they'd taken Shiravan technology back to the Polity that was much more advanced than when they'd found it, but she still felt that they were holding something back. Human ships seemed to take much less damage than Shiravan ships. The firepower difference was easily explained by the fact that the humans had totally reconfigured the inside of a battlecruiser to accommodate their shorter stature, giving them more room to install heavier weapons and more of them per vessel. This also gave a cruiser the power of a battleship that somehow managed to resist incoming impacts much more readily than Shiravan vessels. This was most certainly another incidence of humans bending applications of existing technology in different directions and one they hadn't deemed necessary to inform the Shiravans of.

In their place, I would certainly do the same, she thought. *It's never a good thing to put all of your assets on the table at the same time. I wonder who's really orchestrating the human's movements. A worthy adversary, indeed.*

Kitty spent her days learning the Shiravan language. She already knew what she wanted to say to the Matriarch, but she felt it would show respect if she could be at least semi-fluent before the interview. Rentec smiled when she told him of both her intentions and her dilemma. "Madam Herald," he said, radiating pure pleasure, "it would be my great pleasure to help you. I'd like to use a method your Dom Spencer taught me when he learned our language. It's called total immersion."

"I know what you mean, Rentec," Kitty said. "But

how about the basics in a human-to-Shiravan forum for a couple of weeks? Let me get the feel first. I really do apologize for not learning this earlier. I knew this meeting was going to happen sooner or later, but I honestly thought I had more time."

CHAPTER EIGHTEEN

Lucy Grimes wondered if she'd gone totally insane. How had Kitty maneuvered her into being the talking head for the Terran Alliance *again*?

That she'd once been one of them and now led them again seemed so incongruous that she sometimes needed to take more than one aspirin to get the headaches to go away. She closed her eyes and envisioned possible futures unfolding from the solidified past. Simon had once explained how he saw his visions. Now, she thought she could begin to see what it meant to have that kind of ability, knowing that a certain course of action could lead to many different futures, depending on how the first one was handled—chess on a cosmic scale. The thought scared her deeply.

One action could lead to many different conclusions, but not all the actions taken had originated with her, or even with humans, so the conclusions became foggy the further out she looked. Now with *two* alien races in the picture, how was she to tell which way led past the shoals? There were no lighthouses where she was going.

She wondered sometimes if she suffered from megalomania. What right did she have to undertake such a task? Everyone around her told her she was doing the right thing—her cabinet and the people chosen to advise her on matters she had no time to explore in detail herself. That was the key to a good command team, Simon had once told her. She was overjoyed, to say the least, to have Alliance headquarters moved to Vesta. It cut down on pesky reporters. She'd been surprised to find out that at least two different media outlets had already leased space on Vesta in anticipation of the official notification of the changing status of the Alliance.

All she could tell them was what her staff told her anyway—how many ships were ready for crews, how many volunteers were in what stages of readiness, the total number of ships that were now patrolling home space, how many had been assigned to the much more dangerous assignment of checking out the nearer stars, looking for a Korvil presence. Shows that promised realistic representations of the success of the first ships were already being promoted on Earth. Lucy wondered about the accuracy of the reports since she had no idea who would leak what information to the media.

After her third encounter with one of the few microphone-wielding reporters already stationed on Vesta, she decided on a daily press release, charging nothing for transmission of the release with an added commentary by the reporter.

Marsha Kane, recently decanted from her stay in the *Galileo's* med bay, watched as the delayed broadcast played over Alliance receivers. The Alliance had insisted on placing as many of Earth's satellites back in orbit as quickly as possible, a way to show that they cared about their world. Global positioning systems that guided everything from ships to airplanes to hunters and hikers needed to be brought back online, as well as numerous military satellites carried into orbit. At a time when Earth's space program was slowly failing precisely because of the existence of the Alliance, this showed most people the necessity of having the Alliance around. Many even championed their defense of the Earth in the numerous attacks, pointing out, and rightly so, that the death toll could have been much higher if more ships had gotten through or had more time to accurately aim their weapons. Even the astronauts aboard the International Space Station had been saved by the Alliance since Earth had no vehicles ready to launch after the Korvil attack that had savaged the now-redundant habitat. Its mass had gone into the *Galileo's* converter to help build parts for another battlecruiser.

The late-night radio host came on after the top-of-the-hour news. "Ladies and gentlemen, for reasons I am about to explain, things will be a little different tonight."

After a short pause, he said, "It was my privilege to get a reply from the Terran Alliance recently. I've wanted to interview one of them for a long time. So, in a rare moment of generosity, the Alliance has sent a captain of one of the ships currently in orbit to be on tonight's show."

He continued, "In a departure from our normal routine of having multiple guests on the phone, I've invited several people to my studio to form a small discussion group in which the Alliance captain will participate. I guess you could call it an inquisition.

"Tonight, we have with us Captain Louise Garcia of the Terran Alliance battlecruiser *Mira,* which happened to be the ship that saved the astronauts aboard the ISS. Also with us tonight is Dr. Martin Van de Veer from NASA, along with the president's science adviser, Mr. Joseph Blount. Representing Earth's corporate involvement with the Alliance is Mr. Aaron Lee of Virginia, and a regular guest, Mr. Richard C. Hoagland, one-time science adviser to Walter Cronkite. You can find him on the web at EnterpriseMission.com, a well-planned, well-laid-out website for those people who wish to keep abreast of any number of interesting anomalies concerning our planet, our solar system, and out into the vast universe beyond. We'll be asking him about that later in the show.

"Although this will be an extreme departure from our usual show, I'm sure the result will prove to be worth the effort. It was agreed beforehand that I'd act as moderator and have full authority to have anyone, even Captain Garcia, cut out of the loop if things get out of hand." After a few seconds, he said, "I'll start this off with a question of my own. Captain Garcia, how did you come to be the captain of a spaceship capable of devastating an entire planet if you so choose?"

The captain's voice came across steady and clear. "As most other people do. I applied for citizenship in the Alliance and was accepted for testing. I took a very intensive battery of tests, lasting almost a week on Vesta Base in the asteroid belt. That's where Alliance Headquarters and our major training facility are. I excelled in a variety of tests, leading me into the command structure, and after more training, I was awarded the rank of second lieutenant. As more ships became available, I was moved onto one to perfect my newly acquired skills. When a new ship came out of the docks, the person I was training to fill my spot on that first ship took over, and I, more experienced now and having been promoted to first lieutenant, took the position of navigator aboard the new ship. It was a combination of skill and the luck of being in the right place at the right time, and soon I was executive officer until I finally got my own ship, the *Mira.*"

"So which ships did you serve on before getting your own?"

"My first posting as second lieutenant and third shift watch officer was the *Arthur C. Clarke*." A catch could be heard in her voice. "After that, I served aboard the *Heinlein* for a short while, then the *Capella* as executive officer. I received my own ship about six months ago."

The NASA man spoke up. "Captain, if you please, how long will it be before Earth gets ships of their own?"

The captain hesitated before answering. "You're not going to like to hear this, especially those at home and any official of any government on this planet. Earth will get ships of her own when she comes of age and is deemed worthy to join the Alliance as full partners. Before anyone says anything, I mean that this planet will have to be reshaped into a single political unit. I point to the Shiravans, our valiant allies, from whom we acquired the first ship, the *Galileo*, and the Korvils as well. Both of them are unified spacefaring races. And they only became so after uniting under one set of rules and rulers. It requires the GDP of an entire planet to finance the basic infrastructure of a spacefaring race."

Richard C. Hoagland finally got a word in. "It has been known almost from the first that the Alliance wasn't responsible for the devastating attacks on Earth or the massive loss of life that ensued," the calm voice said, indelibly linking the images to the Alliance anyway. "At that stage, the Alliance was three deep-space construction docks, with a fourth under construction. In addition, they had nearly half a dozen warships at their disposal, complete with trained crews. Through data that has been released by the Alliance Office of Public

Information, we know that the attacks came as a total surprise, even though the Alliance upper command knew it was a possibility."

"Now, hold on just a minute," Captain Garcia said, interrupting Hoagland hotly. "The Alliance knew it was under a time limit almost from the first, but they expected the *owners* of the ship to show up and claim it, not to be attacked by a third race. As a matter of fact, it was thought by many that the Builders, as we originally called them and whom we now know to be the Shiravans, were not responsible for the attacks on Earth. Our sole thought was to get as much as possible of the technology duplicated before the rightful owners showed up and demanded their property back. It was also thought that the owners might not like having their property duplicated and essentially stolen, so the decision was made to begin production of warships modified to human scale. In the doing of that, it was found that there was a lot of free space since humans are so much shorter than Shiravans. There was room for more weaponry, more sensitive instruments, and larger missile loads. Another innovation was the use of miniaturization, integrated circuits and microchips, to enhance the power of the weapons and sensor suites. We seem to have a knack for taking an existing Shiravan machine and reworking it to perform at higher levels. Of course, that's because we as a race think a bit differently than the Shiravans do. They feel that if it works, don't mess with it—an old saying I've heard right here on Earth many a time. But humans are like a teenager with an old jalopy. We've just got to get the most out of each part of the machine."

"And from what we've learned," the NASA spokesman said, "that's exactly how the Korvils came onto the galactic stage, by taking technology that wasn't theirs. Can you blame the Shiravans for being fearful of us?"

"As a matter of fact, I can," the captain returned forcefully. "It's also assumed by the Shiravans that the Korvils got their ship by massacring an entire ship's crew after it landed peacefully on their world. But we took possession of what was essentially a deserted ship. There's an enormous difference there that needs to be shouted from the rooftops. If any Earth government had gotten ahold of it, they would have spent years studying it, but we were attacked just after having built our first space dock.

"Apparently the natural inclination of this third race, the Korvil, is to attack anything they perceive as weaker than they are. They were at just the right stage in their evolution to be able to recognize the fact that there was more to the universe than their one small planet. The problem was that their ego wouldn't let them accept anything less than total domination of what they considered their inferiors. Does that remind you of anything in the history of our own world?"

Not allowing the man to speak, Captain Garcia went on. "From the very earliest records, our scientists have found that humans are the highest form of life on this world because we have either killed off the stronger, independent predators by outwitting them or just plain annihilating them, along with more than a few innocent and harmless species along the way, to be sure, but what does one single species mean in the total scheme of things, right?" Sarcasm came easily on this particular topic.

"The problem is that we've come into contact with not one but two different examples of nature's rule governing survival of the fittest. One seeks to overwhelm and destroy us, and the other wants to enter into a partnership against that very threat."

"That's an interesting point, coming as it does from an Alliance representative," the host noted. "What are your opinions on the matter?"

The black-clad captain thought for a moment and answered, "I think we should trust the Korvils to continue as they've begun, and I don't think we should trust them any farther than we can throw one. I also think we should make an alliance with the Shiravans. Attacking the Korvils on two sides will split their forces and cost them more in the way of manpower and machinery than they can spare." There was a short pause, and then the captain added, "We hope."

The host tried to get a word in, but the captain rolled over him. "I, as well as most Alliance members, feel that the Shiravans, while an older race than ours, shouldn't be trusted completely yet, nor should they trust us either. Remember, all three races have an instinct toward racial survival, and we have no idea what will trigger the Shiravans into the same type of attacks the Korvils are making, if any. And the reverse must be true of you. Just how far can you trust us? So, we're making small steps in dealing with them. As we speak, the Herald is aboard a Shiravan vessel, complete with a three-ship human escort, to the Shiravan homeworld to negotiate a deal with their Matriarch on just exactly how we can coordinate our attacks to do the most damage. There are eighteen Shiravan ships in Earth's system right now, integrated with our own ships that are patrolling our outer reaches and making forays into some of the nearer star systems. So far, there have been two skirmishes. Three Alliance ships accompanied by two Shiravan vessels met and destroyed eleven Korvil battlecruisers in a system some thirty lightyears from here. The surprise was so complete that we lost only five Mambas in that fight. On the way home, they overtook inbound Korvil attack craft. At a cost of one destroyed cruiser and forty-five more Mambas and their pilots, we managed to destroy that bunch, too.

"I'd be extremely surprised if such a victory could occur again, though. We're about to get into a slugfest in which the winner will be the one with the greater advantages. We believe we hold the technological edge over both the Korvils and the Shiravans because we've bettered many of their systems and added a few innovations of our own."

"What's to keep the Shiravans from letting us take all the punishment and then finishing us off after we whip the Korvils?" Hoagland asked.

The captain chewed the inner side of her lower lip for a moment, a sign of indecision that, fortunately, couldn't be seen on a television. "That possibility has been put forward, and all I can say is that we won't let ourselves become so weak and distracted from fighting one foe that we will ignore another potential danger. But you must keep in mind that, so far, the Shiravans have shown no inclination to be anything other than completely aboveboard about all of their dealings."

"Ladies and gentlemen, you've just heard from Louise Garcia, Captain of the Alliance battlecruiser *Mira*. After the break, we'll try to get some calls in to the captain." The music rose, the host's voice faded out, and an announcer began to tout a new vitamin package.

"Well, that went better than I expected," Marsha said as she turned the receiver off and poured two drinks for herself and Lucy. "Still just drinking 7-Up, or have you gone back to stronger stuff?"

"Just the pop for me," Lucy answered, watching Marsha pour a bit of Seagram's into her own drink.

Marsha sat down after putting Lucy's drink in front of her and took a long pull on her own. Setting it back down with a grimace she said, "Something's wrong, either with the booze or the pop."

"That's odd," Lucy commented. "Kitty said much the same thing about beer after her stretch in the chamber. It's something to keep an eye on."

Then Marsha just stared at Lucy, and Lucy stared back. Finally, Lucy couldn't take the staring anymore. "What? Have I grown two heads or something?" she asked testily.

"No, Luce, it's not that," Marsha replied quickly. "I just see people staring at *me,* and I get all defensive. I mean, can I help it if that damned machine turned my hair white, too? It also got rid of several dozen scars and two tattoos in the process of healing me. I've had those tats for years, and they both meant something to me. How am I supposed to feel?"

"How about glad to be alive?" Lucy replied sarcastically.

"Well, of course I am," Marsha said hotly. "But I've had my ship reassigned to someone else and haven't been given another assignment yet. I also need to speak face to face with Simon as soon as possible."

"How about taking the next ship out of the yards? From the looks of things, Taurus Base is going to finish our first true battleship in a few weeks," Lucy said, looking over some statistics she brought up on her terminal. "Crew is going to be almost a thousand, with twenty Mambas, greater computer defense for incoming, better coordination on outgoing fire, stronger laser batteries, and larger missile magazines. And you'll have the first ship to come equipped with the new plasma bomb as a standard. That one is going to come as a real surprise to whoever you use it against. You're also going to have a transporter and both tractor and pressor beams—in short, just about all the innovations we've come up with in one ship."

Marsha gaped at Lucy. "I know Kitty put you in charge while she's gone, but isn't that a bit much for a captain who hasn't really proved herself? Shouldn't Shirley get this command instead of me?"

Lucy just smiled at Marsha. Back in the days before the *Galileo*, she and Marsha had been mere acquaintances on the same campus. They rarely appeared at the same parties, their one real intersecting interest being UFOs, or to be more specific, science fiction. Now, Lucy sat behind the Alliance Deputy Herald's desk and was giving instructions to Marsha, who'd been far and away the more popular of the two from the beginning. And now that she had white hair, she was even more striking, making Lucy feel like the ugly sister. "No, Marsha. Shirley has command of another ship. It's not my intention to move captains around any more than it was Kitty's. So, you'll get the next ship out of the yards. You're fit to command her. This three-week notice is so you'll have time to compile your command cadre. You have full access to all computer records concerning recruits and veterans who are currently unassigned. Fill out your command teams and submit them to Personnel for approval, which is just a formality in case someone you choose is slated for some other mission."

"What about the regular crew? Do I get any say in that?" Marsha didn't really expect to and wasn't surprised by the answer.

"No. What you'll get is the highest ranked newbies we can give you, sprinkled with some veterans in slots to ride herd on them until after your shakedown cruise. Now, for the bad news."

Marsha smiled grimly. "I've been looking all around this mess to find the hook in the bait, but I haven't seen it. You're about to set the hook, aren't you?"

"I'm not a fisherman, but if I read your meaning correctly," Lucy said, "then, yes, I'm about to set the hook." Marsha sat there, poker-faced, forcing Lucy to continue without any help. "Your shakedown cruise is going to consist of a patrol into a system we haven't checked out yet. You won't be flying solo, though. Yours will be the task force command ship, with two cruisers and one carrier under your command, as well as two Shiravan ships along for assistance, plus two cruisers under full cloak. One Shiravan has been equipped with the new shields, so that ship can be deployed at your command, giving you seven fighting ships. The other is to be held back as a courier. If anything goes wrong, it can be sent back here to report. We're going to start making forays deeper and deeper into Korvil space, carving out a section of our own. The Shiravans will be doing the same from the other side, but they don't have the shields, heavy-duty lasers, missiles or other innovations that will make the difference in a major battle. We do."

"I already understand that Korvil space is between us and Shiravan space, with the Korvils claiming the space we inhabit," Marsha said, looking at the holograph slowly rotating above Lucy's desk. "Won't the Shiravans be taking the brunt of the damage? I remember something about the Korvils being more suicidal or something. And with the Shiravan fleets not being equipped with our innovations, they're going to be walking into a meat grinder."

Lucy nodded at Marsha's analysis. "True, but that's what your shakedown cruise is for. As soon as you finish your first patrol, you and your task force will be assigned to Shiravan space, an eleven-month journey, to assist the Shiravans in combating the Korvils from their side of the line. If the Korvils start finding that they can't take out ships from either side of their territory, it will cause them plenty of second thoughts before they deliberately attack Shiravan shipping or colonization ships. Once we can send a few more ships their way, the pressure should ease off the Shiravans. Besides, they'll be busy upgrading their ships and missiles from the schematics we'll be providing, making it even harder for the Korvils to do any real harm to either of our races. Of course, we have no idea how the pressure will affect their high command, so we'll just play the cards we're dealt."

CHAPTER NINETEEN

Marcad Korvil sat on his throne in what was left of the Korvil Pit of Justice. Gaping holes let light in through level after level of what had once been his palace. The still undecapitated body of his late war-Minister lay off to one side, tossed aside like an old toy.

"Ruin seems to follow my every move since the arrival of the humanz." His predator's mind closed in on that one fact. Ever since the discovery of their system, the Gods seemed to have turned their backs on him. Two raids and two full-fledged attacks had been beaten back with nearly one-hundred-percent casualties. An entire clan had been destroyed root and branch by the humanz, who'd never before shown the audacity to launch a full-out assault on any Korvil world, not that they'd ever found any before now. Now there'd been an assault on homeworld itself, along with the shipyards on the two moons. Those were an almost total writeoff, reports told him, needing extensive repairs just to put a hull together.

He continued the litany of his worries. The main fueling port was in need of major repair. It had survived merely by being too far away from most of the larger targets around the inner system. And an entire strike patrol was overdue. Two hands and one had been dispatched to scout approaches to the humanz' homeworld, and no sign of their existence had been found.

And now this. He crumpled up the message delivered

by a comm clerk rather than decapitating him. He was, after all, only the bearer of the news, not the instigator. Korgan Garmon had that honor. Ruler of most of the plains clans and a number of coastal clans as well, Garmon carried considerable influence, as well as bankrolling his own fleet of ships. Normally, these ships were the Korvil's to assign, but with the loss of so many ships and crews, it seemed the Korvil mystique was about to have to withstand its first real Challenge in over three generations.

His head came up off his chest when he heard the sounds of a ship landing, something he never should have been able to hear from this spot. That would be Garmon's ship, bringing the plains Lord to the Challenge. Marcad welcomed the coming fight if only to have something to kill personally. Darmag had been no opponent. In the end, even his brilliant mind hadn't been able to withstand the might of his Lord's strong left hand.

Marcad heard boot heels moving his way authoritatively. Somewhere deep inside, a blood lust began to rise. No enemy Lord had ever set foot in the Korvil Pit of Justice, and he was about to have to defend his right to reign. Here, in front of ancestors going back so far that the names on the pillars had been worn smooth, he was going to have to defend his right to rule.

He heaved himself to his feet, left hand holding his immense sword as if it were a wooden practice weapon. The footsteps ceased as the maker stepped across the threshold onto the heated sands of the inner sanctum. Marcad's ears twitched every which way, listening for the betraying sound of feet sliding through the sand surrounding the Pit. He moved slowly from pillar to pillar, letting his senses reach out, searching for the faint sound of a foot compacting sand, an unwary breath, or the odor of the enemy—anything to tell him where his challenger was.

He didn't fear an ambush; that was not the way among the Korvils. Ambush was only for the lower lifeforms. His challenger would step into the light and announce himself, and Marcad would only save face if he was facing his opponent when he entered Korvil's Pit.

There. He'd caught a flicker of firelight off the silvery tips of Garmon's fur, who would enter the Pit between those two pillars. Marcad faced the open space between the pillars, his sword tip in the sand and his hands draped loosely on top of the hilt. *Come, Garmon. Step into my Pit.*

By now the Pit was surrounded by guards from the 'retinues of both Lords, witnesses to the eventual outcome of what was going to be a death match, determining the future course of three different races.

Garmon stepped into the light provided by the flickering torches and sunlight. "Such a gloomy Pit, Korvil. Soon, our Supreme Pit will move to the central plains. It is much more to my taste than this krador." The word evoked thoughts of stinking, slimy sewers, infested by light-hating vermin.

"On what grounds do you bring this Challenge?" Marcad asked for himself. His war-Minister, who would usually ask the question, way lying dead, unable to perform his duty.

"Treason is the charge," Garmon replied. "Almost half of the ships lost in this past farat have been ships paid for by Garmon coffers. Kravar was oath-bound to Garmon, and now they and all their ships are no more. What have you done to avenge their losses?" Garmon roared as his rage increased.

Marcad let his opponent work himself into a frenzy,

subliminally aware of the fact that an angry opponent was one apt to make mistakes. Holding his own temper in check, Marcad replied, "Where were Garmon's ships if they were in league with Kravar? Only Kravar ships were lost at Kravarine. So say the reports."

"Reports," Garmon snorted. "Just words some lackey put together to impress you. The war against the Shiravans is not going well, and if you don't realize it, then the least of the charges against you is incompetence. The Shiravans, and now these humanz, are pushing us on both borders, and you sit and do nothing. I say treason against your own race is the charge."

Treason. Incompetence. Either charge to Garmon's face was a declaration that one of the two would not leave the chamber alive. Marcad studied his opponent. Younger by some twenty farat, the silver tipping his fur was an attribute of the Garmon clan. Scars didn't exist where scars should if this upstart really wanted to win. Experience was a hard taskmaster, and Marcad had been a more than apt pupil. More Challenges had he faced than this not-so-youngling had years.

Marcad watched Garmon draw his sword—almost but not quite a duplicate of his own—in a two-handed grip that no first-farat Korvil would use for fear of having his ears shredded for stupidity. Garmon's sword was a bit lighter and shorter than Marcad's, but Garmon's longer reach offset the difference in length. The one thing Marcad had as an advantage was his sword's weight, almost a third again heavier than his opponent's.

Fearlessly, contemptuously, Marcad moved toward his adversary. A loss now would end the Korvil line forever, and that was something the Gods must not allow. *From the ashes of both enemies, I will fashion an empire like never before.* He shrugged out of his bloody vest, standing as the Gods had made him, and waited.

Garmon slipped out of his own vest and stood, sword forward, at the edge of the Pit. Here, in the shadows, he was about to bring his race out of the dark ages and onto the interstellar scene with Honor. For almost fifteen farats, he had planned this moment, waiting for a chance to Challenge the Korvil. Even now, the taste in his mouth was bitter, just like the day his father's father had stood in this same place... and lost.

His eyes took in the blood-soaked fur of his opponent. "You are injured. This will not be a match of equals. I grant you time to be looked after and rest before we fight. I will not have my victory tainted by the fact that you are already disabled."

He'd known, even before he made the offer, what the response would be. He'd do no less were the situation reversed.

Marcad could not believe his ears! This upstart offering him grace in his own palace was an insult that could not be ignored. "Scratches only, whelp. Do not let that be an excuse to back out now. The Challenge has been made. In front of witnesses, I declare myself fit for combat and waive any rest. Let us begin. My father's father killed your father's father on these very sands, and you will die here as well. Korvil forever!"

Suddenly, he saw the trap he'd almost allowed himself to be led into. Of course, Garmon would try to make him angry, just as he was trying to do in reverse, but there would be no quarter. He'd lay this whelp's skull beside his father's father at the foot of the pillar that would one day hold his own mortal remains. Or not. The Gods will be done, he thought. He moved to cut Garmon off from the center of the Pit because control of the center was the most common way of winning a fight like this. All one had to do was defend until one's opponent made a mistake.

The first flurry of blows startled Marcad. This was no unblooded warrior he faced. A feeling came over him, and he focused onto the moment. He watched the way his opponent's shoulder dipped as he attacked or defended. Time was measured by the space between sword strokes. His superior strength didn't seem to be pressing his enemy back as intended. Instead, he held his ground, weathering each onslaught made by Marcad.

After a short time, the sword in Marcad's hand began to weigh more and more. At some point, he noticed that he'd been scratched on his off shoulder, but when that had happened eluded him. He stopped his attack, studying his foe while trying to find a weak spot in his defenses, but Garmon wouldn't let him be. Each time he stopped, Garmon would make a move of his own, giving Marcad no time to rest. The cuts and blood loss he'd sustained when his ship was blown up began to take their toll.

Garmon had plotted for farats for this moment. He would have manufactured an excuse to fight if he'd had to, but this disaster with the humanz had given him a truly legitimate reason to claim Challenge. Even if his father didn't need to be avenged, he would have had to Challenge for the sake of the race. Two advanced races against their one didn't seem like good odds to the wily hunter. For the sake of the race, he had to make a dangerous move.

Garmon knew that he was no match for the Korvil in a conventional Challenge match, so he had prepared. He'd studied records that hadn't seen sunlight in generations. There was an understood rule that required the opponents to carry only swords, but in a crumbling ledger he found a description of a fight wherein the opponents carried shields on their off-side arms. Sometimes two feet across, these were defensive weapons and perfectly legal under today's codes... maybe.

Now, the Korvil staggered slightly, and Garmon reached his left arm back into the darkness, a prearranged signal for one of his retinue to step forward, still hidden by the shadows. Hadn't the Korvil wondered why he hadn't even tried to gain control of the center of the arena, the best position to defend against an attacker? He felt the first two leather shield straps slide up his arm and he grabbed hold of the third, bolted to the far side of the two-foot round, steel-edged shield, and swung it around in time to block a blow that should have crippled him, at the very least. Left side numb from the blow, he still held the shield high, thrusting around the edge or over the top as conditions dictated. Slowly, the numbness began to subside, and he started using the shield to deflect the Korvil's sword away from his body, leaving openings to exploit. He finally managed to land a serious blow to the Korvil's sword arm.

Marcad felt his opponent's' steel slice through muscles and tendons. His arm dropped to his side, and he barely managed to shift the sword to his right hand before blood made the grip slippery. The fire that burned through his arm told him that he would probably never use it again.

Shields had been out of style for several generations, their banishment the legacy of an emperor who felt them to be too much of a hindrance in battle. Marcad had never fought an opponent who used one, but he quickly spotted one of the weaknesses. To parry one of his blows, Garmon would either have to use his shield to block, trying to counter around his shield—not the best position for a swordsman—or use his sword, hopefully allowing Marcad a chance to get in a killing blow.

The evaluation of his predicament took much less time to assess than to describe, and almost as soon as his right hand held the sword, he swung it in a mighty arc just two feet off the floor. Garmon saw the stroke coming and managed to jump over the swing, causing it to get caught on the bottom of his krath-hide boots instead of the backs of his legs. A real connection would have disabled him. Instead, the blow did nothing more than cause him to lose his balance and fall on the sand. His secret weapon would do him no good.

Landing on his back in the hot, packed sand, Garmon saw the killing blow coming. Marcad had battered at the shield a number of times, and it hung in tatters from the straps on his left arm. This was the time for the Korvil to kill him, and he had switched hands, bringing the sword down one-handed to finish him off.

Parrying the blow with his sword would throw the Korvil off balance, leaving his entire front exposed. Normally, this would be a time for both contestants to retire and refresh before continuing, but Garmon sensed that this would not be the case here. In a desperate move, he slashed across the Korvil's unprotected torso with the finely-honed steel edge of his crumbling shield. Hot blood sprayed him from neck to crotch, and he looked up in amazement as the Korvil, surprise on his face, staggered back. He dropped his sword and slowly fell to his knees in the hot sand.

Garmon stood up, hardly believing his luck. But he couldn't shirk his duty now. He staggered to his feet, lifting the sword that seemed so heavy now, and looked down at his opponent. After a lifetime, he heard the Korvil speak, softly, as if he were unable to speak louder. "Finish it now and be done with it."

Garmon raised his other hand to the sword's hilt, preparing for the blow, his eyesight focused on the Korvil's neck. As the sword came down in a smooth arc, he realized that in this instant he had become *the* Garmon. Leaning over to pick up the severed head of the Korvil, he bit back a groan. It would be unseemly for a warrior to complain about a few cuts and bruises.

He dropped the sword where he stood, switched the head to his other hand, and let the shield fall to the ground as well, walking out of the Pit. As he slowly marched through the corridors of the Korvil's razed palace, each warrior in Korvil livery knelt to the new Lord of the Garmon. Those who didn't were immediately slain by members of Garmon's retinue, laser pistols sounding unaccustomedly inside the crumbling walls of the palace.

He stepped out of the darkened interior onto a raised porch and blinked at the bright light of day. So short a time had actually passed that he was surprised to see the sun still so high in the sky. His gaze returned to earth and the sea of faces before him, all but a few in Korvil livery.

Now was the time to find out if all his planning, plotting and waiting would pay off. He held aloft the severed head of the Korvil and waited. Slowly at first, then in expanding waves, all the beings before him knelt on one knee, acknowledging him as the new Lord of the race. "We are no longer Korvils," he roared. "From this time on we are Garmons, and we will take back what is ours—our pride, our glory, our Honor. Garmons forever!"

His last two words beat back at him as he slowly walked to his shuttle. Even through the closed hatch, he could still hear the chant, and it wasn't until the engines fired up that the noise was blocked out. He handed the trophy to one of his men. "Mount this and send out the appropriate messages and warnings. Also, send out an order for all clan leaders to attend me at my palace as soon as possible. A way must be found to end this war in our lifetimes."

Marsha Kane submitted her command lists to Lucy, surprised to find that of the thirty names she'd requested, only three had been turned down. She'd planned on that eventuality and handed over another list. "Pick any three off that list and I'll be happy," she said.

Lucy looked at Marsha oddly but didn't say anything as she pulled the list toward her and looked it over. Picking up a pen, she put small, neat checkmarks beside three names and slid it back to Marsha. "So, what are you going to do now?" she finally asked.

Marsha picked up the list without looking at it, folded it, and slid it into her pocket. "The first thing I'm going to do is get a suite, take a long, hot soak, and get some sleep. Tomorrow, I'll notify Personnel and let them contact all the appropriate people. Then I'm going to hitch a ride to the *Taurus*. You said she'll be ready in about three weeks. I sent a query to the *Taurus* and found out that power, light, and heat are available on all levels, which means I'll have almost three weeks' head start with my command team. Remember Simon's rule about command—keep your head and stay at least one step ahead of your officers and crew."

"Simon," Lucy said flatly.

"What?" Marsha asked. "Are you having trouble with Simon?"

Lucy shook her head. "No trouble. It's not that." She sat silently, marshaling her thoughts. "He takes orders well, but I wind up feeling like he's pulling the strings somehow." She shook her head. "It's only a feeling. Like he gave in too easily when Kitty announced that she was going to Shiravi, at least in public. And you know, Simon isn't afraid to make a scene. They've been so close in all of this, in spirit if not always in body, that it's hard to see him letting her go without him." She looked Marsha in the eyes. "Sometimes, I have to wonder if I'm being used."

Marsha waved her hand, pushing the thought aside. "That's just Simon," she said. "He always said that all he really wanted was to be a ship's captain."

Lucy looked thoughtfully at a spot on her desk, eyes unfocused for a moment. "That's not all of it, but you've just added another piece to the puzzle. He submitted a request, through channels mind you, to have this new battleship as his flagship. I told him 'no,' and he took it. He just said he'd renew his request when the next one comes online."

Marsha looked at Lucy like she had two heads. "He just took it?" she asked incredulously. "I've only heard him back down from Kitty… wait a minute. Did Kitty give you a handle on him?"

"No," Lucy answered hotly. "And I resent the thought that I would stoop to blackmail to get anything done."

This last came out with a crooked smile on her face.

"This coming from the woman who threatened to drop an asteroid on an NSA agent's house?" Marsha asked, smiling.

Lucy looked sheepishly at the surface of her desk. "Okay, so I'm guilty of holding a double standard, but I'm not going to let Simon get out of hand. And I'm going to have to do that without any help from Kitty. And, yes, I'm going to blackmail him, too. Either he stays in line, or I quit. He won't like having to split his responsibilities between the fleet and governmental matters. He really hates the spotlight, and I'm going to use it against him. He also said that information was power, and he's in a position to know about all that goes on in the fleet *and* the governmental side. That's a lot of information—and a lot of power. I'm not even sure I know all that's going on in the fleet right now. That gives him more power than I have, if you think like him."

"God forbid," Marsha said fervently.

"On the contrary," Lucy said. "If I know he's using me without him finding out that I know, then I have a chance to stay that one step ahead of him."

"Sounds childish to me," Marsha said.

"Or politics." Lucy said the word as if it hurt her mouth. "That's all this job is. I can see why Simon doesn't want it back, and it's the one stick I've got to beat him over the head with, so I'll use it."

"You don't want to make an enemy of Simon, Luce," Marsha warned. "I have a feeling there's a lot more to him than we know about. It's like he hasn't told us yet what his full idea is, you know?"

"That's what I was just saying," Lucy returned. "He keeps saying he didn't get caught on purpose, but I still got stuck with the job, went nuts doing it, and here I am again, all because of his precious 'chain of command.' And Kitty asking me to, of course," she added weakly.

Worry was a weakness, and Simon wasn't about to show any in public. Certain friends he could relax with and talk about how he felt about his wife getting farther away every second. She had that effect on him, making him feel like the protector. He knew in his mind that she was in no more danger than he was—less actually, but his heart ached with the loss, almost as if a part of him had been cut out.

Otherwise, he kept his emotions under tight rein as he worked on getting the fleet ready to take on unknown forces in unknown places and unknown numbers. He interpreted his orders to mean that he should begin to build a buffer zone around Earth, carving out a section of the galaxy from a race that had been an interstellar player for at least two hundred and fifty years.

There was no doubt that these Korvils were bent on either killing or enslaving the human race. Korvil comm chatter had been recorded and decoded after the Shiravan translation program was installed in a computer built and maintained for that one purpose. Demands were never sent to the victims, only orders given to ship commanders and confirmations sent in reply. There'd been no attempt at communication or negotiation.

Okay, so be it, Simon thought. *We may be new on the scene, but we bring new ideas with us.*

CHAPTER TWENTY

The interminable journey was nearing its end, and Kitty couldn't have been happier. She finally went up into what was called the Witches Den, the clear dome on top of all large vessels. The swirling colors made her think of an aurora gone wild, but the story that ran through the Shiravan crew was that to look upon the Spirits was to go mad. Well, if these swirling colors were the Spirits of Space everyone kept referring to, she didn't think they'd make her go insane.

She spent several hours alone in the dome, letting the movement of the colors bring her into a trancelike state. This was the same state Simon used when he wanted to calculate the odds, as he would say. Once there, after great effort, she let her mind roam free. Things she'd seen and heard mingled with the ever clearer impressions she'd received as her command of the Shiravan language increased. She stood up and walked over to the crystal-clear wall separating her from the void beyond, wanting to get a closer look at some of the images her mind had wrought, but nothing came clear. She turned to leave and was startled by the sight of her own body still sitting cross-legged in the middle of the Den.

I'm having a literal out-of-body experience, she thought. *How the hell am I supposed to get back?*

She walked over to and around her body, wondering. *Does Simon go through this? He's never said anything about it.* She finally sat down in her body, making sure that both were correctly aligned as her mind continued to think through all the possibilities.

Basically, the Shiravans were a good people, she'd learned over the two years the First Fleet had been in Earth space. Now and then, there was a bad apple in the barrel, but that was the way it was when so many different personalities spent too much time too close together. The problem wasn't usually this noticeable, she was given to understand, because extremely long contra-space excursions were relatively rare, except for the Exploration Corps, a group of misfits dedicated to extending the Shiravan frontier under the Matriarch's mandate.

Kitty let her mind ponder the question of contact with the Shiravans. Certainly, Earth, or at least the Alliance, was now up to par and then some, technologically if not numerically, but what of economics, politics, and *religion*, for Christ's sake! She recognized her blasphemy and offered a silent prayer of forgiveness, just in case.

Back on track, she continued looking ahead, much like Simon had shown her, letting her mind wander down each path it found. Some led to closer ties, some to more dire consequences. After a time, she came to the conclusion that the Shiravans would probably opt for a more distant relationship, owing mostly to the fact that they would someday have to deal with a male ruler, something that was still a long way off.

She laughed quietly at the reversal of fortune between the genders of the two races. Then, an unsettling thought rose to the top of her mind. In both cases—one led by females and one primarily by males—neither worked as well as the leaders would like.

Expansionists versus Isolationists. Republicans versus Democrats. Young versus old. Good versus evil. Male versus female. On her own world, matriarchies, patriarchies, monarchies, theocracies, and almost every other form of government had been tried.

So far, democracy seemed to be the top dog, and more countries had begun to institute reforms in that direction. The idea that most of the people would be right most of the time was an appealing one, but it just felt wrong somehow, as wrong as one man deciding for millions. Still, one worked with what one had.

Granted, this newer, updated version was only a little over two hundred years old, and so far, the world hadn't come to an end, although there'd been several close calls in the mid-twentieth century. Now, in the opening years of the twenty-first, racial genocide had raised its head again under the guise of terrorism and antiterrorism.

She let her mind wander down darker paths with severe reservations. The Korvils were there on more than one path. On some, they overpowered all opposition, though just barely, and humanity and the Shiravans had become a part of the past. Other paths changed from dark to light with the eradication or control of the Korvils. One path she followed even gave a hint at a way to let the Korvils survive an interstellar genocidal war. The problem was that at the same time as the threat from the Korvils was ending, the path turned dark again. The one problem remaining was to see the end of that particular path. But the variables became too many for her mind to encompass. She'd definitely have to come back up here and look again after some of what she'd seen either came to pass or didn't.

Kitty's eyes finally refocused, and for a moment, she wondered where she was. Eventually, the design inlay on the floor and the swirling mists told her, and all her memories came flooding back. She stood up slowly. Her cross-legged position had numbed her lower extremities, and it took a minute for the tingling to stop. She felt as if taking a step too soon would bring her back in contact with the floor.

She finally felt fit to walk, so she moved to the stairwell, taking in the sight of the glowing, swirling mists one final time. She tromped down the stairs slowly, thinking about her experience. *I could have achieved the same results just chanting* nam-myo-ho-renge-kyo, she thought. *But I can see its appeal to people who've been experiencing the phenomenon for generations.*

Each downward step brought her body under better control. By the time she reached the door, all her aches were either gone or hidden well enough that no one would know, and she chalked it up to still not being completely comfortable in the lower gravity. She hadn't slept well since the convoy had reached mid-point in their journey. Effectively, they were in the middle of Korvil territory, but not even the Shiravans had figured out how to locate or talk to another ship in hyperspace.

She opened the door and was startled to see a Shiravan officer standing beside the door. "Se el kuvai," she said almost automatically, noticing another Shiravan hurrying away. Almost eleven months of total immersion in the Shiravan language had made the, "'I'm sorry,'" come out almost flawlessly. Heaven knew, she'd had enough chances to use it. "Have you been waiting long?"

"I have been waiting here four hours, Domagera Herald," the officer said.

Kitty stared at her in disbelief. "If you'd wanted to enter," she waved her hand at the stairs, unable to let the words "Witches Den" pass her lips, "you could have come in at any time."

The officer stood up straighter. "It is never wise to interrupt someone in communion with the Spirits. Besides, I was given the duty of asking you to visit the private quarters of Policy Minister sel Garian at your earliest convenience but not to disturb you. If you wish to go to your quarters first, I'll report to the Minister that you'll arrive shortly."

Kitty said, "I wasn't in communion with... Oh, never mind. I guess now would be as good a time as any. You say you've been waiting for four hours?"

The officer nodded. "Aya, Domagera Herald," she said as she led them off into the bowels of the ship.

Kitty shook her head. "My God," she said in English. In Shiravan she continued, "You still should have come in. To keep the Minister waiting that long..." Suddenly, she couldn't finish the sentence.

Over her shoulder, the officer said, "When it was learned that you were with the Spirits, it was Minister sel Garian herself who said you shouldn't be disturbed. I was assigned the duty of seeing that you weren't disturbed and giving you the message. Your staff has been informed of your location and are even now being informed of your return to the ship," Kitty winced at the turn of phrase, as well as the Minister's request for a personal meeting.

Kitty still felt somewhat ill at ease in the dimly lit, high-ceilinged rooms and corridors of the Shiravan battlecruiser, but she had learned to suppress the feeling after so long. The officer stopped at a door, let her palm be read by a screen mounted beside it, and then pressed a button. The door slid open immediately, telling Kitty that this was no low-ranking officer to have such access to sel Garian's private quarters. She stood aside and motioned Kitty forward. "You are expected, Domagera Herald."

For a fraction of a second, Kitty wondered at the advisability of visiting sel Garian's quarters without making sure that at least one member of her staff knew her whereabouts, but she steeled herself and walked into the room. It wouldn't do to let the Shiravan second in command think the Alliance Herald was afraid. After all, she'd been aboard for almost eleven months now. If the old woman wanted her dead, she could have done away with the entire delegation and no one would be the wiser.

The door slid shut behind her, and she looked around the room. A desk, unoccupied, sat against the far wall, and two chairs sat opposing each other, separated by a table that looked odd somehow until she realized that it had been lowered a bit—not to an entirely comfortable level for humans but shorter than the Shiravan average. She also noticed the human-style chair sitting at the table and, seeing no one else in the room, walked over and sat down. There was no telling how long she was going to have to wait.

The wait turned out to be only a matter of minutes. A door slid open and sel Garian walked into the room. Kitty stood up. "Minister sel Garian," she said. "I regret that I did not get your message sooner."

The old woman motioned Kitty to sit back down and stopped at a side table, picking up a small tray bearing a decanter and two wooden cups. Kitty was familiar with the kemwood cups, having a set of her own, a present from the Matriarch. "Do not concern yourself with such things, Domagera Hawke," she said. "When one is conversing with the Spirits, one is not to be disturbed. Of course, the kemwood protects you from poisons and such," the old woman said, changing the subject, "but I'd like to get a human's response to our fire wine."

She set the tray down between them and poured a pale blue liquid into the two cups. "We'll reach Shiravan space in two more days," the Minister said. She sat down and seemed to actually diminish in stature, almost to Kitty's diminutive size. She slid the tray minutely toward Kitty, each cup equidistant from her guest, inviting her to choose whichever cup she wanted—a sign, she'd learned, that the host was well-disposed toward the visitor.

I'm glad she doesn't hate me, Kitty thought. She picked up a cup at random—the right one because she was right-handed—and waited for her companion to pick up the other.

The old woman held her cup and looked into its depths. After a time, she said, "It would appear that exposure to the Spirits does not affect humans as it does some Shiravans."

Kitty stalled, not knowing what sel Garian was looking for. During their many talks, which had never been held in her private quarters before and never occurred without the knowledge of at least one other human, Kitty hadn't known how to react to the woman. Her charisma, for lack of a better word, always seemed to throw Kitty off. "You base this on one human's response to the phenomenon?" Kitty asked, looking into her own cup as well.

The Minister inclined her head toward her right shoulder slightly, "No, Domagera, not just one human's response. Several of your party have been into the Den during our voyage, but none stayed more than a few minutes, until you. Even though the others showed no signs of madness, they all said they felt uneasy or ill at ease. You spent four hours and walked out as if you hadn't even been there." Her voice had a tone Kitty had come to recognize as accusatory.

"Simon taught me quite a bit about meditation," she answered. *Four hours? It only seemed like one.* The words she used came out as inner soul searching. "I actually found the experience a bit disagreeable at first, but when I begin to look inside myself, the outer world just seemed to fade away."

sel Garian looked at Kitty as a toad might look at a fly before dining. "We have a sect, as you know, called the kath-mora. They claim to converse with the Spirits when in the Den. Did you converse with them as well?"

Kitty looked confused. "I don't believe so. What I do is more of an introspective phenomenon. While I'm looking inward, I can see some of the futures that are possible if certain actions are taken." The older woman showed an expression Kitty had come to translate in her own mind as surprise. "It's similar to a chess game," she said, by way of explanation, having taught the Shiravan Second Voice the game during their long voyage. "My problem is that I can only see so far ahead, and then things get muddied by all the variables."

"Explain further, if you please."

Kitty was surprised at the request. Seldom did the old woman ask for clarification on anything these days. She automatically took a sip from the cup and froze as the fiery liquid rolled down her throat. She felt it hit her stomach and flow from there through her entire body in a matter of seconds. At first, she wondered if the cups were really kemwood but then decided that if sel Garian had wanted her dead, she'd surely have done it before they were just two days from their destination. She embraced the sensations and found them agreeable. "I approve of this," she said, nodding to sel Garian. Her nod brought her eyes back to the cup in her hand. Under oath, Kitty wouldn't have said that the liquid actually glowed, but it sure seemed to when she took a second sip.

"We call what Simon and I do 'meditation.' It allows us to process information we wouldn't normally think of as related—actual experiences, mixed with the emotions of the moment, and our instinctive reactions to them, as well as unconscious conclusions we reach because of them. It starts out with one simple action—let's say my travel to Shiravi. There are an almost infinite number of reactions to that back home among my own people and yours, as well. So, I'm already starting out with three variables. Add to that the length of time I'll be gone, almost two years, and anything could happen. Most of those anythings are extremely remote, so I discard them and all their off-shoots, and concentrate on the fewer, more realistic possibilities.

"My trip to your world could be the best thing to happen to both our races, either one of them, or neither. Again, it's like chess. One makes moves and countermoves in hopes of achieving eventual victory over one's opponent. Only in this case, Shiravans are not supposed to be opponents but allies. Still, everyone has their own ulterior motives or agendas, and political maneuvering and positioning will undoubtedly take place."

sel Garian nodded slowly. *No novice, this one*, she thought. "So, did you focus on human/Shiravan relationships?"

Kitty nodded slowly as well. "I see our two races being more like distant friends. We'll do some trading, mostly of ideas, but some tangible things, like these cups and perhaps the gava stone, would be rare attractions on Earth. It's the thought of having to deal with a possible male leader sometime in the future that will be the main stumbling block for most Shiravans. You have for too long, by my estimate, been stratified into a matriarchy, that is, a society ruled by females. We, on the other hand, recognize the inherent need to balance the two genders. Male cannot exist without female, and female cannot exist without male, no matter how hard someone tries. Sometime in our future, a male will lead the Alliance if for no other reason than he is more capable than any woman at the moment.

"That, of course, is determined by more than just aptitude. Luck plays a part in things, as well. So, I see us being distant friends after we decide how to deal with the problem of the Korvils."

sel Garian nodded. "I don't have your connections to the Spirits, Domagera, but I've come to the same conclusions. Perhaps the Matriarch herself will have some impact on your impressions after you meet her."

Kitty shook her head. "I don't have any connection to your Spirits, Minister sel Garian." Her protest was heated. "I have my own supreme power to whom I ascribe. Perhaps theologians from both our races could meet to trade ideas and see if we share a common theology. You seem to have more than one supreme being. We have but one, if you subscribe to the beliefs of most of humanity. We're still divided on just what to call that higher power or who has the right of it. And some even believe that our entire race is a series of cosmic accidents, but both groups point at your race and claim victory for their own point of view."

Kitty stopped speaking as if she'd been struck dumb. "No wonder you think we're barbarians," she said, almost in a whisper. "There's nothing unified about us, nothing rational that you can depend upon."

sel Garian smiled for the first time Kitty could remember. "Maybe our two races have more in common than you think," the Minister said with a hint of amusement on her lips. Kitty's raised eyebrow didn't go unnoticed. "It's common for allies to not trust each other," the older woman lectured to the younger. "Our history is, I think, longer than yours. It also isn't common for potential foes to give away valuable information. But I will tell you this—I have a much deeper insight, I think, to the human psyche than you do of ours. We are much alike, our two races. We are individualists banded together for the common good, finding it a workable enough arrangement that we continue it, but we're volatile enough to bicker and fight for what we believe in, whatever that happens to be at the moment.

"And we aren't above taking on allies of the moment, turning on or being turned on by those allies when whatever perceived threat is defeated. But I digress," she said. "I've been a student of our ancient history for most of my life. That is, perhaps, how I came to be where I am today. Tell me," she said changing the subject, "what you think this influx of advanced technology will do to your world?"

Caught off balance by the question, Kitty hesitated. "Many will lose their livelihoods as old industries collapse with the advent of new ideas. Most will be able to adapt, but some won't be able to accept the new reality. Within one hundred of our years, there won't be any human who doesn't benefit from the knowledge we've already gained from you. We've already demonstrated that we're pretty handy at adapting your technology to new purposes. With those two thoughts in mind, I believe that as we spread, our two races will clash unless we find a way to come to some accord beforehand. But I would expect this is a conversation I should be having with your Matriarch rather than you, Doma sel Garian." Kitty found she didn't like the direction the questioning was heading.

"I only ask now because the Matriarch will ask my opinion as Second Voice before she meets with you. I'm certain she'll want to speak with Dom do' Verlas beforehand as well," sel Garian answered. "Would not your people do the same if they were in our position?"

Kitty agreed somewhat reluctantly that the Minister was probably right. "So, what will you tell her to do after all of our conversations and exposure to each other all this time?"

sel Garian sipped from her cup, waited a few seconds for the feeling of well-being to suffuse her body and said, "I'm not yet certain. I can see much to admire in your race—your forthrightness about your violent past being one thing. We had our own share of it ourselves." Kitty wondered if the kemwood could completely offset the intoxicating effect of the fire wine. She'd never heard sel Garian speak so frankly. And she'd never felt so comfortable in the old woman's presence. "The problem is that, like the Korvils, you are still too close to your wild roots. You haven't yet learned, as a race, to work together toward a common goal."

Kitty recognized the argument. It was one that had come up repeatedly in late-night bull sessions. Her response was the same now as it had been in each of those session. "I don't claim to speak for the majority of humanity, only for those who've followed my mate and myself into this endeavor. That's a truly small portion of our population, but it's my supposition that most of the common folk of our world would welcome a chance to explore the universe. Our only limitation is how fast we can turn out ships. Getting crews isn't a problem. Most of our last two generations have grown up with the idea that our manifest destiny lies somewhere beyond Earth. Our archaeologists have determined that a strike by an asteroid changed life on our world some sixty-five million turns ago, wiping out species that had existed for hundreds of millions of years. This cataclysm led to the eventual rise of what we have come to call human beings, the pinnacle of evolution on our world."

Kitty recognized the sarcasm in her own voice. "I find it extremely prideful to think that the universe would never do such a thing to our world again, and that's why I support our move into space. This way, no single cosmic accident will spell the end of the race. Isn't that why you've colonized fourteen worlds yourselves, in the final analysis?"

sel Garian smiled again. "You learn quickly and well, for such a young race. 'Knowledge is power,' is a saying that dates so far back into our prehistory that its origins are totally lost to us. So. You have successfully ascertained more about us than we have suspected."

Kitty nodded. "We have exactly the same saying in virtually every language on our planet. And that is another count against us, isn't it? Our lack of a unified leadership. But let me suggest to you that you look ahead that same hundred years. Many will join us openly, certainly, and many will support us, either openly or clandestinely, but those who will oppose us are the very ones who wield the power in their various little nations. In effect, we still have a very small group of people who make policy for the rest of the world.

"We have what we call superpowers. Those are nations that have the military and political strength to impose their will on other, smaller nations under the guise of alliances. There are really only three of those, but they have diametrically opposed ideas about how the world should be led. Russia and China are two of those powers. Russia is going through severe internal upheavals as they struggle to move from one economic system to another, but their problem is that too many of the old guard still exist and resent the loss of status for their nation and themselves. The United States, where most Alliance recruits come from, is what we call a democratic republic. That means that the people vote for the ones who will represent them in government, hoping that their interests coincide with the common man's. Each nation has one or more people who make policy for that particular nation. Sometimes their interests mesh; sometimes they clash. A one-world government would eliminate that and so much more..."

Kitty smiled slightly at the thought of the whole world cooperating. "One of the things we have discussed is the fact that if we wield too much influence, the nations of the world will band together to oppose us. If we can keep them aligned against us long enough, then that one-world government is going to become a reality. But as long as they stay fractured, there's no chance at all. Our eventual goal is to become the big, bad enemy that Earth has to band together to oppose."

She waved her hand negligently. "Of course, openly, the governments of our world will appear to accept us. They'll have to at first. Public opinion will force it that way—and has, I might add. We have the embassies where we accept new citizens, bringing the newest volunteers out to our ships. That's for public consumption. There were clashes between our people and members of various governments, early on, but we made one particular group back down with no losses on our side and few, if any, on theirs. We set out to make a point—that we had the power to do whatever we wanted anyway, so why not work with us for now, at least, and see where things go? Then, we can sit back and watch as our world governments coalesce into one. It is already happening, to a small extent. Nations are grouping together for economic reasons, military reasons, and ideological reasons until there are really only the three major groups to contend with. Sooner or later, the smaller nations will have to align themselves with one of the big three, further consolidating the world.

"As we siphon off the best minds to our side, the balance will shift, and we'll become less welcome on Earth for a time. But we even have that covered, I think. Enough money has come under our control from selling or licensing the technology aboard the *Kreth* and we've been able to invest it in a wide enough manner that we couldn't easily be excised from the planet. If we pulled out, Earth's future power base would be gone because we've refused to allow weapons or propulsion technology to be transferred to Earth." She sat back and let her words be digested by the older woman.

sel Garian looked at her and wondered. So far, the truth seemed to be all the human could tell, if her debriefings of do' Verlas and kep Parrasine were any indication. Several other interviews had led to the same conclusion. "Tell me, Domagera, why are you so forthright about your race's shortcomings? I would think that you'd try to hide them."

Kitty smiled openly this time. "With your people coming and going all over our world for the past two years? What could we possibly hide? Some of our outdated military technology, to be sure, but what good is that? Actually, we of the Alliance have a certain knowledge of what things are in the arsenals of the world because some of us come from a background that had access to such information. The only thing I can say for sure is that there are enough nuclear weapons to destroy our world several times over, another reason to move out onto other worlds before we blow ourselves off the pages of galactic history. Of course, with the shielding we've developed from your capture fields, we could deflect some of the missiles but not all. And who would we save? The United States? That would alienate the Alliance members who come from other countries. And we're getting more and more of those every day. We're stuck between the horns of a dilemma." She took another sip of her wine and closed her eyes as the liquid flowed down her throat. "Besides, if we hide our shortcomings now and they're found out later, it would increase misgivings about us from the Shiravan side."

sel Garian tried another tack. "Has anyone told you just why you receive so much deference from the Shiravans you come in contact with?" She watched the human's eyes widen slightly, a sign of shock or surprise she'd come to recognize.

"I can only assume it's because I'm the leader of our particular segment of humanity," Kitty answered uncertainly, but there was something in her gaze. "I've also noticed that people refer to me as Domagera, now. Beyond that, I'm not sure. Why?"

"Because," sel Garian said after another appreciative sip, "your real name sounds the same as one of our deities. do' Verlas and kep Parrasine weren't sure how you'd use the information, so it was kept from you. Though I know you have come by some of the information on your own. We constantly refer to the Spirits of Space, the swirling mists you see from the Den when we are in contra-space." She deliberately shortened the name of the observation bubble, detesting even the sound of the word 'witches.' "There are two major facets of the Spirits, although I personally don't ascribe to the notion. One is the Spirit of Evil, and the other is the Spirit Good—Kath-e-vel and Kath-e-rin. The kath-mora have seen to it that they are the conduits through which the Spirits make their wishes known to Shiravans. For a long time, it was suspected that the kath-mora were involved with the Isolationist movement, trying to keep their positions and power. Now comes an individual who claims the name of the Spirit of Good. Do you think the kath-mora will let that go unchallenged? As long as the Spirits were only accessible to a few, the few could translate what they learned in the Dens and inform the general public as to what the Spirits wanted."

She took a longer pull on her cup and set it aside. "It was my desire all along to dispose of the kath-mora in some way not traceable to the Matriarch. On our trip to Earth, the Witches murdered and disposed of the fleet commander. I took it upon myself to take command, even though our charter expressly forbids my doing so without special dispensation from the Matriarch. That one act alone was enough to condemn all of the Witches on this one ship. But when Rentec and Maratai told me your name, I realized that I had to act quickly before some Witch got to you and ended the threat to their privileges and easy living.

"With the evidence presented by Rentec and Maratai,

added to what I'd already gleaned over the last few years, I decided to act more quickly than I'd planned. I authorized the new Fleet Commander to disable the *Cara Set* so that she'd be able to reach contra-space with a few judicious repairs and arrive at Shiravi a few weeks after us. Then, they'll all be taken into custody as soon as they make orbit."

Kitty's face burned red with indignation. "So, you are using me—us—to solve a major problem on your own world. I don't find that a good way to start an interstellar relationship between two peoples with as much in common as you say."

"Have you not done the same in your own past?" the Minister parried. "Everything from the Trojan Horse to intentional misinformation dealt to enemies to throw them off balance, is what I've heard about your past tactics, not to mention genocide, regicide, patricide, matricide, and dozens of other ways to dispose of unwanted peoples. Need I remind you of your World War II?"

sel Garian saw Kitty visibly shudder and knew she'd scored a point in this meeting, finally. She smiled at Kitty. "I don't say these things to discomfit you but merely to illustrate the fact that we're more alike than you know. We've experienced many of the same types of events in our own past—much longer ago, of course—and we learned from them, I think, more quickly than you and yours to live in peace with ourselves. Given a few more centuries, you might achieve our level of understanding as a world and not just as an isolated few.

"It wasn't until the Korvils came on the scene that the Witches became a problem," sel Garian continued. "Until then, they'd been a sect of psychics plying their trades—scrying, finding lost people and objects, determining whether two people were compatible for marriage, and many other functions—a real use among our people. Then the Korvils came and the Witches decided we should leave them alone so they'd leave us alone.

"I have only two problems with that decision—one, it's not the belief of the Matriarch or any of her counselors, including myself; and two, it's not the belief of the people who've had their worlds attacked, ships destroyed, and loved ones killed." The old woman sipped from her cup again. "The fallacy of that argument has been proven over and over again for two hundred and fifty turns, but still they try. It would seem that whosoever screams the loudest is right, and the Witches scream very loudly indeed. I used you, yes, but I would have done the same sooner or later, even if you'd never existed. Your name just gave me the incentive to push my timetable up a bit."

Kitty shook her head. "I don't see how a name can do that much damage," she said slowly. "Especially mine. There are thousands, hundreds of thousands of people with the same name in some variation or other."

sel Garian looked at her as if she were a child, which she might just be to these long-lived creatures. "I'll say only two names to illustrate my point," she announced. "Mahatma Ghandi and Adolph Hitler. One is the epitome of good, and he got assassinated. The other is your worldwide symbol of evil, and he was hunted down and eliminated as well. A name means a lot to some people. Some names bring hope, others despair. Yours will bring hope to many, and despair to a few. It's the few that we must prepare for."

"It would seem," Kitty said quietly, angrily, "that

you've been studying our situation far longer than you've let on until now. An alliance against a common foe, certainly, but I don't wish us to be drawn into your personal politics. We're doing our damnedest to keep it that way on Earth, as well, staying out of their politics until they decide to unify and prove it. I wonder if we should abort this mission and return to Earth to battle the Korvils on our own."

Kitty thought, *She's trying to kill two birds with one stone', and I have to wonder if she really cares what happens to the stone afterwards.* She set her cup down and leaned back in the chair. For some reason, the memory of the first Shiravan chair she'd ever sat in—the shuttle seat—came to mind, and she smiled slightly. Now, she was sitting in a comfortable chair, talking with an alien being nearly forty lightyears from Earth.

"I find it very disturbing to be getting this information now, two days before arriving at a destination it took eleven months to reach, rather than before we left Earth. And don't think that because we're a younger race than yours that we aren't very familiar with the art of intrigue." The word she actually used could also be interpreted as something akin to cowardly skulking.

The not-so-veiled insult didn't seem to faze the Minister. "If your race was in danger, and it is, wouldn't you do whatever you had to, to protect its existence? Yes, you would," the old woman said, answering her own question. "You're here for that very purpose. You could have chosen to stay home and help build up your ship strength, and what you have accomplished in five of your years is truly impressive, by the way. Even the Korvils couldn't match you. At your rate of production, by the time you get home, there should be nearly twenty more Alliance ships making farther and farther patrols around your star, locating and eliminating any Korvils they may find. This will give you a both buffer zone and a breathing spell."

Kitty let her eyes un-focus into the thousand-yard stare, a condition that was once applied to snipers on Earth in the last century, and a condition many people fell into when they began to think or remember. She let her mind process the information she was receiving, disregarding the feelings of her adversary. In the back of her mind, *nam-myo-ho-renge-kyo* echoed, a chant she used at times to help calm her mind and emotions. She let herself think about, of all things, evolution and how it applied to everything. Nothing survived evolution. It either adapted or died out. It was a simple concept.

Even religion evolved. Consider Christianity. At one time, God was almighty and vengeful, smiting the wicked and turning the disobedient into pillars of salt. Today, God was a just and loving being, accepting of almost all things. All the wrath and fire and brimstone had been excised from man's definition of God, the only way to stay afloat in changing times. And politics had evolved as well. Kitty was truly a neophyte on the subject, which was why she'd insisted on Baron von Schlenker accompanying her. And considering his age and a two-year absence, she invited Margit along as well, officially as her personal aide, although Diana Ross filled that post admirably. She just couldn't see the two separated for so long in their twilight years.

Kitty settled even deeper into the chair and brought her attention back to the present. "I'm going to tell you our history from what I was taught in school and learned afterward. We have people we call archaeologists, and their job is to find out as much as they can about our past. One of our wisest men once said that the culture that forgets its past has no future. So. Some two hundred years ago, the first dinosaurs were found. It was surmised from the first few bones that a race of gigantic people had inhabited our world before recorded history had begun and were somehow wiped out.

"In one respect, they were right. The creatures whose bones they'd found were indeed giants, but they weren't human. Reptilian would be the more acceptable description—some of evolution's first experiments with land-based lifeforms. We call them dinosaurs today. About sixty-five million years ago, an asteroid (the commonly accepted theory) impacted our planet, causing a cataclysmic climate change that the supposedly cold-blooded creature couldn't adapt to quickly enough. Mammalians were far more adaptable, and they managed to survive the ensuing ice age. From them, we trace our own origins.

"From arboreal tree dwellers to two-legged plains dwellers, the climate continued to change slowly, just slowly enough for certain species to continue to successfully adapt. We humans are the pinnacle of that evolution, at least, most of us think so. I have to wonder what the next step will be." Kitty mentally shook herself. "Anyway, the oldest fossil we have of a bipedal creature in the chain of evolution most of our scientists accept is three and a half million years old. And we just reached our only planetary satellite almost forty or so years ago. Are we ready to be out here among the older races? I don't know. But, thanks to an unusual set of coincidences one might call astronomically large, we are.

"I think we're more civilized than the Korvils, but whether we're more or less civilized than your race is yet to be learned. From what I've seen so far, I'd have to say we're dead even. You've got more years in space, but we've recently had more years of strife than you. Will that make us better warriors? Again, I don't know. But I do know that when push comes to shove, humans have taken on and beaten everything nature and the cosmos has thrown at us. And that includes the Korvils—at least so far." Kitty sat back in her chair and gave the Minister a chance to digest what she'd said so far. She picked up her wooden cup and took a sip, setting it down carefully after noticing how thin the wood was in places. This was one of a very old set of cups.

"In truth," the Shiravan said, "I've known about your name almost from the first. I thought it best to keep the knowledge to myself and a few others, although the secret seems to have leaked out aboard this ship. To the crew, you are Kath-e-rin, come to save us from the depredations of the horrible Korvils. I see that you are just a person, no better or worse than any other." She held up her hand to forestall Kitty's expected response. "I know. You see yourself, your friends, and your organization as something altruistic and good, seeking to better the conditions on your own world using our technology.

"But the truth is that you're as mortal as I am and just as dedicated to the preservation of your race." The old woman sat back in her chair, duplicating Kitty's posture. "You look to better the condition of your race and ensure its survival. That is my wish for our race as well, and I'm using your name to instill a sense of hope among our crew. And that same sense of hope will become known to the entire planet almost as quickly as we make orbit around Shiravi. The crew will see to that. For months, the talk has been about nothing more than that we have found one of the Spirits and are bringing her home to be venerated.

"I see two problems with this scenario. First of all, you aren't Kath-e-rin, and secondly, you'll refuse to pose as such. Your central core won't let you lie in that fashion. You'll try to tell everyone you come in contact with that you aren't a Spirit come to life."

The elder woman looked at the younger over the rim of her cup. "How many do you think you'll convince? Especially when I deny that you have ever named yourself as such. My denial will only fuel further speculation that you truly are Kath-e-rin come to free us from the scourge of the Korvils." She drained her cup and set it aside almost without notice. "And you *will* help us destroy the Korvils, further proving to my people that you are truly a Spirit. Besides, look at you— so very different from the only two humans our world has ever seen. The white hair will only confirm the legend.

"Short, with light skin and white hair is the description of Kath-e-rin. And it will grow," the Minister predicted. "The more you deny, the harder people will believe. And look at what you bring with you—three ships that look like ours superficially but are capable of so much more."

Kitty couldn't keep quiet any longer. "All right, that's enough," she said firmly. "The fact is that we just look at things differently. After an unfortunate incident on Earth, I was lost for a time in some kind of limbo in the medical section of the ship. We don't have the technology to repair the kind of injuries I sustained that day, so I spent ten months in isolation from the rest of the world while your computer cured me. And my hair used to be yellow, or what we call blonde. Now look at it. And it's not going back to its natural color. I've been like this long enough to figure that out.

"So, I look like what your culture thinks this Kath-e-rin looks like? Most races invent a god that looks like them. Our ancient Romans, the Greeks before them, and the Sumerians before that all depicted their gods as being much like themselves, only with greater powers."

The Second Voice smiled. "Why must a deity look like the race they protect? Is it a requirement? I think not. Look to some of your own religions for the answer to that question. All that is needed is for that deity to come to the aid of her people when needed. And you are arriving at just the right time."

Kitty was finally beginning to feel the effects of her prolonged visit to the Den, along with her verbal battle with the Shiravan Minister. "I need time to think about this. There are ramifications I need to discuss with my staff before we continue this discussion." She stood up, an insult if she were of a status lower than sel Garian, but since she was the leader of her people, it went unremarked upon.

sel Garian stood as well. "If you need the insight of your people, Domagera Hawke, then by all means, seek them out and discuss the situation. Are you a person willing to wager on the outcome of a set of circumstances?" she asked, changing the subject.

Kitty thought for a moment. "Under the right circumstances, yes. But those circumstances require that I have a better than even chance of being right. What are you proposing?"

"Better than even?" sel Garian asked with a smile. "You truly are a beginner, aren't you? Very well. If you succeed in convincing our people that you're not Kath-e-rin, I'll present you with enough gava stone to make you a rich person on your own world. If I'm right," she continued, "you'll personally conduct me on an unrestricted tour of your world, excepting, of course, military installations or other sensitive locations. I want to see your literature, art, architecture, and anything else that might come to mind while I spend an extended amount of time on your world sometime in the future. This will enable me to better decide whether we wish to have any closer contact with your world."

"Done," Kitty said immediately. "With one exception."

"And what might that one exception be?" sel Garian asked suspiciously.

"If I win," Kitty said, "I'll ask for nothing more than you've asked of me—a full tour of your world, minus the sensitive areas."

sel Garian looked closely at Kitty. The impression Kitty got was of a cat sizing up a mouse before dinner. "Done," she said, "although I'm sure our Matriarch will give you that tour anyway."

"True," Kitty replied, "but she'd only show me the brighter side of your culture. I want to see how the common folk live. That's the true measure of a race. And I'll see, before you have a chance to throw it in my face, that we humans are woefully lacking in taking proper care of our underprivileged."

The entire exchange had taken place in Shiravan, since sel Garian had not had time to learn English, and Kitty felt extremely proud of herself. On only three occasions had she or sel Garian had to resort to looking for a different way to say something. She held out her hand and said, "A handshake, as you know, is used upon meeting friends or strangers but also when two parties have come to an agreement or when they are going their separate ways under conditions of mutual respect."

sel Garian slowly took the cooler human hand in her own. Kitty felt slightly awkward with the longer, hotter Shiravan digits wrapping almost completely around her hand. She pumped her hand up and down three times. "And now it's time that I return to my staff before they begin to worry that something bad has happened to me." She held her own hand up to forestall a comment by the Minister. "It's just that humans have, over the centuries, come to believe the worst in most cases, until proven otherwise. I've already been gone too long."

"Then I shall keep you no longer," sel Garian stated. "Return to your people and discuss what we've said here. Perhaps we'll have another chance to talk privately before we arrive at Shiravi."

Kitty walked to the door, and just before it could slide aside, she turned back to the Minister. "Let me ask a question for you to think on." When sel Garian nodded, she continued, "You say that Kath-e-rin and Kath-e-vel are two aspects of the same being—one good, one evil. Even if I were to pose as Kath-e-rin, wouldn't some of your people seize upon the notion that I could be bringing ruin and destruction to your race rather than salvation?" The look on sel Garian's face spoke volumes, now that Kitty was a bit more adept at reading the Shiravan people, and it said she'd already considered the possibility.

Kitty moved a pace forward and let the door open. *Score one for me!* she thought. Stepping through, she looked back at the old woman behind her desk and said, "It is impossible to figure all the variables, no matter how hard you try, isn't it?"

The door closed on a face as devoid of expression as she hoped hers was.

CHAPTER TWENTY-ONE

Kitty Hawke stood on the bridge of the *Shumara Vacht* as the four ships warped into Shiravan space. The small fleet stopped just inside the local Oort Cloud and sent messages to Shiravi, explaining the return of the *Shumara Vacht,* along with three Earth ships that had come to join the war effort from the Shiravan side of Korvil space. The fleet commander waited patiently until they got the proper response.

Considering the distances involved to the dim red sun, the smaller system, and the relatively close proximity of Shiravi to both the sun and the cloud, the reply came within a week, having been intercepted and rushed to the Matriarch long before the actual transmission could arrive. The four ships, now with a two-destroyer escort, began their preparations for their inward journey. Before the *Shumara Vacht's* captain could issue the order, though, Kitty spoke to sel Garian. "Why not let our ships take the lead going in? Not physically, but if you slave your controls to one of our ships, we can jump all four into orbit within a matter of minutes, almost literally. That will surely give the tongue-waggers something to keep themselves busy, and those who need to know will get a better approximation of our capabilities. It will also save us days of travel time."

sel Garian thought for a moment and then ordered Captain do' Sirkis to do as Kitty asked. Reluctantly, the captain passed the proper orders, allowing Kitty's flagship, the *Vega*, to override the *Shumara Vacht*'s controls. The other two Earth ships, the *Federal Case* and the carrier *Canopus*, did the same, bringing them all into close orbit as a tightknit group mere minutes after receipt of the confirmation to continue.

To say that the almost magical appearance of four ships caused a major furor among Shiravan Space Command was nothing short of an understatement. Captain do' Sirkis spent the next several minutes identifying himself and his ship, casting an occasional glare in Kitty's direction. Her declarations were met with outright disbelief until sel Garian stepped in front of the screen, pulling Kitty along with her.

"Do you recognize me, Commander?" she asked in her grating, mechanical voice.

The officer on the other end of the link stammered, "Yes, M-minister sel Garian. It's just that we've never experienced such an event before, four ships appearing out of nowhere, and three of them alien in the bargain. I was afraid Captain do' Sirkis was under some kind of coercion." During her entire apology, her eyes never left Kitty, barring the initial recognition of sel Garian.

The Minister essayed a smile that Kitty was glad she wasn't on the receiving end of. "You will immediately assign the *Shumara Vacht* and her escort ships a lower orbit so we can transport to the surface." Her tone said that dire consequences awaited whoever didn't comply on the spot. The hapless commander looked down at something out of view of the camera and began to rattle off a series of numbers, immediately granting the *Shumara Vacht* a lower orbit. The navigator signed that she had received and understood the instructions, and sel

Garian nodded her head once. "We'll descend to the new orbit shortly. You are to be commended for your diligence, Commander."

She reached down and pressed a button that cut off the comm link. "Sometimes it's good to be feared, but it's not always the best way to get things done. I don't like to pressure those who are only doing their jobs any more than I have to, but I know that family—an officious bunch and very jealous of their positions. This is not a time to dally, though. If you'd like your officers to accompany you to the surface, we'll beam them first to the *Shumara Vacht* and then to the Matriarch's personal estate."

Kitty nodded and sat down at a vacant station. She called the three human ships, explaining the situation and invitation, while the *Shumara Vacht* led them to the new orbit. Presently, she and sel Garian were in the *Shumara Vacht's* transporter room greeting Shirley Dahlquist of the *Vega*, Thomas Breen of the *Federal Case*, and Miranda Lee of the *Canopus*. Although the four ships had been traveling together for almost eleven months, she hadn't spoken to them personally, since it was impossible to do so in hyperspace.

"Captain do' Sirkis will accompany us to the surface," she said after greeting each captain individually. The four humans made a distinctive group since the captains were in their dress blacks and Kitty was in a white pants suit, the midnight blue trim around her collar and sleeves matching the blue of the Alliance banner.

The Minister stepped onto one of the three hexes on the far side of the room and Kitty followed suit, motioning Miranda Lee to the third hex. "I'll see you two on the surface in a few minutes," she said to the others, and sel Garian motioned for the transporter tech to activate the transmitter.

The room Kitty, Miranda, and sel Garian transported into was bare of furnishings but open to the outside, more of a pavilion than a real room. It was attached to a much larger structure, but Kitty looked outward at her first view of an alien world. For all that she'd been in space for over almost eight years now, this was the first non-Earth planet or satellite she'd set foot on. Only Derek Carter and Maggie Spencer had been here before, and their travels had been farther and their travails worse by far.

The light from the Shiravan sun duplicated the lighting aboard the Shiravan vessel. During their voyage, Kitty had almost succumbed to a type of depression until one of her staff had noticed the slowly deteriorating morale of the humans aboard the *Shumara Vacht* and she remembered when they'd first discovered the *Dalgor Kreth*. Once the human suite had the lighting adjusted to Earth-norm, everybody began to feel better. Knowing there was a haven of yellow light to escape to had given everyone the fortitude to leave their quarters more willingly. If their stay there was to be of any length, the same would have to be done planetside as well.

In the distance, a range of mountains separated the ground from the sky, and she could almost swear she saw the glow she'd heard so much about and seen with her own eyes in the pendant she now wore in place of the larger one Simon had found so long ago. It wasn't possible yet, of course, because the reddish sun was still too high in the sky, but she eagerly awaited the spectacle she'd been assured existed nowhere else in the explored galaxy.

She felt a tug on her arm and brought her attention back to the pavilion. sel Garian pulled both her and Miranda away from the hexes imbedded in the pavilion's floor so the rest of the group could transport down as well. Kitty let herself be moved and continued moving until she stood at one of the open sides, getting a better view of the mountains and the small city nestled between two arms of the immense mountain range.

A slight noise she recognized as a gasp of surprise turned her around. The last sparkles were fading away as Captains Breen and Dahlquist got their first look at the alien landscape. Captain do' Sirkis ignored the view and watched the reactions of the humans instead. "Welcome to Shiravi, honored guests," sel Garian said formally when the last arrivals appeared. After they'd had a few moments to gaze in awe at the sight before them, sel Garian said, "If you'll follow me, I'll lead you to your suite to freshen up while I report your arrival to the Matriarch."

Five minutes of walking down corridors with too-high ceilings brought the group to a set of doors nearly ten feet tall, the ceiling another five feet higher. Opening the doors herself, sel Garian ushered the humans into what was apparently a common room. Several doors opened off the main room, all ajar and all leading to what appeared to be individual bedrooms. The old woman said, "Please, relax here while I report to the Matriarch. I'm afraid that may take some time as she has many other concerns on her mind, and we *have* arrived a week early." Her voice was almost accusatory.

As the door closed behind her, Thomas was the first to speak. "You spent the most time with her, Madam Herald. How do you assess the situation?"

Kitty wondered for a moment at the odd phrasing of

Thomas's question, then put it on the back burner along with several other items jumbling around in her subconscious. As she worked to bring the three captains up to date on what she'd learned while aboard the *Shumara Vacht*, she forgot about it. "Well, I'm not one hundred percent sure, but I think we've made a favorable impression on the Minister. At least, we're no longer considered to be barbarians," she said slowly. "Once I managed to get a better grip on the basics of the Shiravan language, sel Garian and I had many talks. She's good at turning the conversation into channels she wants to pursue, of course, but I think I convinced her that we're better as an ally, especially considering their present situation.

"You realize," she continued, "that sel Garian is the second most powerful person in the Shiravan hierarchy. That means that not only will she be giving a full report on what she's learned while with us, but she'll have to be brought up to speed on what's been happening during her absence. That woman has more irons in the fire than we know about, I'm sure. Her opinions will be listened to, assessed, and reassessed. And she'll want to know how her plans have matured during her extended absence. Also, she'll be anxious to get back to what she does best—spying on the opposition. We could be here for a while, so make yourselves comfortable."

The four humans began a systematic search of the area assigned to them, finding that all the doors except the one they'd entered by led to separate, smaller suites, complete with bathing facilities and all the amenities. Windows gave them a view of the same mountain range they'd seen upon arrival—all built to Shiravan standards, of course, making the humans feel that much more like little children in the presence of adults.

Hours passed with no word, and the four humans began to relax into their new surroundings. Early on, Shirley discovered that the food processors had been adjusted for humans and sat with a glass of apple juice in her hand. She'd also called her ship to see if their comm links worked. To her surprise, she was able to get through to the *Vega* without any problem. Thomas and Miranda tried their links as well and found them in working order.

"So, we're not cut off from our own ships," Kitty noted. "We can call down a shuttle if we decide to leave."

She glanced out the window for perhaps the hundredth time, remembering Maratai's stories of the fabled Stala Mountains, and noticed the glow. None of the lights had been turned on yet, but still, an hour after the last rays of the red sun had faded from the sky, the room was comfortably lit, only now the color had slowly changed to a greener cast, unnoticed by the group. She got up and walked over to one of the windows. Her sharp intake of breath pulled the others after her. For as far as the eye could see in both directions, the mountains actually glowed, releasing the built-up heat back into the atmosphere, along with enough light to see fairly clearly even without the room's lighting turned on.

"Assuming the shuttle isn't shot down by some overly efficient weapons control officer," Thomas growled, unimpressed by the sight. "I don't like this at all—all of us in one place and effectively quarantined until such time as sel Garian decides to let us out of our gilded cage."

That release wasn't much longer in coming. Kitty had stretched out on a lounger in the common room while the others selected rooms of their own and took the opportunity to rest as much as possible. Their own body clocks told them it was the middle of the night, but on-planet it was early evening. Kitty dozed fitfully, starting at the slightest noise until a knock at the door sat her straight up. Thinking it was a dream, she did nothing until another, more insistent knock sounded. "Ta hai," she said automatically, standing up and straightening her clothes.

A tall female entered the suite, reminding Kitty of Maratai for some reason. "It is my understanding that you speak Shiravan, Domagera," the newcomer said. "Is that truly the case?"

"Aya, Doma," Kitty responded as her companions straggled into the room. "I've had the privilege of studying under Minister sel Garian for almost a turning. It's my hope that I'm not mangling your language beyond comprehension."

"Oh no, Domagera," the alien woman replied. "I can hardly detect any accent at all. Your grasp of our language is impressive."

"Segala vin, Doma," Kitty said. "Thank you." A moment's hesitation. "Whom do I have the honor of addressing?"

"I am Sitha kep Parrasine, Domagera, personal attendant to the Matriarch. She wishes to speak with you at your convenience."

"kep Parrasine," Kitty repeated. "We left a Maratai kep Parrasine behind to help coordinate human/Shiravan relations during my absence. Is she any relation to you?"

"I have the privilege of calling Maratai my older sister, Domagera," the stranger answered. "Was she well when you left?"

"Quite well, Doma," Kitty answered, "and of

invaluable assistance to our efforts to bring humans and Shiravans together under one cause, along, of course, with Ambassador do' Verlas."

"What's up, Madam Herald?" Thomas asked, walking into the room and running his hands through his hair.

"It would seem that the Matriarch has found time to see us now," Kitty replied. She motioned toward the door and addressed the red woman. "By all means, let's not keep her waiting."

When the entire group of humans had begun to move toward the door, Sitha said, "I beg your indulgence, Domagera, but the invitation is only for you. Domagera to Domagera. It is understood that your companions do not speak Shiravan well, and the Matriarch feels that too much time would be lost translating to your captains."

Kitty repeated the statement in English for the benefit of the others. "I'm not sure I like this, Madam Herald," Thomas said. "Splitting us up at this time isn't in the best interests of your protection."

"I have been separated from your protection for almost a year now, Thomas, while I traveled aboard the *Shumara Vacht*. I don't believe any harm will come to me at this point. And Doma kep Parrasine has a point. A lot of time would be wasted translating back and forth. I'll fill you in as soon as I return." Something about Thomas's manner bothered her, but she couldn't put a finger on it.

Realizing her decision wasn't popular with the others, she said, "We're all at the mercy of the Shiravans at this point, us and our ships. Trust has to start somewhere, and I say that time is now."

Bowing to the inevitable, the others sat down slowly, one at a time. Kitty turned back to Sitha. "My captains were voicing their protestations that it would be unwise to separate at this point, but I've told them we're under the protection of your Matriarch and nothing untoward will happen. Personally, I have no problem with placing my safety in the hands of your Matriarch. Please, lead the way."

Linnas des Harras, Matriarch of the Shiravan Polity, including fourteen colony worlds and some three trillion people, sat in her chair and looked down at her shaking hands. Here she was, about to meet with the leader of a branch of the humans, and her hands shook. She'd listened to the reports of both her Second Voice and Rentec. Granted, she'd met and come to know two other humans, but by their own accounts, they were only hired labor or, more accurately, volunteers in humanity's attempt to duplicate Shiravan technology.

Those reports, as well as the conclusions drawn, worried her. Dom do' Verlas was ecstatic in his praise, as was the long letter he hand-delivered from Doma kep Parrasine, who'd remained behind. Manura, on the other hand, was considerably more cautious in her estimation of humanity's ability to render assistance and certainly dourer in her assessment of their capabilities. Too many innovations had been implemented by the humans too quickly. It was as if their minds saw things in a different manner, a situation, she realized, that could lead to the same result they were headed for anyway.

Proof of their inventiveness rode in orbit around her own homeworld in the shape of three alien-built ships, one of a totally innovative design. None of her military had ever considered building a ship to carry only fighters, opting, instead, for larger ships carrying stronger weapons. Now, just above her head were two ships of battlecruiser class, each capable of taking on any two, and possibly more, full-fledged battleships of Shiravan make. Also, each one carried ten fighters, as opposed to seven on a Shiravan battleship. And the third ship. Why had none of her engineers ever suggested such a thing? In retrospect, it seemed obvious. A "carrier," the humans called it, capable of launching fifty fighters at once. Add that to the ten carried on the two cruisers, and the humans could put seventy fighters into space in a matter of moments, overpowering most ships' defensive capabilities. And even the fighters were of superior design.

And now, the Domagera of the humans, who'd chosen to follow her mate into space, was approaching. She checked again that all was in readiness. The ceremonial kemwood cups sat beside a bottle of fire wine, a drink she'd been told was acceptable to the human metabolism. A chair, built for Doma Spencer and Dom Carter, had been brought in and placed opposite her own. Set on a raised dais, it would let the smaller human sit eye to eye with her. And this human was already quite conversant in the Shiravan language.

The knock at her door broke her reverie. "Ta hai," she said, trying to hide the unaccustomed quiver in her voice. Sitha entered the room and Linnas stood up in anticipation of the next entrant. The reality of what she saw shook her deeply, even after seeing the reports and secretly acquired pictures. Even smaller than Doma Spencer or Dom Carter, she'd still stand out in any crowd. The absolutely white fur on top of her head, called hair, hung nearly to her hips and swayed as she walked into the room. The tiny human moved daintily, almost as if she expected the floor to open beneath her feet at any moment.

Linnas moved from her position on the patio into the center of the room. "Welcome to Shiravi, Domagera Hawke," she said. "I regret that you have had to wait so long. Please, come sit with me and let us talk."

The human female moved forward with more confidence, glancing around the room as she entered it. "Think nothing of it, Domagera des Harras. You needed to hear from Minister sel Garian and Ambassador do' Verlas first. In your position, I would have done the same." She held out her hand in what the humans called a handshake.

Linnas tentatively took the cooler human hand, pumped her own hand up and down twice as she had been instructed, and let go. She turned toward the patio and the table and chairs waiting there. "I thought perhaps to sit under the stars, since they are what symbolize our two cultures most." Secretly, she was a bit shocked at the perceptiveness of this human.

The human—Domagera Hawke, she reminded herself--nodded once in Shiravan fashion and walked first onto the patio, leaving her back exposed. Although this could be taken as a sign of trust, from earlier experience with the only other two humans she'd met, she could tell by the set of the shoulders that the alien wasn't the least bit at ease. Even so, the show of confidence wasn't lost on her, nor was the fact that the human carried two small packages that she set on the table without any explanation. Security had scanned the packages before the human's arrival and pronounced them safe, being merely some type of minerals.

Linnas waved to the chair she'd set aside for her guest and settled into her own. "You're probably quite tired of looking at metal walls for almost a full turning of your own world. I thought this might be more pleasant."

"Aya, Domagera," the alien responded easily. "I've heard stories of your Stala Mountains. They are, in truth, even more impressive than I'd been told."

So, the reports of her ability to speak our language were not exaggerated, Linnas thought. She busied herself with the small ritual of pouring wine into the cups, hoping that her shaking hands would go unnoticed.

"They are the source of the pendant you sent as a gift, are they not?" the human asked.

"That is so, Domagera," Linnas replied. "And the main source of income for my family for almost a thousand turnings. As is custom, I went into the mountains and personally selected the stone for the gift that was sent to you. The less informed still believe that the glow has healing properties, and tradition dictates that any marriage be sealed with a gava stone pendant. It makes for a lucrative income, even if I weren't Matriarch."

The human sat down in the chair that was obviously placed there for her and waited for Linnas to sit. She set a cup beside the small human and finally lowered herself into her own chair. "Do you find this situation as uncomfortable as I do?" Linnas asked bluntly.

"Oh, yes," Domagera Hawke replied quickly, a small smile crossing her face. "Although I've had extensive contact with your people for almost three turns now and learned some little bit of your language during our voyage here, this is an extremely uncomfortable position I find myself in."

Linnas tilted her head from side to side, a Shiravan shrug. "I, too, find it a difficult situation. I have never been in the position of hosting an equal."

The alien woman waved her hand slightly. "I would hardly call myself your equal, Domagera. After all, you are the ruler of fourteen worlds, not counting this one. All I control is four bases and several thousand people. Not anywhere near your exalted position."

"But you do control what happens beyond the boundaries of your own world," Linnas countered. "You decide what happens with all of your space-based economy and dictate the movement of forces that your own world cannot match. By all reports, even the other leaders of your world defer to you."

"'Defer' is hardly the word I'd use," the alien said with a small sound Linnas had come to recognize as laughter. "They fear what we could do if we don't get our way. Not that we try to influence anything, but our power base is stronger than any military power that is strictly ground, sea, or air based. It's our mobility and unknown potential that gives us our edge, so to speak, and causes our various militaries to have sleepless nights."

"And more people flocking to your banner every day," Linnas noted dryly.

"And how many of them are spies?" Kitty countered. "Learning our secrets, which we plan to give to our world anyway but at a rate that won't totally disrupt the economy of our world. It's fragile enough with so many different countries, each with their own currency based on differing values, and none of it really backed up by anything but promises. The world used to be on what we call the 'gold standard.' That meant that we printed what we call money on worthless paper with the promise of having enough of a mineral called 'gold' to back it up. All it would take is just a few of the right people to upset that balance and our entire economic structure would fall."

Linnas looked at the small human. "What is this 'gold' you speak of?"

Her guest twisted a small band of yellowish metal from a finger of her left hand and passed it over. "This is what we call a wedding ring. It serves the same purpose as the pendant my mate found aboard the *Gal... Kreth*. In our case, both parties exchange rings in a mating ceremony. It's not the rarest metal on our world, but it's imbued with the most significance, much like your gava stone, I believe. The worth is mostly symbolic."

Linnas turned the ring over in her hand, feeling the heft and noting the color. "I believe we have the same metal here, Domagera, but we only use it for electronic components. Something about it working better, but I'm not an expert in that area. Perhaps in my second career..." She handed the artifact back and watched as the human put it back on her finger. Something about the way she did so prompted her to ask, "You miss your mate greatly, don't you?"

Staring at the band now back on her hand, the Domagera slowly nodded in the human fashion. "Aya," she said. "Yes, I do. He's in charge of the defense of our entire solar system. The ships your Minister sel Garian left behind, some eighteen vessels, are under his control at her orders, and he was beginning to integrate them into the human fleet even as we left. You might be interested to know that, one at a time, all the Shiravan ships are being what we call upgraded. In other words, they're getting the same shields we've developed from your capture field technology. Also, we're outfitting them with new torpedoes. It's our belief that once the Korvils realize their torpedoes can't penetrate our shields, they'll work to develop the same technology.

We're trying to stay one step ahead of them by building a missile that will penetrate our own shields. Of course, the 'how' will be passed along as well."

Linnas picked up her cup and looked over the rim at her guest. "Building a defense and then building a counter to it. That is most circuitous thinking. Are all humans this devious?"

"Oh, no, Domagera. Most humans are as straightforward as most Shiravans. It takes a person on the level of Minister sel Garian to think in that fashion. Or a group who get together and spend all of their time playing 'what if.'" She picked up her own cup and took a sip. "Fire wine, if I don't miss my guess," she said appreciatively. She inspected the cup, a virtual duplicate of the set she'd been gifted when sel Garian arrived in Earth space.

Kitty set her cup down and looked at the woman who controlled fifteen worlds. "This cup reminds me," she said. "It's an Earth custom to return a gift with a gift. As you sent me two gifts unique to your world, it's my pleasure to present you with two gifts I hope are unique to our own planet." She reached out and pushed the two wrapped packages partway across the table.

Kitty watched as the other woman reached out and pulled the two packages toward her. Her host lifted first one then the other. One was heavier by far, and that was the one the red woman opened first. Two birds, sculpted from the purest white alabaster, emerged. "This is a sculpture of a pair of doves, flying creatures of our world. Over the centuries, they've come to stand for peace or love. It's my hope that you'll accept them as a symbol of peace between our two races." She watched as the Shiravan monarch studied the specially commissioned piece. "The work was done by one of our world's most accomplished artists and is a perfect replica of the birds."

Kitty watched her host's eyes widen. "The detail is exquisite," she said. "I can only think that it took you much time and effort to get the details perfected. We have something similar on Shiravi, but evolution is bound to follow similar paths under similar circumstances. This is something I, and subsequent Matriarchs, will treasure beyond price. Thank you."

Kitty watched as her host set the sculpture carefully in the center of the table and reached for the second package. Kitty, knowing what was in the other package, waited until the gift was unwrapped. She was amused at the Matriarch's slow examination of the gaily wrapped package. "On our world, anticipation makes the gift more special. That's why it's wrapped in what we call 'gift wrap.'"

The alien leader slowly worked her fingers under the tape that was holding the wrap on the package. Finally removing the last of the paper, she was holding a square white box, the lid a separate piece from the bottom. Pulling the top off, she gasped at the sight within. Carefully, she lifted the string of pearls out of the box, studying first the pearls themselves and then the clasp.

Kitty stood up and walked around the table. "These are what we call pearls. They are made by shelled sea creatures called oysters. First, a grain of sand gets inside the oyster—a source of food that's considered a delicacy, by the way—then the oyster coats it with a substance called nacre in an effort to prevent irritation. It doesn't work, and more layers are added in an effort to reduce the irritation. The end result is what we call a pearl. You hold in your hands a matched set of pearls. Most are white, although a few are black. The biggest is the largest black pearl I could find, with two more of a slightly smaller size on each side. The rest are white pearls, graduated in size to make a necklace. This gift is for you, personally, and not to be handed down to your successor. On our world it is quite valuable, and not one person in ten thousand would be able to afford it." She showed her host how to work the clasp, then placed it herself around Linnas' neck, closing the clasp behind.

Kitty watched as her host looked at the pearls and felt them with her fingers. "We have nothing like this on our world or any of the others we've colonized. I cannot accept such a precious treasure."

"Of course, you can," Kitty said firmly. "We have nothing like gava stone or kemwood on our world, making them the two most unique things in human existence. I accepted your kemwood cups and gava stone pendant. It's my idea that the two gifts cancel each other out, making each one priceless in its own right."

A few seconds passed before Linnas nodded her head once, firmly. "You are right, Domagera. Each of these gifts is unique to our respective worlds, and I accept with gratitude." Kitty watched as her host's fingers moved over the smooth surfaces of the pearls, an unreadable expression crossing her face.

"So," Kitty said firmly, "we've established that we are to be friends, I hope. I've accepted your gifts, and you've accepted mine. What will be the next step in our negotiations?"

"Deciding how we can best assist each other in our war against the Korvils, I would suppose," the red woman answered.

Kitty looked at her host. "As I'm sure you know, I

brought three of our ships with me to show you that we're able to duplicate, use, and improve upon your technology. Much of it we still don't understand yet, but we can and do use it. Our best scientists are working on the underlying principles, but they're having a hard time with the mathematics involved. It's not enough for us to be able to duplicate it; we need to understand it as well."

She hesitated for a second. "As I told your Minister, just point us at an adversary and let us show you what we can accomplish. And remember, the advances you'll see are already being installed on the ships you left in our system, whether we can stand up to the test or not. And I've already turned a set of detailed plans on how to construct every modification over to your Chief Engineer right after he inspected one of our ships and asked for schematics on the changes. Either way, you win."

The Matriarch looked over the rim of her cup, an obvious affectation since she'd done so several times already.

An attempt to hide her features and therefore what she's thinking? guessed Kitty.

"You speak much about winning, Domagera Hawke. What if you lose?"

Kitty had been waiting for that question for eleven months. "If I lose—humans, that is—then you'll lose also shortly thereafter. That leaves this entire section of the galaxy to a totally feral, predatory race. We have many old sayings on our world, as I'm sure you do here. One is 'divide and conquer.' If you allow the Korvils take us out, which is extremely possible, where will they turn their attentions next?

"The problem is that I don't have a clue as to whether or not we can win. Each time they attack, they use a larger force. Three more waves, even with the addition of your two fleets, could wipe us out. Even with our innovations, we have our weaknesses, and an overabundance of enemies is something no race can handle alone. One of our great leaders of the past said that if you only defend, you'll eventually lose because, sooner or later, a killing blow will get through. A combination of defense and offense is what's required to accomplish any mission, or total offense, which can be a bad move in its own right. Such a move would, of course, result in major losses on our side, with no way of knowing in advance how much damage would be inflicted on the Korvils. If we gamble wrongly, both of our races are in peril."

Kitty sat back and let her host digest the information and speculations she had set out. There were too many variables for her to properly assess a safe course through the minefield of possibilities. Lord knew, she'd spent enough time in the *Shumara Vacht's* Den, trying to do just that, but the possibilities were endless, and she couldn't even decide which of the nearer paths to follow. She sipped from her cup once more, finishing the last dregs, and reached for the bottle to refill her cup. After doing so, she indicated the Matriarch's cup with an eyebrow raised. Linnas absently pushed her cup over a bit, more out of habit than any real desire to have the cup refilled.

Kitty was more than a bit frustrated at the situation. She'd come here hoping that the Shiravan leader would have a plan or battle tactic ready to be presented for consideration, but it appeared that she was going to have to be the one to make that move herself. She took a deep breath. "Listen, Domagera, if you would. We need to get onto the same page here." At the alien woman's blank look, Kitty said, "We need to come up with a plan that will keep the Korvils off the offensive and on the defensive. Remember, he who only defends ultimately loses. And I have another proposition to put to you, if it doesn't offend any of your customs."

The alien woman set her cup down carefully and looked Kitty squarely in the eye. "Although we have many customs it would be a terrible breach of protocol to ignore, I feel that with your lack of knowledge of such, some latitude would not be remiss. What do you have in mind?"

Kitty hesitated for a moment. "I have a problem with us as equals, for one thing. You control so much more power and so many more people. Trillions, I'm told, in contrast to our slowly growing thousands. In any event, I think that if we're going to act as equals, we should be at least on a first-name basis. I'd be greatly pleased if you'd call me Kitty instead of Domagera."

The alien nodded. "I agree. I have the name of Linnas and would be proud to have you refer to me by that name, at least in private."

"Agreed, Linnas," Kitty immediately decided. "It's often the custom on our world to use first names among equals, and since you consider me an equal for some reason I still haven't figured out, I'd consider the use of your name an honor."

Linnas looked closely at her guest. She sat up straighter in her chair, obviously coming to a decision. "I've been informed that Kitty is a diminutive of a longer name, and that the longer name could play chaos among our people."

"Oh, not that 'kath-e-rin' thing again," Kitty groaned. "On our world, there are many people named Katherine, and it was just my luck to have been named so by my parents. Here, Kath-e-rin, which sounds amazingly like my name, is a deity, and two-sided at that. I asked your sel Garian what she thought about what people would think. First, they have the goddess of peace amongst them, but the other side of that coin is something not quite so easily digested—Kath-e-vel."

CHAPTER TWENTY-TWO

Linnas looked closely at her guest. It wasn't often that she met someone with whom she could speak this easily—Manura, of course, and lately, of necessity, Manura's protege, Sitha kep Parrasine. A real enigma, that pair. Now here was a totally alien being, speaking the Matriarch's own language and discussing esoterica like the Spirits of Space.

She shook her head to clear her thoughts, a mannerism she had acquired from Doma Spencer, she realized. "I don't recognize this coin you speak of, but if you mean two aspects of the same thing, I agree. Without the presence of bad, you have nothing to gauge good by. Virtually everything has to have an opposite— peace and war, love and hate, female and male. One cannot exist without the presence of the other. Normally, these are things one would discuss with the local Spirit Witch, if one were so inclined. But that's no longer going to be the case."

The small, white-haired woman—Kitty, she reminded herself—shrugged her head in the Shiravan fashion. "I'm not so sure about that, Linnas. Minister sel Garian and I spoke at length about that very subject, and I have an idea that your race won't be long without spiritual guidance." Kitty first settled back in her chair and picked up her cup. Finding it empty, she sat back up and reached for the bottle. She poured a respectable measure into her own cup and glanced at the twin cup on the table. A twitch of the hair-covered skin above one eye led Linnas to think that the human was asking if she wanted a refill. Nodding once, she slid her cup a few inches closer to the center of the table.

As she poured an equal measure into the second cup, Kitty spoke. "I'm sure your scientists have observed that nature hates a vacuum. With the removal of the Spirit Witches, someone will come forward to fill the void. All people want to be told that what they're doing is right and that their deity is happy with the direction they've chosen to follow." The small woman settled back in her chair, warming her cup between the palms of her hands. "sel Garian has made it plain that there are two types of Witches—those with power who wish to rule through their 'special connection' to the Spirits and those who have those same powers and use them for the good of your people. I believe the former to be a blight on your society, much like several we have on our own world, but the other... Now, that's a different story altogether. I've never had personal experience with what we call extra-sensory perception, but I've also never discounted its existence or power. It's just something that, on Earth, has never been satisfactorily proven to exist in the general populace. Here, it would seem, it not only exists for real but has been integrated into normal life."

Linnas nodded. "We use the Witches to perform such things as findings, future searches, and whether or not two people are matched for a mating ceremony, just to name a few. They weren't among those chosen to accompany the two contact fleets." She sat silently for a short time, twirling her own cup in her hands. "I'll tell you some things I've never divulged to anyone else, Kitty," Linnas said slowly. "Of course, Manura will know immediately, but I no longer care. A ruler must have those she can count on to give her advice that will keep her on the throne and in the hearts of the people. Despite her reputation, Manura sel Garian has never given me cause to regret the trust I've placed in her. She's been known as the Butcher of Harusel for so long that the reasons are almost lost to the younger generations. When I ascended to the leadership of our people, there were those who opposed the appointment. Isolationists, we call them. I came from a background that would almost certainly assure them that Expansionism would be the order of the day, and it has been so. There have been several attempts on my life, all foiled by the foresight of Minister sel Garian, although she did miss the attempt on the father of Rentec do' Verlas.

"All of us are fallible, and Manura is as susceptible to that as any of us. She earned her name in my defense. Shortly after my ascension to the throne, the sel Garian clan attempted to overthrow my regime, planning to install one of their own in my place. Manura went along with her clan leaders' instructions except that she informed me of the planned uprising. At the proper moment, she quashed the uprising by calling out the Matriarch's Guard and trapping her own clan, along with dozens of members of several affiliated clans, in the open. The loss of life was devastating. Only a double handful of the sel Garian clan survived, and several of the allied clans were completely decimated, earning her the name Butcher of Harusel. Since that time, there has definitely been no love lost between the factions. It's only been in the past few turnings that we've come to realize it was the Spirit Witches orchestrating all the opposition, their strings being pulled by the sel Garian clan."

Linnas finally took another sip to quench her parched throat. "So it was that when the contact fleets that were looking for your homeworld set out, Manura, with the assistance of the Office of Exploration, set the rosters for the crews of the twenty ships. It was no accident that so many of the Witches' top echelons were assigned to the fleets. Actually, most were anxious to go in hopes of influencing your leadership that it would be a bad idea to associate with us, but sel Garian's plot bore fruit first. Now, they return in a disabled ship. When they arrive, their fate should be no surprise to them. They'll all spend the rest of their lives on the moons or in the asteroid factories, working toward the furtherance of Expansionism." A fleeting thought crossed her mind. "That is, of course, unless you wish to speak with them. It wouldn't be fair to let you hear only one side of their story."

Kitty waved her hand in dismissal of the idea. "If what you say is true, they're guilty of enough crimes that it would do me no good to speak to them. Besides, Minister sel Garian has given me a fairly accurate description of them and their practices. I spent much time talking to the crew as well, and the general consensus is that these Witches should be treated as renegades to your regime. You say that only the top leaders of the Witches were sent on the two fleets. What of the lesser Witches?" Kitty asked, changing the subject.

Linnas was surprised at her guest's thoroughness and quickness. "The lesser Witches, as you call them, are crucial to our plan to restructure the Shiravan people away from dependence on the guidance they receive from the Witches. As we speak, one of the lesser Witches is, with my gratitude, reorganizing the remaining Witches into a less politically active role and moving them into a role more suited to serving the Polity."

"It would seem," Kitty observed, "that you have your internal situation well under control. Of course, that's due to having one ruler, something we're still working toward on my own homeworld." The small alien went on, "It seems that we've now arrived at the most crucial junction of our meeting—how we can help you, and you, us."

Linnas sipped from her cup carefully. Even kemwood couldn't completely dissipate the effect of fire wine. "We can help you by providing more support as your bases turn out more ships, and you can help us in two ways. First, you can show our people that all aliens aren't necessarily bad, and second, you can show the Korvils that they can't just walk all over us. With the addition of your three ships and the schematics for the upgrades, we can take the war to the Korvils on two separate fronts. Their empire is between ours and yours. Actually, they claim the space your world lies in, although they've never gotten around to surveying it or subjugating it.

"If we, using technology superior to theirs, attack on both of their borders, it will surely give their hierarchy pause to reconsider their actions."

"I agree," Kitty said. "Although I've never been in a war, except this one, of course, I've read a bit about some of our major conflicts. Any time two allies can squeeze their opponent between them, the opponent goes on the defensive, and that's never a winning position."

The look of surprise was becoming common on Linnas' face. "You claim not to be a warrior, yet you speak of tactics as if you were born to them. Are all of your people like this?"

"No," Kitty said with a smile on her face. "I have the good fortune to be married to a man who's familiar with wars and how to fight them. The only difference, he says, is that there's now an extra dimension to the conflict, and if we don't learn fast, we won't even be a footnote in history." The smile disappeared. "It's my job to see to it that that doesn't happen."

Linnas felt a shiver run down her spine—not from the cool night air but from her very similar response to a question Manura had posed to her before the departure of the fleets. "It would seem that your mate and I think much alike in this matter, Kitty. I, too, don't want my people to become extinct, especially at the hands of something as despicable as the Korvils."

For a time Linnas stared into the depths of her cup, wishing for the scrying abilities some of the Witches claimed to have. She looked up to find her guest staring at the Stala's as the final glow faded and true night began to fall. She watched as the little woman pulled the pendant she'd been gifted from beneath her tunic, the glow brightening her face. "I don't believe I've thanked you for the beautiful gifts you sent," she said quietly. "I understand that the cups are far rarer, yet this one small stone seems to represent your people more. The glow that comes from the warmth of a body or sun represents your inner strength. The diminishing glow, as it loses touch with either a living body or the sun, represents fallibility, and the rebirth of the glow each day represents hope for the future."

Linnas' next words stunned Kitty, her cup halfway to her lips. "Perhaps you truly are Kath-e-rin, after all. All reports say that you've had no contact with any of the Witches or their works beyond your questioning of the

Shumara Vacht's crew, none of whom are associated with the Witches, yet you just very nearly, word for word, expressed their core belief about the stone."

"Wait a minute," she protested. "I'm most definitely not your Kath-e-rin. Just a simple human who's had no contact with anything remotely connected to their beliefs."

"What do you call the hours spent in the Witches Den aboard the *Shumara Vacht*? You emerged wholly sane after five hours alone with the Spirits," Linnas countered.

"I can do the same thing in any room, whether it be exposed to hyperspace or not," Kitty answered quickly. She took another sip of the wine and felt it burn all the way down. "We call it meditation, and it's one of our ways to find either peace and tranquility or answers to questions. What it does is lets the mind explore all the events, emotions, and feelings one has picked up and process them in a more intuitive manner, coming to conclusions one wouldn't necessarily come to otherwise. There's no magic in it, and there's no talking to your Spirits or ours, either. It's just a technique we've developed over thousands of years to get in touch with our inner selves."

"I don't understand this meditation you speak of," came a voice from the darkness, startling Kitty and making her spill a bit of her wine, "but I do agree that you couldn't have received this knowledge from the Witches." sel Garian stepped out of the shadows and walked over to stand behind her Matriarch. "It remains to be seen what real effect you can have on our enemies, and I fear for the effect you'll have on our people in general. Will you be a boon to us or the destruction of a way of life we've cherished for a thousand turns?"

"Minister sel Garian," Kitty said, showing an extreme

attempt to restrain what was possibly anger, "it's considered rude to eavesdrop on private conversations on our world, and while I know I'm not on my world, I still find it rude. In the future, if you wish to join a conversation with me, please do so from the outset." Where her nerve to speak so to the Second Voice came from, she didn't know, but now she couldn't back down. She stood up and looked over the head of the Matriarch directly into the red eyes of the Minister, a possible protocol gaffe. "Do you want proof of our abilities? I asked you to point us at a target and stand back. Do so and quit making veiled innuendos. I also promised you data on how to transform your existing technology into shields so no Korvil missile can touch your ships. That will come, along with several other ideas we've come up with, as soon as you make a computer available for us to download the specifications into. In no time at all, you should be able to retrofit many of your ships to accept them and begin to attack on your own. Until then, our three ships are the Matriarch's to command. I expect that computer to be ready tomorrow and a target designated shortly thereafter. Designate any two or more ships to accompany us and see how well we fare against the Korvils; then judge us. And if you wish to learn about meditation, you need but ask. I'll be happy to personally instruct you in how to do so. Of course, it will require that you empty your mind of all other considerations, so you'd be a most unlikely candidate, but I *am* willing to try."

With her last words, Kitty reached down, picked up her cup and drained it. Standing, she looked ever so slightly down at the still-seated Shiravan leader. "I really don't think these cups can take out all the intoxicants or I wouldn't have spoken so. I apologize for any insult to you personally and ask your indulgence. And I ask for a guide back to my quarters. The company has just become unbearable."

Once the human Domagera had been led off by the night orderly, Linnas turned to her Second. "Are you deliberately trying to offend our only hope of defeating our enemy, Minister sel Garian?" she asked formally, anger tingeing her voice. "You've spent the last turning with her and should know by now the capabilities of her race, as well as their quickness to take insult. That last one even *I* picked up on almost immediately."

"Of course, I've studied them, Your Grace, and this was just another test to see how far they'll go on our behalf. And you'll notice how quickly she returned the insult. If it weren't for the fact that we've extended them a grace period to learn our ways, I would've challenged her right then," Manura answered. "I distrust anyone who asks for nothing in return for their help. These people are willing to turn the *Kreth* back over to us as soon as they've consolidated their bases and industries. The only thing they want is our technology. I fear that they'll become worse than the Korvils in time."

"We must face one enemy at a time, Manura. Otherwise, both races will be devoured by the Korvils," Linnas lectured as if to a child, even though her Second was many turns older. "You've spent too many years looking for the worst in people, and it has affected you far more than you realize. And as for your challenge, I heard you insult her first. I'd rule that she has the right to challenge first, if it should come to that." She held up her hand, forestalling a response. "I grant that your paranoia has saved the Polity on more than one occasion, but you mustn't let it become a permanent mindset. There are people of our own world who act out of altruism. Why cannot that be the case with another race? Just because the Korvils don't, doesn't mean that these humans won't."

"I've already seen the greed and deviousness of some of these humans, Your Grace," Manura said. "It bodes ill for future relations, especially with so many different leaders on their one world and so many of them males. I tried to act in such a manner that they wouldn't learn of my misgivings, but I can never trust them completely."

"But this one is female and amenable to working *with* us, not against us. I suggest that you expedite the technology transfer immediately and do as Domagera Hawke asked, which is to point them at a target and see what happens," Linnas replied. "Once we see their technology and tactics in action, we can form a more complete picture of how we wish to continue to interact with them. And," she continued, "we have enough people of our own who act out of greed and a sense of self-serving to understand that it's probably a universal constant."

"Yes, Your Grace," was all the answer she got.

Kitty had stopped Sitha by placing a hand on her arm. Gesturing for silence, she listened to the conversation on the balcony. Not wanting to get caught or appear hurried, she took her hand from Sitha's arm, allowing herself to be escorted back to her quarters. The argument she'd intentionally stopped to hear had given her much to think about and much to confer with her staff about. As soon as morning came, she'd beam back up to the *Shumara Vacht*, transfer to the *Vega*, and begin to prepare her small fleet for battle, both against the Korvils and, apparently, against the subtle bigotry of Linnas' Second Voice. This revelation stunned her, thinking the Policy Minister to be a gracious host and an excellent interrogator/adversary, especially with eleven months to question the six humans aboard the *Shumara Vacht*.

She shook her head at her off-base ideas. Kitty looked up at her guide as she followed her back to the human's' quarters. The lighter gravity made her feel more upbeat than she should, she was sure, along with the slight feeling of euphoria from the fire wine, but still, the question remained: who would Sitha kep Parrasine report to? Who'd find out first that she'd deliberately stopped in the next room and listened in on the ensuing conversation?

The answer to those questions and others would only come with time, and reactions to both scenarios would have to be worked out. That would require certain privacy, which could only happen aboard one of the human ships, so a quick assault on something Korvil was of the utmost importance at the moment.

As she finished the thought, Sitha stopped beside a door and palmed a panel beside it.

"Your quarters, Domagera Hawke," she said formally.

"My thanks, Doma kep Parrasine," Kitty replied as the door slid open. "I'm sure your elder sister would be proud of the job you're doing, having risen so far in the Matriarch's service." It never hurt to fish a little, if it could be done discreetly. And even though these people knew she spoke their language, it was an even bet that even sel Garian wouldn't guess to what extent she'd come to learn Shiravan body language.

"Thank you, Domagera," the tall young woman

responded, standing a little straighter, her chin held a little higher. "Perhaps you can tell me later how she fares."

"It would be my honor," Kitty replied, nodding deeply. "But let me ask a question first. It seems that we of Earth tend toward less formality than your people, for the most part, but there are a few who view pomp and ceremony to have more value than it really does. I'm more open to less formality. I feel as the second group does, so it would please me if you'd call me Kitty in situations where it wouldn't be improper to do so. I really don't like the whole 'Domagera' thing. To me, it seems like a hereditary title and one vested with a great deal of power, and that's truly not my position among our people. I have a staff that helps me decide what's best to do. True, the final decision is mine, and sometimes, although rarely, I'll just tell them what I want done with no room for discussion, but on most sensitive matters, I'd rather have more input than my own intuition."

The tall red woman nodded once, curtly, in the Shiravan fashion. "It's true of us as well, Domag... Kitty. The Matriarch has her own staff to assist her in making decisions on difficult matters. To do otherwise would be folly, since no one can know all that transpires in situations as complex as the ones we find ourselves in now."

Kitty held out her hand in the human sign for a handshake. Sitha took it gingerly, her fingers wrapping almost completely around the tiny hand of the white-haired human. "I wish to thank you for your assistance in this matter. You've been more help than you know."

A look Kitty had come to recognize as puzzlement passed over Sitha's face, quickly stifled. "It's my honor to assist you any way I can, Domagera. If I can be of any further assistance, just let me know."

Kitty released her hold on Sitha's hand. "As a matter of fact, Sitha, there's one other thing you can do, if it doesn't conflict with any instructions from your Matriarch. How would you like to accompany me on our first patrol against the Korvils as a guest aboard our lead ship, the *Vega*?"

"I'd be honored to say yes immediately, Domagera Hawke," Sitha said formally, standing her straightest.

A quick image of Mutt and Jeff, an old Sunday newspaper cartoon from the fifties and sixties, ran through Kitty's mind, and she had to fight not to giggle.

"But that's a decision only the Matriarch can make." Sitha continued, "I'll pass on your request." She hesitated a moment. "You do realize that a professional team has been delegated to accompany you in any event to assess your tactics and degree of... excuse my words... 'expertise,' don't you?"

"I would have expected nothing less. Those observers do realize that if we fail, their lives are forfeit, don't they?" Kitty asked in return.

"Of course," Sitha replied, almost casually. "Such are the fortunes of war."

CHAPTER TWENTY-THREE

Kitty stood in the doorway for a moment, watching Sitha depart. She had a feeling as to whom she would be reporting, but there couldn't be any real certainty for a while. Her supposed personal loyalty was to the Matriarch, but she'd been trained by sel Garian. Oh, well, she'd find out soon enough. And knowing which way the wind blew was always an advantage.

She turned to face the common room, squared her shoulders and walked into what she knew was going to be a royal ass chewing, unless she put a quick stop to it. "See, I told you not to worry. Let me say right up front that sel Garian showed up, but I think the Matriarch and I are on the same wavelength. Where's Miranda?"

"She's taking a nap," Shirley answered stiffly, "as you might have known if you hadn't been gone for over three hours. Anything could have happened, and we'd never have known about it. If it weren't for what Simon would do to me, I'd turn you over my knee and spank you right here."

"You forget," Kitty said, smiling, "that Simon not only married me, he trained me to protect myself. I don't think you'd get very far in the spanking department, but it might just be fun for you to try. I haven't had a good workout in months. Now, would one of you please go wake Miranda? We've got plans to make."

Thomas, still silent, got up and knocked on a closed door. At the muffled response, he said, "Kitty's back and wants you out here, pronto."

Miranda walked into the common room, buttoning her shirt. "Well, you're back in one piece, I see. These two owe me money." She looked at her companions and said, "I'll collect later." Looking back at Kitty, she asked, "So what's the drill, boss?"

"The drill is," Kitty said, sitting down in a chair that would let her look out at a subtly different starfield, "that the Shiravans and I have an idea how to get the Korvils off both our backs. We all discussed some of the possibilities before we left Earth, and we've all had that much time to do some thinking about those possibilities. Our return to the *Vega* will give us the chance to discuss this in absolute privacy. But in general, the decision is that we are now allied in a two-front war and Earth space is one of the fronts. With our present superiority in weapons and shield technology and their larger infrastructure, perhaps we have a chance. Alone, well, I'm not so sure." She looked at her team and commented, "I do get the feeling that they're holding something back, but then so are we. At the moment, one cancels out the other."

She went on to relate her discussion with Domagera des Harras and the late intrusion of sel Garian. "She tossed an insult at me, so I gave her one back, along with a challenge to point us at a target and see how we fare. We'll carry observers on each ship, and a couple of ships will follow at a safe distance to report back if we don't make it. I set a deadline of tomorrow."

She turned to Shirley. "Call the *Vega* and have a shuttle land about an hour after local sunrise. Also, contact the tactical and ops staff aboard the *Vega* and have them start our preliminaries, with special attention to ship maintenance. I'm sure sel Garian won't hesitate long since I didn't give her any leeway in front of her boss. Then I left, saying that the company was no longer acceptable to me."

"Was that the wise thing to do, Kitty, antagonizing the Second Voice?" Miranda asked worriedly.

"That remains to be seen, but I did manage to deliberately overhear part of the conversation the two had after I left. The Matriarch dressed her down pretty well, in fact. It seems that they have a challenge system here, and according to what I overheard, Linnas would have ruled in my favor just because sel Garian was out of line, by their standards. One of the things I want to find out is who our guide reports to. She was trained by sel Garian but is a part of the Matriarch's personal guard and the little sister of Maratai. As for sel Garian, I think she was trying to see just how far she could push me."

"Oh, Christ!" Thomas exclaimed, finally breaking his silence. "You have the second hardest head in the Alliance, and she wants to butt heads after spending eleven months locked up on a ship with you? Is she out of her mind?"

"I hardly think so, Thomas. And thank you for the compliment. I think. It seemed to me like she was just playing more of her spy games." Kitty watched a small twitch appear on Thomas's cheek for a second and disappear.

"So, do we have any idea what or where we're going to attack yet?" Miranda asked.

"No, but I want all three ships on standby in the event that we don't get much notice. That would be just like sel Garian. I'm certain it won't be before we download our specs into one of their computers first, though," she said cynically.

"Well, in that case," Miranda said, pulling a small

box out of her purse, "would anyone care for a game of chess?"

"Why do you insist on carrying a purse in this day and age?" Shirley asked, looking contemptuously at the offending object.

"In this day and age? Is that what I just heard you say? You of all people, Shirley Dahlquist? Did you forget that it was only eight years ago that we even got the *Galileo* in the first place?" Miranda turned on her companion captain and shook the purse in her face. "Did you carry one before? If you tell me 'no,' I'll call you a liar to your face and bet that I'll get away with it. Besides, there are no rules expressly forbidding them. I've thought about submitting a proposal that fanny packs—call them utility belts—be made an optional piece of the uniform. Through proper channels, of course, but since you brought it up, let me show you the real use of this 'purse,'" she said, mocking Shirley's tone. "We know that we're going to be here all night. The shuttle will be here to pick us up just after dawn. Did you even think about that before beaming down? I did, so who's gonna have clean teeth at bedtime besides me?" Turning toward her private room, she waved the brush over her shoulder. "Nighty-night, y'all."

Rentec listened to the conversation going on in the guest suite uncomfortably. As the only Shiravan available with extensive knowledge of the language, he'd been summoned for just this purpose. Over his objections, he began. "Your Grace, it would seem that Domagera Hawke doesn't trust Minister sel Garian. She stayed behind and overheard the conversation after she left the balcony. She feels that we are holding something back and readily admits that they have a few secrets held back of their own. The conversation is lighthearted and bantering for the most part, but she's essentially giving an account of your meeting from a strongly slanted and slightly angry point of view, I believe. Apparently various scenarios were discussed before leaving Earth, and now they wish to discuss their feelings and findings in private. To that end, it seems that Domagera Hawke has scheduled a shuttle to land just after dawn since she plans to begin to get her crews ready for whatever target Minister sel Garian designates. To that end, she has just ordered all three ships onto standby, a condition where all posts are permanently manned, all systems are online, and full power can be acquired within seconds."

"A not unwise decision to come to, considering their parting," Linnas observed wryly. She turned to her second in command. "Now, Manura, before you say one word about having three armed, powered-up alien warships riding in our lowest orbit, I want to remind you that it was your interruption and provocation that precipitated the matter. So, nothing will be said. As for our ships, you'll order them to disregard the situation. I expect the same of your other staff members, both overt and convert. Continue, Rentec."

"Your Grace," Rentec said uncomfortably, "the rest consists of general acceptance that Minister sel Garian has what humans call a hidden agenda, and they're letting the matter drop. One is even suggesting that they play a game."

"Well," Linnas said to the silent third person seated in the room. "It was a good idea to put a microphone in their room, Second Voice. I applaud your ingenuity. But it would seem that the humans have a staggeringly different perspective of you than I do. Why is that, do you think?"

sel Garian didn't hesitate. "Your Grace, I cannot say what it is that triggers my…" she stumbled for words for almost the first time in her life. "I'm just not comfortable around them. I grant that they've done no harm and that they've freely given aid and assistance to Shiravans in their territory when it was well within their rights to deny it. And I agree that their giving us the specifications to upgrade our ships to their levels will be of tremendous help in our ability to take the war to the Korvils and save Shiravan lives and property, which is another point in their favor. The human Domagera is right—stand together or die separately." The old woman hesitated. "I just cannot make myself like them."

Rentec cleared his throat. "Your Grace, if I might interrupt?" At her nod, he went on, "The humans are having the same problem, some of them. They just cannot make themselves trust an intelligent, alien life form. They developed a word for it long before they left their own world. It means fear of that which is different or strange: Xenophobia. And if you'll forgive me, it seems that our exalted Second Voice might have a small dose of it."

Kitty decided that she should at least inform the Matriarch's staff that she'd called for a morning shuttle. Her deep feelings were that their suite was bugged. Since Rentec had accompanied them back to Shiravi, so the Matriarch, or sel Garian, she thought uncharitably, would know soon enough, but proper protocol must be maintained.

She picked up the comm link in the common room and said, "Is this unit being monitored?"

"Aya, Domagera Hawke," came back almost instantly. "How may I be of service?"

"I'd like to speak to Doma Sitha kep Parrasine, if she hasn't already gone to bed," Kitty requested. "Anyone assigned to her shift will be acceptable if she isn't available."

"I'll see to it at once, Domagera," the unidentified voice responded. "It may be a few minutes... unless it's an emergency?"

"No emergency, thank you. As soon as she's able will be fine." She heard the transmission cut off and laid the device back on the small table at the end of the couch.

"So, what's up, Madam Herald?" Thomas asked. He was the only one who wouldn't unbend enough to call her Kitty.

"I think it would be polite to let our hosts know that a shuttle will be landing here in the morning. A matter of courtesy, Thomas. Besides, I don't want an incident with our new allies this far from home if I can help it."

Kitty was sitting in a chair, sipping from a glass of apple juice and nibbling on a portion of the foodstuffs they'd beamed down with, when she heard a light knock. Setting the glass down, she tiredly stood up and walked over to the door, passing her hand over the plate beside it, and the door slid open. Sitha stood there, dressed, but somehow not quite at her best. Kitty said, "I told them that your relief would do just as well, Sitha. There was no real need for you to get out of bed for this."

"It's of no consequence, Kitty. The Matriarch has assigned me as your personal aide while with us, and it's my pleasure to assist you."

"I feel bad, regardless," Kitty confessed. "Everyone needs their sleep. It's just that I've ordered a shuttle to pick us up just after sunrise in the morning, and I didn't want your defenses firing on it. If you'd be so kind as to inform them that it will be arriving, I'll make sure the pilots, who are fluent in Shiravan, announce their flight plan and arrival time when they depart the *Vega*."

"You are wise to do so, Kitty," Sitha said sleepily. "Defense Command should be apprised of the flight, especially since it's coming straight here. I'll first inform the Matriarch and then Defense Command. Will there be anything else?"

"I don't think so, Sitha," Kitty said. "But I do want to thank you for coming here so late at night."

"It is nothing. There are always people awake to handle the business of the Polity these days," Sitha responded.

"But each one is not on twenty-four-hour call," Kitty said. "That defeats the purpose of rest, which is to be at your sharpest. And you must admit that this particular request could have been handled by a subordinate."

"True," the woman said. "But we take our obligations very seriously in light of these troubled times. It's been my pleasure to serve you. Will there be anything else?"

Kitty could tell from the curtness of the conversation that it would be best to let Sitha get back to sleep. "Thank you, Sitha. I apologize for dragging you out of bed, and I hope it won't be necessary to do so again anytime soon." The woman nodded once and turned to leave. Kitty watched as she moved down the corridor. After almost three years among the red aliens, she could tell when one of them was short of sleep and promised herself not to be so inconsiderate in the future.

"Your Grace, Sitha will be here momentarily to inform you that Domagera Hawke has requested a shuttle to arrive just after local first light. Sitha has notified the Domagera that she will inform Defense Command of the impending arrival as well."

"I had hoped as much. It shows respect and consideration, as well as forethought," Linnas responded. "Your services will no longer be required tonight, Rentec. Get some rest, and you can add anything you might find necessary after your visit tomorrow and after listening to the rest of the recordings."

Rentec nodded, acknowledging his leader's command, and almost stumbled out of the room. Linnas turned to her Second. "Manura, you will expedite the acquisition of the human's technical data and find an appropriate target for them to engage. During your absence, we've located several possible worlds that might harbor Korvil outposts." She sat silently for a few moments before coming to a decision. "Choose several, and I'll make the final decision. It would be best Domagera to Domagera. Now, leave me and let me think."

Linnas poured a not inconsiderable amount of fire wine into a crystal glass, eagerly anticipating the effects, and waited for Sitha to arrive.

The next morning, the door chime woke all four humans with its insistence. Shirley was the first to the door, though not by much. It slid open to reveal Sitha, this time appearing as if she'd had time to make herself presentable and ready to tackle whatever the day might hold. "I beg your forgiveness, Doma Dahlquist," she said formally, "but it's one hour before your shuttle lands, and they've already contacted Defense Command for permission to do so. Should I give them permission to land?"

Shirley looked sleepily over her shoulder. Seeing Kitty, she raised an eyebrow, and Kitty just nodded. "That would be acceptable, Doma kep Parrasine," Shirley said, stumbling through the Shiravan translation. "We'll be ready. Thank you."

The door slid shut as the Shiravan woman turned away. Kitty said loudly, so as to be heard throughout the suite, "Okay, people, we've got a long day ahead of us. Let's get cracking." She turned back to her room and an eagerly anticipated shower. Twenty minutes later, changed into her duty blacks, she walked out of her room, overnight case in hand, and looked at her watch. Thomas, always one of the first for almost all functions, was already waiting. "Apple juice, Madam Herald?" he asked, holding out a glass to Kitty.

"Thank you, Thomas," Kitty said taking the glass and draining it in two swallows. "Have we heard anything else from our hosts or the shuttle?"

"Not yet, Madam Herald," he answered. "But I expect to hear something soon. The *Federal Case* is aware of the situation, as well as the other two ships. I took the liberty of calling as soon as the Shiravan left." Kitty's eyebrows rose slightly at his wording, but she said nothing. Facing away from him, he never noticed.

Shortly, Miranda and Shirley joined them, waiting impatiently like many passengers throughout the centuries must have felt before a momentous voyage.

Kitty picked up the comm link, and without triggering it, she said, "This is Domagera Hawke. How long before our shuttle arrives?"

The response was almost immediate. "Your transport will arrive within the half hour, Domagera. Can I be of any further assistance?"

"Yes. I'd like to speak to Domagera des Harras, if she

has risen for her day. Also, would you inform Doma Sitha that we're about to depart?"

"At once, Domagera," came back over the unit. This time no telltale cut-off informed her that the circuit had gone dead, and the fact that she hadn't triggered the unit didn't go unnoticed by her companions. She made a show of indicating that the unit was still active and set it back down on the table.

Ten minutes passed and the door chimed. Kitty passed her hand over the wall-plate and admitted Sitha. "Domagera des Harras is awaiting you at the landing field," Sitha informed her. "She wishes to see for herself some of the modifications you've made to your vessels."

"Am I to understand that she wishes to inspect one of our ships personally?" Kitty asked, formally.

"Yes, Domagera. And she wishes to ride up to the *Vega* with you, if you have no objections. I'll also accompany her."

"If your security has no objections, then neither do I," Kitty said, a bit nonplussed. "Shall we go wait for the shuttle to land?"

Sitha turned and walked slowly away, trusting that all the humans were ready to go. A short walk took them to a side door leading onto a large, open expanse. "The auxiliary landing field," she said. "The main field is for far larger ships than mere shuttles."

Kitty looked around and saw a small group some hundred yards away, the Domagera evident by her separation from the rest. Rentec was present, along with Minister sel Garian, who stood closest to her leader. Kitty gripped her overnight case a bit more tightly and started across the alien landscape. The grass felt the same under her shoes, but the color was so different that the alien nature of the situation was driven even deeper.

The shuttle hadn't landed yet, so she walked up to Linnas and set her case on the grass. "I understand you wish to personally inspect one of our ships," Kitty said conversationally.

"I'd consider it an honor, if you agree, Kitty." The Matriarch seemed in higher spirits than the night before.

"Of course, Linnas, but you must remember that our ceilings are considerably lower than yours. And the lighting is considerably brighter. You might find the tour somewhat uncomfortable," Kitty warned.

"No matter. I've been briefed on those aspects of your ships. I want to see the innovations you've made to our technology firsthand. Dry statistics in a computer just won't do," the Shiravan leader answered lightly.

Moments later, Miranda pointed toward the east, almost directly into the reddish ball that was starting to show itself above the Stala's. Kitty finally saw the speck that was the *Vega's* shuttle and glanced over at her guests. If she were a betting person, she expected sel Garian to accompany the Domagera, along with the two obvious security personnel and three other so far unidentified Shiravans. Kitty turned to Sitha. "I assume these others are going along as well to see what they can make of the innovations your Domagera wishes to see?"

"Yes, Madam Herald," Sitha answered in English but then switched to Shiravan. "Two are captains of ships currently in orbit, and the other is one of our physicists. It's hoped that they might be able to understand the thinking processes that led to these innovations and help us begin to learn how to think a bit differently about what we have."

"I see," Kitty said. "Rentec will do a superb job as translator. He's worked very hard to understand not only our words but their meanings in different contexts, but your input might be invaluable as well—to your Domagera, that is."

"I'd be honored," Sitha said, any other response excluded by the request from the human Domagera herself.

The trip to the *Vega* went much as Kitty had expected. The ride up in the shuttle was uncomfortable for the Shiravans since they hadn't requested any special accommodations beforehand. Kitty was quietly pleased that sel Garian was uncomfortable, and not just because of the lower ceilings and chairs suited only to human bodies. For the Shiravans, it was much like a parent visiting his child's kindergarten class and having to sit in one of the small chairs.

Linnas had apparently anticipated a longer trip to the *Vega*, but the entire trip, from liftoff to clearance to landing, had taken only twenty-two minutes. "It would seem that your people take to our technology well," Linnas said as she looked out into the shuttle bay. "I'm interested in what my people have told me about your new ideas for some of our older technology."

Kitty already knew from two years with Rentec, Maratai, and Captain do' Sirkis that the level of technology aboard the *Galileo* was at least state of the art for when she'd left port just eight years before. Not so much could change in that time, knowing how the Shiravans dedicated themselves to maintaining the status quo.

The shuttle let itself be pulled into its berth, the pilots wisely deciding not to show off with so many high-ranking persons aboard. The ramp touched the deck, and Kitty made sure she was at the doorway as each passenger got off. Her own captains waited until the guests had stepped off the ramp before descending themselves.

"I was expecting much lower ceilings," Linnas said to Kitty as she waited for the last person to disembark.

"You'll find them soon enough," Kitty said, "throughout the entire rest of the ship, excepting the engine rooms, I'm afraid," Kitty apologized. "This is just the docking bay. Each ship that lands is inspected and rearmed and/or repaired each time it comes in. Then, it's moved to its own launch tube, except for the shuttles that remain here. The extra headroom is if we need to tear a shuttle or Mamba apart for some reason. Now, we're about in the middle of the ship. We can either begin our tour with the engines or the forward torpedo bays and sensor arrays."

Rentec had been keeping up a running translation, shortened only to expedite time. Kitty decided to speak a bit slower, letting him keep up more easily. One of the captains made a quiet comment. Kitty understood it but let Rentec translate for the other humans present who might not understand. "Captain des Gara would be most interested in your engine room first, if no one else objects," he said.

"By all means then, let's go to the engine room," she said merrily, her voice hiding the ennui that always accompanied these tours. "You know the layout as well as the rest of us, Mister Ambassador," Kitty said. "Why don't you lead the way and tell our guests what they're seeing as we go?"

With a slight nod to Kitty, Rentec led off toward a distant hatch. He described the various stations they passed along the way, as well as their analogous relationship to Shiravan stations. He reached the closed door, a red sign beside it spelling out the fact that the area beyond was restricted. Kitty stepped forward and held her armband against a sensor below the sign, and the door slid open, revealing the *Vega's* heart.

Several technicians looked around at the sound of the door opening but turned back to their jobs without a word until they realized that half a dozen Shiravans had entered with the Herald. Surreptitious straightening of uniforms went on, along with quickly updated entries in various logs.

Silence reigned as the two strange Shiravan captains moved slowly throughout the room. Linnas and sel Garian moved from one area to another as well. Kitty had no trouble with those two, but Rentec was being run ragged by the two captains calling him to translate some esoteric answer they couldn't fathom for themselves.

One of the Shiravan captains, frustrated by the slowness of the translations, came over to Kitty. "Please forgive the rudeness, Domagera Hawke," he said, bowing deeply, "but I've heard your fluency with our tongue and am eager to hear the answers to my questions from someone with an intimate knowledge so I can get to the kernel of the matter without double translations, if it will not trouble you greatly."

Kitty waved her hand expansively. "Ask whatever you will, Captain. It will be my honor to enlighten you or accept enlightenment if we've overstepped the limits of the technology."

"I cannot see the necessity of the third power core, Domagera. Please enlighten me, if you're able." The captain was so engrossed in the subtle differences and the huge addition of an entirely—to him, at least—unnecessary power core that he never noticed that he'd voiced the near-disastrous assumption that a superior might not know something.

Having spent almost a year playing protocol games

with sel Garian, Kitty recognized the captain's gaffe. Not one to want to see talent wasted just because of one mistake, she overlooked the unintentional insult and just gave the same answer she'd given to so many captains in the First and Second contact fleets. "With your design, your two power cores supply power to the engines and the weapons, with a small bit shunted off for what we call essential services, life support, power to sensor arrays and essential controls, which in a warship means all systems and little else. That gives you a finite amount of power for each function, with no thought to borrowing power to move it from one system to another.

"Once we were able to actually project shields around ships, necessitating the third core, it was a logical leap for one of our technicians to crosswire the three cores to provide additional power to whichever system needed it. You must remember," she noted dryly, "that this was at a time when we'd lost all of the higher functions of the computer. If the designs for the bases and various ships hadn't been duplicated in another area of the *Kreth*, we might not even have had those available to us. We'd expanded on your own technology, remember, and installed shields against high-powered, incoming missiles, so we felt it necessary to have a separate power source for that system as well. You've possibly noticed that our sterns are somewhat larger than yours. The generators and extra power core account for that. Also, as I've said, we have them all cross-connected so we can divert power from less necessary places to critical areas as needed. Suppose we needed to harden our shields against an unexpectedly high number of incoming missiles? Our active antimissile defenses, what we call point defense, can only handle so much. Even the shields can be overwhelmed if enough missiles are thrown at us. We aren't invulnerable, just harder to kill, so we temporarily divert power from, say weapons to shields, you see?"

The other captain, Maragon, strolled around, looking at the various command consoles, much as Kitty had upon her first visit to the *Galileo's* bridge. At one, Maragon stopped and scanned it closely. She looked at several dials, all labeled, of course, in English.

"Chudara do' Verlas," she called. She waved at the console and asked, "Errocerra, se jimana?" Translating for the sake of Kitty's companions, Rentec said, "May I, please? I believe she's requesting to test out the board. I believe that's the one controlling cooling and heating to this one room."

"As long as she doesn't blow us up or start a war, she's welcome to play with it as much as she wants. It looks like something she knows." She waved her hand at the console in question. "Aya, Sorgala," acknowledging the captain's rank.

Bowing a bit distractedly, the captain turned back to the console and began hesitantly, at first, pressing buttons.

Kitty looked around. "For those of you who wish to move on, I'll leave a guide to bring Sorgala Maragon along when she finishes her analysis of our hardware here." Receiving a semi-cognizant wave at her suggestion, Kitty nodded at one of her security team. He nodded back and moved over against the wall.

Linnas spoke up. "I, for one, would like to see a fully functional… what do you call them? Mambas? But I guess decorum would have us examine your bridge first to see how your ship is run. We could inspect the weapons on the way out and save the best for last."

Linnas was a bit surprised when Kitty made the sound she'd been told was a polite chuckle. "We think much alike, you and I," Kitty said, a smile creasing her face. "Come, let's do things in the proper manner." She moved off toward what was obviously a lift door. Truly, the humans had copied much without making many changes. The ceilings were lower to accommodate their more diminutive stature, true, but the ship was no smaller. This gave them room for two or more extra decks and an unknown number of additional point-defense units, which wasn't an idea Linnas cared to follow at the moment.

Deck Three proved to be the central command point for the humans as well, Linnas noted as she walked into a scene of quiet competence. The arrival of several aliens didn't slow the muted chatter of the operators at their various stations. Doing so would have surprised her completely. She'd come to think of these humans as more focused, more vibrant, and more confident rather than younger. The almost universal dismissal of the Shiravan presence showed her their level of competence. Only the shift commander even acknowledged their presence, and that with a slightly raised eyebrow. Her hosts easily missed the wave of her hand that told the duty officer to go about her business.

Rentec translated whenever he was specifically requested to do so but remained in the background as much as possible. The efficient functioning of a ship holding orbit was obvious enough to the two captains that they soon wanted to see more of the ship, with their eventual arrival at one of the Mambas.

The tour passed through one of the forward torpedo bays. Captain Maragon, having returned to the tour, walked over to one of the tables where she looked down at one of the torpedoes, strapped into place and opened up for servicing. Kitty stepped forward and said, "Regular maintenance makes sure we have a high on-target rate of active missiles."

Maragon looked down at Kitty and asked, "Does it also include a power core both front and rear? I see no connections that might send power to the engines, and the power core takes up the place of the explosive package we always install on..." She ran down, and an expression others might call a smile crossed Kitty's face. Linnas had come to know that expression well as Maggie and Derek prepared for their journeys home and sincerely prayed to the Spirits that it never be directed her way.

Linnas watched as Kitty let the captain arrive at her own conclusion. "The first core breaches their exterior hull, and the actual power core detonates that much further inside the target, multiplying the amount of damage exponentially. Our conventional explosive wastes itself on the thicker Korvil hull so the power core won't breach the inner hull." Captain Maragon looked down at the Herald. "I'm very glad you're on our side, Domagera," she said sincerely, bowing slightly.

"Thank you, Captain," Kitty said, smiling. "I'll take that as a compliment." She turned to her other guests. "Well, would anyone care to see a parda kellin, human style?"

Getting positive responses all round, Kitty pulled her comm link off her belt and keyed in a call code. "This is the Herald," she announced to a tiny voice that came out of the unit. "Please ask the Officer of the Deck to have a Mamba moved to the shuttle deck for inspection. Any one will do, just make sure all the controls are locked."

Linnas suppressed a moment of… was it anger?... at the translation. Then she realized that the controls would surely be labeled in English, and she'd be sitting in an armed vessel inside another vessel. Kitty was nothing if not pragmatic. She and Kitty led the group back down the elevators to the shuttle deck to find what she could only describe as a close cousin of the fighters she'd once flown on her own. Longer by at least a third, the entire stern was more massive, with three engine nacelles rather than the standard two.

The only other obvious changes were the relative size—to match the engines, she supposed—and three torpedo launch tubes per side. Climbing the ladder provided, she looked down into the smaller, human-sized space and asked, "Why all the extra room surrounding the pilot?"

Kitty answered, "Not all of the changes are purely external, Your Grace. Just as the engines are larger, so is the top speed, necessitating a larger grav sump. This ship also employs shields, admittedly not of the class that can be installed on a full-sized ship but enough to get a pilot out of a lot of scrapes in combat. Also, we now carry a total of thirty missiles, allowing each pilot five six-torpedo runs at any given target or just a longer mission, firing singly or in pairs. The missiles are housed around and below the pilot. You'll also notice that the nose of the vessel is a bit longer than your parda kellin, allowing a larger sensor array and a slightly larger computer."

Rentec translated, and Captain Gara asked, "You surround your pilots with all of their torpedoes? How can you get someone to fly in such a deathtrap?"

Kitty's laugh was almost musical. "Captain Gara, where do you keep the torpedoes on your fighters?"

"In the nose, where they can be cycled into the launch tubes more efficiently," he answered indignantly.

Kitty walked over to a wooden stand. On it sat a pad of papers of an exceedingly large size. She lifted the first one over the back and revealed what turned out to be a diagram of the parda kellin before humanity got their hands on it. Clearly shown was the location of the torpedoes, grouped around their launch chambers, complete with the assemblies that moved the weapons into position—number of missiles, time to reload, reacquire targets, top speeds, and ability to reach those speeds delineated for all to see.

This sheet was moved over the back of the stand, and the newer version was shown. "Tell me, Captain," Kitty asked, "What would happen if an enemy made a direct hit on your torpedo storage area?"

"The entire vessel and pilot would be vaporized, of course," the captain answered as if he was speaking to a youngling. Linnas started to speak to his audacity, but Kitty caught her eye and she stilled her tongue. Not sure what was coming, she waited in anticipation.

Kitty waved to the ladder on the other side. "Please, Captain, climb up and answer one question for me, if you would be so kind." Her voice left no room for dissension, so the captain did as he was bid, although slowly, as if he were going to his death. From the ground, Kitty's voice still resonated. "If you find yourself able, Captain, I'd be most pleased if you'd sit down in the cockpit. I realize this ship has been redesigned for humans, but you should still be able to fit for these few moments."

Linnas looked across from the ladder on the other side. "If you won't sit in her, Captain, I surely will, although I don't know if I'd be able to answer

Domagera Hawke's questions as well as you would."
The Matriarch's remark left the captain no room to back
out. He slowly stepped onto the seat and squirmed into
the chair, finding that there was enough leg and hip
room if he slid his feet past the lower controls. He
looked up at the canopy, judging, Linnas believed,
whether or not it would leave him head room once
closed.

He looked down at the human, feet spread, hands on
hips, looking up, waiting. "What is your question,
Domagera?"

"What would happen if this vessel took a direct hit in
its torpedo storage area?"

"Why, it would explode as surely as one of..." His
face reddened even further than normal. "My apologies,
Domagera. Your point is made and made well, I might
add. It just seems so," he searched for a word, "unsafe to
have all the torpedoes surrounding the pilot. Of course,
you did mention that this vessel has shields to prevent
just that occurrence."

"You may come down now, Captain. And yes, it does
carry shields, primarily forward only. There isn't enough
room to provide generators to completely protect the
craft."

Linnas helped the captain extricate himself from the
cockpit and eased into his place. "Come look at this,
Captain," she heard Kitty say. The two made their way
to the strange board of papers, and Kitty's descriptions
and justifications faded into the background as she lost
herself in a world she'd thought permanently behind her.
Her hand caressed the central control, what the humans
called a joystick, and remembered the few missions
she'd been allowed to fly as Domagera-designate.

Some time passed—just how much, she didn't know

until she looked down and found the eyes of Manura staring at her. Resignedly, she awkwardly climbed out of the craft and made her way down the ladder to her Second Voice. "I am surprised to see you here, Manura. I thought you knew all there was to know about their new parda kellin."

"I do, Your Grace," Manura said tersely. "Don't forget, I was able to get engineering reports on the two crippled ships the *Esmit* rescued. As a matter of fact, those two ships are on the surface now, being taken apart with great glee."

"Then, why are you here? There isn't much that can bring you out of your special world, old friend."

"I was issued a challenge, Your Grace," Manura said. "Immediately upon finding the right target, I had a pilot fly me here so that I might discharge my part of the challenge. Only the fact that our new allies don't understand our customs has kept me from answering the challenge in the proper manner. Instead, I've chosen to do exactly as challenged. I have a target for the human battle group."

CHAPTER TWENTY-FOUR

Admiral of the Fleet Simon Hawke felt like tearing something apart with his bare hands, and he didn't much care what it was. The pacing he'd finally broken himself of because of Kitty's nagging was back with a vengeance. And knowing she was forty-odd lightyears away didn't make him feel any better. Half the time he couldn't even remember the number.

Simon often found himself on Vesta as more and more of his duties kept him groundside, overseeing operations rapidly increasing in size. With the addition of the Shiravan translation program and their star charts, it had just become a matter of securing the immediate area and starting to systematically attack anything that even smelled Korvil.

Of course, all of these plans rested on their ability to produce ships without disruption and the good luck to not make too many mistakes too early in the game. Simon spent many an hour behind his desk, but a lot of his interaction was networking—*God how I hate that word*—at dinner or at meetings scheduled by practically everybody at just about all times.

One evening, while making rounds after dinner, he ran into Lucy's psychiatrist and casually asked, "And she's still okay, except for not wanting to return to Earth?" Getting a definitively positive answer again, except for that one particular point, Simon nodded. He made a casual reference to his memory problem. When the psychiatrist called it a classic case of denial, Simon retorted, "I hope you don't expect to be paid for those kinds of diagnoses. I'll tell you something right now, Doctor. Even though I may not be able to tell you how many lightyears separate us, I can feel each and every foot of the distance. We've been separated before, and this isn't denial. I'd suggest that you get to know me a whole lot better before you start tossing conclusions around."

The room had gone totally silent as Simon's voice went up. He looked around and then back at the doctor sheepishly. "Or maybe it is. How about we discuss it over coffee or something?"

A clumsy silence followed Simon around for a few minutes until people felt less like he was going to explode. Maratai took that moment to walk up, handing him a glass. "I asked your bartender for something nonalcoholic and he called this a coke." Simon took the glass and looked up at the alien woman. "We're both of us apart from one for whom we care deeply, Admiral. Any time you wish to talk, I'm available, if you'll make the same concession."

"Agreed, Doma. We have a saying, 'misery loves company.'"

"It seems that your people have many sayings, Admiral."

Simon laughed for the first time in what felt like years. "I do believe you're right. I'll bet that someone somewhere could go a whole day without speaking anything but old sayings."

Maratai took his arm, and despite her height, she seemed no more notable than he did. She led them to a group that was discussing the running of Vesta. Simon caught, "...but she's doing marvelous things with the administrative side of things."

Simon looked around at the various people in the group—most commanders by their rank, with one captains, Robert Greene, and a lieutenant—and decided to listen a bit before adding his own two cents' worth. "You know that she has Marsha Kane's friend, Jackson Potter, acting as treasury secretary, and from what I hear, he's making money for the Alliance hand over fist."

The speaker, a lieutenant he only recognized vaguely, said, "Admiral, welcome to our little ad hoc meeting. We were all of us wondering what was next after our destruction of that Korvil attack squadron."

Simon looked the lieutenant over. Seeing that his nametag read Alvarez, he remembered that he was the first Hispanic to graduate from the first formal classes held entirely on Vesta and was slotted to be a captain in short order.

"I don't know if you've reviewed the records of that action, lieutenant," Simon said a bit stiffly, "but if you do, you'll see that we caught the enemy totally unawares. That reason, and that reason alone, accounts for the total destruction of eleven Korvil raiders with a cost so minimal to us—three, or maybe it was four, Mamba pilots. I almost wish I could be there when you come up against an entrenched and well-prepared adversary. But, unless you *can* come up with something miraculous, we'd all be dead with that attitude. Never forget, we are not invulnerable. We're just as capable of being erased from the galaxy as the Korvils. And we're starting out with a deficit in ships, training, personnel, and I don't have any idea how many other areas. Our only hope is to revert to the animal cunning that first led us to pick up a stick and turn it into a club."

Simon's dressing down of the soon-to-be promoted

lieutenant brought all conversation to a halt. "Lieutenant Alvarez, I'd appreciate it very much if you'd start attending some of our planning sessions starting tomorrow morning."

He continued speaking to the circle in general. "We have a total of fifty-three ships available to protect our system, and that includes the generous loan of eighteen Shiravan battleships, cruisers, and destroyers, all of which are receiving or have received upgrades to their internal systems to make them as potent and defensible as possible. We've started making forays into local star systems, lowering the number of ships available for local defense, and we're expected to start sending some of our ships to Shiravan space to help take some of the pressure off our new allies. Remember, we only have one world to protect; the Shiravans have fifteen."

He looked around the circle of faces. "All of you need to do some number crunching. We've been in space for what, eight years now? The Shiravans have been out here for over four hundred and the Korvils, by all accounts, in the vicinity of three hundred. Now yes, we've beaten off all attacks so far at a truly minimal cost in manpower and machines, but that doesn't include the loss of over twenty million on Earth because we weren't experienced enough to keep all incoming attackers from reaching their goal. Looked at the right way, we really *have* lost a lot in the last eight years in terms of damage to the planet that will take centuries to heal, if that fast, and lives lost that we'll be blamed for without having an answer. And, of course, there's the *Clarke* and most of her crew, along with various other personnel up until now."

No one was ready to contradict Simon when he got wound up, least of all those who knew him well. Robert

Greene and Maratai looked at each other and let him have his head. Simon turned back to Alvarez. "Lieutenant, I've invited you to the meetings because you'll be getting the next ship to come out of the yards, and you're already working with assigned bridge crews laying the groundwork for filling out a crew. How would you like to be part of a wolf pack foray into Korvil space? Captain Greene will command, of course, and there'll be a carrier along, so the action should be short once you find a target to engage. The trouble is that by now, the Korvils must know that one of their heavy squadrons has been lost with all hands. That's eleven ships plus the fourth attack that never made it in. Every time we've kicked their asses, they've come back with a larger force, and look at what happened to Earth the second time."

He couldn't drill that scenario into enough heads enough times. All most people could see was the glamour and glitz of shiny new powerful toys and not the cost of acquiring them, maintaining them, increasing them, or using them. "Sheer power is one thing, people," he said, "but we're badly outnumbered so we have to use our brains. Think strategy. Think tactics. Think survival with minimal losses. But think about the losses, because there *are* going to be losses. Soon enough we'll start noticing that some face we were used to seeing around isn't anymore. We'll start adding more names to the roster of ships lost in combat, and I, for one, don't want that list to grow any longer or faster than it has. We'll take hits due to our inexperience, but we, as humans, have a history of fighting against overpowering odds and coming out on top. And let me point out one last thing before I end my tirade.

"In the beginning, the Korvils would attack and keep on until they felt they were outnumbered. The Orion debacle is a case in point. One single ship turned tail and ran from three fighters—Marks One's at that. But it took two battlecruisers and their fighters to corner it in the asteroid belt and kill it. Our adversary is a strong one people, and one that we have no way of understanding. They won't talk with us, and they haven't talked to the Shiravans for over two hundred years. It's just attack, attack, attack. Now, though, they skulk around our system, looking for a weak point, and they're much more wary and wily about how they go about an assault. We *have* made a difference people, and we'll continue to do so as long as we stay alert and in production of newer, more powerful ships.

"Soon, we'll be starting to lay the keel for our first true battleship. It'll be damn near the size of the *Galileo* without the factory section, but I want two more carriers first. Imagine in conjunction with two battlecruisers, a carrier and a farrier going up against, say a Korvil outpost. The amount of firepower would be devastating to any ground-based defenses, and unless they have more ships to spare than I think they do, we'd kick their asses all the way back to the Korvil homeworld, which is a planet we're desperately looking to find."

The Garmon sat on the throne that had been grown by his ancestors so long ago it was lost in the mists of time. He watched as the line of sub-leaders made their way slowly forward to profess their allegiance. The end of the line was finally in sight, so the ceremony wouldn't take much longer. Then he could get down to the business of finding out how many space-worthy ships were available to him. The yards on the outer moon of Korvilene were almost ready to start turning out ships again—one at a time, of course, until the other two yards could be repaired and refurbished.

This line of sub-leaders was composed of those who hadn't given their oath to him earlier. It had long been Korgan's dream to overcome the Korvil. For many farats, he'd been binding more and more tribes to his own power base. For just as many farats, he'd envisioned the battle that would bring him ascendancy, but it hadn't happened quite as expected. The Korvil had been weakened by wounds sustained when the Shiravans attacked, so his victory was tainted. Already, he was hearing it said that he shouldn't be the leader, but let anyone say it to his face and they could join the criminals and politically untrustworthy who'd been sent to the two moons to operate and repair the bases. Or they could die. It was no matter to him, except for those few he'd cultivated as his inner circle.

Finally, the boring fealty ceremony was over. The only leaders who hadn't shown up were off-planet, supervising their holdings in other areas of space, and, of course, the leaders of the two fleets sent out to keep track of the humanz. After the last sub-leader had passed through the Garmon's Pit of Justice, he carefully laid the sword he'd used to vanquish his foe across the arms of the chair, declaring the ceremony ended, and stalked off to his palace.

Why the Korvil's palace had suffered so much more than his own was a mystery to him but not one he was willing to look at too closely. The Gods had already favored him with the leadership of the Garmon people, and he was determined that they shouldn't suffer further if it was within his power to stop it.

He strode into his council chamber, finding the expected leaders waiting for him. Talk subsided as he strode to the slightly raised chair that was his. "Very well, we are met. Report." The tone was the same as he had heard the Korvil use on more than one occasion, and it worked just as well now. His eyes speared the clan leader.

"Sire, it's clan Gubarak's pleasure to provide over ten hands of ships to our endeavor to destroy the humanz." The count rose with each leader, some with more ships, some with less.

Finally, clan Grimat's leader stood up. "Lord, Grimat places two hands and two ships at your disposal. I'm at a loss as to why two other hands and one ship have not reported in after trying to search out another way to get to the humanz's inner system. Their return is overdue by several weeks now."

Korgan looked over at his personal scribe. "Lord, with clan Grimat's addition, we have almost thirty double hands of vessels available for attacks on various targets."

"Almost thirty double hands?" he roared at the assembled leaders. "It was only two farats ago that the Korvil was able to field over *fifty* double hands of vessels. Are you saying that we've lost over twenty double hands of vessels attacking these humanz?"

"Not just the humanz, Lord," one of the assembled leaders said deferentially. "It would seem that the Shiravans have gotten bolder or luckier than usual as well. We're now fighting on two fronts. Trying to take colonies away from defended planets is a costly endeavor, and the Shiravans are beginning to leave more ships on-station at each colony world. We're still able to destroy them, but we're losing a few ships with each attack. As for the humanz, we have no idea why these newcomers are able to repel us so effectively. Virtually no ships return from any assignment concerning them, leaving us with no knowledge of their tactics or armament. the Korvil sent one clan out to scout the outer fringes of their system, but that was clan Grimat, and I believe that would be the two hands and one that are unaccounted for. Perhaps they were trapped or caught unawares. All is speculation."

"Speculation," The Garmon said, "is for amateurs. We are seasoned hunters. We need to know all there is to know about our prey—their habits, their habitat, and especially their weapons. If these humanz have developed new claws, we need to know about it, conclusively. I therefore decree that all attacks against Shiravan targets will cease unless we are attacked first. We'll devote our full attention to this new threat, these humanz."

Korgan Garmon stood up to his full height, a bit shorter than the Korvil, but the Korvil was dead by his hand. He reached out and grasped his staff, on which rested the only thing brought from the Korvil's palace—his head. At Korgan's leisure, the rest of the palace would be razed, taking even his enemy's ancestor's names away. What more fitting punishment for one to let so many ships be destroyed? He'd decree that all mention of the Korvil be removed from all records and the land made into a public hunting preserve after sufficient landscaping. In a few generations, all remembrance of his line would be completely forgotten, as if they'd never been—a fitting end for one who would underestimate prey and bring the race close to extinction. Even now, the extermination squads were tracking down the last remnants of the clan of he who no longer existed.

He pounded the staff twice, bringing silence to the room. Clan leaders, ship captains, fleet commanders, and civilian leaders, such as those who controlled the production of food and those who controlled its distribution, as well as anyone else who thought they might lay claim to some portion of the new political hierarchy, all turned to face him, seeing the head of the deposed monarch. The scent of fear was almost overpowering.

Fear was something a Garmon could understand. Everything with any intelligence was afraid of the Garmons. Their cunning attacks could not be predicted until now, for some reason, by these humanz. Only this fear was of *him*. The feeling of power was almost so overwhelming that he felt the need to kill something. Instead, he dredged up the ancient words, "By the power of my own arm, by the power of my own mind, I claim the leadership of our people."

He transferred the staff to his left hand, picked up the sword he'd earlier carried, and waited. Some few, his closest associates, knelt immediately. A slow wave moved outward from each kneeling clan leader he'd convinced to join him whatever the outcome. The wave also consisted of the sub-leaders admitting fealty only moments ago.

Normally, Garmons had only two reactions—fight or flight, the latter seldom occurring. Now, a new element had been added—acceptance. The choice of flight had been beaten down by the very obviously positioned guards who not only didn't kneel but carried large, unsheathed swords in his presence. More guards stood amongst the shadows, these carrying the new power pistols. The choice of fight was defeated by those same guards and weapons. In such cases, a Garmon would defer to the alpha male as the only viable alternative, but even under the best conditions, that kind of obedience was suspect since it was coerced. Positive results would have to follow quickly to bind the clans to him unquestioningly.

He finally spoke. "We'll scout out these humanz and discover their strengths and weaknesses, and we'll find a way to use that information to our advantage. To that end, I declare that while I'll make the final decision, I'll also accept input and discussion of a rational nature. Therefore, we'll be sending out patrols to scout out the enemy on both our borders. Half will find out how badly the Shiravans have interposed into our space, and the other half will determine the exact location and full power of the humanz. Each patrol will be followed by a single small ship. If the patrol attacks or is attacked, the single ship will wait out the battle from a safe distance and return here with the information so we can devise a plan. We must know their abilities as a first priority."

He stared around the room at all the kneeling leaders. He had noticed who the last few to do so were, though. "You may rise," he said, having made his point.

"The target I've selected," Manura said to her Matriarch, "isn't far from here. Its defense consists of only seven ships, all of cruiser class or higher. If we send two of our ships, along with an observer, we should be able to assess the abilities of the humans. That will give a force of five versus seven. The humans claim that their shields are so much better that no other ships need be risked at this time."

"Very well," the Matriarch said slowly. "The *Shumara Vacht* will be one of the two ships sent as assistance. You'll choose the other, as well as the observer ship. You'll go with the *Shumara Vacht*, subject to the Herald's orders. Assuming any of you survive, I'll expect a full accounting of the humans' ability to conduct an attack scenario with full knowledge beforehand," Linnas shook her finger in Manura's face. "There will be no duplicity, Manura. I know you have an irrational fear of these new aliens, but so far they've acted fairly with us, so we'll do the same with them. Is that understood?"

"Perfectly, Your Grace," Manura said quietly, face blank. "I would do no other. It's true that I don't completely trust these humans, but they haven't led me to believe that they're in any way duplicitous. I just have a bad feeling about the future. I'm willing to commit two ships to the coming conflict, with my own person in the line of fire to prove that these humans can't be trusted to complete a mission without turning tail and running at the first sign of superior firepower. They have two battlecruisers, and the target is invested with three fully functional Korvil battleships. It will be interesting to see how the humans fare against such odds." She thought, *Overlooking the fact that they haven't told us about some of their more recent weapons modifications.*

Linnas looked her Second Voice in the eye and said, "I better not hear that you withheld assistance at an inappropriate time just to bolster your own agenda. I'm as capable of determining that as anyone else. Don't make me have to reconsider my decision to depend on your acumen just because you're afraid of a bunch of aliens who are giving our own technology a boost, making us capable of standing off the Korvils for the first time in our history. Just by virtue of coming here in person, you've been subject to the increased abilities our human allies have added to our techno-base."

Manura bowed slightly to her Matriarch. "I've never

given less that my all to you personally or as my leader, and I'll do no less now. I've chosen this target because it has those three battleships, which the humans claim their cruisers to be the equal of, and because it lies between Shiravi and Harlo where some still hold out hope that there are survivors. Should the humans win, the way lies open to send a mission to see. In actuality, since one of their ships is a carrier, there will only be four capital ships in the fight. But that carrier has a total of fifty parda kellin aboard. Add to that the ten on each cruiser, and the humans field eighty fighters."

Linnas waved her hand at a chair and invited her old friend to sit. Manura did so gratefully, continuing, "The *Shumara Vacht* will, of course, not hold back, nor will the *Seppigorn*, taking our chances right along with the humans. It's my intention to use them, the humans, as shields as much as possible because of *their* shields, while getting off shots and parda kellin of our own to add to the fight. All will be recorded by the observer ship for your perusal as soon as the battle is over, one way or the other, and some of our crews will get real combat experience without being blown out of space immediately afterward."

Linnas hosted the human leader in her own quarters, although protocol strictly forbade it. All that was needed was one misunderstanding and the new alliance could fall apart.

Kitty brought a bottle with her. "On our world, it's the custom for the one who's invited to bring the drinks. You'll be happy to know that this beverage is acceptable to Shiravan metabolisms without the necessity of the kemwood cups. Both Ambassador do' Verlas and Doma kep Parrasine have pronounced it fit to drink."

Linnas stood up, waving her guest to the seat that had been set up for her. "I'll get a pair of ceremonial goblets, then, and test your beverage."

Kitty settled into the chair, turning it slightly so she could look over the patio railing at the mountains. As her host returned with the two glasses, she admonished, "This is made from a fruit we call grapes and is known as cognac after it has… aged. This particular vintage is a dangerous one since its taste doesn't begin to hint at the pain and suffering to come if one were to drink too much, too quickly. Please, small sips until you can tell that what I say is so. Both Rentec and Maratai were surprised by its effects." She poured a small amount into each of the two delicate goblets.

Linnas took up her goblet and, following Kitty's lead, swirled the liquid around and then inhaled the bouquet of the wine. She raised the glass to her lips and took a cautious, tiny sip, barely letting the liquid touch her tongue. It would be highly embarrassing to, say, have to leave the room immediately for a moment. Finding the taste exceedingly mild, she asked, "You are certain of its potency?"

"Oh, yes, Linnas," Kitty said with a small laugh. "So, before you get the full effects of it without kemwood cups, why don't you tell me why you've asked me here at this time of night?" She turned to look at the sun setting behind the Stalas, an image she'd have to capture on video for her own sense of peace in stressful situations.

Linnas set her glass down, afraid the brew would make her lose her tongue if she wasn't careful. "I have the somewhat dubious honor of informing you that Doma sel Garian has found a target where your ships can show their mettle. One of my demands on the subject was that the target not be too big but still big enough to make you work for your victory. I'm afraid she's pushing my meanings to their limits, but I must either accept her choice of target, since she knows more about your technology than I, or assign one of my own. And I at least appear to remain neutral in the matter.

"Two of our own ships will be traveling with you, under your command. It is my hope that you'll hold those two ships behind your own, letting them have the secondhand use of your shields while they launch missiles and parda kellin to assist in the attack. They are not to just sit it out and see how you fare. sel Garian wishes them to be in or near the forefront so they can get some combat training and pass it along to future crew persons."

She took another small sip of the wine, feeling the small explosion that went off in her stomach. "The system you're going to attack will have three full-sized Korvil battleships, which we only recently discovered to exist, along with a number of smaller support vessels. Basically, they're just oversized cruisers, but that's enough of a description that it could be applied to one of our own battleships. Our main goal is to see how well your innovations fare against that which we haven't been able to defeat without serious losses on our side versus minimal losses to the Korvils. It's estimated that you'll face around seven ships, some of them larger than any of yours. Is this acceptable to you?"

Kitty looked over the rim of her delicate blue glass at Linnas. To back out now would have this alliance fold before it ever got started, and she was sure that was what sel Garian wanted. She let some of Simon's confidence well up in her words. "Only seven ships? And only three of them battleships? We've got them surrounded and whipped, and the battle hasn't even started yet. When do we leave orbit?" She downed the last dribble in her own glass and added a considerably larger dollop for her second round. "The outcome will depend on what their state of readiness is, how much they expect an attack, how many personnel are actually aboard when we shift into their inner system, and how fast they can get their weapons to bear. We have an old saying, 'When battle is joined, all plans go out the window.'"

Linnas looked a bit perplexed for a moment, then smiled. "We have a saying that is much the same, I think." She reached over and picked up the bottle. Pouring a considerably smaller amount into her own glass, she said, "Dom Carter introduced us to the toast." She raised her glass high. "To surprise and victory, my new friend." She waited about two beats, not long enough for Kitty to respond. "Your fleet leaves in two days. We can do over the exact details later."

Kitty raised her glass as well as an eyebrow. "To surprise and victory," she repeated. She drained her glass and stood up. "If you'll forgive me, Linnas, since I only have two days, I need to go inform my crews that they're going hunting. There's a lot to get done in a short time, and we need to be ready for departure. Besides, I need to get some sleep. There won't be much time for that once we get under way."

Kitty walked to the door, and just before she could put her hand on it, it opened at one of Linnas ever-present retainer's touch. *How do they do that?* she thought. *It would be nice if my people could see how things should be done.* She turned, placing one hand on the door sill. "The rest of the cognac is a gift, my friend," she said. "Perhaps you and Manura can sample it together while you talk over our conversation. Sleep well." Turning toward the corridor, she stepped through and let her guide lead her back to her quarters.

Manura stepped out of the shadows. "That one bears watching, Linnas," she said, pulling a second, Shiravan-sized chair over to the table.

"Oh, piffle, as Doma Spencer used to say, Manura," Linnas admonished. "If you keep this up, I might just start believing that you are—what do the humans call it—xenophobic?" She reached over and grabbed the bottle Kitty had left behind, still more than half full. She set the two glasses she and her previous guest had shared next to each other in the center and filled them each halfway.

Manura looked at the two glasses and said, "Linnas, I've served the des Harras dynasty since the beginning of my second vocation. I chose to serve my third in the same position as well, and your predecessor agreed that it was the wisest choice. You know I've given up family and clan to fulfill the sel Garian obligation to the des Harras clan though, few others even recognize that it exists."

Linnas raised her hand. "Let me finish for you, old friend. Over three thousand died on the day of my coronation because you committed an act of treason against your clan, which was, in effect, an act of loyalty to the succession, and that act was to inform on the leaders of the impending insurrection. Your actions cost the lives of three thousand and more of your own kin and allies, earning you the epithet Butcher of Harusel.

"You, as attack commander, called a last-minute meeting of the top opposition commanders and clan leaders, bringing them together in one place. You gave the location of those troops positioned to attack the Capitol building during my coronation to troops loyal to the des Harras dynasty, and you spearheaded the attacks against those troops after slaughtering at least twenty clan leaders and military commanders in single combat while your handpicked security teams finished off the rest, leaving those troops leaderless.

"Your sacrifice has not gone unrewarded these past twenty turnings. And I won't pretend to understand what you've had to go through to make the decisions you've made. It cost you what was left of the rest of your living kin and earned you my eternal gratitude. Elsewise, I wouldn't have depended on your loyalty. Spirits know, you've had opportunity enough to do to me what you did you your own, but not once have you let me down. To this moment you are a source of strength that I'd be loath to give up." She looked across the table and said, "Taste this cognac old friend, and think on the matter, for I must know. Can you be objective about the humans or not?"

The old woman looked again at the two glasses, the nearer one having been used by the human. For a time, she looked away, out at the stars, the patterns subtly altered from those she'd recently seen in human space. She looked deep within herself for the answer to the question her monarch had just posed. Could she be relied upon to be impartial, thinking of race above self? She recognized the symbolism of the fact that the human had drunk from the glass nearest her and couldn't resist a small jibe even as she admitted defeat. "You have learned well, Your Grace."

She reached out and took the glass farthest from her and swirled it in the fashion she'd seen from the shadows. "I don't see them to be as bad as the Korvils, but I see a dark side to coexistence with this human race. I see too much of us in them—us as we were five hundred turnings ago. They're energetic, inquisitive, and willing to take a risk where others weren't, but they're also motivated by what we call a higher imperative—the furtherance of the race. The Korvils are much like that as well, although they're closer to their primal ancestors than even the humans. These humans are just beginning to reach in the right direction.

"They recognize a higher power, but still they kill themselves by the millions in the names of their varied and benevolent gods. There are those who don't believe in a higher power at all, preferring to believe they're the end result of natural selection. We are, both races, much alike, but ours is more settled and theirs more growth oriented. Remember, they've seen that we have fourteen colony worlds and that the Korvils have claimed another twenty-one before we broke off negotiations.

"They have reason to get themselves scattered out as much as possible in as short a time as possible. In their position, I would do no less. I think, as well, that they might be smarter than we are. Certainly more inventive, at least at present, although one would think that the Korvils alone would be enough to bring our own inventiveness to the fore. Instead, we just keep building more of the same kind of ships and weapons and throwing them at the Korvils, losing that many more ships, and not so incidentally, their crews as well. These humans think differently, perhaps from necessity. I don't know. Suppose they'd gotten the *Kreth* and then never been visited by the Korvils? Would they be as far along as they are? Would they have incorporated the changes they have? By the time I arrived, they had four functioning bases in their asteroid belt and were churning out ships, missiles, and parda kellin capable of sending us back to the Stone Age if they so desired and were left unchecked. They scare the Spirits out of me."

She sniffed the liquid in the glass, then took a sip as cautiously as her mistress had. "And she says this is potent? How does it affect you?" Linnas had taken perhaps three sips after her initial testing.

"I would treat that with great respect, old friend," Linnas said. Manura took another, larger swallow, and let it slide slowly down her throat, admiring the taste but not getting a feeling even as potent as fire wine. Less so, in fact. It had a fruity tang that invigorated one's mouth. "I'd also treat these humans with the same respect you're going to come to have for their liquor."

Manura looked at her Matriarch and friend in wonder at the comment. "This?" Then the bomb went off in her stomach. She felt the heat radiate outwards until it passed through her skin. Sweat broke out on her forehead, and the room seemed to spin.

"I used the pretext of gazing at the stars in contemplation while Domagera Hawke was here," Linnas said. "You have my permission to try it yourself. The worst effects should wear off in just a few minutes, and then you should be able to stand. I'm certainly not going to try it for a while, though."

Manura finally caught her breath and grated, "What in the name of the Spirits is this stuff?"

Linnas laughed lightly, then groaned. "She called it cognac, and she warned me in advance that it was potent but drinkable. She said Rentec and Maratai both considered it was suitable, and since it wouldn't have done her any good to poison me this far from home, I believed her. But I'll certainly have to have a talk with Rentec about what he considers 'potent.'"

Manura shook her head, fighting to clear it of the cobwebs that threatened to slow her thoughts. "Who have you chosen as my successor, might I ask, Your Grace?"

"There will be no more 'Your Grace' coming from you, Manura. You'll live out your days here, if you wish. I refuse to coerce you into anything, my revered aunt— my revered aunt to whom I may sometimes come for advice." She held up her hand as the old woman started to speak. "I said, 'may,' Domina Manura. And don't think you're being set aside for a younger person. You'll be instrumental in shaping your successor, so you'll be putting in as many hours a day as you always have been for some time yet. Just training your successor until she's ready will keep you busy for some time to come and let you keep your hand in the pot while you're at it."

The old woman held her glass up to the younger almost in a gesture of contempt. From anyone else, it would have been, but this was Manura sel Garian, and Linnas chose to ignore to semi-insult. "And that would be Sitha kep Parrasine, by my guess," she grated out. "Not much for me to be teaching that one, Linnas. I wondered, how she would acquit herself while we were away. Worried actually, because your life depended on her doing her job with little actual field training. And you do know I was loath to leave and wouldn't have done so without specific orders. Even then, I might have stayed behind except for the need to curb those accursed kath-mora.

"Then I read the raid reports about rounding up the Spirit Witches left behind. An ugly mess, even for me.

And she handled herself respectably. Who would have suspected so many could have amassed so much weaponry in this day and age? The arrest squads took almost thirty percent casualties and the Witches over fifty percent, and Sitha stood at the front of enough of the major assaults to become well recognized." Manura stood up and looked down at the leader of fifteen worlds. "And if I should decide not to help train your pet kep Parrasine?"

Linnas stood up as well, glass in hand. "She gets the job anyway," she said positively. "But, if you accept my invitation to live here at Cho-An, you can help oversee the polishing of a very adept young woman, Manura. I'd be so grateful that I'd wipe sel Garian's debt off the des Harras ledgers, Domina," she said, staring into the red eyes before her. "I'd be grateful enough to sponsor Clan sel Garian's restoration to Great Clan status."

Manura looked stunned. "You mean the debt is cleared?"

Linnas nodded. "Yes, Domina, the debt is forgiven, assuming your student can stand up to the meat grinder I know you'll put her through. It will be posted in tomorrow's dispatches if you agree here and now to finish the training of Sitha kep Parrasine."

"I still won't be able to go home, you know," Manura said conversationally.

"I know, and I regret it more than you can imagine for one who's never gone through what you have. That's why you're being invited to join my family. I already think of you as Domina, and have since I was a child. Why should that change now just because you're nearing the end of your third vocation?"

The older woman looked deeply into the ruby eyes of her Matriarch. "Even though my relatives will not acknowledge my participation, I'm sure they'll accept the restoration and clearance of the debt. Great Clan status is a great incentive, especially since it was once in their hands and then was yanked away, and now it's about to be restored."

Linnas smiled slightly. "They'll have no *choice* but to acknowledge your contributions since they'll be part and parcel of the postings. You know I have to post all reasons for my decision to restore sel Garian to Great Clan status. If I don't, it'll get tied up in council debate for turnings, and I won't tolerate that when we'll need to be spending our time on other more important matters. So, are we agreed?"

The old woman tossed back the last of her drink and waited for the explosion in her stomach, and its aftermath, to pass. The only outward sign she showed was when she reached one hand out to the table to steady herself. After a moment, she said, "Agreed, and without reservation. Sitha's training begins in two days. She'll be observer aboard the human ship *Vega* when it leaves orbit for its first patrol. I, of course, will be in the same position aboard the other human battlecruiser, the *Federal Case*. You'll note that the humans consider the *Vega* to be their flagship, and I've already moved myself into second position. We have nothing equivalent to their carrier the *Canopus*, so we'll post two captains aboard as observers, both of whom have some parda kellin experience, having come up through the ranks."

Linnas stamped her foot angrily, childishly, she realized. "So, you knew you were being replaced even before I knew I was going to do it. Is that what you're telling me?"

Manura looked with new respect at the odd-shaped bottle on the table and remembered Linnas's warning earlier. She smiled at her friend of so many years. "It was my intention to resign anyway, Your Grace, if you'll excuse the title one more time. My resignation has been written and was in the queue to be sent when our patrol returned with the human refugees. I barely managed to stop the transmission because I knew my contributions were going to be needed for a while longer. I now have no reason not to resubmit that resignation once you're satisfied with the training of my student."

CHAPTER TWENTY-FIVE

Simon Hawke, Admiral of the Terran/Shiravan combined fleet, was bored to death. He'd spent two years sitting behind a desk once the DIA had taken him out of the field after his marriage to Kitty. He'd hated paperwork then, and he wasn't any fonder of it now. It wasn't that he didn't have anything to do, what with the personnel rosters, production reports, security reports, patrol reports, and upgrade statistics on Shiravan ships, ad infinitum, ad nauseum, that crossed his desk; it was just that he was bored with the whole business.

It wasn't even the reports from the now fully functional academy for ship personnel hopefuls. Those were beginning to make him feel more like a commandant than an Admiral. Staring at a viewscreen of the surrounding space because no windows were available this far inside the asteroid, he finally realized what the problem was. Loneliness.

And not even the loneliness of sleeping alone at night, not having Kitty to hold. It was the loneliness that came when one had no peers to talk to. Kitty, of course, was off on her diplomatic mission, and Gayle had taken command, finally, of a ship—the *Stephen Walker;* she'd named it in honor of her dead almost-husband. And Stephen, of course had died in the explosion that crippled the *Clarke*. That took care of all the Firsters, as the four had become known. There were other Firsters, but they were known for being the first group to join, such as Lucy, Shirley Dahlquist, and over two dozen others.

He snapped shut the folder he wasn't reading, set it aside, and checked his urgent file. Empty, as was his stomach, or so he interpreted the noises coming from that direction. He stood up and left his office, finding the outer office empty. He remembered something about his secretary calling him some hours earlier, saying that it was end of shift and did he need anything before she left. He'd answered almost automatically that he wouldn't be too much longer and that she should go. A quick glance at his watch told him that almost three hours had passed since then.

He made his way to the officer's mess, picked up a tray, and stood at the end of the serving line. It ran twenty-four hours a day, what with three shifts constantly rotating. The two tech officers he stood behind barely gave him a glance, busy discussing some problem down in hydroponics—something about a yeast culture that wouldn't work as it should. He was sure he'd see the report in the coming days.

He made his way slowly down the line, pointing at one thing and another, finally ending up with mashed potatoes, gravy, vegetables, and something that resembled turkey. He took two rolls from a basket at the end of the line and looked for a place to sit. Junior officers immediately stopped talking if he chose to sit with them, perhaps afraid of saying the wrong thing or just awed by his rank and Firster status. He was surprised to see an arm waving at him from one of the corners of the room. When he saw that it belonged to Robert Greene, he muttered, "What the hell," and walked in that direction.

"Just the person I've been looking for," Robert said,

indicating the chair across from him. "Have a seat, Admiral. You look like you could use someone to talk to. I feel pretty much the same."

"Really?" Simon asked setting his tray down on the table. A steward, noticing the Admiral sitting down in his section, hurried over to fill two glasses with water.

"Really, Admiral," Robert said firmly. "I think we have a similar problem." He looked at the steward. "Iced tea for me, please, and I think the Admiral will have a Pepsi." He looked at Simon, one eyebrow quirked up, and Simon just nodded. The steward moved off as quickly as he could.

Simon looked at his plate and took an experimental bite of the potatoes and gravy. "What similar problem could that be? I don't see you stuck behind a desk with all of your friends off doing god knows what."

Robert stuck a spoon into what looked like an oversized bowl of tapioca. "No, but just listen. I'm not trying to open old wounds, so don't take offense. I think we should call this an informal officer's call and go to first names. Standing on formality is so tiring, don't you think?" Simon nodded slowly, looking for the trap. "We all have our jobs to do, Simon," Robert started to say and stopped until the steward had deposited their drinks on the table.

"Unfortunately, we've gotten spread out kind of thin. At least the first three waves of volunteers have. Those are the ones you've used, for the most part, as ship captains and the more sensitive positions." He took a bite of the dessert in front of him and continued, "You Firsters have lost one of your number, bringing the number down from four to three. The second wave, which I'm part of, was almost forty in number. Do you have any idea how many Seconds are on Vesta at the moment? I checked the registry when I brought the *Nova* into orbit. Exactly three—me, Lucy, and one other. We, neither of us, have anybody we can talk to."

Simon cut through the rubbery turkey, took a bite and said, "I've had the same thoughts lately, Bob. Are you saying you have a solution?"

"I think so, but the final decision is up to you," Robert said. "How would you like to get out of here and go on a patrol? *Nova Group* is scheduled to leave in three days for a patrol in one of the sectors nearer the center of what the Shiravans have told us is Korvil space. Our objective is to hyper to the nearside of their local Oort Cloud, about a three-month trip, and slip in under minimal power. Add to that directive. Make us more like privateers. If we can find a suitable target, either ground based or flight capable, we are to engage, unless the opposing force appears overwhelming. And we won't be using Shasta Group's success to make our decisions by, either.

"Most of the captain's believe it's about time for the Korvils to start coming to the parties a little more heavily armed than before. And if not heavier armed, then more of them and more aware of what to expect. So far, we've taken out every ship we've encountered. That's got to have become apparent to their leaders by now. All of a sudden, a particular portion of their empire is swallowing up every ship that enters it. A spatial Bermuda Triangle? Or something worse? We know that two humans were in Korvil hands for almost a year before they were saved by the Shiravans, so they know we exist and where we are.

"Sooner or later—and my money is on sooner— someone on their side of the fence is going to realize that none of their balls are coming back. I mean, we know that has to be the case since the attacks have grown stronger and more…" he searched for a word, "desperate each time. Sooner or later we're gonna get our asses kicked, but I think we'll learn as much as we lose in the long run. It's going to cost ships and lives, but what are our choices? Unless the Shiravans are lying to us about the size of Korvil space."

Simon nodded, pushing his food around his plate without really eating it. "So, what are you suggesting, Bob?" Simon asked, a forkful of peas mixed with potatoes and gravy halfway to his mouth and his eyes boring into the captain's.

"What I'm suggesting, Simon, is that you're in need of something to get your adrenaline flowing. And rubber-stamping reports isn't going to do it." Robert looked surreptitiously around the room, noting all those who seemed to be paying more attention to the two officers than they should. "You know," he said, lowering his voice a bit, "we seem to be attracting a bit more attention than I'd anticipated. What say I come to your quarters sometime tomorrow afternoon? We can discuss my idea in more detail and a lot more privacy."

Simon, years of DIA indoctrination and training coming to the fore, never even looked around. "I'll take your word for that, Bob," he said quietly. "I've kinda gotten out of the habit of thinking that way. Tomorrow, I'll make sure to finish my day at a more normal hour and expect your arrival shortly after shift change. Okay?"

For once, Simon left his office at a more decent hour, actually a bit ahead of his secretary, who was busy revising notes on the various classroom and space-side studies of the crewmen and officers in training. The idea was to make it more easily readable by Simon, not that he couldn't wade through all the details and make the right decisions. This way just made it easier.

He stopped by her desk on his way out and looked down at what she was working on. "Demeter, don't you ever feel that this isn't what we're supposed to be doing?" he asked.

"Daily, boss, daily," she said in the informality of the empty office.

He smiled down at her. "Well, don't fret about it. I'm working on a plan to start a new department—one that's strictly designed to keep track of the students and their progress, taking it completely out of our hands except for a weekly briefing for me by our soon-to-be-found-and-hired training commandant. I think he should be attached to the personnel department, don't you?" he asked rhetorically. "Just don't spend too much more time here, okay?"

"No problem there, boss. I've got a date with a specialist from logistics in about two hours, and you know how long girls need to get ready," she answered. "You're leaving early tonight, yourself," she noted. "Can't be a date, so what's up?" She closed the folder she'd been working on and set it aside.

"Actually," he said, "I do have a date, but it's just with one of the captains so I'm not going to be having as much fun as you are. I figure on dinner and then the meeting, all about patrols, acceptable casualties, and all that kind of heartrending stuff. And for once, I'd like to climb into a Mamba and just cut loose for a while. It's something I haven't done in a long time."

"It's something I've never done," she answered. "I'm second wave, you know, and my first ship assignment was actually under Captain Kitty. Really drove her nuts for a while, since my twin was assigned to the same ship, only she got lucky and wound up in a command position earlier than I did. I started out in one of the forward missile rooms. Diana, that's my twin, said Captain Kitty had made some kind of comment about redheaded twins aboard her first ship. Neither of us could ever figure that out. Do you know what she meant? Or can't you say?"

Simon sat down in one of the chairs usually reserved for those waiting to see him. *Have to get more comfortable chairs in here*, he noted to himself. He wasn't about to interrupt this conversation right now. "Kitty, Gayle, and I all read for relaxation, but I got started on science fiction, well, actually because I had to. That's another story all by itself. Anyway, once the *Galileo* got crewed and onto her first trip to the asteroid belt, we, along with just about anyone who wasn't already an avid sci-fi fan, started reading more science fiction. Kitty and I both became fans of Robert Heinlein, often called the Grand Master of Science Fiction, and in one of his series, he wrote about the, shall we say, misadventures of a pair of redheaded twins. I highly recommend it for pure entertainment. I'm sure there was no other reason for her comment. I remember quite well that she'd just finished reading the series a short while before she took command of her first ship. I would probably have responded in the same way. So where is your twin assigned now?"

Demeter Ross, Commander, and private secretary to the Admiral, personally selected by the Herald herself, looked down and bit her lip. "She's assigned to the *Canopus* as a Flight Commander," she answered quietly.

Simon's heart sank a bit. A Flight Commander was in command of four other Mambas—combat, patrol, or attack—one of the highest casualty rates in the Alliance.

"Then believe me when I say I understand and wish you and your sister the best."

Demeter nodded. "Thank you, sir. And I'm sure Diana would, as well. She told me the night before she left that she looked forward to this mission. She felt that up until now—no offense meant, sir—we were just playing at Star Trek. Now, she has a chance to really live the dream and be one of the first to go where no man has gone before and make a difference. She was proud, sir. And I am too, don't get me wrong, but I do hope we can start sending some more ships their way soon. I'm working towards a berth, studying myself to death, but I want a position on the bridge. And to learn to fly a Mamba." The last was more an afterthought than a real request.

Manura sel Garian was not at her best this day. Instead of the normal sea of red faces looking at her, each face showing respect, these faces were mostly white, black, brown and yellow. Very few red faces sat in this audience chamber today. The eyes varied as well. A few were of that blue that so attracted a Shiravan's attention, but the vast majority were brown, black, a few green, and any number of shades of each. And none of the expressions showed a great deal of respect right now.

Yet, she was up to the challenge. One last time into the breach, so she must make it count. Rentec stood nearby; ready to translate into English what she was about to say, but enough of the humans spoke Shiravan well enough that it would be a good double-check for their peace of mind. She looked out at the faces and said, "Herald Hawke, Captains Lee, Breen and Dahlquist, Ambassador von Schlenker and your wonderful wife

Margit, Wing Commanders of the parda kellin coming to our aid, I bid you welcome. I wish it were possible to shake hands in the human fashion and reach a relationship. Unfortunately for both our races, this will not be an easy thing to do. We've both met the Korvils before meeting each other, and we look for the dark side before the light. And there's enough dark on both sides, as we all know, having been as open and complete as we have.

"You perceive us as static and... I believe the Earth word is stodgy, and we see you as headstrong, independent youngsters, just coming of age. We wish to see the status quo remain pretty much as it is, trading human for Korvil residency on a number of worlds suitable to your kind."

All who attended these meetings were urged to speak up regardless of rank, and a wing commander, said, "Not meaning any disrespect, but we already have the technology of the *Galileo*. What's to keep us from sitting out the battle between you and the Korvils and finish off the winner?"

"Your innate sense of decency, if I don't misread humanity and their core beliefs. We're the underdog, and you got the technology from us in the first place," sel Garian answered plainly. "You, yourselves have said that you've only been in space for eight years, something like nine of our turnings, and we really need to see for ourselves how your adapted uses of our technology fare against an enemy you can barely hold at the gate."

Kitty sat quietly for a moment after sel Garian's last statement, then stood up. "Doma sel Garian," she said, her anger barely contained, "I find that last comment to be insulting on so many levels that I don't even know where to begin. It wasn't so very long ago that something like that would have had the two of us meeting at dawn, swords in hand. Instead, I find myself on an alien world, having to tolerate obnoxious behavior and snide remarks." The murmur of voices died down as people realized what Kitty was saying.

"I know you've received reports on all that's transpired since we came into possession of the *Galileo*," she said, her use of the human name deliberate, "because I gave you most of that information myself, what you didn't get from Dom do' Verlas, and I know you're aware that we've destroyed every ship the Korvils have set upon us, as well as a few unlucky enough to get caught unawares. True, we've sustained severe casualties on our homeworld, but so far, we've lost only one battlecruiser and an unacceptably large number of Mamba pilots. Your tactics had gotten you nowhere until you formed your Reprisal Fleets. And that has been, by your own words, just one small outpost.

"We have even, out of the goodness of our hearts, given you the specifications to upgrade your ships to *our* levels." The stressed pronoun didn't go unnoticed. "And we made modifications to the *Shumara Vacht* before coming here, so your technicians could see what was going on, not to mention two complete new cruisers to replace your losses on our behalf. I'm beginning to wonder if we shouldn't just return home and let you fight your own battles from this side of Korvil space while we do the same from ours without any further collaboration. I'm going to have to speak to my advisers in private before these discussions continue."

Kitty settled into her favorite chair in the common room and said, "Ladies and gentlemen, I think we should return to our respective ships and let tempers cool down. All advisers and staff will meet aboard the *Vega* in…" she looked at her watch, "one hour." She turned towards the door. "I'm headed for my shuttle. Anyone traveling with me be there before we lift off or find other rides."

Outside, Kitty met Sitha. She wondered if the woman had been listening to the conversations going on inside but refused to ask. Instead she said, "We'll be returning to our ships. Are our shuttles still waiting?"

"Yes, Domagera," Sitha answered. "May I ask why the discussions have broken off so abruptly?"

Kitty said through gritted teeth, "Please lead us to the shuttle field, if you'd be so kind."

Sitha, recognizing the anger in Kitty's response, turned and started walking down the corridor, the crowd of humans following.

"The discussions broke off," Kitty said testily, "before I had to challenge your Second Voice to a duel. It just seemed inappropriate to kill the second in command of such an otherwise decent people. We'll discuss how to go about the next phase of the negotiations, if there is one, in private. The only place to do that is aboard one of our own ships, so we'll go there. Please deliver my apologies to Domagera des Harras, along with any personal commentary you feel necessary on what happened. I will relay my decision to the Domagera as soon as we've reached a consensus." Somehow, she had a feeling that Sitha kep Parrasine was better informed than she let on.

Inside the meeting chamber, sel Garian let no expression reach her face but one hand clenched into a fist unseen behind the podium. "This special session is dismissed."

"Freddie, Margit, did I misread the situation down there?" Kitty asked as soon as she was alone with the two older folks and her three ship's captains.

"I don't believe so, Kitty," the Baron replied. "I wasn't on board the *Shumara Vacht* during our journey here, so I don't know what went on and probably even wouldn't if I had been, but she was definitely baiting you. I'd be very careful before accepting any directions from that one in the future."

Margit asked, "Did anything untoward happen while you were on that ship? Some reason the Second Voice might have decided she wouldn't be the friend we'd all hoped for when she first arrived in Earth space?"

"No," Kitty said definitely. "We spoke about the customs and histories of our peoples, and I taught her how to play chess. Beat her silly for the first few months and then we split wins for a while, but in the last two months, I haven't won a single match. She's good."

Miranda Lee, of the *Canopus*, asked, "Did she give you any reason, before today, to suspect she was less than open to us?"

"None to speak of," Kitty temporized. "I have to wonder though. While she was in Earth space, she came to Earth only once, meeting Maggie's family, and then only traveling as far as Vesta. Not once did she let herself be surrounded by as many humans as she was confronted with today. I think she's a xenophobe. I think she tried to hide it by waiting until we were on her home court, so to speak, to confront so many of us at one time, and it still wasn't enough. I truly don't know what to do." She sat slumped in her chair, the picture of total dejection.

"Xenophobia has been a deeply rooted part of human

existence almost since the beginning of time," Thomas said. "It would appear that it's as much a part of Shiravan society as it is for humanity." He looked around the room. Six humans, himself included, sat in various postures of depression. "If I may make a suggestion? I think we should deal with someone else rather than sel Garian. Perhaps the Matriarch herself. You said she seemed to be more amenable to human/Shiravan interaction than you'd expected."

"A good idea," the baron added thoughtfully. "Perhaps Sitha could be a go-between to set up such a meeting, leaving the Second Voice out of the loop, so to speak. Of course, that'll only serve to infuriate sel Garian, if she's so inclined. Just remember, we have no real idea what their social structure is. No matter what they've told us, we have to take everything with a grain of salt. It may be that this Sitha will report directly to sel Garian first before going to the Matriarch. If she does, we'll know soon enough who the power behind the throne is or if des Harras is truly the ruler of all she claims."

"So, what do we do next?" Kitty asked, knowing she was in over her head. Give her something to shoot at, and she'd be all right. Her long talk with Toni Putnam had seen to that. But this was politics, which wasn't her forte, hence the presence of Freddie, the baron. And of course, Maggie—Margit—his wife, who was an incorrigible political savant in her own right.

"We do nothing," the baroness said firmly. "The ball is in their court, as I once heard someone say. It means that it's their move. Soon, if we don't contact them, we'll begin to receive calls from the surface concerning our discussions." She smiled at the group. "We'll have a junior officer receive the call, and when one of us is requested by name, he or she will just tell them that the discussions are ongoing and whoever they ask for doesn't wish to be disturbed.

"Sooner or later, the Matriarch herself will call to request to speak to Kitty at the earliest possible moment," Margit prophesied. "It will be couched in terms that won't assume an urgent request, and that's the time that whoever's on comm duty will say the meeting has ended and Kitty will be available momentarily. Keeping Domagera des Harras waiting for a short time will do her no harm and give her more time to rethink her options."

"What options?" Kitty asked, fists propped on her hips. "I mean, we know where home is and how to get there, so we can always just leave, but we came here to find allies. Just because one old woman doesn't like us isn't reason enough to run home with our tails tucked between our legs," she said, finishing up and breathing heavily.

Miranda clapped her hands. "Now, that's the Kitty I remember," she exclaimed delightedly. "I say we take whatever mission they set us, and if you get bored on the *Vega*, come over to the *Canopus*. I'll set you up as a wing commander and turn you loose on the totally unsuspecting Korvils. The bastards won't stand a chance."

"And the Herald's chances of survival go down correspondingly," Freddie admonished, effectively scotching that idea. "I'm afraid that a combat option will be unavailable to our leader for a while yet." Kitty glared in his direction. Before she could say anything, the baron added, "Do you have any idea what Simon would do to the survivors if we let anything happen to you? Especially if it occurred while doing something as dumb as flying this kind of mission against an enemy in their own territory?"

Thomas stirred in his chair. "I agree. That's one man I never want to have to face with really bad news."

"Oh, you are such a wuss, Tom," Miranda said, acid dripping from her tone. "How did you ever get to be a captain in the first place?"

"I did it by being the best at everything I was assigned," he replied. "How did you get *your* post?" His acrimonious tone dripped even more than Miranda's.

"That's enough, you two," Kitty snapped. "We'll get nowhere by sniping and backbiting." She looked at her watch. "I don't know about you guys, but I've had a long day, and I'm going to bed. Tomorrow will be time enough to see if Margit's right, although I'm not going to bet against her even if we're dealing with a totally alien mentality. I suggest the rest of you do the same."

CHAPTER TWENTY-SIX

Simon's door chimed on the stroke of eighteen hundred hours, and he said, "Enter," without moving from his chair. One of the channels that was beamed out from Earth was showing a documentary about the restoration of the South American forests and the American Northwest. Several shots showed what was obviously Alliance equipment and personnel working alongside downsiders in their efforts to bring a semblance of normalcy back to the area.

The South American ecology was most delicate, and biologists and biological research specialists were hard pressed to get the planting done that would restore the area to livability. But it was the tsunamis from the Bering Sea strike that had done the most damage. Tsunamis had raced back and forth across the North Pacific for days, their surges slowly decreasing with each oscillation. The original waves from such a deep, violent explosion had ripped through almost everything manmade within two hundred fifty miles of the shoreline. This was true for Russia, Japan, South Korea, parts of Canada, Alaska, Washington, Oregon and some of Northern California. Hawaii might never be the same.

Anyplace that acted as an outlet for a river, stream, or creek had been subjected to near-apocalyptic incursions of fast-moving, highly salted waters, each successive inundation smaller and smaller until at last the seas decided to take pity on the devastated landscape. Huge earthmovers rolled across a landscape ripped straight from the minds of all the doomsayers ever to spout their philosophies. Power poles were set back in place and lines strung in preparation for the eventual restoration of power to the areas. Most nuclear reactors had gone into automatic shutdown, but some had been as effectively demolished as any other structure. It was with some small bit of happiness that the authority assigned to clean up the radioactive mess found that most of the material had been swept out to sea—not that it wasn't of concern there, but at least it wasn't polluting the land. On the other hand, the seas were the source of all life, so new measures had to be enacted to deal with the new problem. Other power producers had in some cases been effectively scoured from the face of the Earth. Anyone living along the Pacific coast had largely returned to early nineteenth-century lifestyles and accommodations.

Hope, unity, and a sense of righteous outrage were keeping people working on bringing back the lost infrastructure. Roads had to be rebuilt from the very lowest levels to allow some of the larger vehicles to get in. Eighteen-wheelers formed solid lines, bringing supplies in and carrying wreckage and debris out.

Simon turned his head from the screen when someone set a glass of amber liquid down beside him. He hadn't even looked up from the scenes being played out on the screen until then. "How much time do you spend watching this stuff?" Robert asked.

Simon shook his head slowly. "Not all that much really. Just the morning news and only the top five or six stories. If we aren't there, or we're getting good press, I'm happy. It's the protests that get to me. It reminds me that we can't let our guard down again. Against anyone."

Robert settled himself into a chair that made Simon

turn away from the viewscreen to talk to his guest. He took a sip from his glass and grimaced. "I don't see how anyone can drink scotch," he said. "It's a horrid habit."

Simon picked up his glass and sniffed the amber liquid. "At least you brought Chivas." He looked at the amount of fluid in Robert's glass and said, "That one and one more and you'll begin to like the taste."

"Or my taste buds will be so ruined that I won't know the difference," Robert retorted.

"Or you'll be too drunk to care," Simon snickered as he took an appreciative sip of his own drink. "Me, I'm going to enjoy this without asking where it came from. Kitty said she couldn't stand anything but wines and such after coming out of the chamber, but I can still handle my scotch."

"Good. That way I won't have to lie to you."

Simon picked up the viewscreen remote and shut it off. "Okay, I've been appropriately bribed with my favorite alcohol, and we've traded witticisms. What's this about me going out on a patrol with you? You know Lucy won't go for me being gone that long."

"True enough, under normal conditions," Robert responded. "But these are not normal times. That's one of the reasons I went over your head to talk to Lucy last week about this very subject." He took another sip of fortification, scowled slightly, and went on. "I finally persuaded her to have an independent person decide whether or not you'd benefit from an extended working vacation, so to speak."

Simon laughed out loud, the first good laugh he'd experienced since Kitty left for Shiravi, he realized. "And how is someone going to evaluate me now that I know what they're doing?"

The humor of the question seemed infectious. Even

Robert started laughing. "The way I understand it, the absolute best way is for the one being evaluated *not* to know about it."

Something in Robert's expression made the hair stand up on the back of Simon's neck. He got up and began to pace, a sign of deep thought. "You know, of course, that I spent almost ten years as a DIA agent before retiring to Montana. It's been something like fifteen years since I was an active agent, but my position in the Alliance has helped me keep some of the skills I brought with me sharpened, such as knowing when I'm being followed or led, as the case may be, or when I'm being interrogated, debriefed, or pumped for information."

Robert looked him squarely in the eyes and took another sip of the scotch in his glass. This time, the taste didn't catch him by surprise, but there was still a less-than-pleasant look on his face. "Do people really develop a taste for this stuff?" he asked, deliberately not offering any information. Simon scowled. "That doesn't work on me right now since we're in a Simon/Robert moment," Robert admonished. "I'm offering you an observer post with Nova Group on a patrol that could last from six months to an indefinite period beyond that. The group will consist of the *Nova*, the *Pollux*, and as a carrier we get the newest out of the Taurus yards, the *Teton*. Rumor has it the captain thought about naming her the *Chicken Coop*, but her exec talked her out of it."

"Who's the exec?" Simon asked casually, letting the matter of how he'd been evaluated drop for the time being. "He or she has a lot of nerve standing up to Gayle when she gets her mind set. Especially after I had to practically pry her out of the *Stephen Walker* with a crowbar."

Hesitating for a second, Robert answered, "Bruce

Grimes, Lt. Commander, fast tracked into a combat position—not by his sister or his name but by his talent alone. He applied under his mother's maiden name so he wouldn't get any special treatment."

"Does Lucy know about this? I mean, she has to know that he joined the academy, but does she know about his assignment?"

Robert shook his head slightly. "The Deputy Herald doesn't get all of the paperwork we generate. If she did, nothing would get done. You were the one who preached delegation of authority, you know. I'm pretty sure she hasn't got a clue."

"Oh, shit," was all Simon would say about the matter.

After a brief silence, Robert said, "We'll have the Shiravan ships *Stigarn* and *Berra Feigh* along for the ride, both outfitted with the new shields and extra power cores, as well as the newer missiles. That will make four nearly impregnable ships plus a fifty-Mamba carrier. Do you want to go?"

"Hell, yes," Simon said, finally. "I'd do almost anything to get out from behind that damned desk and out of this rock. The only question is: who's going to be in charge while I'm gone?"

That answer wasn't long in coming. Two hours later, after Robert had definitely developed a taste for scotch (at least until he sobered up), he agreed to Simon's idea that Lloyd Pike should take over, "He's a natural, Simon," Robert said. "Just like a robot. Give him an assignment and he'll carry it out without question and to the best of his ability. I think he's still showing off for daddy."

Simon's comm link went off. "Hawke here," he said, a slight slur in his voice. He'd been in the process of pouring two more glasses, finishing off the bottle of

Chivas that Robert had arrived with. What he heard made him set the bottle down with a thump. "That's good news, Lieutenant," he said thoughtfully and closed the circuit. "Marsha Kane has just returned from her first patrol with the new battleship. Seems that she has a report to make and wants to see me at my earliest convenience. I need to talk to her and then send her and her battlegroup home for a short break because they're going to be the next group to head to Shiravi to lighten the load on Kitty. Once I get her briefed, we can go play cowboys and Korvils." He sat for a moment longer, deciding that tomorrow would be soon enough to meet with Marsha.

"I'm too drunk to do more than be thankful she's back," he said to Robert and flicked the switch on his comm link. "This is Admiral Hawke. Please send the following to the *Raptor*: Congratulations on your trials and first patrol, Captain Kane. Get some rest and meet me on Vesta at 0900. Hawke out." He looked over at Robert. "That's one of the few really nice things about being the Admiral. Very few people tell you no."

"Absolutely not," Marsha said in answer to Simon's question about problems, and she did so with absolute conviction in her voice. "Everything went just like clockwork, Simon. Raptor Group is ready to take on any mission you set us. You'll send at least one Shiravan ship to establish our bona fides, is my guess. I'll swap crew with any ship willing to do so to get crews that are ready to leave now."

She looked across the expanse of Simon's desk and secretly thanked her lucky stars that she didn't have his job. "I'm a ship captain. You set me a mission, and I'll go try my best to get it done. My people feel the same way. It's time to go really kick some Korvil ass." She didn't even mention the destruction of three Korvil ships in the second system they entered. It was all in the mission report lying on Simon's desk. She could see the last page with her signature on it.

"You're right about being a ship captain, Marsha," Simon said to her, "but you're also now the head of an entire combat patrol group. So far, we've only been sending out wolfpacks, and that only infrequently until we build up our ship strength. We'll keep on doing so, but your group will be fulfilling a promise to send help as soon as we were able. A second human fighting force should help make good on that promise."

Simon leaned back in his chair and said conversationally, "Well, we've got the big stuff out of the way. Your people get a bit of R&R. Go ahead and transfer whatever crew you need to get under way in about two weeks. I have the privilege of going out on one of Nova Group's next patrols and get an almost real, first-time-feel for what it is we're actually doing out here. I mean, I'm no stranger to the idea of killing someone if I have to, but I like my motives to be clear. This is my first chance to do something really meaningful since we started this whole thing."

Marsha looked at Simon steadily. "I'll never figure men out. You figure deliberately putting yourself in harm's way is meaningful?" She shook her head slowly. "And my uncle is how many lightyears from here?"

"About fifty, Marsha. He was assigned to the *Canopus* to keep her fighters flying while Kitty leads the diplomatic mission to Shiravi. We sent the best we had. Miranda Lee captained the *Canopus* and Shirley Dahlquist the *Vega*, along with Thomas Breen of the

Federal Case. They were escorted by the number two Shiravan, who showed up with the second fleet aboard a ship that we sorta rebuilt for them, showing them how to better utilize their own equipment. Plus, they got two Mambas to play with. I expect we'll be seeing more ships with shields and the new torpedoes pretty soon."

"I've got to let my mom know about this," she said. "She worries, you know. There's not much of our family left. Me, my mom, my uncle, and that's it."

"I saw to it that your uncle got leave before he shipped out, so your Mom knows about him."

"All right, Simon," Marsha finally said, "I'll do it. But I'll take you up on the 'home first' part. Take a few days to reassure mom."

"Agreed," Simon said immediately. "Make it a week, or make it two if necessary to make sure she's comfortable with this, and we'll get your crew situations straightened out. I just need a list of people you want and a list of alternates. If we can't fill all your requests, you'll just have to get used to new faces. And if you have any more questions, you'll have to go see Personnel."

Kitty sat at the head of the table, looking at her staff—the baron, Margit, three ship captains, and still, disconcertingly, Brandon Galway. "Okay, we've had three calls from the surface now. Do you still say we should wait for the Domagera to call personally? And do you think she will?"

"Of course, she will," Margit answered immediately, waving a hand negligently. "We may be of different species, but she's still a woman *and* the Matriarch. And she'll follow Shiravan protocol. If I had money to bet with, I'd bet the next message is from Linnas herself."

It was lucky for Kitty that no dollar value was mentioned because eight hours later, the Shiravan Domagera herself requested an audience with Kitty. The baroness intervened before Kitty could say much of anything. "Invite her aboard for the audience, since she's the one requesting it. It will establish your dominance and allow her to see again how we've modified her peoples' ideas. It is my guess that she's been secretly fascinated with the modifications all along."

Kitty took the microphone almost as if it were about to bite her and said, "Domagera des Harras?"

"Aya, Domagera Hawke," came back almost immediately.

Kitty looked at Margit, who only nodded. "Let me invite you aboard the *Vega* to finalize our arrangements," she said. "Would you do me the honor of coming aboard tomorrow morning?"

The few seconds' delay was almost negligible at this distance from the planet. "I'd be honored to visit your ship, Kitty. Do you mind if I bring another with me?"

Kitty raised an eyebrow questioningly at Margit, who just shook her head and shrugged. "That will be quite all right, Linnas," she replied. "I'll expect you sometime shortly after first meal, Cho-An time." She cut the circuit somewhat hesitantly, but firmly.

"It is difficult to refrain from saying I told you so, but I did, you know," Margit said, giving her husband a superior glare. "And ending communication that way," she said to Kitty, "was pure genius. You have established yourself as an equal, even though you control only a few thousand people to her fourteen worlds."

Kitty grimaced. "I wish you wouldn't keep reminding me of that," she said morosely.

The baron grinned at his wife and said, "Even the greatest Roman emperors had a slave following them around, reminding them that they were only human, my dear," he said. "I'll readily agree that any one ship of yours—ours—is more than a match for one of theirs or a Korvil ship, but each of those star empires have more ships than we do. Do you really think you can do anything but bluff until our strength is built up to their level? And what is their level, or the Korvil's for that matter?" His expression turned serious. "What do we really know about what we're in the middle of? Certainly, I agree that we should be helping the Shiravans, but to what degree? Should we not hold something in reserve? This is a case of the pupil bettering the master, in a way, and I want to be sure the master isn't going to be displeased."

Kitty said, "We'll know tomorrow. She's bringing sel Garian with her. I'm guessing we'll get our target then." She sat for a moment, letting the idea sink in, and then started to stretch. First, she extended her fingers, holding the extension hard, and then balled her hands into fists. Twice she repeated this, then went on to stretch each muscle group in her arms, neck, and shoulders. Finished, she said, "I think we should all get something to eat and then get some rest. I intend to ask the doctor for something to help me sleep; otherwise, I'll second-guess myself all night and be in no shape to act as hostess tomorrow."

The informal end to the meeting was met with approval all around, the day having been a long one. The entire group shuffled off to the officer's mess, eating mostly out of habit and not saying much in the presence of the odd officer who passed by at that late hour. Kitty finished and said, "First meal on Cho-An, what they call their planet, is about seven a.m. our time, so we should expect our guests to arrive at about nine."

She triggered her comm link to the Officer of the Watch. "This is the Herald. I want you to pick out about a dozen personnel to act as honor guard for the arrival of the Shiravan leader sometime around nine in the morning." Looking back at her group, she said, "Well, that's about all I can think of at this time. We should meet for breakfast about seven in the morning. Until then, I'll leave you to yourselves." She stood up, and the males in the group did the same. "Good night, ladies and gentlemen," she said and left the table, not looking back, her mind on a hot shower and a good night's sleep after a short visit to the dispensary.

Kitty's alarm went off a half hour earlier than those of everyone else on the day shift. This was intentional since she wanted the extra time to get herself under control. Never had Simon felt so far away. She desperately wished that life hadn't dealt them the hand it had, but here she was anyway, without his quiet assurance to hold her up. She climbed out of bed and shuffled into the bathroom. Half an hour later, washed, dried, and made up, she walked back into her bedroom and found that her ever-vigilant aide had anticipated her somehow, finding her bed made and closet opened. She wondered with some degree of amusement how the girl had overridden the room's security to find out when she was awake.

She wanted to wear the gava stone pendant in honor of the occasion, so she chose a black turtleneck over a black skirt that reached her upper knees. She strapped on a pair of three-inch heels, laughing at the thought.

Nothing would ever bring her up to eye level of even another human, much less a Shiravan, but they did make her calves stand out, and Simon always said she had nice legs.

She shook herself out of her reverie and hung the silvery chain around her neck, looking into the full-length mirror on the back of the closet door. An elf looked back. The creature was dressed exactly as she was, in all black and topped with the whitest of hair. There were times when her new appearance caught up with her, and she'd freeze up. Her reflection showed hair that reached her waist and bangs that stopped just short of her equally white eyebrows. Long white lashes framed her light-blue eyes. Her appearance made her remember what she'd learned from the computer. If she was going to live as long as these Shiravans, she needed to figure out how to get the regeneration chamber to work on people who hadn't been wounded to one degree or another.

She turned at the sound of a knock. *How does she do that?* She closed the closet door and crossed the room, stopping just short of the door. She took a deep breath. *Lord, just let me get through this one day*. She pressed the button that slid the door open and stepped through, hearing it slide shut behind her, cutting off her last retreat.

Kitty looked at her aide—she'd never refer to her as a personal assistant—and said, "Good morning, Glenda."

The lieutenant nodded respectfully, "Good morning, Madam Herald. It would seem that most of your staff had the same idea last night. Several are already in the officer's mess."

"Thank you, Glenda. I guess I'll be off then." She didn't know how to take this new aide. Even after a full eleven months, she seldom spoke about herself, other than her time at the Academy (which had now achieved the status of a capital A) and her time aboard the *Federal Case* before being reassigned just before departure. It had been nice of Thomas to let such a highly rated and classified person go just to fill out her own staff. What was her last name? It had been so long now that she almost didn't remember. Hallawell, Glenda Hallawell. She'd been his intelligence officer, a position that had originally been called the tactical officer. Mostly, it was a position that required second guessing one's opponent, and since the Alliance had no real data on Korvil tactics beyond three slash-and-run attacks, almost anybody with any higher-level gaming skills would do at the outset.

"Good luck with your meeting, Madam Herald, and may I say that you look stunning. Very yin/yang, if you know what I mean."

"I remember a saying my grandfather used when it was time to make a decision," she said, knowing the wording would be found vaguely offensive by her inherited aide. "Shit or git off the pot." Her reminiscence achieved the expected results from the prim and proper lieutenant. "His colorful way of saying lead, follow, or get out of the way."

She reached the door and placed her palm on the doorplate, exposing herself to the outside world. Anticlimactically, all she faced was an empty corridor. Shaking her head slightly, she turned left and headed off to fill the growing void in her middle.

CHAPTER TWENTY-SEVEN

Linnas gathered her nerve as she stepped into her personal shuttle. The coordinates for the *Vega* were well known, but the ceilings these shorter beings used made visiting difficult, unless one spent most of one's time seated, and she was supposed to get the whole tour. Of a battlecruiser. With more decks. She was sure the Herald would show off the wonders of her ships and then try to strike some kind of bargain for their use after wearing her down with all the stooping and tromping from one area to another.

It was with a great deal of surprise then that she watched her shuttle's controls being overridden and the whole craft being sucked into the side of the visiting warship and set down perilously close to one of the walls. She was even more surprised to find that an impromptu greeting/meeting area had been set up in one corner of the bay. The Herald stood there, oddly enough, with her chief opponent on this mission, Brandon Galway. She'd described him as a "friendly enemy" and shrugged it off on most occasions.

Rentec had come along just in case, but the Herald's Shiravan was almost flawless now, and only the occasional odd word needed to be translated. It was her guest that she wanted to see the Herald's reaction to. Sitha followed her down the ramp in the place usually held by the Second Voice. She watched with interest as the Herald spoke quietly to her companion, a look of bemusement on her face, if she'd learned to read human expressions at all. His expression was—the only word she could find—guarded.

"Permission to come aboard?" she asked before she stepped off the ramp.

"Granted," the Herald answered back, "and welcome aboard the *Vega*, Domagera. Come sit and let us talk." Her eyes kept returning to Sitha, whom she'd met on her first visit to the Shiravan homeworld. It didn't keep her from following the amenities, though. "I've had two chairs brought down for our meeting, and since Rentec is here, another is on the way. I must confess that I, we, that is, were expecting Doma sel Garian."

It almost seemed as if the Herald was asking why Sitha was present without quite asking. Time to see how badly she could shake up the status quo. "Doma sel Garian has decided that it's time for a change. She has, of her own free will, chosen to end her third vocation. She'll spend the rest of her days at Cho-An as a revered aunt. Sitha kep Parrasine has agreed to fill the post at my request."

The Herald translated for Dom Galway, and then looked Sitha in the eye, a difficult feat for someone of her diminutive stature. "Congratulations on your new position, Policy Minister. It brings honor to the kep Parrasine clan."

"Segala vin," Sitha answered automatically. "Thank you, Domagera Hawke. I will strive to fulfill my Matriarch's trust in me."

"Of course," Linnas said conversationally as she sat down, "Doma sel Garian will be available to her replacement for several turnings until she's comfortable in her new position." This was a thinly veiled hint that the mind of sel Garian wasn't going to be wasted in retirement.

Several thousand miles away, Manura sel Garian looked at the captains of four of the most powerful battleships in the Shiravan fleet. "You're to reach this system with all possible speed and make one, and only one, pass through it. I want the inhabitants aroused and looking for a fight when the human fleet arrives."

"But Doma sel Garian, two of our own will be with that fleet," one captain protested. "Won't that be putting more of our own people at risk? And in a ship equipped with some of the latest innovations the humans have installed."

"True, Captain, but remember that we have all the specifications on file now, and the loss of the *Shumara Vacht*, if it happens, while deplorable, wouldn't be totally devastating to our cause. And I'll be aboard that fleet as well." Once more, she stressed her orders. "You are to take no chances on getting caught or sustaining more than minimal damage. One high-speed pass to stir up the thitura's nest before the arrival of the humans, and then return here by a roundabout route as if you'd been on a normal patrol." Her eyes pierced the captain's. "You'll report to me and me alone as soon as I return, and none of you will reveal your part in what you are about to do, *ever*. I'll accept no disobedience and no deviation from my orders. Is that clear?"

The captain looked at her peers, and after a long, silent glance at each one, she said, "We are yours to command, Doma. All shall be as you wish."

sel Garian nodded curtly. "Very well. You are dismissed. Get under way as soon as possible, and speak of none of this except to your officers until just before you enter otherspace. And impress upon them that the orders come directly from me. That should be enough to keep them quiet long enough to bury your involvement completely." She appeared to forget that the four were present as she turned her attention to papers stacked on the corner of her desk. Raggedly, the four captains stood up and filed out of the room.

Kitty wondered what could have caused such a high-level shakeup in the Shiravan hierarchy in such a short time. She badly wanted to ask but decided to let it go for another time. "I chose the landing bay because I didn't want you to have to stoop over for hours at a time. I have no intention of taking you on a tour of the entire ship since you already know what most of this stuff is all about, anyway. Let me know what you wish to see specifically, and I'll escort you to that section. Or, if you wish to experience the whole ship, you can. I'll leave that decision up to you. Otherwise, this is the only space on the *Vega* that has ceilings high enough for you to stand straight and relax."

"No, Domagera Hawke, this will be just fine. Unless Sitha wishes to see anything, I'm perfectly comfortable right here."

The new Second Voice, seeming a bit uncomfortable in her new role, said, "I see no need to explore at this time, Your Grace."

Can it be that she is almost as surprised as I am? Kitty thought.

Brandon finally spoke up in Shiravan, surprising Kitty. "I beg your indulgence, Domagera des Harras. During the voyage here, I spoke at length with Doma sel Garian about the differences between the Alliance and the United Nations of Earth."

Kitty had never heard quite that turn of phrase before but let it pass, filing it away under things to discuss with Freddie.

Almost before Kitty could finish filing, the Shiravan Matriarch slapped him down. Hard. "I have had extensive conversations with Domina sel Garian, Captain do' Sirkis, and my ambassador, Dom do' Verlas. You have a United Nations, but they are never in agreement on anything important, so why the lie? And you are lying to yourselves, at that. Maybe our kath-mora have a greater impact than I thought. At least we are never so deluded as to think that we'll all always think alike on all matters. That's why I have a council. I cannot know everything."

Brandon looked her in the eye. Seated, it was much easier to do. "We have councils as well," Brandon said.

"Yes, you do, and that is all well and good, as Doma Spencer used to say. But in our case—it is better to say in *my* case—I can make a decision right here, right now, and you can only go back and convey my words to your councils. If I choose to ally my people with yours, and my council decides that the basic philosophies of our two cultures are too disparate for further contact, I can overrule them without even having to give a reason. Or the reverse.

"Perhaps your race will mature more, or mine will learn to accept a culture that has a male for a supreme ruler. We are too well acquainted with male-dominated cultures—our own, in the past, and the Korvils—and even though we're bringing our males back into the general population, we're doing so at a controlled rate. And Dom do' Verlas impressed me enough to make him the Ambassador to the humans. He spent almost a full turning with Doma Spencer and Dom Carter, learning your language. In the process, Maggie and Derek, as they liked to be called, learned more than a bit of Shiravan. And that is as it should be, but it isn't why we're here."

Kitty eyed the woman speculatively, wondering what was next. Pushing, she asked, "Is it to set a target so we can prove we're worthy of being your allies? Because if it is, we're ready to leave orbit almost immediately, although I was given to understand that you'd be sending observers on each ship, as well as the *Shumara Vacht* herself. A battleship, two cruisers, and a carrier equipped with the innovations we have at our disposal should be able to take on almost anything in an even match."

The Matriarch nodded in the human fashion. "Yes, that's why we're here." She reached out a hand, and Sitha placed a data cube in it. Linnas set the cube in the middle of the table and pressed a button on one side. Almost immediately, a starfield formed above the cube. The supreme leader took out a collapsible pointer, human enough in design to make Kitty's lips twitch into a small smile.

The tip of the pointer lit up as it was pushed into the pattern of stars above the cube. "Here's the star we have in mind." A white point turned to red. "Here is Shiravi." Another point turned blue. "You'll spend almost two of your weeks in transit, and, as of our last intelligence report indicates, you'll face between five and nine ships ranging in size from destroyer-class to battleship. *Korvil* battleship." She looked directly at Kitty, and just as if she was giving a lecture, continued. "The *Shumara Vacht* and one other will be under your command. Of course, there can be only one commander of any group of any size. So, you'll have a battleship, admittedly Shiravan but enhanced by some of your technology, two Alliance cruisers, a Shiravan cruiser, and one of your carriers." The last word was in English as the Shiravans had no word for what the humans had made from their technology.

"That means," the Matriarch went on, "that you'll bring seventy parda kellin to any confrontation." She paused for a moment. "I feel that the name parda kellin doesn't do your superb fighters justice. What do you call them?"

"Mambas, Domagera des Harras," Brandon put in before Kitty could speak up. "Named after one of the most deadly creatures on our world—a thing called a snake. A body about this big around." His forefinger and thumb made a circle that almost touched. "About this long," he said and held his hands about four feet apart, spreading them out and back to show that the length varied, "and one bite from this snake will kill a full grown human in seconds. The venom attacks the central nervous system and paralyzes every muscle in the body, voluntary and involuntary. The heart stops, breathing stops, and you die. Quickly. Painfully."

"You seem to know a lot about Alliance technology, Dom Galway," the Matriarch noted. She looked at Kitty. "Is it a common thing to tell your potential enemies things about your weapons?"

"You still haven't grasped the core difference between our factions," Kitty said. She looked at Brandon when she said it, including him in the comment. "We of the Alliance believe that at some time or other, the nations of Earth will outlaw us, making it almost impossible to bring in new recruits. They are going to consider us their enemies because they can't control us.

It's a failing humans have. But here's the difference: *we* won't consider them to be *our* enemies. They are, after all, where we came from, where some of us plan to retire to, and where most of us have relatives. It's going to be an adventure to get new recruits, much like our first batches, Brandon. I hope you don't think we're going to let ourselves be cut off at the knees.

"Besides, it will be harder to sneak in spies. We know you have them in place now; we just don't know who or how many. Actually, it doesn't matter. As you have been told in the past, we're going to keep the propulsion technology and weapons technology away from the bargaining table. We just don't trust you enough. Even if you have the data and somehow manage to build a ship and weapons systems, you don't have the technology to get the material and process it to make power cores. And you need those because nothing else on Earth will produce enough power to energize either the weapons or propulsion systems."

Brandon just looked her in the eye and said nothing. Kitty shrugged mentally and turned back to the Matriarch. "We'll be ready to leave orbit as soon as your observers are aboard. We have crews modifying at least one room on each vessel to accommodate your added height. Also, the gravity and lighting in those rooms will be individually controlled. We don't want to cause any undue stress on your people."

Aside from taking them into combat with a bunch of primitive aliens who are likely to kill them, Kitty thought.

The Matriarch stood up to her full height, with Sitha duplicating her move immediately and Kitty and Brandon a bit slower. "This time tomorrow morning, expect a small shuttle to approach each ship. Sitha will board the *Vega* and Domina sel Garian will board the

Federal Case. The carrier gets two because both generals were equally qualified and eager to fill the post, and neither would back down."

"So, you allowed both to go," Kitty finished for her. "A good way to get two opinions and keep your officers happy. I approve."

The Matriarch nodded once, acknowledging the compliment. She reached down and pressed a button on one side of the cube and the image vanished. "Take this to your Navigator and she will be able to program your course. And know this, Domagera: I already consider you an ally. It is not for my people to determine. Remember that it's far better to have complete control than have to debate endlessly a course of action."

She looked down at the smaller woman. "Despite what you or anyone else may think of Domina sel Garian, she has shown through her sacrifices that she has the best interests of the Shiravan people at heart, and she'll continue with me for turnings to come. Now, we'll leave you to your preparations. May the Spirits of Space fly with you, Katherine Hawke." She placed her right hand on Kitty's left shoulder. "I know what we lost in our first meeting with your people, and I have a better idea than you might think about what you're about to sacrifice for our people. The gratitude of the Shiravan people rides with you as well."

The matriarchal blessing apparently at an end, Linnas moved slowly toward her shuttle, Sitha accompanying her. Kitty and Brandon scrambled to get around the table and catch up with the longer-legged beings. Linnas and Sitha stepped onto the ramp of their shuttle and turned to the smaller beings. Linnas said, "Fingatha kesh, Domagera Hawke. I know that phrase is one you can't translate, so I will tell you that it means: Fight well and die with honor. Should you not return, your name will be inscribed on the des Harras family dusterna for all to know of your bravery and sacrifice."

Kitty looked up at her opposite, an even more difficult business since they were now on the ramp of their shuttle. "I don't think you'll be adding my name to your dusterna, whatever that is, anytime soon," Kitty said. "You told me a two-week transit. That means two weeks back as well. Add in the time it takes to scout the system, discern if your intelligence is still good, make a plan of action, and execute it. See you in eight weeks, tops."

The Matriarch looked down at the human, a strange look on her face. "Eight weeks it is. Then I order the carvers to start on your names." She turned and walked into the shuttle, followed by Rentec. Sitha passed the portal last, and the ramp began to rise, forcing the two humans back until it sealed itself into place as a part of the ship's hull. Seconds later, the shuttle was lifted off the deck by the internal repulsor beams, sliding through the forcefield and into space. The nose of the craft pointed down relative to the occupants of the shuttle bay and slid out of sight.

Kitty rounded on Brandon as soon as the Shiravan shuttle was out of sight and the outer doors began to slide shut. "What is this 'United Nations of Earth' crap, Brandon? I thought we were going to keep this legit. The United Nations isn't in any position to handle policy for a situation like this. Just which United Nations of Earth were you referring to?"

"That's not a subject I'm allowed to discuss," he said, sidestepping the issue. "I'm sorry, really I am, but you've known from the first that I was sent along to get the best deal I could for Earth. To use your own words, we just don't trust you enough."

Kitty's mouth moved, but no sound came out. She just couldn't find the words to express her indignation. Finally, she turned and headed for the elevator. "I need to get this cube to Navigation and then see about a captain's meeting. I'll call you if I need your input, Mister Galway." The last frosty words were spoken as the elevator door slid shut on her scowling face.

Her side trip to Navigation completed, Kitty slouched in a chair in her dayroom, looking at the faces of her captains and the baron and baroness. Freddie was the first to speak. "It seems that you have something pressing on your mind, Kitty," he said, "or is this a Madam Herald moment?"

Kitty didn't answer for a moment, almost as if the comment hadn't registered. "No, Freddie, Kitty is fine. I just don't like the feel of this—sel Garian stepping down at a critical time in Shiravan history, our Mister Galway suddenly speaking for the 'United Nations of Earth,' whatever that may be, and us getting our traveling papers, so to speak. I've taken the coordinates to Navigation, and we'll be leaving orbit tomorrow morning after we take on the Shiravan observers we've agreed to host. By Shiravan estimates, we'll face between five and nine ships, mostly destroyers like we're used to, but at least one much larger. It's my guess that it will be just a bigger version of a destroyer since that's all they've ever shown us and, supposedly, the only thing they have the plans to build. It would seem that the Korvils are no greater fans of innovation than the Shiravans.

She slouched even lower into her chair. "I heard the Matriarch say that the *Shumara Vacht* will accompany us because we've upgraded her with, and I quote, 'some of your technology.' Has anyone let slip that we haven't released all of our upgrades to them?"

Thomas, Miranda, and Shirley all shook their heads in unison, and Freddie and Margit joined in. "We all understand the necessity of keeping an edge on the competition, Kitty," the baron said. "I believe the Matriarch was just on a fishing expedition with her comment. If you didn't react, then she's none the wiser. She may have her suspicions based on what she'd do if our positions were reversed, but she has no real, hard data to base her assumptions on. Of course, that'll probably change as soon as we return from our mission."

"Hmmph," was all Kitty would say to that. "Anyway, you three should return to your ships and get your crews ready to leave orbit. And prepare for visitors, of course. I'm glad Sitha kep Parrasine will be the observer aboard the *Vega*. I'd rather have her where I can keep an eye on her, and besides, it'll make her more uncomfortable during this mission. She, in her inexperience, may make a mistake we can use later. As for the rest of the day, I'll be in my cabin unless I'm needed. By the way, someone call Engineering to have a suite set up for Shiravan standards on each ship that a Shiravan will be on."

She worked her way out of the chair and to her feet, the rest of her group doing the same.

CHAPTER TWENTY-EIGHT

The Garmon stalked a krath on the open plains miles from his palace on the newly named planet, Garmon. Having killed the Korvil in single combat, he worked quickly to assure his powerbase and inform the rest of the race that he was now the leader. Trial by combat had been the way of ascension since time had begun. The race took the name of the ruler, and the home planet did as well. Now would be the time for someone to try to wrest control away from him. Shrewdly, he'd foreseen the necessity of making the kind of alliances that would ensure his dominance. Secret meetings with clan leaders who'd have had him beheaded before the attack on Korvilene now stood him in good stead.

As he slowly moved in on the unsuspecting animal, he thought about more than just the hunt. The danger from that was real enough. He had no weapons except his teeth, claws, and brain against a creature almost as wily as he was. Stronger, faster, and armed with two wicked horns, the krath was at least twice his own four-hundred-plus pounds. All muscle and bad temper, the beast would scent him soon enough and charge. He wondered why the beast had ever become associated with cowardly actions. Like a Garmon, it wouldn't back down from a fight but would struggle on until it either won or was destroyed.

The problem was that the beast was so single minded that it was nearing extinction due to those very qualities the Garmon so revered. Perhaps he should order that no more be killed until their numbers had risen somewhat. Killing one singlehanded was a rite of passage, and tackling one barehanded was folly at best, unless one had something to prove, and as the new leader of the race, a new krath-hide vest would be necessary to prove his fitness to rule and hold all the Honors he'd acquired in his life.

He moved slowly closer from downwind until the animal's head came up, wide nostrils reacting to the faint scent drifting on the fickle breeze. In the back of his mind was the thought that some distance away waited the Court of Ascension, watching to make sure that he used no weapons other than those nature had provided.

Lowering himself closer to the ground to escape the sharp eyes of the giant beast, he moved closer still. With luck and the will of the Gods, he'd be able to get close enough for a throat strike with his foreclaws or a disemboweling stroke with his hind claws. Either would work just as well. Then all he'd have to do would be stay out of reach of hooves and horns until blood loss did the rest of his job for him.

But the Gods didn't smile on him this day. Either the wind gave him away, or the keen eyes spotted his movement through the tall grass. No matter. With a snort, the beast charged his position without any thought to its own survival. On Garmon, the rule was kill or be killed, and this beast had survived many a conflict. The scars on his hide gave evidence of that, and the many rings of his horns attested to his long life. This was no junior krath, herdless and alone. This was a cagey veteran of many battles, probably driven off by a younger, stronger male but no less dangerous for all that.

The two long, straight horns of the krath zeroed in on his position as the animal got closer. Korgan Garmon stood up to his full height. Not quite the equal of he who was nameless but being of sturdier stock, his stance was more solid. That was what had given him his ultimate edge over the nameless one in the long run, and that was what he was going to risk his life and his race's future on. He would stand his ground and try to sidestep the lethal horns, maybe scoring a debilitating stroke, if not a killing one. A thought crossed his suddenly clear mind. Why not hamstring the animal and finish it off at his leisure? If the opportunity presented itself…

During the two weeks it took Kitty's battle group to traverse the distance to the target planet, she had come to know the new Second Voice a bit. Not as secretive as sel Garian, at least yet, she was able to talk openly with the young woman.

Young for her race, that was to say. It turned out that Sitha was almost one hundred turnings old and had been in some form of training for her position for almost twenty years by Earth reckoning. From her, Kitty learned a lot about Shiravan culture and much more—things she passed on to the baron, the baroness, and the *Vega's* captain, Shirley Dahlquist, for discussion late at night.

The Shiravans had constructed a true matriarchy in every sense of the word. From the moment when the females had taken control of the planet away from the males and separated and sequestered them until only one hundred years before, no male was seen outside a clan compound unless escorted by a female relative. Social dynamics dictated that males be in attendance at most social functions to prove the viability of each clan.

Normally, Kitty was given to understand, male children were not allowed to be born. Some form of genetic manipulation was used to keep the male birth rate down, squelching any chances of an uprising and upheaval of society by males. Some Shiravan clans, Sitha had said, had specialized in genetics after the wars, while others gave themselves over to the exploration of space, colonizing nearly twenty worlds before the Korvils had come onto the scene. Still other clans devoted themselves to the inner sciences of the mind, spawning the kath-mora.

It was the discovery of otherspace that had set the kath-mora on the road to their present position. Once one clanswoman had testified that she'd communed with the Spirits of Space while studying the ethereal drifts of light found in otherspace, others soon followed suit. Whether it was true or not, some believed, and that was enough to bring together any Shiravan female who had any powers that could be used to drive the agenda of the kath-mora forward.

It was that agenda that led to the loss of the *Kreth*, and its eventual arrival in human space. That same agenda had eventually led to the Isolationist movement not long after Shiravi's first contact with the Korvils, also leading to the schism that was slowly fracturing the whole planet. That was the reason sel Garian had gone with the Second Fleet. She'd loaded the ship rosters with known and suspected kath-mora—the higher ranking, the better—to get them off the planet and let the des Harras government deal with the lower ranks.

It was sel Garian who convinced the Matriarch that those same lower orders weren't responsible for all the damage to their society. Indeed, most of them were true believers in the Spirits of Space and their eventual triumph over the Korvils. But as more and more attacks occurred, the Witches pushed their juniors to greater acts of violence against the Expansionist des Harras government. That was why the leaders had been removed from the main body of Witches.

Most of the lower orders were just what they seemed—finders, futurists, matrimonial consultants, and spiritual guardians. sel Garian had even suggested that, in her absence, a lower order kath-mora be appointed to the Matriarch's staff to supervise the whole remaining body of Witches. Surprisingly, she had named Tira do' Verlas, mother of Rentec and wife of the assassinated Kirel do' Verlas, as the best choice to fill the new post. It was a move designed to appease the remaining Witches and, at the same time, defuse the entire network of clandestine meetings and subversive actions that were sure to be promoted by the few remaining unidentified Witches.

The revelation to Rentec of his mother's elevation to the Matriarch's staff had been quite the sight for Kitty. The do' Verlas line had made many significant contributions to Shiravi over the past thousand years. It just seemed like the right thing to do after Manura explained it in detail, along, of course, with easing the restrictions on males in the general population, a necessary move to free up more females for duty aboard the slowly growing fleets of ships being sent out to protect the colonies from attack. The problem was that the Shiravans had no experience with warfare and hadn't had since the wars of a thousand years ago. But they were learning fast. Even though ship losses were on the order of four of theirs to one of the Korvils, they were learning.

Witness the attack and ground assault that had resulted in the rescue of Carter and Spencer. Ten Shiravan ships, two of them full-fledged battleships, had attacked a newly discovered Korvil outpost. Almost a dozen Korvil raiders were destroyed at a loss of two Shiravan ships, one of those a battleship. Granted, eight of those ships had been grounded, but of the other four, two had been caught completely unawares on landing approach, but the other two managed to take out two Shiravan ships by ramming. However, it was still a considerable victory and was treated as such.

Just before jumping into hyperspace, Kitty ordered that all ships drop out one day earlier than originally planned. It was her intention to use the sensor arrays to try to determine what state the target system was in and whether any intelligence could be gathered on the amount of traffic and number of ships they were about to face. She'd wanted to arrive sooner than the Matriarch expected so she'd ordered that each ship, including the *Shumara Vacht*, transfer power from their third power core to the engines, effectively cutting travel time by about twenty percent.

The end result was that the battle group arrived far enough outside the Korvil system that, hopefully, no sensors could detect them. Unexpectedly, their own more refined sensor arrays spotted not only a thoroughly agitated system, with Korvil ships—apparently eight in all—scurrying about the system, but an unnerving anomaly as well. Navigation said, "Madam Herald, I don't understand why my instruments would show this, but it seems that at least four Shiravan ships have just left the system as we were entering. There's nothing as distinctive as a Shiravan engine signature. Even ours are now different enough to distinguish without too much difficulty. The Korvils are thoroughly stirred up, and there's no chance of surprising them now."

Kitty looked at her own display, confirming the information, and then looked at Sitha, who'd come onto the bridge to watch the breakout from hyperspace. She just tilted her head left and right in a Shiravan shrug. "Someone is going to get cut off at the knees if this was some kind of set up," Kitty promised. "We'll wait here for a while to see what happens and whether the Korvils settle down. If they do, so much the better. If not, we'll formulate another plan to accomplish our mission. We do at least have an accurate count on the number of Korvil ships in the area, their sizes and capabilities. That's to our advantage, but we can't get cocky. We have too few ships to make assumptions that may be unfounded. I want to see if any more ships begin to patrol the outer reaches. If they do, we take them out one at a time. And we won't play fair. Any advantage is acceptable. Four to one odds are the best we can expect, not counting the carrier. That will stay in reserve until we need it and its cargo. Now, Comm, get me in touch with the *Federal Case* via whisker laser. Ask specifically for Domina sel Garian, and don't take no for an answer."

During the coming study period while the Korvils calmed down, she intended to have a full and in-depth discussion with sel Garian about just what constituted keeping one's nose out of her attack plans. And she didn't expect it to be pretty, so she planned on observers and hidden cameras.

Two days were spent watching the inner system. The Korvil ships continued to move about in seemingly random patterns, but none came close to the battlegroup holding position outside the system. One ship appeared from hyperspace near the end of the second day, entering almost halfway across the system and leaving the dirty footprint indicative of Korvil engines, destroyer class. It stayed in-system for almost twelve hours, and then jumped out on a different heading. Several hours went by before the results of the single ship's arrival and departure made themselves felt by the *Vega's* passive scans. Six of the eight enemy ships headed for the planet that had been designated as most likely to be the main outpost. The other two kept up their patrols.

Kitty looked again at her display and made a decision. "Captain Dahlquist, order all ships to start moving in slowly using the *Vega* as their reference. Once we're spotted, we're going to even the odds at the last second by launching all seventy Mambas and letting the *Canopus* back off for the duration of the fight. If we have at least ten Mambas in close proximity to each other, it will look like we have ten ships to their eight. Knowing what we do about their psychology, it will make them attack, thinking that their superior ability to stand grav stress and battle damage will give them the advantage. They won't know what hit them when the Mambas break up and start after individual targets. The confusion should allow us to get the upper hand with a minimum of loss of life to our Mamba pilots."

Before the ships could do much more than begin to power up, Comm said, "I have a tentative translation on a transmission from the single ship, Madam Herald."

Kitty looked up from the seat she occupied in one corner of the bridge. "What do you have, Comm?"

"Ma'am, the computer says that the single ship was carrying a message that there's been a change in leadership among the Korvils. They are no longer Korvils but something called Garmon. Apparently, someone named Korgan Garmon has staged a coup and taken power from the previous leader, demanding that all Korvils now call themselves Garmons."

Kitty looked at Sitha. "Doma kep Parrasine, do you think this will make any difference in how we proceed against the enemy?"

Sitha made the little headshake that passed for a shrug and said, "When we first met the Korvils, they called themselves by another name, still. The only difference we could determine was the name change. Their tactics remained the same. This sheds some light on why the name changed, but I have no idea what a change in leaders will do to their policy towards anyone not Korvil. It made no difference last time, and I see no reason to suspect that it will change anything now."

Shirley had waited throughout the exchange between Kitty and her Comm officer before beginning the mission she'd been given. She raised one eyebrow at Kitty, who just said, "Captain, you have your orders. You're in charge of the attack and retreat from this system. I'm now officially an observer."

Captain Shirley Dahlquist, once a student at Denver Community College, commanded more firepower than any fleet in human history when the Shiravan battleship *Shumara Vacht* and her destroyer escort, a last-minute replacement called *Ligara Keer-sa,* were added in. Now, she sat in command of a full battle group over forty lightyears from Earth and prepared to issue orders that would get some of her best friends killed. She looked around the bridge of the *Vega* and said, "Comm, send this tight beam to all ships: move into the inner system dead slow until we are spotted. At that time, the *Canopus* will launch all Mambas and back off. Mambas will form as five tight groups of ten and keep that formation until I order otherwise. We've rehearsed this enough times that no more need be said at this time. *Shumara Vacht*, you'll enter behind the *Vega* and the *Federal Case*, and *Ligara Keer-sa*, save yourself for emergencies."

The ships began to move forward slowly as a group, spreading out in a preplanned fan that would require the enemy to split their forces. The *Canopus* moved along with the rest until the two ships on patrol noticed the battle group several hours later than Shirley figured they should have. The *Canopus* launched her chicks and slowed her forward momentum, letting the main group outpace her. In five groups of ten, the Mambas drove toward the two enemy ships. Twenty more Mambas sat in readiness in the launch tubes of the *Vega* and the *Federal Case* in the event they were needed.

The two Korvil patrol ships, now Garmon, moved with a swiftness that had to be causing stress on their power systems. They moved directly toward the oncoming threat, sending messages back to the planet that an attack was in progress, but not one message was directed toward the invaders. The two Garmon ships never slowed down. Sensors showed that all offensive systems of the enemy were fully powered up, as well as several defensive systems.

Shirley looked at her screens and ordered, "*Vega*, *Federal Case*, attack at will. Take out those two ships. You have the shields to offset their weapons, and I want them destroyed in total before we have to deal with their reinforcements as well."

Without hesitation, the *Vega's* helm officer moved the ship into the path of the oncoming enemy. Kitty silently congratulated her. The *Federal Case* was noticeably slower in moving into position, but she was still in place before the enemy ships arrived. The *Vega's* point defense took out the missiles aimed at her with ease, the *Federal Case* doing the same. The return fire crippled both ships, leaving them twisted, drifting wrecks bleeding air, hardware, and flash-frozen bodies.

The five ships moved farther into the system, watching for a response from the planet. The five groups of Mambas moved along with them, the *Canopus* bringing up the rear in the event that a fighter that hadn't been totally destroyed could be rescued. To anyone who might be manning sensors planet-side, it looked like eight ships were moving in on the outpost planet, and it wasn't long before six more ships were headed out toward the invading fleet.

Seven ships moved away from the planet, one more than anticipated, but Shirley deployed her forces to meet the oncoming threat. The newly named Garmon fleet followed the same attack pattern as usual, depending on their unusually high tolerance of gravity changes to accomplish their objectives. It was a shame for them that they ignored the human propensity to improve on existing technology.

The *Vega's* Comm officer reported the departure of a small ship headed in the general direction of what was assumed to be the Garmon homeworld.

It was obvious from the quick response and the attack

pattern that the Garmons didn't expect any reaction other than what they were used to. It never occurred to the clan leader that humans would be working in concert with the Shiravans at this early stage of the war on this side of Garmon space. The only problem was that that particular assumption was so very wrong.

The Garmon fleet commander saw eight ships inbound and, working under the assumption that the attackers were solely Shiravans, sent his entire fleet out to attack and destroy the presumptuous interlopers. Somehow, the fact that two over-gunned destroyers had failed to report in after their initial contact with this fleet apparently never made it to the fleet commander's attention before he ordered his forces to attack—that, or it made less than no difference. A report to his clan leader describing the destruction of eight enemy ships was sure to earn him another Honor for his vest.

Clan Leader Zerrk Bardak expected no less than what normally occurred in the event that Garmon and Shiravan forces collided—victory for the Garmons and total, unreported defeat for the Shiravans. Either way, seven more ships flew into the human/Shiravan meatgrinder.

In the normal course of events for the Garmons, seven ships versus eight was virtual suicide for the eight, if they were Shiravan. And it was actually six Garmon to seven Shiravan as far as the Garmon clan leader was concerned. One of the Shiravan ships was slowly falling behind, an easy target once the others were disposed of.

He'd already sent word of the attack to the new homeworld. It would take several days for the small courier ship to make the passage, but with luck, there would be survivors for him to send to his new Lord as a gesture of fealty, since he'd been unable to attend the oath-binding ceremony in person. One thing aboard the courier was his written oath, but he'd soon have to make the journey in person. What better way than with a hold full of captives for the new Lord to play with?

The clan leader sat in his command center, watching the battle unfold in as close to real time as possible, and the closer the enemy came, the shorter the delay. The battle would take place too far out for him to make personal decisions. Several minutes would pass before his words could reach the fleet commander, and the same would pass before he could receive a reply. So, all he could do was rely on one of the best commanders in the Garmon fleet, no small Honor, to apply the proper tactics to the situation.

Garmon ships were far more heavily armored than Shiravan ships. Missiles that would penetrate a Shiravan ship just dented Garmon hulls, and the ability of the Garmons to operate in higher grav conditions was a direct result of living on a high-gravity world. Those two advantages had stood the Garmons in good stead for over two hundred cycles. There was no reason to think that anything different would happen now. It was just bad luck on the enemy fleet commander's part that he'd happened to pick this particular system to invade.

It was almost with a sense of boredom that watched the screens as the two fleets closed upon each other. The first indication that all was not well was when five of the enemy ships broke apart without a shot being fired. What had been five distinct ships suddenly turned into a cloud of smaller ships all darting in different directions.

No, not different directions, he realized too late. He also realized what his fleet commander had already found out the hard way, but there was still no way he could influence the outcome of the battle. Frustration made him jump to his feet, his chair falling over, the clatter unnoticed. The small ships that had held so tightly together that they seemed like separate, distinct ships, now began to move around the space occupied by his six clan ships, trying to move in on their more unprotected rear. He could see a few, too few, being destroyed as they tried to flank his fleet.

His one bit of joy came from the fact that they'd have too hard a time trying catching up to the battle to do any significant damage before the remaining three ships were destroyed. All Garmons feared the little fighters the Shiravans used. They'd been tried on several occasions, but being alone was something the Garmons weren't able to accept for prolonged periods of time. Even the courier had a crew that numbered almost twenty, providing enough companionship to prevent the Gods from taking the minds of the crew. Pilots who flew alone were too susceptible to going mad from the solitude, and the fighter angle had been discarded decades before.

He reseated himself, an aide setting the chair back in place, until he saw the small ships performing maneuvers he knew were patently impossible for Shiravans to manage. Only Garmons could handle the stress these ships were putting themselves through, but it was happening nevertheless. Weapons fire poured from his ships toward the enemy fleet, doing remarkably little damage. Conversely, the fire coming from the three ships still in front of his fleet was making itself visibly felt. Even at this distance, he could see that two of his ships were already starting to lag behind, a sure sign that they were experiencing severe difficulties. And the two forward patrol ships were noticeably absent.

It was at that same moment he noticed that the small fighters had made very high-speed turns, coming in behind his ships almost in unison. Now his instruments could make out almost fifty of the small enemy ships flying up behind his ships, and he realized he'd been outmaneuvered. The fleet discovered the same thing, but they could do no more than he.

Two of his ships were vaporized by repeated salvos of some kind of missile he'd never seen before, and two others were taken out by the swarm of tiny ships plaguing their unprotected rears. All Honor left him was to take some of these demon ships with him into the Great Dark as a tribute to the Gods.

"Send to the fleet commander: ram the lead ship," he ordered. His comm officer didn't even hesitate but only repeated the orders that would be received minutes later by the slowly deteriorating fleet of Garmon ships.

The fleet commander didn't even bother to send an acknowledgment. He ordered their course corrected to do as ordered, followed by the last remaining ship in his until then undefeated fleet. "Point defense, take out as many of those damnable missiles as possible. We go to the Gods with slaves to serve us for all of eternity."

CHAPTER TWENTY-NINE

The *Vega's* navigator, helm officer, and comm officer clamored for attention at the same time. Shirley chose Nav first. "Report," she said, knowing from her own scans what was happening.

"Ma'am, the last two ships have adjusted course to ram us."

"Comm, what do you have?"

"Ma'am, translation agrees with Nav. We've been targeted for ramming by the two remaining ships."

Kitty found out what the extra bridge crew was for at Shirley's next set of orders. She'd thought they were there in the event that someone needed to be replaced, but she hadn't figured on Shirley's planning. "Execute plan Alpha," Shirley said, and three crewmen standing positions behind several stations moved to surround Kitty and move her off the bridge.

"Shirley, what are you doing?" she demanded.

"Keeping the Terran Herald safe at all costs, per my orders from Admiral Hawke, Madam Herald," she replied. "You're being removed to the safest spot in the fleet, along with the Shiravan observer. That means you're being sent to the *Canopus* until the last chance of any harm to either of you passes." Throwing a short, stony gaze Kitty's way, she added, "Don't even think about fighting this, Kitty. I have my orders and priorities, and so do my crew. Don't make their job any harder than it already is. And I'm truly more afraid of Simon than I am of you."

It seemed the work of seconds only before she was being hustled aboard an already prepped shuttle, waiting for Sitha and the rest of her staff, the baron and baroness, to arrive from other parts of the ship. In the meantime, she felt the telltale vibration of the *Vega's* launch tubes spitting out more Mambas to interpose between the oncoming collision. Tears in her eyes, she watched as Sitha was hustled aboard and the hatch closed.

She looked into the cockpit and said, "Patch us in to the *Vega's* comm system, please."

"Aye, Ma'am," the pilot said. "*Vega* control, this is shuttle one launching solo. All passengers are accounted for." The vibrations that followed proved to her that this wasn't a drill. Soon, she could see on the pilot's screen that the shuttle was clear. Oddly, she could only count nine Mambas pulling away from the *Vega*, firing selectively at the oncoming hostiles. She was about to sit down and try to explain to Sitha what was happening when one more dot escaped from the *Vega's* proximity—the tenth Mamba she hadn't been able to account for.

"Vega, this is Dahlquist," she heard over the comm system. "I'm taking charge of forward point defense. All Mambas form on me and stop those two ships. *Canopus* Mambas, target engine compartments and missile storage areas. Stop those two ships before they reach the *Canopus*. We need to have somewhere for you to land after this is over."

Kitty felt her heart sink. "God damn it, Shirley," she muttered. "If you live through this, I'm gonna kill you."

Sitha, having a working knowledge of human language, asked, "What transpires, Katherine?"

"We're being moved to a position of safety," she answered bitterly, "while the *Vega's* captain is taking the lead Mamba out to stop those ships from ramming her own ship. She started out as a Mamba pilot and seems to want to end as one as well."

"A noble gesture, Madam Herald," Sitha said quietly. "Her name will be inscribed on the dusterna of the Matriarch, as well as the kep Parrasine dusterna. Her story will be told for generations and her memory will not die."

The shuttle pilot interrupted. "Madam Herald, the *Vega* is attempting to evade the ram, but the enemy is adjusting course. Mambas from behind are trying to get shots at the engines, but it looks like the emissions from those Korvil engines are fouling their sensors. No one is getting a good lock. I predict collision in twenty seconds."

"I've got to watch this," Kitty apologized to her guest, the words choking her. "Please excuse me for a few minutes." She slipped into the cockpit and stood between the two chairs as the shuttle moved toward the *Canopus*. Dots of light, Mambas from the *Canopus* and the *Vega*, winked out one at a time as the two ships drew closer together. One, not totally destroyed by some freak chance, spiraled away from the battle and drifted in the direction of the target planet.

Not knowing Kitty stood behind him, the co-pilot exclaimed loudly, "Direct hit on enemy engines! The vessel is no longer under power. It looks like a near miss instead of a direct ram." At that moment, the two dots of light collided in the display and silence reigned in the cockpit.

Both vessels appeared to be unpowered now, drifting apart like a couple of billiard balls. The swarm of Mambas finally took out the last ship and then made short work of the drifting attacker, its dot disappearing from the screen in a small flash as its atoms were spread among the stars.

Kitty reached out and grabbed the microphone. "*Vega*, this is Hawke. Status report." The voice she used was the one Simon had taught her, with difficulty, over the years. Now, under stress, it came naturally.

"Madam Herald, this is the *Vega*. We've suffered massive damage to our port side and multiple casualties throughout the ship. Landing bays are nonfunctional. Surviving Mambas should attempt to rendezvous with the *Canopus*. Internal systems are failing. It's possible that we've had a power core breach. Four Mambas do not respond, including Captain Dahlquist's. We'll hold on as long as possible. *Vega* out."

By this time, the shuttle had reached the *Canopus*, and Kitty was off the shuttle, heading for the bridge so fast that the longer-legged Sitha was hard pressed to keep up. Kitty spoke into her wristband. "*Canopus* Control, this is the Herald. Move forward and pick up your chicks. Assign ten to follow the damaged Mamba toward the planet and intercept if possible. Also, send to the *Federal Case*: launch all shuttles and save as many of the *Vega's* crew as possible. Launch yours as well. There may be a power core breach and we need to get that ship evacuated as soon as possible."

"Aye, Madam Herald," came back almost immediately. "Shuttle crews have been alerted to report to their stations on the double. Contact with the *Vega* is spotty, but they understand that rescue efforts are under way."

Shortly, Kitty walked onto the bridge and found a solidly functioning crew bringing ships into the bays while others worked to coordinate the rescue attempt of the damaged fighter still drifting toward the hostile planet. She found Miranda Lee trying to stay on top of all aspects of the various operations. "How goes it?" she asked quietly.

"As well as can be expected, Kitty," she said informally. "You know that the single Mamba is Shirley's?"

A cold wave passed up Kitty's spine. "No, I didn't. Let me have a microphone." She took Comm's seat and keyed the mike. "*Federal Case*, this is the Herald. Launch all Mambas to provide cover for the rescue efforts for the Mamba headed for the planet. Shirley's flying it. I want her back here in one piece so I can kill her personally."

The response astonished her. "Madam Herald, this is Captain Breen. Launching all Mambas will leave this ship without any mobile defense. Do you wish to reconsider?"

Kitty looked at Miranda in astonishment. She keyed the mike and said harshly, "Captain Breen, if all of your Mambas are not headed for that planet within two minutes, I'll have you relieved and placed under arrest. Captain Dahlquist needs your assistance, and you will respond with all due haste. Have I made myself clear?"

Interstellar static hissed through the speakers for five seconds until the response came. "All Mambas are launching now, as you command, Madam Herald." Did she hear annoyance in his voice? "Nav says it won't be possible to interdict before the damaged ship reaches the planet's atmosphere. Do you have any further instructions?"

"Yes," Kitty said, keying the mike with something close to anger. "Send your captain's gig along to pick Shirley up if she makes it to the surface alive. We'll speak in private later. Hawke out."

Something like nine years had passed since Kitty had first set foot aboard a Shiravan ship. During that time, she'd learned many things—some of them from Simon and some of them from those she chose to surround herself with. Among those were people with military training, be it Army, Navy, Marines, or Air Force, and one lesson she'd learned was that a stern chase was the longest, hardest maneuver to execute. This was precisely because, usually, the leader was under power. In this case, however, the Mamba carrying Shirley was not under power, and it wasn't even known if she was still alive. Scans of her ship gave no clue since the distance was too great, only reporting that minimal power remained, possibly having been rerouted to life support or just the normal functioning of a damaged craft devoid of a living pilot.

A total of twenty Mambas, followed at a distance by the *Federal Case's* captain's gig, arrowed in toward the planet and the sole Mamba trapped by the gravity well of the slightly larger than Earth-sized planet. Kitty ached to be in one of the small fighters but resigned herself to being held hostage to her position. Nonetheless, the bitter taste in her mouth stayed.

She ordered Miranda to move the carrier closer to the planet to facilitate the recovery of the Mambas on their return and allow something closer to real-time information on the rescue attempt. In the meantime, shuttles from the stricken *Vega* began to arrive with survivors of the ramming. Most were not hurt at all, some few needed attention, and a very few needed more complicated attention. The sad fact of space combat was that in most cases, you either lived or died. There was very little middle ground. Still, the loss of life astonished her, as well as the number of survivors.

Of almost five hundred personnel aboard, only three hundred and forty-one had been transferred to the *Canopus* before the *Vega* was declared clear of survivors. Intensive scans and room-to-room searches confirmed that fact, and Kitty finally ordered the ship scuttled—a wet navy term, she knew, but appropriate. Charges were set to destroy the magnetic containment fields on the three power cores, and any piece larger than a car was blasted by Mambas with laser fire to deprive the enemy of any technical data from the wreckage.

Still, the more important issue was the lone Mamba. An astonished bridge crew came to life when sensor data reported that the little ship had applied power to enter the atmosphere at an angle that would let it reach the surface intact. "It's still going to require a lot of luck on Shirley's part, Kitty," Miranda warned.

"Not as much as you might think, Miranda," Kitty replied. "Remember, Shirley qualified almost as high as you in Mamba training. What I see is a pilot who's shepherding her power. She kept to minimal life support until she needed power to the engines. My bet is that she's going to try to glide as far as she can, reserving as much as possible right up until the last minute." She was silent for a moment, then added, "Of course, her speed will have to remain high to have any control if she's dead-sticking, but once she nears the ground, she should be able to use her antigravs to set down."

"Assuming she has that much power left," Miranda responded. "It's just what I would do of course, but we don't know the extent of her damage or what kind of terrain she'll have to land on."

Miranda's Comm officer broke in. "Reports coming

in from the rescue ships now. They've got her power-up on sensors and are following her down. Still no comm chatter. The first ship should be hitting atmosphere ten minutes behind Captain Dahlquist."

If the confines of a Mamba's cockpit had let her, Shirley Dahlquist would be kicking herself. Hard. Her computer and comm system were out, power reserves were minimal, and she was going down on a planet that was populated by over-sized man-killing aliens with bad attitudes. As she dipped farther into the atmosphere, she could literally see the power indicator dropping. She cut all shields, hoping to reserve that power for the landing she prayed to survive. How she was going to get back was problematic.

Everything would depend on her skill at repairing whatever damage she'd sustained, and she wouldn't know that until she got down and inspected the ship. Of course, that was if she didn't have to fight off giant predatory teddy bears while she was doing it. Passive scans of the surface showed the high-grav planet was only lightly populated, or at least there was very little in the way of infrastructure except near the coastlines. She aimed her ship into the interior of the largest continent below her and looked for a level space to set down.

A high-pitched whine insinuated itself as she dipped low enough to make out distinct features of the alien landscape. A hurried examination revealed that her cockpit seal was beginning to melt away. At the same time, she noticed the rosy glow coming from the front of her ship. Friction was heating the super-hardened metal of her ship's skin to the point that it was melting seals that weren't composed of the same material. A Mamba was not, after all, designed to fly through atmosphere without the extra protection of at least the forward shields to dissipate the heat.

She decided to sacrifice speed and maneuverability in hopes that the seal would last until she could get down. It was certain that she wasn't going to be flying that ship back into space without the seal, and she knew her spares compartment didn't carry anything that would serve. Her prospects looked grimmer as she got closer to the ground. She determined that she'd save the last shot in her pistol for herself. The stories she'd heard about Carter and Spencer's treatment at the hands of these aliens were bad enough, and the pictures just fortified her resolve.

Scans showed no indications of life in a large flat area directly ahead, and she aimed her craft toward it. The ground came up at alarming speed until she cut in her antigravs. Power levels dropped drastically as soon as she did, but she was only about two hundred feet above the ground at that point. She deployed her landing gear and aimed for an opening in a grove of trees.

Recalled from a hunt, Zagrrt Bardak—son to the clan leader—studied the scans and watched as one small fighter dropped toward his domain. He called the landing field and ordered his flyer readied for flight. With his only courier already past his ability to recall, all he could do was take out this one alien and hope that he survived long enough to report to homeworld the ignominious defeat of his hand and two of ships. These accursed humanz—for that was all they could be— weren't predictable enough to use standard tactics on. Much like the krath he hadn't had time to finish earlier due to the arrival of this fleet of ships, it appeared that the only way to win was to use vastly superior numbers, which he'd never had. Why they were so much more adept at combat was a mystery to him. All reports said that they'd only been in space for a handful of years. How had these humanz gained the expertise to fight so well? Certainly not from the Shiravans, whom they'd been beating at will for over two hundred cycles.

Still, this one would be a diversion while he awaited a reply from Homeworld Sensor Security. Sensor techs kept him apprised of the intruder's path as it fell lower into the atmosphere. He'd be minutes behind the alien, taking great pains to make his demise last long enough to appease his own anger at the loss of his clan's ships.

Shirley pried her cockpit open, cursing the failed seal, and climbed out onto alien soil. "I wish it didn't have to be here," she muttered, staring at the partially melted seal. She walked around her ship, gauging the damage. The engines appeared to be intact, but there was a gaping hole in the skin of the ship just forward of the flux converter. Not an impossible problem to fix, given time, but she feared she didn't have that much time to spare. And the damage had effectively welded her repair compartment shut so she couldn't reach her tools.

Her only hope now was to get a message out to the fleet and hope for rescue if they hadn't written her off and moved on out of the system after taking out all the enemy ships. So. Power she had aplenty; the problem was to get it to her comm system. Another look at the damaged hatch gave her an idea. She pulled her laser out and checked the charge level. Full. Twenty full-power shots.

Dialing the intensity down, she aimed at the access hatch, hoping to open it without damaging the internal systems. Three shots and she had a hole she could reach into and hopefully reroute power to the comm system. Holstering the weapon, she reached inside the jagged hole, ignoring the burns to her forearms as she tried to feel her way through the process of getting power from the core to the cockpit while a part of her mind listened for any unusual sounds, although she had no idea what was unusual on an alien planet.

After a short time, she climbed back into the cockpit to see if she'd made any progress, not being able to tell through the ragged hole in the side of her ship. As she pulled herself up, she felt the full effects of this larger planet—twenty percent more than she was used to she guessed as she grunted with the effort of getting back into the ship. Her heart leapt at the sight of the lights aglow on her comm panel. Not only had she restored power to her comm system, but she could get the ship off the ground, although the melted seal still wouldn't let her get back into space.

Cockpit still open, she keyed her mic, calling for the fleet she hoped was still in the vicinity. "Battle Group Vega, this is Dahlquist. Respond. I repeat, this is Dahlquist. Respond."

Not really expecting a reply, her heart skipped a beat when an answer came. "Captain, this is Flight Leader Simms. We are inbound for your position. Be aware that we have a bogey on our screens that will arrive at your position ten minutes before we're able to get there. Are you able to move your ship?"

"I am now," she replied, her voice choking on the words. "But I'm not able to get above atmosphere. I'll need another ship to get out of here in one piece."

"Captain, this is Simms. We're escorting a gig to pick you up, but you'll have to protect yourself until we arrive. Good luck and good hunting. Simms out."

The curt response told her that she'd better not waste any time getting airborne. Fighting to get her cockpit as sealed as possible, she also hit her scans and immediately saw the incoming bogey—a bit larger than her own ship but certainly not faster or more maneuverable. Pouring power to the antigravs, she lifted above the treetops and visually searched for the bogey. Gaining altitude, she finally saw with her own eyes what her screens had shown for the last minute—a single ship heading in her direction at high speed. She activated her forward shields and accelerated directly toward the bogey, firing her lasers. Early, it seemed, since they missed by a fair percentage, or perhaps her targeting computer needed to be realigned as well.

The two ships passed each other, and Shirley got the impression that her opponent's vessel wasn't designed for extra-atmospheric flight. "Just as well," Shirley muttered to herself as she turned her ship for a second pass. This time, she armed two of her torpedoes and, shields at maximum, decided to take a page from her enemy's book. "If you like to play chicken, then let's go ahead and play," she said aloud. Realizing that talking to herself was a bad sign, she shut up and monitored the rescue frequency with a small part of her mind while the rest closed down into the moment.

Advantages, she thought, were that she was more maneuverable, faster, and had more powerful weapons. Her disadvantages were being stranded on an alien planet, her lack of knowledge of the terrain, her inability to disengage from the enemy, and no backup against an enemy who thought mutual suicide was preferable to a win/lose situation. She checked her scans and found the bogey closer than she'd anticipated, barely finding time to fire at pointblank range as they passed again, wingtips almost touching. Both missiles missed and streaked off into the distance. She hadn't had time to set them for target acquisition.

Snapping her ship around, she found that her opponent had anticipated her move and was boring in on her before she'd time to even twitch the controls. Only her forward shields kept her from becoming a mangled wreck as the aircraft was deflected to one side, striking her port stabilizer instead of hitting her head on. The ground came up at her unbelievably fast, and she barely had time or control enough to get her ship level before she hit the ground, skipping like a stone on a pond until her nose plowed a long, narrow furrow in the ground.

She jolted to a stop as her ship's nose hit some underground impediment, bruising her everywhere a strap was holding her in her seat. She tried to raise the canopy and found that her left arm wasn't answering her commands. Unbuckling herself, she stood up, bent over, and pressed her back against the clear material until it finally gave way. Without landing gear deployed, the drop to the ground was a lot less, a good thing considering the higher gravity. With her left arm hanging limply at her side, she grabbed her comm link and survival pack and slid down the skin of the once-beautiful ship, moving into the tall grasses surrounding her on all sides.

Her enemy's aircraft passed directly overhead, and she raised her laser, dialed to full power, and scorched a line from nose to tail, hearing a change in the engines as the beam reached the aft portion of the craft. Whether this was because of her shot or because he was landing, she didn't know and didn't care. Changing directions at random, she moved away from the spot she'd been standing in, stopping only when the sound of the damaged aircraft scraping up dirt and rocks died away. Silence reigned, and she imagined the pictures of the dead Korvils she'd been shown during orientation classes so long ago. Remembering the face, she focused her mind on the nose. These aliens had to have a very good sense of smell, and she was leaving a trail a baby Korvil could follow.

Pawing onehanded through her pack, she found a long-bladed knife and slid it into her right boot. Taking a second laser she stuck it into her belt after checking the charge—three-quarters full, not unusual for a weapon stored for as long as this one had surely been. It matched her own after that last full-powered shot against the aircraft. Looping a fifty-foot length of rope over her good right shoulder, she tossed the rest of the pack aside and moved again, keeping low to the ground, hoping that the grasses, taller than she by far, weren't giving her position away. Where she was, not a single breath of air stirred the thick stalks, but her passage had to cause some of the tops to move. If her opponent was tall enough to see the movement...

Zagrrt climbed out of his craft, flexing his muscles and assessing the damage he'd sustained in the landing, but it was nothing that would keep him from stalking and killing this puny human. Senses alert for any sign of its movement, his ears swiveled independently of each other, much like radar as he attempted to locate his prey. It would surely have moved from its last position by now. He'd start at the downed craft and trace its path from there.

The tall prairie grasses kept him from locating it by the movement of the grass tops from the ground, so he jumped up onto the highest point of the alien's craft and scanned the area. Some distance off, he could see the grasses moving. He watched for a short time, lips skinned back in a feral grin. The alien was lost and moving in circles. This wasn't going to be as hard as he'd expected. Somehow, the thought didn't please him as much as he'd thought it would. A worthy adversary would earn him another Honor, but a stumbling human, lost and alone, wasn't enough for that.

Shirley expected to be tracked by smell rather than sight, so she made it as hard as possible for her enemy. She moved in a large circle, actually surprising herself by coming back to her starting point, and slid the rope off her shoulder. Tying one end to a tightly packed clump of grasses about four feet off the ground outside her circle, she ran the rope out into the center where she hid. Hopefully, she'd confused her trail enough that if she could just get the Korvil to stand in one particular spot and look away from her position, she could shoot him in the back. She had no compunctions about it at all. Injured and tiring rapidly from the higher gravity, it was the only recourse she had left in this terrain. If only she could have faced him on open ground.

Zagrrt's sense of smell, excellent at the worst of times, magnified itself as he went into hunting mode. Sight was no help in this environment, but he only needed his nose and bare hands. Already, he'd scented what he could only deduce was the smell of human fear. He pulled a single stalk of grass out of the ground and smelled its length carefully. His mind's eye gave him a description of the alien. Male or female didn't matter, but size did. This one was small by his standards, standing less than shoulder height. He dropped the stalk and moved on. Crossing the alien's trail, he moved onto it, looking down for footprints.

Finding a depression in the packed soil, he bent down slowly, all senses alert, and sniffed at the find. Definitely fear, he thought, standing back up and moving along the trace he'd found. Now he stared into the grasses on both sides of the trace, looking at waist level for anything that didn't fit the patterns of grasses he passed through.

Shirley felt the alien as he moved toward her. The ground actually shook a bit as he strode along her path, perhaps feeling himself to be the king of his domain and not needing to resort to stealthy movement. Perhaps his arrogance would be his downfall. Time would tell. And soon. She'd covered the rope with bits of dirt and detritus where it crossed the path she'd made in the grass, tied a loose loop in the free end, and put her foot into the loop. When he passed, she'd twitch her foot. He'd see the grass move in a spot where she wasn't, and she'd shoot him. Simple plan. Simple ones were the best, Simon had said once, long ago. Unnecessary complexity just messed things up.

Out of the corner of one eye she saw a movement. Tensing up, she held the laser in her lap, pointed up at an angle that would intersect the alien's chest if she had figured things right. As he came even with her position, she held her breath, twitched her foot and let the rope move the grass on the outside of her circle. The alien froze. He started to move away from her but then leapt straight backwards to land in front of her, only a few feet away. Shirley smelled the rancid odor of a Korvil in full hunting mode and fired her laser. Fear caused her to miss the chest shot she'd hoped for, and she only lopped off one arm. The other came down on her like a sledgehammer, knocking her flat on her back and sending her laser flying into the concealing grasses.

She scrabbled for the second pistol in her belt, but the Korvil landed on her chest, his massive arm pressing down on her. Her injured left arm was pinned against her breast leaving her almost defenseless. Close to five hundred pounds of intelligent hunting carnivore leaned down and snarled in her face. She could feel the second laser being pressed into her pelvic bone and her ribs cracking as he leaned down, his breath choking her. Or perhaps it was just his weight on her chest and abdomen. The Korvil's remaining hand grasped her by the throat and squeezed, only this time no sound came out. He leaned closer, lips skinned back, baring a true predator's teeth. He raked his teeth down the side of her face and neck, toying with her.

He sniffed the blood running down the side of her mangled face and licked it, bringing a shudder to her body, pinned as she was. Her right hand, still free, sought the last weapon she had—the knife in her boot. Pulling it loose, she brought it up just as the Korvil let go of her throat. His intent was clear. He meant to tear her throat out and let her bleed to death in the tall grasses of this alien world. As his head came down, mouth open, she brought the knife up and into view just long enough to stab it into one oddly beautiful green eye. He screamed, and she pushed harder, driving it into his brain. Death came instantly… for him. He collapsed on top of her—lifeless, immensely heavy, and totally unmovable.

Her death was going to be slower, she realized. Unable to move the massive body off her, she'd slowly suffocate under the weight. She finally stopped struggling against the inevitable and let herself relax. Death would claim her soon enough anyway. At least she'd taken one more with her. She started feeling light-headed and heard a distant buzzing in her ears.

Then oblivion claimed her.

ABOUT THE AUTHOR

Bob lived in Montana for over thirty years, since late '85. He fell in love with the state almost instantly (who wouldn't after spending the previous twenty or more years trapped in Houston, Texas). Out in the Big Sky Country, he found the "elbow room" he didn't even know he was looking for. He lived quietly with his two cats and library of nearly two thousand books—about 95% Sci-Fi. He discovered that he liked to write as well and could often be found doing just that. Bob passed away in November of 2019 and is survived by his younger brother. Before he passed, he finished his writing project of more than a decade, The Stellar Heritage series, and he will live on in the hearts and minds of his readers.

Learn more at:
bladeoftruthpublishing.com/bob-mauldin

MORE FROM THE PUBLISHER

Blade of Truth Publishing Company specializes in science fiction and fantasy stories that change the way you view the world.

To find more great books head over to:

bladeoftruthpublishing.com/books

Bringing truth into the world, one story at a time.